THE
DISAPPEARANCE
OF
SLOANE
SULLIVAN

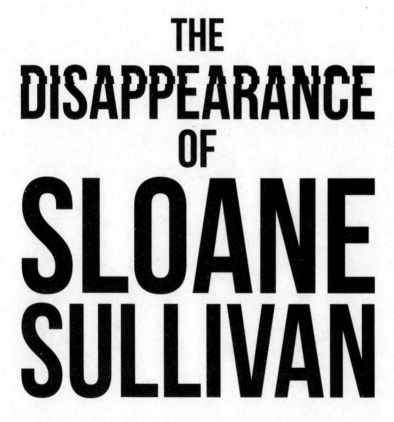

GIA CRIBBS

THE DISAPPEARANCE OF SLOANE SULLIVAN

HARLEQUIN®TEEN

ISBN-13: 978-1-335-01537-2

The Disappearance of Sloane Sullivan

Printed in U.S.A.

For my daughters. Never stop chasing your dreams.

THE
DISAPPEARANCE
OF
SLOANE
SULLIVAN

PROLOGUE

I couldn't shake the feeling of someone watching me.

Dropping the blindfold, I kicked away the ropes by my feet that, a few seconds earlier, had been wrapped a little too loosely around my wrists to keep me bound.

I couldn't see a thing.

Thunder crashed, making something metallic sounding rattle to my right. I held my breath and waited for a flash of lightning to illuminate the pitch-black room, anything to give me a clue about where I was. But when I heard more thunder a minute later, my heart sank. *There are no windows in this room.*

My pulse raced. I had to get out and I didn't have much time.

Taking a deep breath, I forced myself to concentrate, to ignore what I was feeling, and picture every windowless room in the school. The clean, slightly antiseptic edge to the air didn't smell like the gym locker room. *The kitchen?* I inched toward the metallic rattling, arms braced in front of me. Even through my gloves, the metal shelves felt cool when my fingers brushed against them, feeling the buckets and sponges and spray bottles lined up along their edges. *The supply closet.*

I followed the shelving around the room until I came to the door. Without a sound, I eased it open slightly. After a few seconds of blinking furiously at the light that came pouring in, I could see well enough to tell the hallway was empty.

I glanced at the rooms directly across from me. Almost all the classrooms had windows, but most were too high and too small for me to fit through. There were side doors at the end of the hall to the left, a good two hundred feet away. Those doors were the closest exit, but making a run for it down the bright hall, even if the lights were dimmed at night, seemed too risky. I needed to stick to the shadows. Which left the only other way out of this part of the school: the gym.

I inched the supply closet door open farther and slid out, stepping over the rags that had been stuffed under the door to block the light. In only three steps I was in the chemistry lab, the one with doors to two different hallways. I dashed across the dark lab, careful not to bump into anything, and was about to step into the hall that led to the gym when *everything* went completely dark.

I was out of time.

I raced into the hall, willing my outstretched hands to find the gym entrance. Just as one hand skimmed the smooth metal gym door, something behind me squeaked. It was a quick, barely there sound. But it was also immediately identifiable: a sneaker skidding against the floor.

I froze.

The hair on the back of my neck stood up. I couldn't see my hand in front of my face, but I could *feel* him closing in.

I shoved my hand into my pocket and pulled out a handful of pebbles—the only thing I'd been able to grab outside—and threw them down the hall. At the tiny *plink* of stone meeting linoleum, I crept in the opposite direction.

My fingers trailed along the wall, telling me where to turn. As I rounded the corner, an explosive flash of lightning lit up the entire hall. I peeked over my shoulder and saw him kneeling, picking a pebble off the floor. His head was just turning in my direction when the hall went dark again and thunder rattled the windowpanes.

I ran.

A full-on sprint around another corner to the side doors I'd seen earlier. I couldn't hear whether he was chasing me over the sound of my feet pounding against the floor and my heartbeat thumping in my ears. *Where are the damn doors—*

I burst through the double doors with such force they slammed against the brick wall of the school before swinging shut. I took in everything: the trees straight ahead, dense and good for hiding; the sound of a car passing on a nearby street; the lights from a house off in the distance, blurry from the rain. I allowed myself a single second to smile before I reached down and clicked the stopwatch hanging from my neck.

When Mark finally pushed through the doors thirty seconds later, his brown hair escaping from under his black hat and his hazel eyes searching franticly, I was leaning against the brick wall, using the roof's overhang to keep dry. I cocked an eyebrow when his surprised gaze landed on me.

He sighed and nodded at my stopwatch. "What was your time?"

"Three minutes, sixteen seconds. A new record." I fought hard to keep a grin off my face.

"Hmph."

"Don't be a poor sport." There was something about his hat that made him look older, more his age and less the college student he was sometimes mistaken for. I yanked it off in one swift move, leaving his hair wild with static. "You've caught me more times than I've gotten out. Remember Nebraska? You trapped me in the band room in a minute flat."

The corners of Mark's mouth twitched. "Yeah, but that was when you were young and easy to trick. Now you're almost too good. I mean, pebbles? That was a nice touch."

"If it makes you feel better, you almost got me with the blackout. How'd you manage that one?"

His smile grew wider. "Light switches in the front office."

I shook my head. "Did you have to use *all* of them?"

Mark's eyes locked on mine, more serious than they'd been a second before. "Lesson number one."

My smile faltered. It was easy to joke around, to pretend it was only a game, especially this time. But we both knew it wasn't.

It was a test. A way to see how well I knew the school, how fast I could get out if someone was chasing me.

I held Mark's gaze. "Remember how to escape."

When I entered witness protection, it was the first lesson I learned for a reason. Escaping wasn't just about crawling through a window or shimmying down a vent. It was mental. Knowing how to push past the fear and stay calm and *think* was the most important part. Maybe breaking and entering wasn't the best way to start off in a new town, but it was our routine, our way of preparing for every possibility.

Plus, a little extra practice disabling a security system never hurt a girl.

I took a few steps back, letting the rain, which had lightened considerably, mist over me. Everything smelled fresh as I examined the school, shadowy in the moonless night.

Mark moved to my side, his shoulder brushing against mine. "New school, new you," he said, as soft as the rain.

I nodded.

"I'm going to make sure everything's back the way we found it. You coming?"

"In a sec," I whispered as he disappeared back into the school.

I stared at the brick wall in front of me, darker in spots from the rain. The breaking in, the chase, the cleaning up after ourselves—it was all familiar. Yet the more I studied the rough bricks, the more my stomach twisted.

Thunder rumbled low in the distance. For a second, I thought I saw a flash of blue against the faded red of the bricks. But when I blinked, it was gone.

A tight knot settled in my chest.

It was just another wall of just another school. It was all familiar, except for the tiny voice inside my head that warned, *This time's going to be different.*

ONE

Out of all the names I'd had in the last five years, I liked this one the best: *Sloane Sullivan*. It looked right, printed there at the top of my new class schedule. Good thing too, since it was the last one I was ever going to have.

"There's just one more thing I have for you and you're all set," the secretary said. She was a little hard to hear over the buzz of voices coming from the hall on the other side of the glass wall behind me and the incessant ringing of phones inside the front office.

I glanced up from my schedule to find the secretary smiling. Her short, curly white hair and deep crow's feet screamed helpful grandmother. She actually looked a little like our neighbor eight towns back who was a grandmother of eleven. I didn't trust her for a second.

"I figured it must be hard to transfer so late in your senior year," the secretary continued, "so I marked up a map of the school with the location of your classes. That way, at least you won't get lost on your first day."

Okay, I thought. *That's actually kind of sweet.* I peeked at the nameplate sitting on the side of the tall counter separating me from the rest of the office. "Thanks, Mrs. Zalinsky. That's really thoughtful of you."

Little did Mrs. Zalinsky know that, thanks to my adventure with Mark last night, I already knew where every classroom was located. We didn't use our more nefarious skills, like lock picking and camera tampering, just to practice escaping. I'd realized pretty quickly that having to ask for directions or stumbling into classes late didn't help with blending in. And that was always the goal: to blend in. Blend in, follow the rules and don't let anyone get too close. That's what I'd learned after almost six years on the run.

Besides, if we got caught snooping around, Mark could just flash his badge and we'd get off scot-free. Of course, then we'd probably have to move again.

Mrs. Zalinsky grinned, pleased to be appreciated. "You're welcome, Sloane."

The little thrill that always shot through me when I heard someone say my new name for the first time danced in my chest. *Sloane.* I liked the way it sounded too.

"Let me grab the map for you." Mrs. Zalinsky headed for an immaculately clean desk on the other side of the office.

I gazed at my name again, still surprised Mark had agreed to it. I'd thrown Sloane out on a whim and he didn't even blink. He just nodded in that slow way of his, which made his thick hair, which was dark brown at the time, fall into his eyes, and said, "Sure." I knew he would've preferred Sara or Samantha or something more mainstream for my nineteenth identity. He'd totally vetoed some of my more unusual suggestions—

being Leia like the princess from *Star Wars* would've rocked—but he let Sloane slide by. Maybe it was because we were both counting on this being the last time we had to switch names.

I rubbed my thumb over my name. *God, nineteen different people in almost six years. Well, twenty if you count my real name. But I don't remember who that girl was anymore.*

"Here you go," Mrs. Zalinsky said, interrupting my thoughts. She handed me a map. "I circled your classrooms in order based on the colors of the rainbow. You know, Roy G. Biv? Red for first period, orange for second, and so forth. Except since we only have four periods, I stopped at green."

I let out a low whistle. "That's some serious organization. I'm impressed." And I was. It sounded like something Mark would do, and I didn't think anyone was as anal as he was.

"It takes a lot of organization to keep a school of more than 1,800 kids running smoothly," Mrs. Zalinsky explained as she straightened an already perfectly aligned stack of papers.

I grinned. *1,800 kids.* It was going to be so easy to be invisible in a school this size. All I had to do was coast through these last nine weeks of my senior year without any complications and I was free. In more ways than one. I'd be Sloane Sullivan forever. There was no going back to the person I was for the first twelve years of my life. I'd asked, but the Marshals felt dropping me back into my old life so soon after the confession was too risky, even with a plausible cover story. But honestly, I didn't care. If being Sloane was what it took to get out of witness protection, I'd do it.

Out of WITSEC. I never thought it was possible.

"I'm not sure you're going to need the map, pretty girl like you." Mrs. Zalinsky nodded in my direction. "You'll have the boys lining up to escort you to class if you smile at them like that."

I took a moment to let the compliment sink in. Usually, I ignored anything people said about my appearance because it was never about me. Not the real me anyway. It was about a person with dyed hair or colored contacts or—after one horrendous experience with a hairdresser who had to have forgotten her glasses that day—a frizzy black wig that felt like a steel wool scouring pad. But this was the closest I'd looked to my true self in almost six years.

I was wearing contacts that turned my green eyes dark brown, but my hair was its natural pale blond. "The color of real lemonade," my mom always said when I was a kid. Mark had never agreed to my natural color before. He'd deemed it "too light and distinctive," and I hadn't seen it since we left New Jersey. But since this was the person I was going to be for the rest of my life, I'd begged to go back to my roots. Washing my hair seventeen times in a single shower to get out the temporary auburn color I'd had as Ruby had been totally worth it.

I shook the piece of paper in my hand. "Thanks, but I don't need any boys. I've got a color-coded map!"

"You're welcome, dear. And if you ever have any trouble, just come to me. I marked the office with a bee." Mrs. Zalinsky pointed at her nameplate on the counter. Two bumblebees were drawn hovering around the *Z* in her name.

I examined the map. Sure enough, there was a little black-and-yellow bee floating next to the office. "I'll *bee* sure to do that," I joked.

Mrs. Zalinsky chuckled as she reached for a ringing phone.

17

I waved over my shoulder and opened the office door. The volume level rose considerably as I entered the bustling hallway. I glanced at the map just in case Mrs. Zalinsky was watching—I'd been well trained to keep up appearances— and turned left toward physics, my first class of the day.

Despite the fact that I'd arrived early, people were everywhere: crowding the hall, cramming books into lockers, making out in front of classrooms. They were just like the students at the six other high schools I'd attended, except here there were more of them. I loved it.

A sudden burst of sound to my left caught my attention. A group of about twelve guys, standing in a slightly curved line and wearing matching navy blazers, had started singing. *An a cappella group? That's new.* A crowd surrounded them, snapping and nodding along to something I recognized after a few seconds: "The Longest Time" by Billy Joel. A song I hadn't heard in years wasn't exactly what I expected from high school boys. Homesickness pricked my chest as I tried to figure out where I'd last heard it.

I slowed, watching the tallest guy singing lead in the center of the group as I passed. He had light brown skin and short dark brown hair, but even seeing the words come out of his mouth couldn't make the memory hovering at the edge of my brain come into focus. When his eyes met mine, I ducked my head. I hadn't even been watching him for a full minute, but it was all the time I needed to see it: the way the other boys took their cues from him; the slightly larger amount of space around him than any of the other guys, like his all-around awesomeness needed room to breathe; how every eye in the crowd followed him. He was popular. Charismatic. *Not* one to blend in. Therefore, not someone I wanted to know.

I kept my head down and studied my feet—lack of eye contact makes you more forgettable—as I turned the corner to the hall that would take me to physics. Which is why I didn't see the person barreling toward me until right before we collided.

I had just enough time to spread my feet and bend my knees slightly. I felt the crash in my whole body, muscles tensing, air rushing out of me in a muffled *umph*, but a tiny step back was all I needed to absorb the impact. The other person hit the floor with a loud thud, knocking everything I was holding in my hands across the hall. Before I could even cringe at the lack of blending in, a prickly sensation crept up my neck at the feeling of eyes on my back.

My chest tightened as the velvety a cappella voices, the mass of students, the entire hall disappeared. Fragmented images flashed in my mind: feet pounding on concrete, a hand tight on my arm, a broken piece of wood. Then, as fast as the images had come, they were gone, replaced with the hum of conversations and a person sprawled on the ground in front of me and too many students gathered around us. I swallowed hard. *They're not watching you, they're just curious. No one here knows you.*

I took a deep breath, trying to loosen the knot in my chest. "Walk much?" I mumbled, quiet enough I knew the guy who'd run into me wouldn't be able to hear. And I was certain it was a guy. The level of solidness I felt before he bounced off wasn't something a girl could achieve unless she was a professional bodybuilder from Russia.

"I'm *so* sorry," a deep voice said. "I shouldn't have been running. Are you okay?"

I didn't glance at him or any of the people now whispering about us as I bent down to gather my stuff. "I'm fine," I replied without any malice. I wasn't really annoyed at him, I was annoyed at myself. *That's what you get for letting some stupid Billy Joel song distract you. Remembering never helps anything.*

"Here." The guy shifted on the floor and collected the map from where it had landed a few feet away. He smoothed it out, even though it didn't have a mark on it, reached around the legs of a few nosy onlookers and held it out to me.

I grabbed it and shoved it into my bag. All I wanted was to get to physics and disappear into a seat in the back.

"Sloane Sullivan?"

My heart skipped a beat at hearing my name from some random guy. I flexed my hands, my always-on-alert muscles ready to put my self-defense skills to use. Then his hand came into my field of vision. He was holding my schedule, his thumb resting next to my name, and I almost laughed at how jumpy I was being. *Get a grip. It's not like you haven't done this first day thing before.*

"Cool," the boy said. "My grandfather's first name was Sullivan."

My eyes locked on the scuffed floor as my breath caught in my throat.

"Everyone should have two first names."

Every inch of my body froze as a completely different image popped into my head: black hair sticking up in all directions, deep blue eyes bright with amusement, mouth quirked into the same goofy grin it always wore when he said those words, words he'd said so many times before.

My pulse took off as the guy crouched in front of me, making it all but impossible to stand without facing him. "Let me help you up. It's the least I can do for a fellow double-first-namer."

The whole world slowed to a crawl as I forced myself to look up.

Right into the unmistakable deep blue eyes of Jason Thomas.

TWO

I studied the wide eyes staring back at me from only a foot away. It was impossible they belonged to Jason. But the pools of almost green around his pupils that melted into a deep ocean blue set against an even darker blue ring around the edges were exactly like I remembered. Exactly like I'd stared into a million times before.

This is bad. Very, very bad.

It had happened once before. Three and a half years ago, when we were living in Flagstaff. I thought I'd seen Ms. Jenkins, the elderly widow who lived across the street from me in New Jersey, come out of a gift shop one Thursday afternoon. I'd been inside a bookstore next door and was certain Ms. Jenkins hadn't seen me, but I still took the long way home and told Mark. Three hours later, we were in the car on the way to our next lives.

And I hadn't known Ms. Jenkins nearly as well as I knew Jason.

A crease appeared in between his eyebrows. He opened his mouth slightly then closed it, all while searching my face.

The contacts! I prayed the brown would be enough to throw him off. But when his gaze dropped to the left side of my neck, I knew I was in trouble. Mark's voice sounded in my head, as clear as if he was standing right next to me: *Lesson number six: take control of the situation.*

I shifted my hair to cover the faint pink scar on the side of my neck—the only proof I'd once had a large dark brown mole there—and stood. "Sorry about that. I wasn't watching where I was going." I grabbed my schedule with one hand and took hold of Jason's outstretched hand with the other, helping him up. "I'm Sloane, but you already know that." I nodded at my schedule.

The crease in between his eyebrows deepened. "Jason," he replied, still holding my hand.

I wanted to laugh at the deepness of his voice as I took in the rest of him. *What happened to the scrawny twelve-year-old I left behind?* Sure, his eyes were the same. And his black hair was still disheveled, only now it was tousled in a bed-head kind of way that could only be described as sexy. Which pretty much described the rest of him too. He'd filled out and grown super tall and it made my stomach flip as all the ways I'd changed from my twelve-year-old self ran through my head.

A husky voice interrupted the silence hanging between us. "Well, hel-lo."

I yanked my hand out of Jason's. A tall, slender guy with deep red hair was leaning against the lockers right next to me, holding a football. He inclined his head toward me and smiled. "Do you believe in love at first sight, or should I walk by again?"

I glanced from the boy to Jason and back again. "Um…"

A petite girl with olive skin materialized in between the boys. "Ignore him," she told me, shaking her head at Mr. Love-at-First-Sight. "He tries his lines out on every female he sees." She had shoulder-length, wavy dark brown hair with long bangs that swept across her forehead, partially covering one of her brown eyes. She turned to Jason and whacked him on the chest. "Babe! You practically mowed this poor girl down. How many times have I told you two playing football in the halls was going to end in bodily injury?"

Babe?

The girl turned back to me. "I'm Livie." She paused, peeking at the guys on either side of her, then sighed. "And if these two Neanderthals haven't properly introduced themselves yet, this is Sawyer—" she pointed to the pale redhead "—and this is my boyfriend, Jason." She wrapped her hands around Jason's arm.

The movement seemed to snap Jason out of his daze. "Oh, sorry, guys. This is Sloane." He gestured toward me.

I gave them the look of self-deprecation I'd perfected from constantly being the new girl. "You know, I expected to embarrass myself on my first day but I had no idea it was going to happen so quickly."

"It wasn't *your* fault," Livie insisted. "It's these two who should be embarrassed."

Out of the corner of my eye, I saw a flash of blue against a red background. Something twisted in my chest as I remembered the flash I thought I'd seen the night before outside the school. I turned my head, half expecting to see another brick wall.

Sawyer was on one knee in front of the row of red lockers,

his blue shirt still fluttering from his sudden movement. I shook my head. *Of course there isn't a brick wall.*

Sawyer gazed up at me, batting his eyelashes. "I, dear Sloane, offer my humblest of apologizes for causing you embarrassment by using my considerable strength to throw this football farther than Jason expected, making him run to catch it and crash into you. I promise to find a way to make up for my superhero-like muscles."

I glanced around. Most of the crowd that had stopped to watch the aftermath of my collision with Jason had moved on, but several girls were still hovering, giggling at Sawyer's spectacle. I tugged on his arm. "You can start by getting up," I hissed.

Livie helped pull Sawyer to his feet. "She's trying *not* to draw more attention to herself, genius."

Sawyer grinned at me, totally not sorry for making a scene, then leaned toward Jason. "Bet you can't top that apology."

Jason didn't respond. He was still studying me, head tilted to one side.

My eyes locked on Jason's and my pulse raced, pounding a rhythm in my head that sounded suspiciously like *it's not working.* I knew what I had to do.

I peered around Jason at the door to the girls' bathroom, barely visible down the hall. Thanks to my recon mission the night before (and lesson number two: notice every possible exit), I knew that bathroom had a window large enough to climb out of. I'd simply politely extract myself from the conversation, go into the bathroom and vanish without a trace. I'd be a new person in a new state by morning.

It wasn't a choice, it was a rule. And for good reason. Even

25

though I couldn't remember what I saw the day I entered WITSEC—a little online research at a public library one day when no one else was around told me I'd probably repressed the memories—I'd always known being discovered wouldn't be a good thing. The creepy flashes I got whenever it felt like someone was watching me. The way my dad and Mark had always refused to discuss what happened in front of me, whispering about my dad's testimony in hushed tones. How Mark once told me he never wanted me to remember. Disappearing was the safest thing to do.

I inched away from Jason, eyes on the bathroom, preparing to make my escape.

"Wait!" Livie blurted, pulling my attention back to the group. She dug in her bag, pulled out a wrinkled sheet of paper, and glanced at it before grinning at me. "You're Sloane Sullivan."

What is it with everyone here knowing my name?

Livie bounced a little on her toes. "I'm your First Day Buddy."

"My what?"

"You know, someone who shows you around on your first day, makes sure you don't eat the fish sandwich in the cafeteria, answers any questions that pop up. You have physics first period, right?"

No. No, no, no. I nod.

"Mrs. Zalinsky came into class yesterday and asked for a volunteer—" Livie looked pointedly at Sawyer "—which *some* people rolled their eyes at."

"If I had known it was going to be a cute girl, I would've

volunteered first," he grumbled. "Superheroes make great First Day Buddies."

Livie turned to me and lowered her voice. "Then it's lucky you got me."

I knew I shouldn't have trusted Mrs. Zalinsky. "You don't really have to do anything. I have a map. I'll be fine. And I'll totally tell everyone you did a great job."

"You might not need me, but I need you," Livie insisted. "Mr. Pruitt offered extra credit for volunteering, and I need all the help I can get in that class. And he *always* knows when someone's cheating, right, Jason?"

Jason nodded, his eyes slow to leave me and find Livie.

"Hey," Livie said, focusing on him. "You okay?"

"Yeah, sorry," Jason said with a slight chuckle. "I was momentarily horrified imagining Sawyer in a superhero costume."

"Shut up," Sawyer muttered, his cheeks turning pink.

Jason smirked and my breath caught in my throat.

The girl I'd been before WITSEC had faded from my memory quickly, buried beneath new girl after new girl. But Jason's smirk—that same irritatingly cute little smile he'd worn when we were kids—was like magic, breaking through the layers and shaking off the dirt on a hundred different memories at once. On all the times *I'd* been the one to sneak out and come up with ridiculous adventures for us, and he'd try to shoot them down even though he was just as excited as I was. A tiny piece of the girl I used to be, the girl who made up her own rules, sparked to life somewhere deep inside me and the craziest question popped into my head: *Could I stay?*

Livie grabbed my hand and pulled me closer, as if protecting me from Sawyer. "Don't worry," she fake whispered. "There are plenty of cute guys in this school to help erase the mental image of Sawyer in superhero spandex."

I gave a little shrug. "I don't know. *Superhero Sawyer* has a nice ring to it."

Sawyer grinned and Jason rolled his eyes and my mind kicked into overdrive.

Everything was riding on making it through this placement without a hitch. The alternative, not lasting only nine weeks in such a large school, hadn't seemed possible before today. I'd taken the SAT and filled out college applications as Sloane Sullivan months ago, before I even became Sloane Sullivan. I'd used a fake transcript painstakingly created from classes I'd actually taken, with grades I'd actually received, because I was tired of working hard for good grades that became pointless every time I became someone new. I was determined to get into college on my merit, like a normal person would. Well, as normally as I possibly could anyway.

And if we left North Carolina now, all my planning would be for nothing. Because Sloane Sullivan wouldn't exist anymore. I'd have to reapply as the girl I became next, and all the application deadlines had passed. Which meant I'd have to wait another year to apply to college. Another year to get out of WITSEC. Another year to start my life.

I couldn't wait another year.

Besides, disappearing had been the safest thing to do when there was no end in sight. When the threat of someone coming after me was more real. Now things were different. Thanks to the confession, the threat was basically nonexistent. And I was just a few weeks shy of getting out anyway. All I had to do was turn eighteen, graduate and have college lined up and ready to go. Those were Mark's conditions, and I was *so* close. Too close to let it all slip away by following the rules this time.

Livie groaned and released my hand to shove Sawyer gently into the bank of lockers. "There is no such thing as a 'super-human ability to attract hotties.'"

Jason glanced at me, one eyebrow raised and eyes sparkling. Even though I knew it was only his amusement at Sawyer's made-up superpower, it looked almost like a challenge. And just like that, my mind was made up. I was going to stay. I was going to convince Jason I wasn't the girl who used to live next door. I was going to get out of WITSEC on time.

No matter what.

THREE

I surveyed the cafeteria. Hundreds of voices floated through the air, wrapping around me like a cocoon. This was normally the part of my first day where I'd hang back and observe so I could find the perfect group to join: the one not too big and not too small; not overly popular, but not outsiders; not so involved in school activities as to draw attention to themselves, yet not so anti-school they stood out. Then I'd emerge from my cocoon as the girl I was going to be. The type of girl that, no matter who she was, would steer clear of anyone who looked at her with even the tiniest hint of familiarity. But this time was different.

This time I had a First Day Buddy who swore eating lunch together was a nonnegotiable part of the First Day Buddy contract. Which meant this time I'd be sitting with the only person in almost six years who knew the real me.

I eyed the table of artsy-looking kids across the room and sighed. They were laughing and teasing each other, saying hello to people walking by yet ignoring the attempts of the table of guys beside them to engage in some sort of food fight. I'd been artsy before, I could do it again. And sitting with them—acting like I not only didn't know Jason, but had no desire to get to know him—was the safest way to convince him I wasn't the girl he possibly remembered, the girl he'd grown up with. Instead, I was about to have lunch with him.

I took a deep breath. It was just one lunch, just one first day to get through, then I could get back to my plan of lying low. *You can do this.* But first, I needed something to eat.

I grabbed a tray and followed the familiar scent of cafeteria food to the open area at the back of the room where lunch ladies with hairnets were serving the day's options. The pizza looked surprisingly good, but it had a line at least fifty people deep. My stomach rumbled, protesting the wait. I went to the other end of the counter and thanked the lunch lady for a plate of what appeared to be roasted chicken, salad and a glop of orange mush. I wrinkled my nose.

Someone chuckled. "It's not as bad as it looks."

Startled, I turned to find the tall a cappella guy standing next to me. I stared for a second, mesmerized by his piercing green eyes. Then I quickly peered back at the orange goop. "What is it?"

"Mashed sweet potatoes."

I wrinkled my nose again.

He laughed, flashing two dimples. "I'm glad I came over. Now I have something else to call you."

I tilted my head in confusion.

"I've been referring to you as New Girl in my head all morning," he clarified. "But now I can add Hater of Sweet Potatoes to the list."

"Ah." I took a step closer to him to avoid the line forming for the chicken, glancing around at the same time. No one seemed to be paying any attention to us. "And what should I call you?" I pointed at his empty hands. "Disrespecter of Lunch Trays?"

He grinned. "I already bought my lunch. I came over just to talk to you."

A wave of apprehension flowed through me. *This better not be some kind of prank on the new girl.*

"I saw your collision this morning and just wanted to make sure you were okay," he said with a shrug. "I thought maybe you could use a friend who isn't trying to body slam you."

Okay, not what I was expecting at all. "You saw that, huh?"

"You know, maybe I should call you Receiver of a Completely Uncalled-For Hallway Football Smackdown. Believe it or not, that's not the way most of us welcome a new student."

A tiny smile formed on my lips. "Maybe I should be Creator of the Full-Contact First-Day Meet and Greet. Guaranteed to get you up close and personal with your new classmates."

He bit back his own smile. "Actually, I was hoping you'd be Needer of a Place to Sit?" He nodded at a table over his shoulder that was surprisingly empty.

My reply was interrupted by a husky voice shouting, "There you are!" over the cafeteria chatter. I turned and saw Sawyer rushing over.

Sawyer placed his hands on my shoulders. "Livie was afraid you got lost. Come on, you can pay over here and then I'll show you to our table." He nodded at the a cappella guy and muttered, "Hey, man," before steering me away.

I peeked back over my shoulder.

"Watch out for flying sports equipment!" the guy called after me.

I grinned until I spotted a girl with a short black pixie haircut glaring at me from a nearby table full of girls now watching me. I knew what that glare meant: Mr. Welcoming Committee probably once belonged at that table and according to its current occupants, he was off-limits. The smile disappeared from my face.

"What do you want to drink?" Sawyer asked, drawing my attention back to him. "Water, juice, milk?"

"Water." I pressed my lips together, annoyed at myself for forgetting I was in ground zero of high school social cliques. I already had Jason to deal with. I didn't need any other complications.

Sawyer placed a bottle of water on my tray and took the tray out of my hands. "Let me pay for this."

"What? Sawyer, no." I tried unsuccessfully to pry the tray away from him.

He pulled a card out of his pocket and held it against a scanner by the cashier. "Already done."

"You didn't have to do that," I protested as I followed him across the cafeteria.

"I was the one who convinced Jason to play football this morning. This is my way of apologizing." He shrugged, but his expression showed he considered it something more than an apology.

I hoped he wasn't considering it a date.

Sawyer led me to the end of a table where Jason and Livie were already sitting next to each other. Livie slipped her hand out of Jason's and waved when she saw us.

"So." Sawyer settled into the seat next to me, across from Jason and Livie, and slid my tray over. "Are you from Tennessee?"

My heart skipped a beat. I had lived in Tennessee. Granted, it had only been for two months, but it hadn't even been a year since we'd left. *Please don't tell me I have to worry about someone in addition to Jason recognizing me.*

"Because you're the only *ten I see*," Sawyer continued without giving me the chance to reply.

I let out a shaky laugh. I could've hugged the person who created such a corny joke right then.

Livie groaned. "At least let her eat before you pile on the pickup lines. They're hard to take on an empty stomach."

Sawyer reached over and snatched a piece of pepperoni off Livie's pizza. "You're just jealous I found someone new to pick up. Plus, I think Sloane likes them."

"I think you're delusional," Livie fired back. "And I'm actually *thrilled* you've found someone else to practice on."

Jason leaned across the table toward me, a half smile playing on his lips. "They argue like this all the time. You'll get used to it."

It was a look I remembered now too, like the smirk. The one that always made it seem like he was letting me in on a secret.

Jason popped a tomato from his salad into his mouth. "So where are you really from?"

I hesitated, instinct warning me to tell him as little as possible. But this was why Mark created fictional backstories every time we moved.

"Pierre, South Dakota," I lied.

"Wow," Livie said. "What's it like there?"

I bit back a grin. "Cold." I'd never actually been to South Dakota, but I had lived in four of the six states that bordered it and that much I knew well. I peeked at Jason. "I lived there my whole life though, so I got used to it."

"You probably didn't get to see much water," Sawyer guessed.

I furrowed my eyebrows. "It's on the Missouri River. And there's a large lake nearby." *Thank you, internet research.*

Sawyer's light brown eyes brightened. "But have you seen the ocean yet? The beach is so close. Maybe I can show you."

I glanced down at my plate. I grew up in the Atlantic Ocean, like all the other kids who lived in my beach town on the Jersey Shore. But I hadn't seen it since I left; I hadn't even been back to the East Coast since I left. And I wasn't ready to see it again. "Yeah, maybe."

"Are you a senior?" Livie asked.

I nodded.

She frowned. "It must've been really hard to move this close to graduation. I moved here at the beginning of the school year and it sucked starting my senior year someplace new, even with the First Day Buddy I got."

"It's not that bad. My dad got a new job and he had to start right away."

"But what about your mom?" Livie continued. "I mean, couldn't you two have stayed in South Dakota for a few more weeks until you graduated and then met your dad out here?"

"I don't have a mom," I said.

Sawyer and Livie wore matching shocked expressions but

Jason's eyes were a bit narrowed, more curious than surprised. I pretended not to notice.

"I mean, I *have* one. I just don't know where she is." I stabbed a piece of chicken with my fork. "My parents were only sixteen when they had me. My mom stuck around until I was three but she wanted freedom and parties, not a toddler. So she took off and it's been just my dad and me ever since." It was a variation of the story we used every time Mark pretended to be my father.

Livie sat straighter. "Your dad's been taking care of you by himself since he was nineteen? That's so sweet." She fiddled with the edge of Jason's shirt around his bicep. "We should set him up with your mom."

I put my fork down. "What?"

"Jason's parents are divorced and his mom's the best. She totally needs a sweetheart to sweep her off her feet."

Disbelief coursed through me. I never would've thought it was possible for Jason's parents to be anything other than fairy-tale happily-ever-after in love. *What happened?*

Jason rubbed the back of his neck. "You know she doesn't like blind dates."

"So we'll have a welcome party for Sloane and her dad," Livie said. She wrapped her hands around Jason's arm and scooted closer to him. "I can help your mom cook and she can get to know Sloane's dad before they go out. Then it won't be a blind date."

Even if Mark would've gone for that, Jason looked uncomfortable with the idea. And there was no way I was putting the two of them in the same room together. "My dad's really busy with his new job. It might be a while before he has any free time."

Livie's shoulders fell. "Oh."

Jason gave me a grateful smile. "I think you came at the perfect time. All the senior stuff is about to start."

"That's right," Sawyer agreed. He bumped my shoulder with his own. "Tomorrow's the senior scavenger hunt. Every team has to get pictures of different things around school and the team that completes their list the fastest gets to pick the music that plays when we march out of graduation."

I inched my chair away from his. "Really? You can pick any song?"

Jason nodded. "As long as it doesn't have curse words, anything goes." He turned to Sawyer. "Remember last year was that continuous loop of the theme song to *Mister Rogers' Neighborhood*?"

"If we win we should pick 'Fight for Your Right' by the Beastie Boys," Sawyer declared.

Jason pointed his fork at Sawyer. "Can't go wrong with a classic."

"Come on!" Livie whined. "Don't Sloane and I get a say?"

I choked on a bite of chicken. "You want me on your team?" I'd already been plotting ways to avoid the whole thing.

"It's part of your First Day Buddy experience. Mrs. Zalinsky was adamant about me including you on my team."

Damn Mrs. Zalinsky and her thoughtfulness. "You really don't have to—"

"Nope," Sawyer interrupted. "There's no getting out of it.

You *have* to be on our team." He patted my arm like he was comforting a confused senior citizen. "You're part of the club."

I opened my mouth then closed it, trying to figure out where he was going with this. "What club?"

Sawyer widened his ever-present grin. "You are *Sloane Sullivan*, right?"

My heart stuttered, but I plastered on a teasing smile. "Who else would I be?"

Jason's eyes lit up as he held my gaze. "Two first names," he explained.

I tore my eyes away from Jason to study Sawyer and Livie. "Wait. Do all of you have two first names?"

Livie pointed as she identified each of them. "Jason Thomas, Sawyer James, and Liv Dawson."

Leave it to Jason to find a whole club. "Okay, but does Sullivan really count as a first name?"

Jason nodded. "It was my grandpa's first name, remember?"

Memories I hadn't thought of in years danced in my head: Jason's grandpa dressed like Santa every Christmas, the way he'd pull quarters from behind my ear, going to his funeral when we were nine. My pulse raced. *Is he asking if I remember all that?*

"I said that when I saw your schedule this morning," Jason continued.

I blew out a silent breath.

"There's that cute actor from the FBI show with the tattoos. His first name is Sullivan," Livie added, unaware of my momentary panic. "Oh, and the singer for some punk band I've never heard of before. Some girls were talking about him in class the other day."

"Plus," Jason said, "your first and last name start with the same sound. That cancels out the fact you think it doesn't count."

When Jason smiled, I couldn't help but smile back. An obsession with both Superman and Spider-Man when we were little made him believe that anyone with first and last names that started with the same sound could really be a superhero in disguise.

Livie made a dismissive noise. "Of course they'll count Sullivan. My last name's *Dawson* and they let me in."

"Dawson's a first name," Sawyer insisted. "What about *Dawson's Creek*?"

"It's a *fictional* first name," Livie said. "Have you ever met a real person named Dawson?"

Sawyer laughed. "Some of us like having a first name based on a fictional character, right, Sloane?"

I turned to Sawyer. "How'd you know my name is based on a fictional character?"

He shrugged. "The only Sloane I've heard of before is from that movie *Ferris Bueller's Day Off.*"

My skin tingled as the very first time I had to pick a name—the time I'd accidentally started naming myself after fictional characters—popped into my head.

My dad spun in a circle, his eyes bouncing around the room without ever landing on anything, like he was in a daze. "What else?" He wrung his hands together. "Underwear. Did you pack underwear?"

My gaze darted to two burly guys in suits huddled between my twin bed and the desk Jason helped paint blue and purple. They were mumbling to each other, oblivious to the underwear comment. I studied the tiny duffel bag on top of my flower bedspread. "Yes."

"We really need to get going," one man insisted, examining his watch.

Dad nodded. He leaned toward me, beads of sweat collecting on his forehead. "Pick the thing you want to bring as your personal item, okay? I'm going to go pack a few things for Mom." He rushed out of the room, leaving me with strangers.

The two guys by the desk glanced at each other, then followed Dad into the hall.

"What do you want your name to be?"

I jumped. I hadn't heard the third guy, who'd been keeping watch by my window, sneak up on me. He smelled sweaty and I swallowed hard, trying not to throw up again.

"Well?" he prompted in his thick Jersey accent.

I balled my shaking hands into fists and blinked uncomprehendingly in his direction. Over his shoulder, I spotted Alice's Adventures in Wonderland sitting on my bookshelf. "Alice," I muttered. Because that was how I felt: like I was falling down a rabbit hole.

It was easier the second time, even though I was still terrified.

Mark turned off the TV and knelt in front of me. Something about his cologne calmed my pounding heart. I took a deep breath. The spicy scent was so much better than the stale-smelling lumpy couch I was lying on.

"I know it's only been three weeks, but we need to move again," he said in a soothing voice. "So you're going to have to pick a new name."

I gazed over his shoulder at Dad, who was leaning against the cramped motel room wall. His dyed brown hair was matted to his head and his brown eyes were bloodshot. He looked like he hadn't slept in days, but he gave me a slight nod of encouragement.

I closed my eyes and imagined who I wanted to be. Because any-one had to be better than the broken girl Alice was.

"Beth," *I whispered. I'd just started reading* Little Women *and Beth's character was described as living in a happy world of her own. That's just what I needed.*

"Hmm." *Mark rubbed his chin.* "You picked Alice from the Wonderland book, right?"

I nodded, surprised he knew that. He hadn't been in my room that day.

"Did you know Lewis Carroll based that character on a real girl named Alice Liddell?"

I sat up. "No."

"What if we use Beth Liddell?" *He stood.* "It'll be our little se-cret, the connection between your names."

A hint of a smile formed on my lips. "Okay."

And even though I soon found out Beth ended up dying in *Little Women*, that was how the tradition was born. I picked the first name and Mark picked the last. I went alphabetically, because it helped me remember what letter my name started with every time we moved, and he chose something related to my prior first name. Which was simple, given it always came from a book or movie or song. It gave me an easy answer when someone asked about my name. Because, like Sawyer, someone always asked. It was the one constant I found everywhere we went: people were curious.

I'd been Charlotte from *Charlotte's Web*, Elise from The Cure's "A Letter to Elise," and Jenny from *Forrest Gump*. And now Sloane from *Ferris Bueller's Day Off*. Hey, it was on TV when I was picking. And who wouldn't want to be the girl having a fun ditch day with her boyfriend?

I nodded at Sawyer. "You guessed it—I'm named after Ferris Bueller's girlfriend. And you—" I tapped a finger against my lip "—must be named after Tom Sawyer."

Sawyer's mouth dropped open in offense. "No. I'm named after Sawyer from the TV show *Lost*."

I snickered. "That show wasn't on TV yet when we were born."

Jason chuckled.

"Busted," Livie sang.

Sawyer blushed. "Okay, fine. I thought it would go over better with the ladies if I was named after a sensitive bad boy rather than some kid in a boring old book."

I placed a hand over my heart. "I happen to like that boring old book. And if your *ladies* can't figure out how to Google when a TV show first aired, maybe you need to find some smarter ones."

Sawyer gave me a lazy smile as his eyes roamed up and down my body. "Maybe I should."

Livie's eyes danced. "It's going to be so entertaining to watch you crash and burn again."

Sawyer glared at her.

Dial it back, Sloane. Blend in. Be forgettable. Start asking them the questions. "So," I said, "what other senior stuff is coming up?"

Sawyer wiggled his eyebrows at me. "Prom."

"Career day," Livie added.

"The senior trip," Jason said.

Livie gasped and released Jason's arm to point at me. "You and I can room together! This is perfect!"

Good God, how far is she going to take this First Day Buddy thing? "What's the senior trip?"

Jason straightened a stack of napkins on his tray. "It's a school tradition that all seniors take an overnight field trip to Charleston the last weekend in April. Everyone goes. We visit Fort Sumter and tour the city and eat good food."

"And people smuggle alcohol along and party in their hotel rooms," Sawyer said.

Jason shot him a pointed look. "But not too much alcohol, right?"

"What?" Sawyer's voice was a little too innocent.

"Last time you drank, you got pissed someone beat you at cards and punched a hole in the drywall in your basement." Livie shook her head. "I know you haven't forgotten being grounded for a month."

"Whatever," Sawyer muttered. A blush crept up his neck.

Livie turned back to me. "So what do you think?"

School traditions and parties and alcohol were all things I tended to stay away from. Plus, I wasn't sure how Mark would react to an overnight field trip. But a tiny flutter of excitement ran through me. Because traveling, actually going to a new place just to sightsee and hang out and *not* have to change names to do it, sounded amazing. "Is it too late for me to sign up?"

"Not at all. The forms are due in two days. You have to room with someone of the same sex and I've been having trouble finding someone."

She must seriously be in need of some female friends.

"But the roommates don't really matter," Livie continued,

"because I heard the chaperones go to bed early and every-one sneaks out and hooks up." She peeked sideways at Jason.

Jason's shoulders tensed. He picked up a napkin, scrunched it into a ball and held it out to Sawyer. "Bet you can't get this into that trash can." His eyes brightened as he pointed at an open, industrial-sized, round plastic trash can sitting about twelve feet away.

Livie rolled her eyes and pulled her phone out of her pocket.

I suppressed a smile as more memories came flooding back. When Jason and I were little, we made bets about everything, like who could run around his house three times the fastest or who had the longest french fry in their Happy Meal or who could knock the most action figures off the deck railing with a Nerf gun. Making goofy bets was one of the things about the old me that had disappeared the fastest.

Sawyer cocked an eyebrow. "Loser has to make all the shirts for the scavenger hunt?"

"You're on," Jason replied.

Sawyer took the napkin from Jason.

My hands itched to snatch it from him and shoot it my-self. The girl Jason knew had been a horrible basketball player who never could've made the shot they were talking about. But I'd just left Lexington, Kentucky, home of the University of Kentucky, where basketball is king. Mark and I had really gotten into the Wildcats' season, and had even gotten a basket-ball hoop at our house. We'd spent hours playing each other. I tucked my fingers under my legs so I couldn't grab a napkin and turn it into a ball.

The boys each made their first shots and missed their sec-ond, Sawyer's by a good two feet. At the start of round three,

Sawyer got a lucky bounce, his ball ricocheting off the rim and disappearing inside. But as soon as Jason lined up for his shot, I could tell his trajectory was off. The napkin hit the side of the trash can and landed on the floor.

"Yes!" Sawyer raised his hands in triumph.

I so could've beaten them both.

"Your gloating is childish," Livie said without glancing up from her phone. For a second I thought she was talking to me.

Jason turned to Sawyer. "Looks like I'll be decorating T-shirts."

"T-shirts?" I asked.

"Every scavenger hunt team wears matching shirts," Sawyer explained. "It's not a rule or anything, but people take it pretty seriously."

"We're going to my house after school to make them," Jason said. "You should come since you'll need one too."

No way. Jason's house meant Jason's mom and that was just…no. I couldn't risk being seen by anyone else who knew me. I opened my mouth to give them an excuse.

"No excuses," Livie said, pointing at me. "You say no to everything, but we want you to come."

The boys nodded their agreement.

"Let me guess, it's a required part of the First Day Buddy contract?"

Livie grinned. "You catch on quick."

Sawyer peeked at me. "We could do it at my house instead. I can give you a ride if you need one, Sloane."

I internally winced. I *couldn't* go to Jason's house, yet I didn't want to encourage Sawyer by taking him up on his offer.

"We can't do it at your house," Jason said. "You said your mom was hosting some book club thing."

"Crap. I forgot about that."

"Besides," Jason continued, "my mom will be at work. We'll have the place to ourselves." He gave me a half smile. "Want to come over and help us decide what to put on the shirts?"

His mom wasn't going to be there. That changed things. I wanted to see where he lived and what his room looked like and maybe find out what happened to his parents. "I can come for a little while."

"Great!" Sawyer exclaimed with such enthusiasm you would've thought I'd just agreed to go to the prom with him. "I can still give you a ride if you want." He grabbed his phone out of his bag. "Or I can text you directions to J's." He frowned at the phone for a moment. "There's something wrong with my phone." Then he looked up and gave me a lopsided grin. "It doesn't have your number in it."

I snorted. "I can't fix that."

Livie shot Sawyer a smug look. "Crash and burn."

"No," I insisted, "I meant I don't have a phone." Under the table, I ran a hand over the pocket where my phone was hiding. My secret only-use-to-keep-in-touch-with-Mark-and-never-share-the-number-under-strict-penalty-of-death phone.

All three stared at me like I'd just sprouted wings.

"I had one," I mumbled. "I got really addicted to it a few years ago and gave it up cold turkey. No social media accounts either. You should try it. I have so much more free time now."

Livie's mouth dropped open. "I could never live without my

phone." From the seriousness of her voice, she clearly ranked *phone* on her list of necessities right next to *food* and *oxygen*.

I reached into my backpack, pulled out a piece of paper and a pen and slid them over to Jason. "You can be old-school and write your address down. I'll find my way there."

He scribbled something, folded the paper, and slid it back to me just as a middle-aged woman wearing a suit and stiletto heels approached us. "Gentlemen, I expect you to clean up the remnants of your little basketball game." She rapped a knuckle on our table as she walked by.

"Yes, Principal Thompson," Jason and Sawyer replied in unison.

They both jumped up to collect the trash. As soon as they were out of earshot, Livie leaned across the table, her voice low so the boys wouldn't hear. "How'd you get Oliver Clarke to talk to you?"

"Who?"

She made an impatient sound. "Oliver Clarke? Voice so smooth you just want to eat him up? Eyes so green they make everyone else's jealous?"

Um, okay. I'd admired his voice earlier, but eating him hadn't popped into my head. "Oh, him."

"Yes, *him*." Livie sighed. "He broke up with his girlfriend about a week ago. Or maybe she broke up with him. No one knows exactly what happened, but the rumors are flying. He basically hasn't been talking to anyone since. They'd been dating forever, even though she's probably the worst person in this school, so it was kind of a big deal."

"Let me guess. His ex-girlfriend has short black hair?"

"Yeah. How'd you know?"

"She didn't seem to like it when I talked to him."

Livie slapped a hand on the table. "I knew it! He must've dumped her."

"What's her deal?"

Livie watched Oliver's ex for a few seconds, eyes serious. "She knows everyone's secrets and likes to share."

I peered over my shoulder at Oliver, reading quietly at his deserted table. *He's in some kind of self-imposed social exile because of a gossip-inducing breakup with the secret-sharing "worst person" in the school? There are so many reasons to stay away from him.*

"Nobody in their right mind would break up with Oliver," Livie said. "I mean, there are definitely hotter guys here." Her gaze darted around the cafeteria, presumably landing on all the boys she thought were better looking, but she never once glanced in Jason's direction. "But that *voice*." She looked at me. "I would do absolutely anything he asked if he sang it to me."

Hold up. Did she just imply Oliver was a better catch than her boyfriend? He was kind of cute. And apparently single, not that I would've done anything about it. I'd learned the hard way not to get attached to anyone because I never knew when I'd have to leave at the worst possible time. But Oliver didn't have anything on Jason.

Livie launched into a story about some elaborate revenge Oliver's ex got on the last girl to hit on him, but I wasn't listening. I unfolded the piece of paper in my hands. Under his address, Jason had written two sentences: *Bet you Sawyer uses at least five inappropriate pickup lines on you while you're at my house. Loser has to teach him the meaning of moderation?*

I smiled. Oliver definitely didn't have anything on Jason.

FOUR

The back screen door slammed shut behind me. "Mark?"

"In here, Kid."

I smiled at the nickname and followed his voice to the family room of our rental house. It was smaller and a little more run-down than some of the other places we'd lived in, but it had the beachy feel of home. Mark was sprawled on the blue couch, legs propped up on the square glass coffee table next to a pile of mail.

"Did you hear about this one?" he asked, shaking his head at his laptop. "Nineteen-year-old broke into a condo, stole a bunch of electronics, including a cell phone, and left his own phone *sitting on the condo's kitchen table.*"

I snorted.

"Wait! There's more. When he realized what he did about an hour later, he called his phone. The condo's owner, who had since come home and realized she'd been burglarized, answered and he *gave her his name* and asked if he could have his phone back." Mark grinned widely. "The cops arrested him half an hour later."

I plopped on the couch next to him. "Amateur."

"Seriously. What's happening to criminals these days?"

I watched Mark laugh as he set his laptop aside. I'd always been amazed at how much older or younger he could look with a few little changes. When he let his hair grow longer and was clean-shaven, he could easily pass as someone in his early twenties. But when he looked like he did now, with a shorter haircut and a few days' worth of facial hair, he seemed fifteen years older. It was a skill that let him pose as a wide variety of men in my life, from father to uncle to older brother. Which was funny, because he'd never felt like an actual father or uncle or older brother, not even when I was younger. He'd always been more like the older brother's best friend you see in the movies, the one who's always around, teasing and annoying you, but who'll beat up the guy who's mean to you at school without blinking an eye. The one you choose to count as family. That's Mark.

"What?" he asked, realizing I was staring.

"Just admiring my old man." I ruffled his hair, which was its natural medium brown color. The only thing about him that wasn't natural were the contacts that turned his brown eyes hazel. "It's been a while since I've seen you look so distinguished."

"Shut up," he muttered with a laugh as he smoothed out his hair. "So how was the first day?"

I studied my feet resting next to his on the coffee table. "The usual. Nothing exciting." Guilt flared red hot in my chest.

I'd only ever lied to him once before, and even that was more of an omission of a detail than a full-blown lie. The desire to tell him about Jason was stronger than I'd been ex-pecting. Mark was my *person*, the one I could tell anything to, the only one who'd always been there for me. Lying to him sucked.

Then I remembered *why* I wasn't telling him the truth. No one had ever been officially released from WITSEC before. Once you're in, you're in for life. But I was special. A "one-of-a-kind situation," Mark had said when we started plan-ning Sloane and Mark Sullivan. But if the Marshals knew I'd been seen by someone from my past? Who knows how long it would be before they thought it was safe enough again to let me out.

Mark bumped my shoulder, trying to get my attention. "Any stalkers?"

My heart fluttered as I smiled. It sounded like a joke, but he was serious. I hadn't been smart about someone once before, and I'd promised to never make that mistake again. "No. I did get forced into a group of overly friendly people though."

He pretended to wipe a tear from his eye. "I'm so proud of my little girl, making friends on her first day."

I whacked him on the arm. "I'm actually about to head over to one of their houses in a few minutes."

His smile faltered. "Going to someone's house already? Is that a good idea?"

"They gave me a First Day Buddy."

"Oh." It came out like a laugh, like he knew how much it would annoy me.

"Exactly. There's this senior scavenger hunt thing tomor-row, and I'm on her team and I have to help with something for it. But don't worry, I won't stay long. Wouldn't want to come home late and disturb your beauty sleep, not with the new job starting tomorrow."

"Ah, yes. The rigorous demands of a college maintenance man require much rest."

"Don't make fun of your fake profession. It's served us well."

"That's true," he agreed, stretching his arms above his head. "Who knew there were so many colleges and universities across this great land of ours? Plus, I never feel guilty when we skip out without giving notice." He stood, scattering a few pieces of junk mail to the floor.

I crumpled an ad into a ball and threw it into the middle of the small trash can across the room. "Ha!"

Mark chuckled. "Are you going to be back for dinner? I'm making fettuccine alfredo."

I followed him into the kitchen, groaning with pleasure the whole way. "I would *never* miss your fettuccine. It's one of your best dishes."

"Well, at least not having any friends has paid off. I don't have to answer their nosey questions, and I've had all this free time to master my cooking skills."

I frowned. I knew he'd given up everything for me. I wondered, not for the first time, whether he regretted it. "We have each other for a friend. Who needs anyone else?"

The corners of his mouth turned up slightly as he studied me. Something I didn't recognize flashed in his eyes.

I pursed my lips. "You know I appreciate everything you do for me, right? Including making fabulous food."

Mark dropped his eyes. "I know." He was quiet for a moment. "I like doing things for you." He patted his ridiculously toned stomach. "*I* certainly don't need the extra calories."

"Please," I scoffed. "Like you have an inch of fat on you."

"I do!" He looked up, eyes bright. "We've been slacking on lesson number eleven lately."

I placed my hands flat against the small kitchen island and glared at him. "We have not been slacking on our long distance running! And I've played many a basketball game with you shirtless recently, and you've got nothing to worry about."

He flashed a grin, the one where the right side of his mouth rose more than the left. It was the grin he used when he was giving me a hard time, and guilt spread through my chest again.

I intertwined my fingers and examined the lines across one of my palms, tracing them with my thumb. "So apparently there's a senior trip coming up."

Mark had his head buried in the refrigerator. "Like a beach trip after graduation? Do seniors still do that?"

"No, like a chaperoned overnight field trip to Charleston the last weekend in April. It sounds like all the seniors go. It's a school tradition."

The sounds of his rummaging stopped. "I don't know." There was a long pause before he spoke again. "What if something goes wrong? What about your eyes?"

"I can keep my contacts in. It's just one night." I continued to study my palm, afraid of looking at him when I said what I'd been rehearsing all afternoon in my head. "Plus, I was kind of thinking this placement could be like a test. Once I'm out, I'm going to have to deal with things myself. It might be good to get some practice making my own decisions while you're still around to back me up. And I think I want to go."

The silence made my heart race until I finally glanced up, unable to take it any longer. Mark was leaning against the speckled laminate countertop, nodding his head slowly. "You're right." His eyes locked on mine. "You're prepared, but you need to be confident you can handle yourself. And I want you to make your own decisions. So if you want to go, go."

I was surprised at how much lighter I felt. He may not have known about Jason or that I'd already begun making my own decisions, but it felt like he was telling me I'd done the right thing. And I trusted his judgment without question.

I walked up the path to the small blue house with a bounce in my step. I felt empowered by Mark's approval to go on the trip, and the sight of Jason's house, with flowerpots scattered across the front porch and lace curtains in the windows, reminded me of New Jersey. I rang the doorbell.

Sawyer answered the door with his usual lazy grin. He stepped aside and swept an arm toward the inside of Jason's house. "Sloane Sullivan, come on down. You're the next contestant in the Sawyer James game of love."

Jason stood behind Sawyer. He flashed me a half smile and mouthed, *One.*

The excited buzz of being in on a secret Jason bet shot through me as I stepped inside. Jason's half smile wasn't the only familiar thing I saw. Walking through his house was like taking a trip back in time. The overstuffed yellow chair in the living room was the same one we used to build forts around. The large round wooden table in the kitchen was the same one I'd eaten at a thousand times. And the brown couch I saw as I followed the guys into the rec room in the basement still had the tear on the edge of the right cushion I'd made with a pair of scissors during a bet to see who could make the most paper snowflakes in five minutes.

I peeked around the rec room. Besides the comfy brown couch, there was a coffee table, a couple of beanbag chairs facing a flat-screen TV, a bar with a mini refrigerator in one corner of the room and a Ping-Pong table that dominated the back half. A DVD collection spilled out of the entertainment center onto the floor and two different video game consoles competed for space on the entertainment center's shelves. I could see why they hung out here.

"Hey, Sloane!" Livie called from a fuzzy beanbag chair.

"Hey," I replied as I noticed the movie on TV. I raised an eyebrow at Jason. *"Ferris Bueller's Day Off?"*

"Sawyer brought it over. He's got a thing for '80s movies. We put it on in your honor, but Livie's been skipping around to her favorite parts."

It was on one of my favorite parts too: where Ferris leaves Sloane at the end to make his mad dash through people's backyards in order to beat his parents home. As movie Sloane watches him go, she says, "He's gonna marry me." That scene was the real reason I'd picked the name Sloane, because I'd been jealous of that Sloane's certainty about the future, or at least her ability to even plan for the future. That's what I wanted as Sloane.

Livie sighed and glanced up at me. "I forgot how good this movie is."

I studied her as she turned back to the TV. Mark actually said yes to the senior trip. I had the chance to go somewhere by myself for two glorious days and all I needed was a roommate. I knew it wasn't the smartest idea, but neither was standing in the middle of Jason's house and nothing bad had happened yet. "I talked to my dad and I'm in for the senior trip."

Livie squealed and jumped up, spinning me around in a giant hug.

"You're making my dizzy!"

Livie pulled back and clapped. "We're going to have so much fun!"

My plastered-on grin mirrored her own. I was definitely not used to this much girl time. *Two days of freedom better be worth this.* I stepped away from Livie and nodded at the plain white T-shirts and permanent markers scattered across the coffee table. "So what's the plan for the shirts?"

Sawyer fell into the couch with a sigh. "We have no idea. We've been trying to come up with something related to our double first names for weeks, but we can't think of anything good."

"Just do whatever," Livie said as she reclaimed her spot in the beanbag chair and pulled out her phone. "It's not that big a deal."

As I walked behind her on my way to the couch, I caught sight of a photo Livie had open on her phone: sunset over the brightest blue water I'd ever seen. The sun was a fiery ball at the edge of the sky, turning the clouds around it amazing shades of orange and pink and purple. "That picture's beautiful."

Livie glanced up. "Oh, thanks."

"Where is it?"

"Um, nowhere, really. Not like this." She tapped the screen and frowned. "I've been editing it, trying to make the colors really pop, but I can't get it right." Her eyes narrowed at something I couldn't see. "I like to get creative with reality."

I sat next to Sawyer on the couch and smoothed out a T-shirt. If Livie could be creative, so could I. "What if we do something that's not related to first names?"

Jason pulled a beanbag chair to the edge of the coffee table and sat. "Like what?"

I eyed Sawyer. "Superheroes."

His eyebrows furrowed. "Superheroes?"

"Yeah. I mean, I got run into in the hall today because someone here *supposedly* has superhero muscles."

Livie snorted.

Sawyer flexed his arm, which was surprisingly muscular for such a skinny guy. "There's no *supposedly* about it." He leaned closer to me. "Wanna touch it?"

I pushed his arm away with one finger. "Why don't you use that muscle to draw a superhero symbol?"

Jason tapped a marker on the coffee table. His eyes locked on mine and that half smile appeared.

Livie plopped onto the couch next to me, her phone nowhere in sight for once. "I'm totally being Black Widow."

"Are Superman and Supergirl a thing?" Sawyer shifted so his leg was pressed against mine. "Because that's who we should be."

I leaned in and whispered in his ear, "I'm pretty sure Superman and Supergirl are cousins."

He chuckled. "Ooh, naughty."

Livie gave me an amused smile, one eyebrow slightly raised in question. My cheeks grew hot. I hadn't been trying to flirt—just to give a smartass answer like I'd give to Mark at home—but maybe that's how it looked. "Um, where's the bathroom?"

Livie pointed over her shoulder. "Down that hall, first door on your right."

"Don't try the door on the left," Sawyer warned. "It's like the Room of Requirement or platform nine and three-quarters or something else that requires magical blood to enter."

I paused at the entrance to the hall, a slight smile on my lips. "Should I have brought my wand?"

Sawyer grinned. "Nope. The Door That Must Not Be Opened is wand-proof."

"What if I had the special platform nine and three-quarters ticket? Could I walk through it?"

"Even that wouldn't work." Sawyer snatched a marker out of Livie's hand. "It's J's room, which is strictly off-limits to anyone but him."

I opened my mouth but Livie spoke first. "Don't ask. Neither of us has ever been inside. It's a weird *Jason* thing, like the bets."

I peeked at Jason, who was studying a blank T-shirt and biting the inside of his cheek. *It's not weird, it's sweet.*

"But if you come back over here," Sawyer drawled, "I'll show you something that's nine and three-quarters."

"Gross!" Livie smacked him on the back of his head. "That's no way to talk to someone you just met. And physically impossible."

"Fine," he grunted. "Would it be better if I said, 'Come back over, I need help whomping my willow.'"

"Oh my God!" I exclaimed. "You did not just turn Harry Potter into something dirty!"

"Oh, come on!" Sawyer responded. "You can come back. I promise I'll be gentle when I *Slytherin*."

My eyes grew wide.

"My name may not be Luna, but I sure can Lovegood."

I clamped my hands over my ears. "Stop! You're ruining one of my favorite book series!"

I looked at Jason. His eyes were gleaming. *Two, three, four, five*, he mouthed in quick succession. *I win*.

I groaned, but couldn't help laughing as I turned into the hall. My smile grew even larger when I realized it was lined with framed photographs.

There were some I didn't recognize, but many more I did. Five-year-old Jason on Christmas morning straddling a bike that matched the one I'd found under my tree. Seven-year-old Jason with a wide front-teeth-missing smile and a dripping ice cream cone. Ten-year-old Jason sitting in the lifeguard chair at sunset, laughing that giant childhood laugh of his I hadn't seen here yet. I'd been there for all of them—I'd even taken the lifeguard picture myself. So when I came to a closed door on the left side of the hall that had to be Jason's room, I didn't care that I couldn't see what it looked like. I *knew* Jason. I didn't need to see inside to find out who he was now. I grinned and whirled around to find the bathroom.

Instead, I found myself staring at a photo of two women at the beach. And not just any beach. *Home*. Jason's mom's long brown hair was blowing in the breeze and she had her arm around a beautiful woman with dirty-blond chin-length hair, a million freckles and a thin scar through her left eyebrow. They were sitting on colorful beach towels, wearing the matching purple bathing suits their kids had given them for Mother's Day the month before. The sides of their heads were resting together and their smiles were as bright as the sun shining down on them. I reached up and touched the blonde's face with a fingertip as tears welled in my eyes. I hadn't seen my mom in almost six years.

I couldn't stop my leg from bouncing as I glanced at the man sitting next to me in the too-cold room. He wore jeans and a navy T-shirt, not a suit like the guy who'd just taken my dad into the motel hallway, but I knew he was one of them. His shaggy brown hair and big brown eyes made him look younger than the rest of the suits I'd seen that day, but he was too serious to be anything other than an agent.

He rubbed the back of his neck and took a deep breath. I decided I liked him, even though he hadn't really said much to me. He was the only one who looked like I felt: sad and exhausted and totally freaked out.

"No…no!"

I flinched at the cries that rang through the paper-thin motel walls. My dad's cries.

I jumped up, heart pounding, desperate to help him, but the man grabbed my arm. I stared at him through tears I couldn't blink away. He silently shook his head.

I hadn't known I'd been asking a question with that stare until he answered, but now I wanted him to take the answer back. "What's your name?" I whispered, my voice cracking.

He held my gaze for a long moment. "Agent Markham. But everyone calls me Mark."

"You're wrong, Mark." I tried to say it as forcefully as I could, but that didn't make it true.

When we'd left home that afternoon, the agents said they were sending someone to get my mom from work to speed things up, and that we'd all meet at this motel. We'd been waiting for hours. She hadn't shown up.

Mark swallowed hard. "They got to her first."

The words were like ice in my veins.

"She left work before we got there. Her boss had given her the afternoon off and she was coming home to surprise you and we didn't know. We tried but…they got to her before we did."

"No." I squeezed my eyes shut, trying to keep the truth out. "No. She's just late, that's all. She's coming."

"I'm sorry."

It was the softness of Mark's voice, barely above a whisper, that made me look at him. And his eyes did me in. They were so full of sorrow and anger and guilt that I couldn't pretend he was lying.

My whole body started to shake as tears streamed down my face.

Mark knelt in front of me and held me tight and even though I'd just met him, I didn't want him to let go. I forced the words out between shaky breaths: "Are they going to find us too?"

This time when he spoke, Mark's voice wasn't gentle. "Not if I have anything to do with it."

I wiped away my tears so I could see the photo more clearly. I hadn't been allowed to take any pictures with me when we left, but it hadn't mattered because my mom was supposed to be with us. Now I tried to soak up her smile and memorize her face. Because I'd forgotten exactly what she looked like.

"You're going down!"

Sawyer's shout from the rec room made me jump. I hurried into the bathroom, flushed the toilet—appearances—and splashed cold water on my face to get rid of the blotchiness the tears had caused. I walked back to the rec room as casually as I could and found Sawyer and Livie in the middle of an intense video-game battle that involved both of them yelling at the TV. I walked over to Jason, who was sitting on the couch, just starting to draw a yellow line on a T-shirt. "Hey, I need to get going."

He frowned. "Already?"

"Yeah. I...I totally forgot the cable guy is supposed to come hook everything up today. I promised my dad I'd be there. Sorry about not helping with the shirts." I started to back away.

"It's okay. Do you want me to walk you out?"

"No. I don't want to interrupt the fun." I gestured to the TV. "I'll show myself out. Tell everyone I said bye, okay? Thanks for having me over." I rushed up the steps before he could stop me.

Because I didn't own a car and Jason's house was only a few blocks from mine, I'd walked there. But as I closed Jason's front door behind me, I cursed my inability to make a quick getaway. I eyed the cars parked along the street, wishing I could start one up and escape faster. Instead, I hustled down the block and kept crossing streets and ducking through people's backyards, checking over my shoulder as I went, until I ended up several blocks away in the opposite direction of my place. If anyone had tried to follow me, I was pretty sure I'd lost them.

I sat on a bench and buried my face in my hands. The picture of my mom burned bright behind my eyelids. Even though I wasn't near the beach, I could hear the crash of the waves, feel the hot sand on my feet, smell the way my mom's perfume and suntan lotion mixed to create the flower-coconut scent I'd loved. Silent tears ran down my cheeks and I shook my head at my own stupidity for breaking down in the middle of the hall where anyone could've seen.

You're not her. *Just because things felt familiar back there does not mean you're that girl anymore. You can never be her again. Too much has happened. Jason doesn't know you and you don't know him. You're Sloane, and he needs to believe you're Sloane.*

I took a deep breath and wiped away my tears. *Blend in, follow the rules from here on out and don't let anyone get too close. Especially not your former best friend.*

FIVE

"*Shh.*"

The whispered hush sounded loud in the cramped space where I was crouching. My knees scraped against something rough as I covered my nose and mouth with my hands. I was breathing too loud and too fast. I had to be quiet.

Something solid blocked my front and something sharp and jagged was poking my back. I needed to see what was going on, but there was only darkness. Even though it was nearly impossible, I tried to move. A hand clamped down on my arm and it hurt.

Pop! Pop, pop!

The explosions were so loud, so close, that my hands flew to my ears. My dad's face appeared out of the darkness, right in front of me. His nose was practically touching mine and his eyes were wild with fear. He whispered a single word: "Run."

I began to shake. I tried to jerk away from the person holding me down because I had to run. Even though I had no idea where I was, my dad had told me to run.

"Hey," a gentle voice said. "Kid, wake up."

My eyes flew open.

Mark was sitting on the side of my twin bed, studying my face. He squeezed my shoulders. "You're okay."

I shrugged out of his grip and sat up.

"Did you have the nightmare again?"

I nodded and took a deep breath, willing my heart to slow down.

He pursed his lips. "Anything new?"

"No." I ran my fingers through my hair, loosening the sweaty strands stuck to my neck. "Exactly the same as always."

He exhaled and ran his hands along his jeans. "It's been a while since you've had it."

"Yeah."

"I wonder why it happened now."

Yesterday. Jason. My mom. Take your pick. "I don't know."

I hugged my knees, waiting for the pinpricks of unease in my chest to settle. It was the same feeling I got every time I had the nightmare, every time it felt like someone was watching me. And the same feeling I'd had for a split second two nights ago when I thought I saw that flash on the school's brick wall. I frowned. "It wouldn't make a difference if I did remember something, would it? I mean, not now that they have the confession, right?"

"It wouldn't change anything if you remembered." Mark smiled but his voice was almost too confident, like he was trying to convince himself of that fact instead of me.

I took another deep breath.

"Well," he said as he stood, "I've got to get to work." A grin played on his lips. "And you, my friend, are late for school."

I glanced at my alarm clock and winced. I must've slept straight through the alarm. "Shoot! Why didn't you wake me?"

He made a circling gesture around my room with his finger and stopped when he was pointing at a box of tampons sitting on top of my dresser. "Because I don't want to see stuff like *that*. I only come in here if you're yelling 'Run!' at the top of your lungs."

"I wouldn't have to keep *that* in my room if you'd rented a house with more than one bathroom," I grumbled as I jumped out of bed. "I missed the bus. If I'm ready in five minutes, can you drop me off at school?"

He pretended to shield his eyes and fumble his way out of my room. "Why do you think I rented a house with one bathroom? So there was so little space it would force you to corral all of your girly stuff in the one place I never have to enter. No more opening drawers in bathrooms to find curling irons and pink razors and weird things that look like torture devices but I think have to do with eyelashes." He peeked his head around my door frame. "What exactly is the purpose of bronzer? I've always wondered."

I threw one of my Chucks at him. He easily ducked out of the way.

"We're leaving in four minutes!" he called from down the hall.

I swallowed the last of my Pop-Tart as I shoved my way through the crowd of almost five hundred seniors buzzing with excitement in the school's outside courtyard, grateful the scavenger hunt hadn't started yet. Now all I had to do was find my team.

I inched my way around a group of girls wearing matching Everyone Loves a Cheerleader T-shirts, craning my neck to search for Sawyer, Livie and Jason. I spotted them across the courtyard. Both Sawyer and Livie had their backs to me, but Jason was almost facing me. He bit his thumbnail as his eyes jumped from person to person.

"Jason!" I called over the hum of conversation.

His head snapped in my direction. He exhaled and smiled.

I sidestepped a puddle left over from the morning's rain and took a deep breath as I crossed the courtyard. *You can do this, Sloane.* I held my hands up in apology when I reached the three of them. "I'm sorry I'm late. I overslept and literally had four minutes to get ready."

"You got ready in four minutes?" Livie asked.

I self-consciously smoothed my ponytail, which already had tendrils of hair escaping around my face. I hoped the Chucks, jeans and white tank top I'd thrown on after brushing my teeth and splashing cold water on my face in record time didn't look too horrible. "Um, yeah."

Livie smiled. "I could never look that good in four minutes."

Sawyer leaned toward me. "If I told you you had a great body, would you hold it against me?"

I rolled my eyes. "Do you know the meaning of moderation?"

Jason coughed at the same time Sawyer said, "Huh?"

"It's too soon, Sawyer. I'm still traumatized from the Harry Potter lines yesterday. You have to space them out more. When they come rapid fire like this, they lose their effect."

"Huh," Sawyer repeated, like the thought had never occurred to him.

Livie threw an arm around my shoulder. "Thank God you made it. They just announced we can't have teams this year. Apparently, last year the teams were too big and everyone split up their lists and sent people off individually and the whole scavenger hunt was done in, like, eight minutes. We're only allowed to work in pairs this time, and we were afraid one of us was going to have to go solo if you didn't show."

So that's why Jason looked so worried.

Livie stepped away from me and next to Jason, the back of her hand brushing against his.

Crap. The ramifications of *pairs* suddenly dawned on me. I was going to be stuck with Sawyer and his pickup lines.

Sawyer shook out the T-shirt he had crumpled in one hand and held it out to me. "We can still match though."

I bit my lip to keep from smiling at the drawing on the shirt, the same drawing I realized was on all of their shirts. "What kind of superhero symbol is that?"

But I knew exactly what it was. It was a large yellow lightning bolt, in the middle of which sat a white star on a blue background surrounded by two red rings, and on either side of the last red ring were three yellow lines that looked like wings. It was the same mashup Jason created when we were little because he could never decide which superhero to play, the same one he doodled in notebooks and used as the logo for his dream garage band as we got older.

"No one could agree so Jason came up with this." Livie looked down at her shirt, nose wrinkled.

I slipped my shirt on over my tank top. "It looks awesome."

I traced the *S* in the middle of the star with one finger. "Scavenger Hunt Sloane is ready for action."

Sawyer opened his mouth.

I pointed at him. "No *action* comments from you."

He grinned as Mrs. Thompson, the principal, approached with a large stack of papers in her well-manicured hands. "Jason, how many pairs do you have?"

"Two."

She held out two lists. Jason grabbed one and Sawyer took the other.

They both scanned the lists as Mrs. Thompson moved on to the next cluster of seniors. "Yes!" Jason murmured.

"What'd you get?" Sawyer asked.

Jason held the list flat against his chest. "I'm not telling. You might try to sabotage my items just so you can beat me."

"Oh, it's going to be like that, huh?" The possibility of a wager gleamed in Sawyer's eyes. "We were going to be the group to win it all and now it's me against you?"

Jason's bright eyes flicked to me. "Hey, Sloane, wanna be my partner and help me prove to Sawyer that even with the *new girl*, who knows nothing about this school or where to find anything on this list, I can still beat him?"

My stomach tightened. *Me and Jason. Alone.*

Disappointment flashed on Sawyer's and Livie's faces, but Sawyer rallied first. "Oh, you're on. What do you say, Liv? Should we make these two pay for plotting against us?"

"Hey! I didn't have anything to do with this bet," I reminded him. "New girl, remember?"

"You're right," Sawyer agreed. He bumped Livie with his hip. "Should we make J pay for his poor choice of partner?"

"Hey!" I repeated, a wave of competitiveness flowing through me. "Now you're going down."

Livie chuckled. She entwined her arm with Sawyer's. "Partner, I believe we should."

The whine of microphone feedback interrupted the partner showdown before the stakes of the bet could be set. "Quiet down, people." Mrs. Thompson's voice echoed across the courtyard from where she was precariously balancing on top of a bench in heels taller than I'd ever seen. "Okay. The rules are simple: find each item on your list, take a picture as proof that you found the correct item, and return here where I'll be waiting to check your pictures against your list. The first pair to accurately complete their list wins and gets to pick a song to be played at graduation. Remember, every list has different items so following other teams around won't help you. And if you don't have a phone, I have several digital cameras up here the Photography Club is generously letting us borrow. So see me if you need one. Any questions?" Excited whispers rose from the crowd as people began shuffling toward the edges of the courtyard. "Then let this year's senior scavenger hunt begin!"

Jason motioned to the left as Sawyer and Livie took off running to the right. The mass of seniors thinned fast, and soon we were the only two rounding the school toward the back athletic fields. "What do we need to find first?" I asked. My stomach was a jumble of butterflies and nausea, giddy excitement for the hunt and the bet…and fear of being alone with Jason and being discovered.

"'Evidence of the school's first couple,'" Jason replied.

I stopped walking. I'd been expecting "picture of the school mascot" or "someone wearing school colors," not proof that some historical couple once existed. "How are we going to find that?"

Jason pointed to a large tree, standing alone at the edge of a soccer field in the distance. "See that tree? That's where we need to go."

"We're going to find evidence of a couple at a tree?"

Jason sighed and stopped a few yards ahead of me. "Yes, Ms. Doubtful. Now come on!" He veered off the sidewalk and headed down a grassy hill in the direction of the soccer field.

I watched him for a few seconds, this boy I wasn't supposed to be with but somehow kept ending up with anyway. *Maybe I'm going about this the wrong way.*

If the scavenger hunt had really been it—the last time I was going to be around Jason—I would've quietly followed him, stopped asking questions and let him lead the way just to get it over with. But I had a signed senior trip permission slip burning a hole in my back pocket. I was going to have some level of contact with Livie—with *all* of them—for the next few weeks. And while it didn't seem like Jason remembered who I was, being in his house and seeing those pictures had brought back a flood of memories. Even though I wasn't in any of the photos I'd seen, what if he had something else in his house? Something that would spark a memory that made him wonder about me?

I rubbed my thumb across my bottom lip. Maybe staying away from Jason once all the First Day Buddy stuff was over wasn't the best move. Maybe I needed to keep him close. To know what he was thinking and prove I was a completely different person from the girl he'd grown up with so he'd never believe it was me even if his brain tried to make the connection. And I knew just the way to start.

Anticipation thrilled through me. I bounced on my toes for a beat, a tiny smile creeping its way onto my mouth. *This is going to be fun.*

"Come on, slowpoke," I called over my shoulder as I zoomed past him, running down the hill as fast as I could, "or I'm going to beat you there!"

The girl Jason knew had been a terrible runner, slow and easily winded. But thanks to lesson number eleven, I'd left that girl in the dust.

He made an indignant noise and took off after me. He may have been a few inches taller, but I was fast and had a head start. I was in the lead until about forty feet from the tree, when Jason grabbed a fistful of my shirt, yanked me backward and sprinted in front of me.

I gasped and rushed forward, trying to hip check him out of the way.

Jason wrapped one arm around the front of my body as I got close, angling me behind him and attempting to hold down my arm. "You can't beat me if you can't touch the tree!"

I giggled and spun out of his reach, but before I could get all the way free, he smacked the tree in triumph. "You are such a cheater!" I tried sounding angry, but the fact I was still laughing ruined any chance of that.

Jason's grin in response was deviously unapologetic.

I decided he needed a good hip checking anyway. But instead of knocking the sexy grin off his face, I tripped on an exposed tree root and stumbled into him.

"Whoa," Jason said as he gently placed his hands on my waist to steady me.

My laughter died away and it was suddenly hard to breathe. I watched Jason's chest rising and falling under his superhero shirt. He smelled like my childhood, like cookies and the beach, but there was a spicy boy scent I'd never noticed before. I looked up into his blue eyes.

He chuckled. "I think your attempt at thwarting my totally fair victory messed up your hair." He reached out with one hand and tucked a few strands of hair that had escaped my ponytail behind my ear.

The spot on my waist where his hand had just been tingled.

He held my gaze for a second, then stepped back and cleared his throat. "So this is the Kissing Tree."

I gulped. "Kissing Tree?"

"Take a look."

I turned and my mouth dropped open. "Wow."

Every inch of the tree's bark, from where it disappeared into the ground to taller than even Sawyer could reach, was covered in initials.

"It's another school tradition," Jason explained. "Couples come here to kiss and then carve their initials into the tree."

I circled the tree, letting my fingers trail over the letters. "There are *so* many. How do you know which one is the first?"

"It's this one here." Jason pointed to a spot in front of him at eye level. It was a simple *E loves L* inside a heart with a date below it. "That date is from the first week the school was open. It's the oldest one on here."

I traced the heart with one finger, slowing when the set of initials to the heart's left caught my eye: *J + S.*

"You're killing that tree."

Jason looked up from the base of the oak tree in front of his house. "I am not," he said over the soft sounds of his dad's favorite Billy Joel song wafting from the open windows.

"Then what are you doing?" I bent down and noticed the initials carved into the tree's trunk about two feet off the ground. I smiled.

He brushed off the tiny J + S. "I'm letting everyone know that we're going to be best friends forever." He pushed the tip of his dad's pocket knife into the S, making it deeper.

"You don't have to hurt the poor tree to prove that, Jase. The whole fourth grade knows that already. Everybody knows that already."

Jason glanced up, grinning, and the knife slipped, slicing into his left hand. He jerked his hand away. The knife dropped to the ground, covered in blood.

My heart skipped a beat. "Hold on!" I pressed the edge of my T-shirt against the bloody spot above his left thumb. Blood soaked through the shirt almost instantly.

"Mrs. Stacy!" I yelled, knowing Jason's mom would hear me through the open windows. All the color had drained from Jason's face. "Bet I can annoy more nurses at the hospital than you," I whispered.

He gave me the tiniest hint of a smile.

"It'll be okay," I promised as his mom came rushing down the steps toward us. "We're best friends, remember? I won't leave you."

"Have you ever done that? Carved your initials into a tree?" Jason asked, pulling me out of the memory. He pointed to the Kissing Tree carvings.

I hadn't thought of that day in years. My eyes darted to his left hand, which hung at his side. *Does he still have the scar by his thumb?* "No," I replied. Which was the truth. He had, not me. "Have you?"

He kicked the ground with one of his sneakers. "Yeah."

"Let me guess. There's a *J loves L* on here somewhere." I pretended to search the tree.

"No. Livie and I aren't… It's not…"

I peeked around the tree at him. "I was only teasing. You don't have to explain."

A wrinkle appeared in between his eyebrows. "It's… complicated." His eyes locked on mine. "But I'm not sure it's an immortalize-it-in-wood-forever kind of thing."

"Oh." *Oh.* "I just thought… I mean, Livie was kind of throwing off an it's-serious vibe when she was talking about the senior trip."

Jason's cheeks turned pink. "Yeah. She's got lots of *ideas* about the senior trip that she'll apparently share with anyone."

"I can be your wingman on the trip if you want," I blurted. "If things are still complicated, just give me the secret signal and I'll mummify her in rolls of duct tape so she can't leave our room."

He laughed. "You'd do that for me?"

I shrugged. "Sure. What are friends for?" *Friends.* Saying that word to Jason made my pulse race. I rubbed the back of my neck with one hand as I gestured to the tree with the other. "Well, hopefully friends are for taking pictures of tree carvings when their partners choose to exit the world of cell phone ownership."

Jason pulled his phone out of his pocket. "Friends are definitely for that. Why don't you move closer? I'll get you too."

I took a large step away from the tree. "Nope. I don't do

pictures." *Pictures end up in yearbooks and on the internet and other places immortalized forever where people can find them, with names I don't want them to know.* "I'm not very photogenic. I always blink or make a face. It's a mess."

"I highly doubt that," Jason muttered as he captured proof of the school's first couple.

We got pictures of the next eight items on our list in no time, including Jason's favorite: "Ms. Benton's agreeable band," which turned out to be his science teacher's collection of Beatles bobblehead dolls. "What's the last item?" I asked as we left the chemistry room.

"'The *Z*'s bees,'" Jason read aloud. He stopped walking.

"Oh," I replied, turning toward the hall that would take us to the front office.

Jason stayed still, his eyebrows scrunched together. "Huh." He scratched his head.

"Wait." A slow grin spread across my face. "You don't know what that means?"

"No." He glanced up from the list. "Do you?"

My smile grew wider.

"Tell me."

"Hold on." I held my hands out to my sides. "I want to spend a moment basking in the glory of knowing something about this school you don't. Me, the *new girl*. Who knows *nothing* about finding anything on our list."

Jason shot me a look. "What does it mean?"

I leaned toward him. "Not yet. Still basking."

He reached up and gently yanked twice on my earlobe. It was a familiar gesture, one he'd picked up from his dad, and one that had always annoyed me as a kid.

I smacked his hand away with a laugh. "God, Jase. Cut it out."

He was already reaching for my ear again when he stopped midreach and lowered his hands to his sides.

"What?" I asked.

"You called me Jase."

Crap! Lesson number eight, Sloane, I reminded myself. *Don't get complacent.*

It had always been like that with Jason, easy when everyone else required a little more work. Being around him was effortless. Now, that was dangerous.

You have to stay on your toes if you're going to pull this off. And you need to pull this off. So stop making mistakes!

Before I could come up with an excuse for using my childhood nickname for him, Oliver Clarke appeared trailing behind his scavenger hunt partner. I didn't know where he'd come from, but the deserted hallway was long enough that it was possible he'd seen my whole exchange with Jason, ear yanking and nickname calling included.

Oliver eyed us as he approached, pressing his lips together to hold back a laugh. He remained silent until he was right next to us, then said in a low voice meant only for me, "Hey, Sweet Potato."

The snort escaped me before I could stop it.

Oliver's eyes lit up.

I knew I was supposed to be avoiding him because of the whole gossip and mean ex-girlfriend thing, but no one else was around other than Jason and Oliver's teammate, a guy I recognized from the a cappella group. And I couldn't just ignore him after a reaction like that. I tipped my head in his direction. "Choir Boy."

77

Oliver's mouth dropped open. "Insults are not a good start to our friendship. I think you mean Singer of Very Manly Songs."

I pointed at the corner his partner had just disappeared around. "Or maybe I mean Misplacer of Teammates."

"Oh, shoot," Oliver grumbled as he hurried around the corner.

I shook my head and peeked at Jason, who was biting his lip, watching the spot where Oliver disappeared. "Sorry about the Jase thing," I said. "I have a cousin named Jason and that's what I call him. It just slipped out."

"It's okay. It's what my mom calls me."

I know. She stole it from me. "That's because it's a good nickname."

Jason smiled. "Yeah, it is."

"So." I clapped my hands together. "We need to find some bees, right?"

He raised one eyebrow. "Are you done basking?"

"No, but the basking can continue on our way to the office."

When I opened the office door, Mrs. Zalinsky smiled at me from behind the tall counter. "Sloane, dear. Back so soon?"

The genuine warmth in her voice melted away my lingering annoyance at her part in giving me a First Day Buddy. She was only trying to help and it hadn't been that bad. "We need a picture of your bees for the scavenger hunt," I explained, pointing to Mrs. Zalinsky's nameplate for Jason.

"Ah," he mumbled. "I never would've gotten that. I haven't been in here in forever."

Mrs. Zalinsky eyed Jason as he took the requisite picture. "I told you you wouldn't need that map," she whispered to me.

I leaned closer to Mrs. Zalinsky, like we were old friends sharing secrets. "Trust me, I need a map for that. I have no idea what I'm doing."

"Are you two done chatting?" Jason asked, suppressing a grin. "Because we've got a scavenger hunt to win."

"Thanks, Mrs. Z!" I called as I followed Jason out of the office.

We sprinted for the courtyard, but when we arrived, we found Mrs. Thompson sitting on a bench with a line of about ten pairs already waiting for her to verify their photos, including Sawyer and Livie three groups ahead of us.

I groaned as Sawyer and Livie did a ha-ha-we-beat-you dance. I pulled Jason in line on the off chance everyone in front of us ended up disqualified. "Sorry. I shouldn't have spent so much time basking."

"It's okay," Jason said with a shrug. "We didn't actually bet on anything, so all Sawyer gets is bragging rights. Plus, I liked the basking."

I peeked in Mrs. Thompson's direction, trying to see if she was eliminating anyone, but my gaze caught on the brick wall behind her instead. I rubbed the back of my neck and studied it.

"So what was with you and Mrs. Zalinsky back there?" The smile in Jason's voice didn't match the tightness forming in my chest.

"That was girl talk," I said lightly, not taking my eyes off the faded bricks. It was the same brick wall I'd stood in front of the night we'd broken into the school. It had the same dark wet patches, this time due to the early morning rain. And looking at it again was giving me the same creepy feeling.

"How can you already be having girl talk with the secretary? You just got here."

The air shifted, more thick and humid than it had been a second ago. I sucked in a ragged breath as my fingertips started to tingle, like I'd just scraped them along something rough. I balled my hands into fists.

"Sloane?"

I knew it was coming. But my breath still caught in my throat when I saw a flash of blue against the faded red of the bricks.

Something brushed against my arm and I jumped.

"Did you hear me? The pair with those Team Hot Stuff shirts won." Jason nodded at the students around us, slowly making their way back toward the school.

"Oh yeah, sorry. Let's go."

But as Jason hurried to catch up to Sawyer and Livie, I took one last look at the brick wall and shivered.

Because I hadn't just seen a blue blur against the bricks. I'd heard a voice inside my head. A voice too insubstantial to identify, yet familiar enough to make my heart trip. A voice that said three little words: *You can't hide.*

SIX

I'd remembered something.

Not the recurring nightmare or the flashes I got when it felt like someone was watching me, but something new. I was certain. But I wasn't certain I wanted to tell Mark about it. Not after the conversation we'd had that morning about remembering.

I pulled open the screen door after school, still debating what to do, when Mark's voice stopped me.

"She doesn't know anything."

I froze. *Is someone here?* I scanned the kitchen, the only room I could see from my vantage point at the back door, but there was no sign of Mark. I could hear him, so he had to be close. *The family room?* I hovered in the doorway, one hand propping open the screen, and waited to see if anyone else spoke.

"I'll take care of it." Mark sighed. "You promised I could do this *my* way." There were three quick footsteps, a pause, then three footsteps again.

He's pacing, which means he's on the phone. Is he talking about me?

"Then let me handle it," he snapped. "Yes, it'll be soon. Have a little faith... I've got to go. She'll be home any minute."

The faint sound of a long sigh was followed by what possibly could've been Mark dropping onto the couch, but I wasn't thinking about him on a couch. I was thinking of him in an elevator.

"Thanks for taking me to the carnival." I grinned at Mark. *My hands were sticky from cotton candy and caramel apples and my voice scratchy from hours of screaming on the rides—I'd had fun. Actual fun for the first time since the day we'd left ten months ago. "Which floor?"*

"Three," Mark replied as we stepped into the elevator. "I'll take you back to your place before I tackle the long commute home."

I rolled my eyes. "Yes, because one floor down is sooo long."

He chuckled. "It's too bad your dad wasn't feeling well. I bet he would've had fun too."

"Yeah." My good mood deflated. I wasn't sure whether Dad really hadn't been feeling well or whether that had been an excuse not to leave the apartment. He'd had a lot of excuses lately.

The elevator dinged its arrival on the third floor. "Maybe he'll be feeling better tomorrow and we can go back," Mark suggested.

"Really? That would be great!" I'd make Dad come tomorrow. I'd tell him about all the fun rides and games and he'd have to want to come. "It's too bad the carousel didn't have rings to catch. I bet I could get more than both of you. I've got a secret method."

"Oh really?" Mark knocked on my apartment door. "I'd love to see you try to beat me."

"I'd do more than try," I said, then laughed at his doubtful expression.

He nodded slowly. "I like seeing you smile. It looks good on you, Kid."

I knocked again, eager to tell Dad about the carnival, but he still didn't answer. A slight chill ran down my spine.

Mark pulled his keys out of his pocket, eyebrows furrowed. "Maybe he's asleep." He unlocked the door and pushed it open.

A man wearing a suit and a gun on his hip was standing in my kitchen.

Fear clawed its way up my throat. I took a step back, ready to run, but Mark wrapped a hand around my arm, pulling me close.

He led me into the apartment, shoulders tense, the skin around his eyes wrinkling slightly. "What are you doing here?" he asked as the door swung shut behind us.

Despite the surprise in Mark's voice, he obviously knew the man, and the man wore a suit like all the other Marshals I'd ever seen. An ominous feeling settled in my chest. Mouth dry, I asked, "Where's my dad?"

The man's gaze darted to me and back to Mark in silence.

Mark leaned closer and squeezed my arm once. "Stay here," he whispered. "Don't move. I'll be right back." He motioned for the guy to follow him into the bathroom and closed the door.

I dragged in a few deep breaths, trying to steady my racing heart and trying not to look at the closed door to my dad's bedroom. It didn't work. In the time it took me to take a single breath, I was in front of the door, my eyes searching for any explanation as to where Dad was. I reached out with a shaky hand. My fingers were just about to wrap around the doorknob when the bathroom door flew open.

I jumped away from the bedroom door, my heart nearly exploding out of my chest.

The man in the suit stalked out of the apartment without even glancing at me. Mark locked the door and rested his head against it.

I moved behind him. "What's going on?" I whispered.

Mark turned and I knew. It was like my mom all over again. Tears welled in my eyes.

"Something happened and..."

My throat felt like it was closing but I forced the words out. "He's dead?"

Mark winced.

My heart beat as fast as the possibilities racing through my head. "Did someone find us?"

"No. He..." Mark swallowed hard. "He killed himself while we were at the carnival."

"What?" Hot tears streamed down my face. "Why? Why would he do that?"

Mark tried to wipe my tears away. "That was an agent. Your dad called the emergency hotline before he... He wanted someone to find him before we got home. They tried to talk him out of it and get here to stop him but...it was too late."

I shook my head.

"He told them he couldn't take being on the run anymore. But he wanted you to know that he loved you, very much."

"Yeah, he loved me so much he left me by myself!" I could feel something inside me breaking, shaking into loose bits.

Mark cupped my face in his hands. "No. You have me, do you hear me?" I tried to jerk away but he made me look at him. "Listen to me, Kid. I won't let anything happen to you. I'll take care of you."

He wrapped his arms around me and rocked me as I cried. He started humming something, the sound vibrating in my chest. It wasn't until he began to softly sing the words that I recognized the tune to

"Have a Little Faith in Me" by John Hiatt. It was the song my dad always sang to my mom when she was upset.

I listened, transfixed, until the song ended. I wiped away tears that were still falling and asked, "Where'd you learn that song?"

"I used to sing it to my little sister when we were younger. I took care of her a lot."

It was the first time he'd ever mentioned anything about his real life, but I didn't have any trouble imagining him taking care of a little sister just like he'd often taken care of me. I realized he was right. I had to have faith in him. He was all I had left. "So what are we going to do?"

He wiped more of my tears away. "We'll start over someplace new. We'll live together from now on, okay?"

I took a shaky breath. "I need a new name?"

Mark nodded. "Do you have one in mind?"

"Faith."

I took a deep breath. In the almost five years since that day, I'd only heard Mark say "have a little faith" a handful of times. Only when something was important, when it was *big*. And this time, he'd been talking about me not knowing anything. I buried the echo of the voice I'd heard deep inside my head. *I don't know anything.*

I silently counted to twenty and let the screen door slam behind me in what had quickly become my way of announcing I was home. "Hey!" I called, forcing my voice to be light.

A moment later, Mark poked his head into the kitchen. "Hey! How was your day?" He sounded like he hadn't just been sighing and snapping and *faithing* at someone.

"Good." I tossed my backpack on the island and opened

the refrigerator door, pretending to search for a snack. What I really wanted was to know what was going on.

Mark hopped onto the island and played with the straps of my bag. "How was school? Anything *interesting* happen?"

Cold dread filled my whole body. *They know. They know Jason's here. That's what's big. Mark has to handle telling me I screwed up and we have to move again, and soon.* My shoulders slumped. There had to be a way to reason with him, to get him to understand that I couldn't do it anymore. *But wait. If Mark knew who Jason really was, he wouldn't be making conversation. He'd be telling me we have to leave* right now. *So maybe he doesn't know everything yet.*

I grabbed a yogurt and turned to face him. I was going to find out exactly what he knew. "I invented a nephew for you today."

Mark's eyebrows shot up. "That's…not what I expected you to say."

"I accidentally called my friend Jase instead of Jason, and before I knew it I was explaining the slip by saying that's what I've always called my cousin Jason." *There. I've opened the door to all Jason-related topics. Now tell me what you know.*

Mark nodded in mock seriousness. "I've always loved Jason. He's my favorite fake nephew."

I pursed my lips. *Nothing?* "He's your only fake nephew."

"Oh. Right." He grinned.

Okay. "What did you expect me to say?"

He threw his hands up. "I don't know, something about the senior scavenger hunt perhaps? I mean, how many times does a person get to do something like that, even someone like you who's been in tons of schools?"

"Oh. It was pretty fun, I guess. Better than being stuck in class."

"And?"

"And how was your day? Anything *interesting* happen?"

Mark frowned. "No. Why would it?"

I threw my hands up too. *Because you were talking to the Marshals about me!* "Because it was your first day on the job."

"Oh." The corners of his mouth twitched slyly. "It was pretty fun, I guess. Better than being stuck in the house."

I made an annoyed noise at his use of my own words against me.

He jumped off the island and stole my yogurt and spoon in one swift move. He ate the whole thing in three bites. "I'm going for a run and then I'm playing basketball," he announced as he tossed the empty cup in the trash. "Wanna come? But I'm warning you, if you come I'm making you spill more details about the scavenger hunt than, 'It was pretty fun, I guess.'" He hummed as he left the kitchen.

I watched Mark leave. *What just happened?* I'd given him the perfect opportunity to talk about Jason and he hadn't mentioned a thing. The sound of Mark's bedroom door closing gave me an idea. "I'm coming!" I called as I hustled to my room to change into running clothes, glaring at his closed door as I passed. *If you're not going to tell me what's going on, I'll just have to find out myself.*

SEVEN

The next morning, I was up at the crack of dawn, ready to put some of my lesson-acquired special skills to use. I got dressed for school as silently as I could in my room, all the while listening to Mark getting ready for his early shift at work. When the smell of his coffee followed him out the front door, I snuck down the hall and opened the door to his room.

The what-was-now-becoming-all-too-familiar feeling of guilt made my neck hot as, for the first time ever, I stepped into one of Mark's bedrooms. I'd never snooped through his things before. Our relationship was based on trust, and we didn't keep secrets from each other. Well, except for the giant one I was keeping about Jason. But desperate times called for desperate measures.

My feet padded along the cool wood floor as I scanned the sparse furniture that came with the rental house: queen-size bed with a starfish-patterned bedspread, a single honey-colored wood nightstand and a matching wood dresser complete with a round seashell-appliqued mirror hanging above it. I shook my head. Every place we lived in came furnished, so it's not like we picked the decor, but this room really didn't look like Mark. The extreme level of organization was the only thing that made me think he lived there. My eyes darted around. *Where would Mr. Neat Freak hide something?*

I yanked on the cuffs of my black knit winter gloves to make sure they were snug—lesson number seven: everything you need to know about fingerprints—and started with the nightstand. I wasn't sure what I was looking for, only that I'd know it when I saw it. Other than a few books I wanted to read, there was nothing good on the nightstand. I tried the dresser but only found T-shirts, socks and underwear. Even a search of the closet, which was always the preferred hiding place in movies, turned up nothing.

I plopped on the bed, resting my elbows on my knees and staring down as I tried to think of whether there was anywhere else in the small house he could hide something. My eyes randomly followed grain patterns in the wood floor as I mentally surveyed the rooms, until I realized my gaze kept landing on a hitch in the white eyelet bed skirt surrounding the bed. One tiny section was folded over onto itself, like it had been scrunched up and not properly straightened out. I dropped to my knees and peeked under the bed. *Bingo.*

I pulled out a small black metal safe. It was slightly larger than a ream of paper and had a simple lock, like the kind on a filing cabinet. I ran to my room, grabbed a paper clip and a bobby pin to use as a pick and tension wrench and, thanks to lesson number nine, had the safe unlocked in less than a minute. My pulse raced as I opened the top.

I frowned. It was full of paper. A copy of the lease to our

current house was on top. Underneath that were the print-outs from the real estate website we'd used to pick the house. I remembered looking at several houses in the area with Mark when we decided to come to North Carolina, and I saw print-outs for most of them in the stack. We'd chosen this house because it was the closest to the university, and we'd rented it a few months before we moved just to make sure it would still be available when we were ready to come. I sighed and flipped to the next group of papers.

They were also printouts from a real estate website, only for a different house. I could tell from the abundance of shells in the decor that it was a beach house. I studied the map on one of the sheets and realized it was in a town probably less than half an hour up the coast. I didn't remember looking at this particular house with Mark, but that wasn't strange. He'd narrowed our choices down before letting me help pick the winner. The charming porches and abundance of windows told me it was fancier than the one we were in now, and it was a bit more secluded—on a larger plot of land farther away from the neighbors—all of which would've been pluses. But as soon as I read that it was in a neighborhood called Avalon, I knew why it hadn't been a finalist. I'd thought it was risky enough coming back to the East Coast for the first time, and I definitely would've questioned Mark's sanity if he'd suggested renting a house in a neighborhood that shared a name with the town practically next door to the one I'd grown up in.

The alarm on my phone sounded, reminding me I had fif-teen minutes to catch the bus. I couldn't be late to school two days in a row. I took a quick look at the last piece of paper in the safe, a map of the Avalon neighborhood, and sighed.

"For people on the run, we live very boring lives with very few secrets," I muttered. I neatly stacked the papers back in the safe, relocked it with my makeshift tools, and slid it back into place. After smoothing the bedspread and propping up the bed skirt to erase any sign that I'd been in the room, I closed Mark's door behind me.

As I brushed my teeth, I debated whether it would be worth trying to get a peek at the recent calls on Mark's phone. But what good would a random Marshal's number be? It's not like I could call the person and demand to know whether Mark was suspicious of Jason. I'd pretty much dismissed the idea as pointless when I walked into the kitchen in search of breakfast and saw Mark's phone lying on the middle of the island.

For half a second, excited butterflies filled my stomach, temptation making me reevaluate how quickly I shot down the idea of spying on his phone. Then fear crept up my spine.

"Mark?"

I tossed my backpack on the floor by the coffee table where Mark's cell phone was resting next to an open book and followed the mouthwatering scent of chocolate into the kitchen. Light green walls and dark wood cabinets and a pan of brownies cooling on a rack greeted me—but no Mark.

I paused in front of the brownies. Mark had promised to make them for the eighth grade open house that evening, so they weren't a surprise. But I frowned at the large knife sitting on the counter next to them, so close to the edge it was about to fall off. Mark was usually so anal about putting everything in its place, particularly his prized kitchen gadgets, that I couldn't remember the last time I'd seen a knife lying around. I pushed it more solidly onto the counter, one finger lingering on the handle. "Mark?"

No answer.

I turned into the hall leading to the bedrooms, slowing as I neared my room. I stepped inside, not knowing why. The air felt different somehow, cool and empty and unsettled. A chill passed over me. I needed to find Mark.

I knocked twice on his closed bedroom door. "Mark?"

No answer.

I knocked again, this time a little louder. Nothing.

I pivoted, pressing my back against the end of the hall, and held my breath. The wind blew, making shadows from the tree outside the window dance across the wood floor, but otherwise the house was quiet. Too quiet.

Other than my breath coming too fast, there wasn't a single sound. No footsteps or pages turning or voices coming from a TV.

I moved back down the hall, unease pushing my feet to match the rhythm of my pounding heart. There was still one room to check, one room before I'd have to face whatever was behind Mark's closed door. But when I reached the den, I hesitated.

I'd never liked this room, with its wood paneling and dark corners and lack of windows. The deer head mounted on the wall was disturbing on a normal day, but today its soulless eyes staring at me through the doorway were downright creepy.

Goose bumps trailed up my arms as I crept down the two steps into the room, purposefully avoiding the deer's eyes as they followed me.

"Mark?" It came out as barely a whisper.

My gaze swept toward the couch, but landed on something lumpy sticking out from behind it. It was hard to tell what it was in the dim light, but it was large. Like a pile of blankets. Or a curled up body.

My heart plummeted into my stomach. I swallowed hard and took two steps forward to get a better look.

A hand clamped over my mouth.

I sucked in a sharp breath, ready to try to scream or bite or elbow the body behind me, when a quiet voice next to my ear stopped me cold. "If I was anyone else, it would already be too late."

I spun around, easily slipping out of Mark's grasp, and backed against the wall. Relief flooded through me as I studied him. He looked perfectly normal: work shirt slightly rumpled, black hair neatly in place, a hint of stubble across his jaw, but his green eyes were filled with a determined seriousness that could only mean one thing.

I cleared my throat, but my voice was still rough. "What number are we at again?"

Mark spread out his arms. "Welcome to lesson number eight: don't get complacent."

I nodded and took a deep breath, trying to force my heart to slow down.

Mark's eyebrows pinched together. "Sorry for the dramatic set up. I just..."

"No, don't be sorry. I obviously needed it." I stood a little straighter and glanced around the room. "Because I just walked into a trap, didn't I?"

His eyes lit up. "Yes. Can you tell me why?"

I pointed at the walls. "No windows. There's only one exit, and I came far enough into the room for it to be blocked."

"I saw you pause at the door. How come?"

"Because Bambi freaks me out."

Mark smiled at my joke, but waited for the real reason.

"Because something felt off." And I was afraid you were in here, hurt.

"You need to trust your instincts. Not being complacent means not falling into a routine, staying on your toes and not assuming every-

thing that looks normal is normal." He crossed the room and sat in an overstuffed leather chair. "If someone's tossed one of our houses, it's not always going to look trashed like in the movies. Sometimes, things might be just slightly out of place. But you have to notice."

I fell onto the couch, annoyed at myself for not paying attention.

"What was the first thing that seemed off?"

"The knife in the kitchen."

"Good. What else?"

I retraced my steps, remembering the inexplicable urge to go into my room, and sighed. "The door to my room. I closed it this morning and it was open now."

"What about in here? You should've known before you even came down the stairs that something wasn't right."

I studied the wall opposite the door. I'd been so focused on Creepy Deer Head I missed the fact that the distressed wood bookcase normally centered beneath it had been shifted several feet to the right. I pointed at the bookcase and groaned.

Mark chuckled. "And you missed the most obvious one." He leaned forward, elbows resting on his knees, eyes holding mine. It was a challenge.

I pursed my lips. I'd walked in and put my bag down. Nothing was out of place at first, nothing missing, nothing unusual, except... "Your phone."

He nodded. "You know that phone is our lifeline, our way of being able to reach each other within seconds any time of day. I always have it on me, even if I'm just going in the next room, especially when we're not together." His eyes turned serious again. "That should've been your first clue."

My heart pounded in my ears as I stared at Mark's phone on the island. *Is this a clue?*

I inched forward and silently slid the largest knife from the knife block, the same knife from all those years ago. My fingers tightened around the handle. I scanned the kitchen, taking in every little detail. Nothing besides the phone was out of place.

With the knife ready at my side I slipped into the family room, my steps piercing the silence. The blinds were closed, like Mark had been keeping them in the morning to block out the too-bright sunrise. But even in the darkened room I could tell everything was where it was supposed to be. I crossed to the window and used the tip of the knife to lift a slat in the blinds so I could peek outside. Mark's car was gone.

I let the slat fall back into place with a dull *thwack*. Mark had followed the same routine as always this morning. He'd been humming when he left the house. And I hadn't heard anything unusual since then. I tapped the knife flat against my leg. The only thing that was off was the phone.

Back in the kitchen, I studied the phone for a second. Then slowly, as if touching it was going to set off some kind of booby trap, I picked it up. It was sitting on top of a small piece of paper filled with writing.

Hey, Kid, Mark's cramped, slanted scrawl began. *You're still sleeping, so I'm leaving this note to tell you I dropped my phone in the toilet this morning.*

"Ew," I mumbled as I swiftly put the phone back on the counter.

It's totally fried. Maybe I'll try to stick it in a bag of rice for a few days or whatever you're supposed to do when this happens, but for now I'm using one of the backups. My new number's below (you know the rules: new phone = new number). Do me a favor and text me when you see this so I know you have it. But please don't go dying or anything before then. If you do, you'll miss out on homemade pizza night! And then I'll have no one left to cook for. ☺

I laughed as I put the knife on the counter, then laughed even harder at what I must've looked like stalking through the house with an eight-inch knife for no reason. But my laugh soon morphed into a sigh. *What am I doing?* I trusted Mark with my life, and I was violating his trust in me by going through his things. If there was something he needed to tell me, he would, just like he always had. And if it was bad, we'd deal with it just like we always had: together.

I poured a glass of orange juice, hoping to wash down the shame creeping its way up my throat. But when I went to set the glass on the island, my fingers slipped on the quickly-forming condensation and the glass tipped, spilling juice over everything. Instinctively, I grabbed Mark's phone before it got wet. Then I realized I'd saved the wrong thing. Because Mark's phone was already dead. And his note wasn't water-proof.

Mark's new phone number—the one I hadn't yet memo-rized or programmed into my phone—was washed away by a puddle of juice.

Before I could reach for the note to see if any of the num-bers survived, my phone dinged. *Crap.* I had five minutes to make it to the bus and no way of getting in touch with Mark.

A few hours later, my stomach growled as I shut my locker. The smell of pizza wafting out of the nearby cafeteria didn't help, but I ignored my hunger and studied my locker door. I'd expected Mark to text me when I didn't check in with him. So far my phone had been silent. He'd gotten stuck on big repair jobs a few times in the past where he couldn't look at his phone for a while, and maybe that's what was happening now, but the inability to reach him made me uneasy. Even though I had a strict no-checking-the-phone-at-school policy—it was the easiest way to make sure no one ever saw that I had a phone— I was debating whether to slip into a bathroom to make sure it was on and had a signal when I felt a tap on my shoulder.

I turned around to find Oliver smiling at me from the middle of the hall, his green eyes shining. "So I realized this is your third day here and, despite all my talk, I still haven't properly welcomed you to school yet. Or, you know, actually introduced myself," he announced.

"Oh." I glanced around.

"Don't worry." He held up a hand in my direction. "I promise you'll stay on your feet the entire time. And even though I'm finally going to tell you my actual name, I also made one up for myself in case you like that better." He bounced a little on his toes.

He looked...excited. And completely ignored by everyone in the crowded hallway. And I had to admit, I was more than a little curious about the name he'd chosen for himself.

I slung my backpack over one shoulder. "All right. Let's hear it then."

He pointed at himself. "Oliver Clarke, Master of the Grand Gesture."

Before I could even furrow my eyebrows at what the name

meant, six guys materialized out of nowhere behind Oliver and began snapping and singing doos and bops in a familiar tune.

Oh no! No, no, no.

Oliver locked his green eyes on mine as he started singing the first lines of "Brown Eyed Girl." I barely had time to register that he was singing about something that was, in reality, a nonexistent feature of my appearance before a crowd of students formed a semicircle around us. I got why they stopped to listen. Oliver's voice was smooth and rich and absolutely gorgeous. If I was any other girl, my heart probably would've been melting right then. Instead, I shook my head slightly, trying to signal my discomfort to Oliver. When he didn't notice, I froze, horrified at how much this was *not* blending in, and tried to think of a way to stop Oliver's performance without creating even more of a scene.

I should've moved when Oliver's ex-girlfriend appeared with two of her friends, all staring daggers at me. Or when Jason, Sawyer and Livie arrived and pushed their way to the front of the audience. Jason's eyes widened when he saw me backed against the lockers, trying not to look as freaked out as I was. Sawyer didn't look at me at all. He glared at Oliver, his jaw becoming more set with each new verse Oliver sang. Livie, on the other hand, gave me two thumbs up and mouthed, *So hot!*

It wasn't until the girl standing next to Livie pulled out her phone to start filming that I finally jumped into action. I dashed forward and grabbed Oliver's hand midsnap, making sure to keep my body turned away from the phone. I pulled Oliver down the hall and ducked into the first empty classroom I found. I closed the door behind us and leaned against it. Things like this couldn't happen. Not to me. And I was going to make sure it wouldn't happen again.

"I'm sorry," I sighed. I pushed off the door and began pacing in front of Oliver, the adrenaline from almost being caught on camera making me restless. "I don't like surprises. I don't like being the center of attention. Your ex-girlfriend was out there glaring at me, and I just want to coast through the next few weeks until graduation without any problems from anyone, including her. And I don't even have—"

I took a deep breath. I'd been about to say I didn't even have brown eyes, and in that moment I hated it all. I hated constantly wishing someone could know the real me and at the same time being terrified of anyone finding out who I really was. "I don't think—"

"Has Chloe been giving you a hard time?"

The softness to Oliver's voice made me stop pacing and look at him for the first time. He was leaning against the wall, eyes downcast, with his right thumb tucked into the pocket of his jeans. My breath caught in my throat. I'd once known a boy who'd had the habit of tucking his thumb into his pocket like that when he was nervous. A boy who, like Jason, I'd forced myself to push to the back of my memory. A boy who'd been a friend when I'd really needed one.

"*She* broke up with *me*," Oliver mumbled. "She has no right to say anything to you."

Suddenly, it all clicked into place. He wasn't just some guy who thrived on drama and needed attention from everyone, including the new girl. He was *lonely*. He ate lunch by himself. I hadn't seen him with anyone outside members of his a cappella group in three days. Livie said he hadn't been talking to anyone, yet he kept trying to talk to me. And I'd totally assumed the worst about him.

As if he could read my mind, Oliver continued. "I thought since you were new, you wouldn't know about Chloe or be scared to talk to me because of her like everyone else." He looked up at me with apologetic eyes. "And planning names to call you or songs to sing to you gave me something else to think about, you know?"

I nodded, eyes drifting down to that thumb in his pocket. The reasons to stay away from him hadn't really changed. But he needed a friend and for once, I could be that person for someone instead of the other way around. And Oliver *was* someone I wanted to know, with the goofy names and endearing lack of concern about making a fool of himself, despite his complete inability to blend in. He made me smile, and I wanted to return the favor.

I sat on top of a desk and felt my phone shift in my pocket. The Mark-sized ball of anxiety in my stomach was still there, but I could check my phone as soon as I was done talking to Oliver. "So what happened with you and Chloe?"

He slid onto the desk across from mine. "She's convinced I cheated on her, which I *didn't* do. She said she has proof, but I don't know what she's talking about." He pursed his lips and a tiny wrinkle appeared in the middle of his forehead. "It's what I liked most about her when we first got together. She's just got this complete and unwavering devotion to every single thing she believes in."

His eyes met mine and he paused, as if asking whether that made any sense. I nodded.

"She was the first person to really support my singing, to

tell me I could be famous someday and mean it," he continued. "She practically forced me to join the a cappella group.
And one time she surprised me with tickets to a musical,
and during the whole show she kept whispering things like
'Imagine what it's going to feel like when you're up there,'
and, 'You're better than all of them.' She was relentless." The
tiny smile that had formed on his lips disappeared. "And now
she's absolutely positive I cheated and she's turned the whole
school against me." He sighed. "I don't know. Maybe she's as
bad as everyone says."

I watched Oliver silently run his fingers along the edge of
the desk. "Can I ask you something?"

He nodded.

"Were you using me to try to make her jealous? Because
I'm not okay with that."

His eyes widened. "No."

"You came up to me that first day when I was standing
by her table. And today, that spot in the hall was right where
she'd have to pass on her way to lunch."

"No. Your first day I thought you might need a friend after
the football thing and the lunch line was just the first time I
saw you after that. And then I realized how easy you are to
talk to and…" He winced. "Okay, maybe a little. I mean, the
thought of Chloe seeing me talking to a pretty girl who actually *wanted* to be around me did cross my mind once or twice."

I pressed my lips together to stop from smiling. *He called
me pretty.* "Well, you get points for being honest."

He stared at his lap. "Yeah, look where honesty got me.
You're getting ready to tell me we shouldn't be friends, right?
That you don't want to be dragged into all my crap?"

"I definitely don't want crap-dragging to be a thing with us. Name calling is good. And honesty. I like both of those in my friends."

He lifted his head and grinned, showing off his cute dimples. "Yeah?"

"Yeah." I leaned toward him. "But since we're being honest and just so we're totally clear, even though you have the most adorable dimples I've ever seen, I'm not looking for anything more than a friend right now."

He lifted an eyebrow.

"It's only a few weeks until graduation and then everybody's going different ways for college. It's pointless to start something that can't last."

Oliver nodded. "I get it. After this whole mess with Chloe, I'm swearing off girls for a while. Nothing serious." His eyes danced. "But have you told Sawyer and Jason that?"

"What?"

"Oh, come on," he said with a hint of sarcasm. "Sawyer acted like he owned you that first day, guiding you through the cafeteria and paying for your lunch. And Jason." The sarcasm disappeared from his voice. "You two seemed pretty… close in the hall yesterday."

I picked at one of my nails. *You've got to dial it back, Kid. You're not blending in well enough.* "They're only friends. They're being nice to make up for running into me in the hall."

"I think I'm going to call you Ignorer of Obvious Flirtation."

"Just like you're Ignorer of Obvious Embarrassment during Welcome Serenades?"

Guilt flashed in Oliver's eyes. "I'm sorry. I didn't know you don't like surprises."

"That's because I haven't introduced myself yet either." I pointed at my chest. "Sloane Sullivan, Hater of All Things Surprising."

Oliver made an X over his heart. "I promise to keep that in mind from here on out."

I grinned at what I hoped was a promise he would keep as my stomach growled.

"There's a cure for that problem, my new friend." Oliver stood and held out a hand to me.

"Does it involve pizza?"

Oliver chuckled. "Of course it involves pizza. It's way better than the sweet potatoes."

He helped me off the desk, then gave my hand a quick squeeze before letting go. "You know, you shouldn't set your expectations so low. You already have everyone here failing at friendship so badly that you think you won't be talking to us after graduation. Maybe we'll surprise you." He shot me a smile. "Maybe some of us will be worth keeping as friends for a while."

My phone vibrated in my pocket, silently announcing a text. *Mark.* But instead of the sense of relief I was expecting at finally knowing I could reach Mark again, dread spread through me. Because Oliver was right. For the first time in a long time, I'd made what felt like a real friend. And I wanted to be Oliver's friend as long as he needed one. Then there was Jason. No matter how complicated things were now, he was the kind of friend worth keeping too, the kind that, long ago, I'd wanted to keep forever. And it terrified me.

I wasn't used to making friends this quickly. I wasn't used to settling in and finding people I wanted to keep around instead of push away. Things were happening faster than I'd planned. I could see the end in sight, picture the day I'd be out of WITSEC. The day I'd have to say goodbye to Mark. And while I was more than ready to make my own choices and stop moving around and inventing new people every few months, the thought of not being able to see Mark every day made my stomach twist. I wasn't ready to lose Mark. Not yet. After all these years together, I wanted to keep him around a little longer.

That wasn't asking too much, was it?

EIGHT

I surveyed the contents of my closet and groaned.

I'd spent the last few days lying low and blending in at school. I'd begged off Jason's and Sawyer's invitations to hang out over the weekend and stayed home with Mark instead, watching movies and grumbling about how I hadn't heard back from any colleges despite the passage of the supposed notification date.

But today was the start of a new week and my eighteenth birthday. My *real* birthday—Sloane Sullivan had turned eighteen back in February—and it was a gorgeous spring day outside. I wanted to wear something to celebrate the occasion. The problem was my wardrobe, which consisted only of basics: jeans and T-shirts and hoodies in plain, solid colors. It made it easier every time we moved. Anything too distinctive wasn't allowed to travel with me, and I learned really quickly not to waste money on pretty things that got left behind. But that didn't help with my current desire to wear something sparkly. I wanted the day to feel special, even if no one else knew it was. I sighed. There wasn't a sparkle in sight.

Two short knocks sounded on my bedroom door. "Can I come in?" Mark asked.

I frowned at the back of my door. I was awake and standing in the middle of my room, so I wasn't having the nightmare. *Why does he want to come in? Unless—*

I stopped that train of thought right there. I wasn't even going to *think* about a repeat of last year's birthday, when he'd announced in the morning we had to leave Tennessee that day. I took a deep breath and forced my voice to stay steady. "Come in!"

Mark peeked his head around the door. "Are you decent?"

"No. I always hang out in my room naked."

"Well, the wearing of birthday suits is a possibility when it's your *actual birthday!*" He popped into my room with a little jump and held out a large rectangular box wrapped in brightly colored wrapping paper. "I was too excited to wait for you to come out."

I grinned. "What is it?"

"Open it!"

I grabbed the present and ripped off the wrapping paper as I sat on my bed. I shook the top off the box and pulled out a gray V-neck T-shirt with a large black star on the front. It was edged in gold and had a white capital *V* in the middle of it. I immediately recognized the Vanderbilt University logo. Gripping the shirt in one hand, I peered back in the box. It was filled with letters and printed emails. As I flipped through them as fast as I could, I saw names jumping off the pages: Rice, Georgetown, USC, Dartmouth.

I looked at Mark, my mouth almost too dry to talk. "What does this mean?"

"You did it," he whispered. He hadn't put in his contacts yet, and his brown eyes sparkled. "You got in. I bought one shirt as a symbol, but you got in. Every single one. All five, all yeses, all spread out across the country."

I shook my head. "But I thought…the decisions were supposed to come April 1."

Mark rubbed the back of his neck. "USC's actually came a few days before the first. I hid the letters and deleted the emails after I printed them."

"But…I've been freaking out the past three days! I thought it meant I didn't get in. I moped around the house all weekend!"

"I'm sorry! I just wanted you to be able to see what you did all at once. You did that." He pointed to the box. "Your grades and your essays and your SAT scores. You did it *your* way. I'm so proud of you. And I wanted it to be special when you found out, so I waited until your birthday. I wanted to tell you *my* way."

Mark's voice echoed in my head. *"She doesn't know anything… You promised I could do this* my *way… Yes, it'll be soon. Have a little faith."* So that's what his mystery conversation with the Marshals last week was about! I covered my mouth with my hands as tears formed in my eyes. This *was* big.

Mark shook his head. "You're amazing. Everything you've been through, and you have your pick of futures, Kid. Or maybe I can't call you *Kid* anymore now that you're officially eighteen."

I jumped up and threw my arms around his neck. After a

few seconds, his solid arms closed around me. "Thank you," I whispered into his neck.

Mark exhaled slowly. "Happy Birthday."

A warm salty breeze blew over me as I approached the school's front doors, ruffling my hair and the hem of my new Vanderbilt T-shirt. It was nowhere near what it would've been like if I was actually at the beach, but I took a deep breath. I'd missed the smell of salt in the air, the way salt water stung my eyes and coated my skin when it dried.

A sharp whistle pierced the air. I turned and saw a single pale finger beckoning to me from around the corner of the building. After a quick check to make sure no one was watching, I walked over and found Sawyer and Jason waiting for me. They yanked me into their hiding place.

"Hey!" Sawyer said, grinning. "Lovely day, isn't it?"

I bounced a little on my feet. "Yes."

"I'm glad you agree. We want to skip school."

My eyebrows shot up.

"Wanna join us?" Jason asked. "Livie's coming too."

"Um…" I could feel the excitement radiating off them, but the memory of the last time I'd skipped school made me hesitate.

The rush of water over the falls was louder than I expected, but not as loud as my own heartbeat as Ben wrapped his hands around my waist and pulled my back against his chest. I still couldn't believe that a senior about to graduate wanted to hang out with a freshman.

"I'm surprised you haven't come to Gooseberry Falls yet," he murmured close to my ear. "How long have you been in Two Harbors now? Six months?"

My forehead creased. He'd talked to me for the first time only two weeks ago. I hadn't realized he knew when I'd arrived, although it was a very small town. "Six and a half months," I said. "But most of that was winter. The falls were probably half frozen. I was half frozen."

Ben gave a throaty laugh as he pushed my brown hair off my shoulder and kissed the side of my neck. My heart jumped in my chest. "There's something I want to show you. It's a little place I know that's…off the trail a bit." His grip on me tightened.

The hair on the back of my neck stood up.

"Nora!"

We both jumped at Mark's angry yell. I stumbled forward, the icy spray from the falls shocking the breath out of me. Ben caught my arm and steadied me. "Christ," he mumbled. "How the hell did your brother find us?"

I looked over Ben's shoulder at Mark. His blue eyes were burning a hole through the spot where Ben's hands were wrapped around my arm.

"We're going home, Nora!" Mark called over the sound of the falls. "Now."

I nodded and took two steps away before Ben caught my arm again. Mark tensed.

"Sneak out tonight," Ben whispered. "Meet me by that tree behind your house."

A chill ran down my back.

He leaned in and kissed me right on the mouth, all the while glaring at Mark.

Shock burned through me. I'd done my fair share of imagining my first kiss, even the possibility it might happen with Ben, but I never thought it would happen just to taunt Mark. I yanked my knee up as hard as I could until it landed between Ben's legs. He groaned and doubled over, and I shoved him with both hands. My lips were still tingling as I watched him hit the ground.

I could feel the weight of Mark's silent agitation all the way to the car. He exhaled and shoved his shaggy black hair out of his eyes. "Do you have any idea how worried I was?"

I hung my head.

"The school called this morning and said you weren't there. I thought…" He swallowed hard. "You can't go disappearing like that. I get that you're growing up, but you're not a normal teenager. I'm sorry, but that's the way it is."

"How did you find me?"

Mark started the car. "I tracked your phone. And I know that's a huge violation of your privacy, and I promise I'll never do it again unless I absolutely have to. But I didn't know what else to do."

We drove in silence for a few minutes. "I'm sorry," I said as I studied Lake Superior out the window. "Everyone here is so nice. I thought he was too. But there's something seriously wrong with him."

"What do you mean?"

"He just told me to sneak out tonight and meet him by the tree in the backyard." I turned to Mark. "I never told him where we live."

A muscle in Mark's jaw twitched. "We're leaving as fast as we can."

I nodded—the tightness in my chest loosening a bit. "I'm sorry. I thought…"

Mark examined me and his expression softened. "It's okay. I shouldn't have picked such a small town."

"Maybe I need a refresher on the 'be aware of your surroundings/ know when people are following you' lesson. Ooh, or better yet, I want a self-defense lesson as soon as we get to the next town. Lesson number twelve: how to do more than kick creepy guys in the balls *when they kiss you." The realization of how stupid it was to run off with some guy I hardly knew, how stupid it was to trust* any-one*, hit me like a ton of bricks. I studied Mark's profile. "Thanks for coming to get me."*

He shifted closer to me, eyes on the road. "I promised I'd never let anything happen to you."

The shrill ring of the first bell cut through the silence of the courtyard and snapped me out of the memory. "Um, does the school call home if you're absent?"

Sawyer's mouth dropped open. "No, thank God. What gave you that idea?"

"My old school did that."

He shuddered. "That's horribly unfair to those of us who want to skip."

Jason leaned against the outside wall of the school. "So what do you think? It's a special day."

It was a special day, but he wasn't supposed to know that. I forced a smile. "What's the occasion?"

"We always skip on the first nice day of spring," Sawyer replied. "It's *our* school tradition. At least since we've been able to drive."

"Livie's waiting in the car," Jason added.

My eyes darted between their glowing faces. This wasn't like with Ben. I was with a group. I was going to have to learn to trust people. And it *was* a special day.

"Come on." Sawyer grabbed my hand and pulled me toward the parking lot. "It's only a few hours. No one will ever know we were gone."

NINE

"Just a few more steps." Jason's hands were warm against my closed eyes.

"Why am I the only one being blindfolded?" I asked.

"Because Sawyer already told Livie where we were going. This way, at least I get to surprise *someone*." Jason stopped and turned me a little more to the left. His chest pressed against my back as he leaned close to my ear. "Just humor me," he whispered. He removed his hands and sang, "Ta da!"

I blinked a few times as my eyes adjusted to the brightness of the morning. When I could finally see clearly, I smiled. I was standing in front of a giant carousel.

My eyes swept over the brightly painted horses. They were every color imaginable: pearl white and smoky gray, lemon yellow and sunset orange, pale pink and bloodred. Some had elaborate saddles while others had flowers woven in their manes. Some seemed calm and still and some were frozen midgallop. There was even a turquoise one with the front half of a horse's body and the back half of a seahorse's, tail curled and resting on the carousel's floor.

I glanced around. We were standing at the edge of a grassy square block in the middle of an unfamiliar town. A parking lot with pretty much only Jason's car was behind us, and there were restaurants and stores a few blocks away. But this block looked like someone had plopped a carnival right in the middle of it and didn't even think to add fences or gates. You could walk right up to all the rides, although they were dark right now.

"What do you think?" Jason asked.

I turned. Sawyer and Livie were standing on the other side of Jason, examining the carousel, but Jason was studying me. He ran a hand through his hair.

"It's a carousel, all right," Livie replied. She sounded almost disappointed, like maybe when Sawyer told her they were going to a *carousel* she'd hoped he'd meant *shopping mall*.

I laughed at Livie's reaction. "It's perfect," I told Jason.

He grinned.

Sawyer crossed in front of me and bowed. "Your noble steed awaits, milady."

My eyes widened. "We get to ride it?" There wasn't another person in sight besides the four of us. "How?"

"Watch and learn." Sawyer jumped up onto the carousel and disappeared behind the rows of horses. A minute later, the carousel's lights blinked on and music began to softly float toward us. I closed my eyes and for a second, it was like I was on the boardwalk at home. When I opened them, Sawyer had reappeared and was swinging a key attached to a metal circle around one finger. "I worked here last summer. I figured they hadn't changed the hiding place for the spare key."

"Are you sure no one will catch us?" Livie asked, peering down the block toward the restaurants.

I'd just thought the same thing.

"Nah." Sawyer stepped off the carousel. "Look around. This place is dead in the off-season. Besides, it's just one ride. Who's going to catch us in two minutes?"

I shifted onto my toes. I knew I shouldn't do it. It felt more *not following the rules* than skipping did. But for once, for two minutes on my birthday, I wanted to be normal, to pretend I'd never left home. "I call the purple one with the starfish!" I yelled as I dashed toward the outer ring of horses.

Jason and Livie scrambled after me, fighting over who got the horse in front of mine, which was covered in green scales like a sea monster. Sawyer, however, walked around the outside of the carousel to a small raised platform I hadn't noticed before. He opened a door in the base of the platform, removed a plastic bucket and climbed the stairs to the platform in two giant steps. When he leaned around a tall wood beam extending up from one of the platform's corners and pulled out a long metal arm, it all clicked into place.

I let out a whoop. "Bet I can catch the most rings!"

Jason, who'd won the battle for the scaled horse, turned around. "You're going down."

After Sawyer finished loading brass rings into the metal arm's shoot, he crossed the carousel's deck and flipped a switch. He jumped onto the horse in front of Livie's as we began moving.

No one tried to grab a ring at first because we weren't going fast enough. But by the third rotation, we all reached out as we came around. My heart beat with excitement at the familiar *thwack* of metal sliding against metal as everyone in front of me tried to snag a ring. My finger hooked around one and pulled it free like it was second nature, like it hadn't been almost six years since I'd last done it.

The breeze ruffled Jason's black hair as he spun around on his sea monster, holding up a ring with pride. I lifted mine with a mocking grin until he slowly slid a second ring from behind the first. My mouth dropped open. *Damn him for using my secret technique!*

Jason laughed deeply and I gasped. It was the first time I'd seen his childhood laugh, the one he'd hated because it showed all of his teeth and made his cheeks so full it seemed like they would burst. I thought maybe he'd outgrown it, but there it was. Just like the last time I'd seen it.

I peeked down the hall to where the three agents were talking with Dad in the kitchen, then back at the trophy in my hands. It was one of Jason's old soccer trophies we'd doctored by covering the plaque with a piece of paper that read: #1 Best Superstar at Everything. I was supposed to be picking my personal item, and I knew I only had a few minutes before they'd come looking for me, but I couldn't leave without seeing Jason one last time. I silently opened my bedroom window, pulse racing, and jumped out.

I crossed the short distance between our houses and used the air conditioning unit to boost myself up to Jason's window. I slid it open and prayed he was inside.

"Hey!" He looked up from the graphic novel he was reading on his bed. "What's going on? I thought you were hanging out with your dad this afternoon."

My chest constricted at the sound of his voice, a sound I wouldn't hear again. I climbed through the window and dropped into his room.

"I am. We...have more stuff to do. I just came to give you this." I thrust the trophy in his direction.

He placed the book on his bed and walked over to me. His eyebrows scrunched together as he took the trophy. "What for? I haven't won a bet."

I shrugged, blinking back tears. "Because you're the best friend ever, and I wanted you to know that."

Jason laughed his chipmunk laugh and I couldn't help smiling back. "You're going to have to do something really big to top that and win it back," he teased.

I rushed forward and hugged him as hard as I could. "I can't top that." I let go and backed away before I started crying.

"Are you okay?" Jason asked.

I climbed onto his windowsill. "Yeah. I've just got to go." It physically hurt to look back at him one last time. "I'll see you later, okay?" I lied, then dropped to the ground.

"Are you okay?"

I blinked myself back to the present. Jason was standing next to me holding five rings as the ride slowed down.

I rested my head against my horse's cool metal pole. "I'm great. Just had bad luck with the rings." I held up my single ring as proof.

"Who wants to go again? We can go again, right? New horses!" Livie yelled from a few feet away.

Sawyer hopped off the still-moving carousel. "I'm going to reload the rings."

I climbed off my horse, landing beside Jason. The carousel lurched as it came to a final standstill. I stumbled forward, grabbing Jason's arm to keep from falling, and my hand brushed lightly along the scar by his left thumb, the one he

116

got carving our initials into the tree in front of his house. *He's the same. He's my Jason, with the same goofy laugh and the same scar and the same joyful desire to crush me at everything. I never thought I'd see him again, and he's standing so close I can touch him.*

"J! Sloane! Where are your rings?" Sawyer called.

I glanced up to find Jason watching me with gentle eyes. He slowly reached and yanked twice on my earlobe, his fingers skimming briefly along my neck. My stomach flipped in a way I hadn't felt since Texas, since Duke. Then his hand was back at his side.

He chuckled. "For all your talk, you kind of suck at the ring thing."

I shot him a look. "I'm going to help Sawyer get ready for a rematch." I swiped Jason's rings out of his hand and turned with a smile on my face, giddy at the sheer impossibility of it all.

Sawyer watched me approach the platform. "You're really enjoying yourself, aren't you?"

I nodded and held up the rings. "Can I load these ones in?"

"Be my guest." He stepped back from the metal arm as I climbed onto the platform. "You know, it was my idea to come here."

I paused midreach. "Really?" This seemed more like a Jason thing, maybe because I could picture him on the carousel at home. Then again, Sawyer had said he'd worked here.

His grin widened. "Yup. I wanted to do something special for you."

"Oh." I turned back to the metal arm. "Um, thanks."

I'd just slid the first ring in when Livie called, "You forgot mine, Sawyer!" She stood on the edge of the carousel, blew her long dark brown bangs out of her eyes, and chucked a ring at us like a Frisbee.

It came flying at my head so fast I ducked in instinct. I bumped into Sawyer, who lost his balance and fell backward off the platform. I spun around to try to catch him, but my foot knocked into the ring bucket, sending it over the edge. The sound of Sawyer hitting the ground combined with the dull *thunk* of metal rings landing on top of him made me cringe.

I peered over the platform. Sawyer was flat on his back in the grass with his eyes closed. "Oh my gosh! Are you okay?" I jumped off the back of the platform and began brushing a handful of brass rings off his head and chest. "Sawyer?"

He opened his eyes and blinked at me, a confused expression forming on his face. "Do I know you? Cause you look just like my next girlfriend."

"Ugh!" I whacked him on the chest. "I thought you were hurt!"

He wiggled his eyebrows. "Want to nurse me back to health?"

I picked up a ring, ready to toss it at his head. "I'll show you hur—"

"Freeze!"

The command rang out loud and clear from the direction of the carousel.

Sawyer's eyes widened and he scrambled to fold his long frame into a scrunched up position next to me behind the platform.

"Come on out, you two!" the voice boomed.

I inched up and peeked over the top of the platform. My stomach dropped. Because standing in a grassy patch to the left of the carousel was a police officer who did not look happy.

TEN

I ducked back down. "Crap, it's a cop."

"Did he see us?" Sawyer whispered.

I peeked around the platform. The cop gestured for Jason and Livie to get off the carousel, watching with a tired expression as they worked their way toward him. "I don't think so."

"Good. I'm staying right here."

From the way the cop was angled, I could see the path I could take to escape: sneak around the bumper cars' ticket booth, duck behind the haunted house and I'd be halfway down the next block before anyone knew it.

I looked back at the police officer, at the way Livie was wringing her hands as she came to a stop in front of him, eyes darting in our direction. Escaping would get me out, but not anyone else. And involving the police was *not* blending in.

Mark said local police were never informed when a protected witness moved to town. The fewer people who knew the new resident was in hiding, the less likely that information would be leaked. Thanks to a childhood full of Jason not tattling, I was certain he wouldn't mention me or Sawyer. But I wasn't so sure about Livie. We must've at least trespassed or done something else illegal by riding the carousel. If they got taken in for questioning or whatever cops did to teenage trespassers, I couldn't risk Livie ratting me out. They'd call Mark and he would be pissed about having cops digging into our lives. Probably even mad enough to make us move. Which I couldn't do now, not after getting into college.

The officer's voice floated over to me, less harsh this time. "What were you guys thinking?"

Jason stared at his feet. "We were just…taking a ride."

There was a tug in my chest, a pull toward Jason, rooting me to the ground. I should run. Mark would want me to go. But that's not what a friend would do. It's not what I *wanted* to do.

I squatted next to Sawyer with my back flat against the platform. "We have to help them." A gentle pulling sensation made me look at Sawyer, who was holding a section of my hair to his nose. "Are you *smelling my hair* right now?"

He shrugged. "You smell good."

I smacked his hand away. "That's not creepy at all, Sawyer," I hissed.

Jason said something that sounded like, "Didn't mean to cause any trouble."

Think, think. I looked over and saw Jason's car in the parking lot. For one wild second, a vision of me driving the car right up to the carousel, tires squealing, windows down, yelling, "Get in," with Jason sliding across the hood and Livie jumping through the back door Sawyer was holding open, then fishtailing it out of there, leaving the cop behind in a cloud of dust that rendered him unable to read the license plate flashed through my mind. Practical, no; I didn't even have the keys to Jason's car. But it would've been nice to have options.

Keys. I gripped Sawyer's arm. "Do you still have the key to the carousel?"

He dug it out of his pocket and held it up.

I grabbed the key. "Come on." I stood enough to see that the officer had his back to us.

Sawyer yanked me back down. "What are you doing? There's no way we can help them."

I glared at him. "We can at least try! Now come on and follow my lead."

I stood and quickly crossed the grass to the end of the block, pulling Sawyer behind me, then moved diagonally toward the officer so it would seem like we'd come from the opposite direction instead of from behind the platform. "Bathroom break accomplished!" I called out.

The cop turned in our direction, startled.

Jason's eyes widened at us over the officer's shoulder. He shook his head infinitesimally.

The cop appraised us as we walked closer. For the first time, I wished my hair wasn't so damn blond. Or that Sawyer's wasn't such a memorable shade of red.

"You know these two?" the cop asked, nodding in Jason and Livie's direction.

"Yes, sir," I said as I stopped next to Livie. "What seems to be the problem?"

The officer frowned. "Are there any more of you?"

"No. Just us four," Jason confirmed.

The cop turned to Sawyer and me. "Were you two riding the carousel also? Did you all wake up this morning and decide trespassing was a good idea?"

I put on my best confused expression. "You're certainly more of an expert on what constitutes trespassing, officer, but doesn't it entail being somewhere without permission?"

He arched an eyebrow. "Are you telling me you have permission to be riding this thing?"

I held up the key. "Of course. My uncle runs this place. He gave us the key."

The officer folded his arms across his chest. "What's your name?"

I peeked at Sawyer and saw the T-shirt he was wearing: navy with a silver skull and crossbones that read *I'm a Goonie*. Thanks to Mark's love of all movies ever made, no matter how old, I'd seen what must've been another one of Sawyer's favorite 1980s movies a bunch of times.

"Andy," I replied without hesitation. "And this is Stef, Mikey and Brand." I pointed at Livie, Jason and Sawyer with a smile, as if I truly enjoyed making introductions to the police, but inside I prayed, *prayed*, he didn't know the characters' names from *The Goonies*.

"Do you have some ID, Andy?"

Crap. "No, sir. I don't have a driver's license. I refuse to contribute to the growing epidemic of greenhouse gas emissions by driving. We all have to reduce our carbon footprints."

He studied me, presumably trying to tell whether I was full of it. Then something in his eyes changed. His gaze became more curious than suspicious. I didn't like it.

"I can call my uncle if you want to talk to him," I offered. "I don't own a phone myself—still not sure whether the radiation they emit is going to give me cancer one day—but Brand has one." I wacked Sawyer on the arm.

"Oh yeah." He pulled out his phone. "Here you go, Andy."

I took it and swallowed hard. This was taking my bluff to a level I really wasn't comfortable with. If I called Mark, he'd cover for me for sure. But that would only get rid of the cop problem, not the Mark problem.

The officer's eyes drifted from Sawyer's phone to the key in my other hand.

I let out a slow breath.

"Did your uncle also give you permission to skip school today?"

I laughed, as if just realizing what the problem was. "Oh no. We're not skipping school. We're all part of a homeschool co-op. This is our physics class. We're studying Newton's first law and centripetal force."

"You're studying Newton's first law," the cop repeated, slow and disbelieving.

I nodded. "The carousel's a perfect example."

The officer did another sweep of my face, like he was studying my features. "Homeschooling, huh? Do you live around here?"

"Yes." *This is so going to end in disaster.*

The cop nodded. "With both your parents?"

That's an odd question. "Yes, sir."

His eyes narrowed. *He's not buying it. I need to risk a call again.* I shook Sawyer's phone in my hand. "My uncle can corroborate that too."

Static crackled out of the radio attached to the officer's

shoulder. "We've got a 10-62 in progress. All units respond immediately. Repeat, 10-62 at—"

The officer turned down the volume on the radio. His gaze locked on me. Not Jason or Sawyer or Livie. Only me. He pursed his lips. "Finish your physics thing and clear out of here, okay?"

I nodded.

He jogged over to his patrol car, which was parked at the opposite end of the block from the carousel. He got in, but not before throwing another wary glance in my direction. The lights and sirens flipped on, and the car sped away.

I turned and let out a breath I hadn't even realized I was holding, only to find Jason watching me. For a second, regret and sadness flashed in his eyes. Then, as fast as it appeared, it vanished. He let out a half laugh, half sigh of relief.

"Holy hell," Livie muttered. She leaned against Jason. "I almost peed my pants."

Sawyer whooped. "My girl's a scary good liar!" He slung an arm around my waist and gazed down at me. "Sloane Sullivan, you're my hero," he said in the same nasally voice Cameron used to tell Ferris the very same thing in *Ferris Bueller's Day Off.*

We all laughed in the silly, giddy way of people who've just gotten away with something they shouldn't have. But Jason's laugh was different. It had a resignation to it I didn't like. It wasn't anything like the laugh he'd given me on the carousel. It wasn't *my* Jason.

"I'm home!" I called before the screen door slammed behind me. I was on a mission.

I couldn't do anything to change what happened that morning at the carousel. I'd replayed the conversation with the cop in my head repeatedly and was certain I hadn't given him anything he could use to track any of us down. But I could make sure that if I was ever in that type of situation again, I would have more options available to me. And I needed Mark's help with that.

I crossed the kitchen, eager to find him, when something in my peripheral vision made me pause. I turned and gaped at the cake sitting on the kitchen island. It had a graham cracker crust and caramelized apple slices fanned out across the top in the shape of a gorgeous flower.

"I see you found your birthday cake."

I looked at Mark, leaning casually against the kitchen door frame. "What is it?"

"Caramel apple cheesecake." He pushed off the door frame and stood next to me. "I saw the recipe online and I remembered how much you liked those caramel apples that time we went to the carnival."

My mouth dropped open again. "That was, like, five years ago. And with everything else that happened that day, how did you remember that?"

He shrugged.

"Can we skip dinner and just eat this?"

Mark chuckled. "Sure. You're the birthday girl. You can pick how the rest of your day goes."

"Oh really?" I arched an eyebrow.

He responded with a similar gesture. "Did you have something in mind?"

"I know what I want for my birthday."

"You mean, besides that shirt you're wearing and this awesomeness I baked you on my day off?"

I nodded. "Yes. To mark the occasion of my official exit from childhood, I'm going to be a spoiled brat and ask for one more thing. Something special, on my special day."

"Okay, I'll bite. What do you want?"

I grinned. "A car lesson."

ELEVEN

I tipped the wires together and Mark's car rumbled to life. I did a little happy dance in my seat.

"Don't let go of the starter wires!" Mark chastised. "You'll get shocked if you touch them!" He covered the exposed wires with electrical tape, laughing at my dance. "For once I'm glad I have a crappy old car that's easy to hotwire. You're a natural. I can't believe I didn't think of teaching you this before."

I tsked. "You're slacking on your ways-to-corrupt-the-innocent duties."

He grinned his giving-me-a-hard-time grin. "We're up to lesson number fourteen. I hardly think you qualify as innocent anymore."

My mouth dropped open. "Oh, sure. Teach me how to be a criminal and then hold it against me."

A seriousness crossed over Mark's face that was clearly visible even in the dim light of his flashlight. "I'm not teaching you how to be a criminal."

I studied the wire cutters resting on the seat between us.

As a Marshal, his job was to put bad guys away, not create more of them, and I knew how much he believed in that. "I was only kidding."

Mark sighed and clicked off the flashlight. "I'm trying to teach you ways to escape or defend yourself if you have to. That's what these lessons have been about."

I hesitated. "What about guns? I could use a gun to defend myself."

"No." His voice cut through the darkness. "We've talked about this before. They're too dangerous. It's too easy to make a mistake. The consequences are too...permanent."

I stared out the driver's side window as my eyes adjusted to the darkness of the empty park. This was the only topic we'd ever disagreed on. I knew guns were dangerous. I just also knew they were a lot less dangerous when you knew how to use them properly.

"I can't believe out of all the things we could be doing, you want to practice shooting again." Duke shook his head in mock disappointment, making his floppy dirty-blond hair fall into his eyes.

"My uncle doesn't like guns. You're the only one I can practice with," I explained, hoping he wasn't getting bored.

He picked up a pair of earmuffs from the weathered wooden bench resting against the fence and handed them to me without looking up. "I don't mind. I'd do anything with you," he said so softly I almost didn't hear it.

My stomach flipped as I hung the earmuffs around my arm. I didn't want to put them on yet in case he said anything else.

Duke ran a hand through his hair, then slid a magazine into the handgun and pushed it toward me. He glanced up, all business. "So what are your fundamentals?"

I swallowed my disappointment and picked up the gun. "Um, grip." I placed the webbing in between my thumb and pointer finger on my right hand as high as it would go on the handle of the gun and wrapped my left hand around the other side the way he'd taught me. I gripped as hard as I could. "Sight." I pointed the gun at the target set up across the field and made sure the front sight was centered in the notch of the rear sight. "And trigger." I squeezed out the slack in the trigger until I felt resistance.

Duke took a few steps back and pulled on his own earmuffs. "Let's see what you've got."

I put on my earmuffs, chambered a round, clicked off the safety, lined up my shot and squeezed the trigger. The recoil didn't surprise me anymore. But even with the earmuffs, I wasn't sure I'd ever get used to the sound of gunshots. It brought back too much uncertainty and fear. But that's why I was doing this. Each pop *I caused chipped away a little of the fear.*

"Wow!" Duke said after I'd emptied the magazine into the target, one steady shot at a time. He pulled off his earmuffs. "Every shot hit the center of the target! You're really getting good."

I grinned, proud of myself, but it faltered when I thought of Mark. I wished I could show him how good I was, how careful I was being. I clicked the safety on and set down the gun.

Duke gently pulled my earmuffs off and placed them on the bench next to him. "What does your uncle think we do when you come over, Phoebe?"

I glanced around at the acres of lush green grass and fences and animals and the gorgeous single-story stone rambler at the top of the hill I loved so much. "I don't know, he's never really asked. Tend to the livestock. Ride horses. Whatever else you can do on a ranch in Texas."

When I turned back to Duke, he was closer than he'd been before. He hooked his right thumb into the pocket of his jeans and took a step even closer, so close I could see flecks of green in his light brown eyes. "I can think of something we could do." His gaze dropped to my mouth, a question hanging in the charged space between us.

I reached up and pushed his hair out of his eyes. It was all the invitation he needed. He leaned in and kissed me. It was slow and sweet and steady, just like him. When he pulled away, I thought, That should've been my first kiss.

Duke's smile grew as he brushed a lock of strawberry blond hair off my cheek. "I've wanted to do that for a really long time."

We'd been friends for eight months, ever since I'd latched on to his crowd my first day part-way through my sophomore year, but it didn't surprise me he'd waited. It had taken me months to work up the courage to ask him to teach me how to shoot, and even longer to trust my judgment again after the whole Ben debacle. Things just moved more slowly here, and I liked it.

I grinned at Duke and whispered, "Me too." And I showed him how much I meant it with another kiss.

"…just makes me feel better knowing you have ways to protect yourself," Mark continued as I tuned back into the conversation. "It's the least I can do before…"

He didn't finish his sentence. He didn't have to.

I leaned back and looked out the sunroof at the stars. They were endless and familiar. Those stars were one of the few constants I'd had no matter where we lived. The stars and Mark. Nothing else lasted, no matter how much I wanted it to.

I swallowed the lump in my throat. "What's going to happen when I graduate?" I asked softly.

Mark was silent for a long time. "You'll go to college."

I ignored the way he dodged the question. "What are you going to do without a kid to look after anymore?"

A breathy laugh escaped him. "I might call you that, but I haven't thought of you as a kid in a while."

I turned and studied his profile in the dim light. "You must have friends, a family that misses you. Things you want to do besides teach me how to hotwire cars."

The muscles in his jaw tensed. "I started this job when I was pretty young. This is all I know. I like it."

My ears perked. "How young?"

Mark chuckled. "I'm probably not as old as you think I am."

"Damn. Does that mean I have to return that fortieth birthday card I got you?"

He faced me, one hand spread across his chest. "Do you actually think I'm forty?"

"You're so easy to tease sometimes."

We were both quiet for a bit, curled up in our seats, facing each other. "I want to protect you," Mark said, looking down at his hands. "I'll always want to protect you. That won't stop just because you're out of WITSEC."

Something about the quiet hum of the car and the confined space of the front seat and the way I could only see Mark in shadow made it easier for me to finally ask the question I'd been worried about for months. "Will I be able to see you after I'm out?"

His eyes studied mine. "Would you want to?"

I nodded.

"Then yes."

"Will they allow it?"

Mark reached across and closed the distance between us, placing his hand on top of mine. "I'll make it happen. Whatever you want, I'll make it happen."

TWELVE

I was expecting three things to happen at lunch the following Friday.

First, because sweet potatoes were on the cafeteria menu, I planned on trading some witty banter with Oliver in the lunch line. He always waited for me so we could stand in line together, which was sweet considering he now sat at our table too. We were still making up names for each other, and I had a couple of good ones waiting to be used.

Second, I was looking forward to finally agreeing to hang out with Jason, Livie, Sawyer and Oliver over the weekend. The past four days had been easier knowing that settling in and making friends and getting ready to move on didn't automatically mean losing Mark. And my new friends had been hinting at doing something Saturday night. I had to admit, I was curious what a night out would feel like. It had been a while.

And third, I was anticipating having to fend off more of Sawyer's touchy-feeliness. Apparently, not immediately objecting when he wrapped an arm around me and called me his "girl" at the carousel hadn't been my best call. He'd been finding excuses to touch me all week. I was going to have to let him down gently, I just hadn't figured out the best way to do it yet. Which was why I took a detour to the bathroom before lunch, like I had every other day that week. That and a lengthy chat with Oliver in the lunch line at least shortened Sawyer's how-many-ways-can-I-touch-Sloane window.

What I wasn't expecting? To find Livie crying at the bathroom sink, staring at herself in the mirror.

I froze. My first instinct was to run. Emotional drama is not part of blending in. But the way she was leaning on the sink, shoulders hunched, lost in her reflection like she didn't know I was there, like she didn't know *she* was there, made me pause. I couldn't remember how many times I'd stared into a mirror, searching for myself. I knew what that was like. And if I was really going to do this friend thing, maybe I could help.

"Hey," I said gently, trying not to startle her. "Are you okay?"

Livie blinked and it was like she snapped back into place. She looked at me through the mirror and rolled her eyes. "I'm fine. I can't believe I'm crying over this. It's so stupid." She pushed her bangs to the side and blotted one of the rough bathroom paper towels under her eyes to fix her running mascara.

"What happened?"

The bathroom door squeaked open and a girl with dark skin I recognized from my psychology class, who I thought was named Kiera, walked in. She stood on the other side of

Livie, pulled her black hair away from her face, and began reapplying her lipstick.

Livie continued as if Kiera hadn't just arrived. "Jason broke up with me last night."

My heart did a funny little leap.

"He'd probably say it was never anything *serious*." Livie said the last word in a dopey-sounding boy voice. "But we were together for almost two months. We made out tons of times."

My neck grew warm.

"That counts for something, right?"

Kiera smacked her lips and dropped her lipstick into her bag. "That totally counts for something," she told Livie's reflection in the mirror.

"I know," Livie huffed. "I thought things were going so well. I should've known it wouldn't last."

Kiera faced Livie and leaned against a sink. "You definitely should've with his reputation."

I frowned. "What do you mean?"

"Let's just say he's dated a lot of girls and none of them have lasted very long." Kiera gave me an if-you-know-what-I-mean look.

"More like he's slept with half the girls in the school," Livie muttered, scrubbing away the last of her tears.

What?

Kiera grinned. "Remember Sammy Hayes? Took her to homecoming as their first date and after the postdance party at Josh's house, he never talked to her again."

Livie snorted. "What about Lauren? She made him that romantic New Year's Eve dinner and he didn't even stay long enough for dessert. He got what he wanted from her and left."

That does not sound like the Jason I know. The Jason I know blushed at the Kissing Tree at the mere mention of what Livie wanted the two of them to do on the senior trip.

"I thought I had him figured out," Livie admitted. "He kept going out with all these girls he didn't know well and they only lasted a date or two. So I decided to be his friend first. Friends for a couple of months, then slowly show him I was interested, like I couldn't help developing feelings for my best friend. That was the plan. He would already know we got along and he wouldn't have to toss me like all the others."

Plan? I couldn't believe she'd created step-by-step instructions for seducing Jason.

"Does he like someone else?" Kiera asked.

Livie's eyes flashed to me and back to Kiera. "He said no. He just thinks we're 'better as friends.'"

"That's a crap excuse." Kiera's eyes narrowed and she leaned closer to Livie. "Did you, *you know*?"

"No!" Livie replied, then more wistfully, "No."

"I always thought you were lasting longer than the others because you weren't giving it up." Kiera shrugged one shoulder. "No offense."

Livie let out a single harsh laugh. "And I always thought the fact he *wasn't* trying to sleep with me quickly like all the others meant he actually liked me."

I wasn't sure what to say to that.

Livie stared at herself in the mirror. "I had all these romantic ideas though. Maybe the senior trip, maybe prom. I wanted it to be special." She sighed. "I don't know why I bothered. I don't think Jason has any idea how to do something special for a girl."

I knew for a fact Livie was wrong.

I took a deep breath of salty air. I loved how, even at night, the waves kept crashing, telling their secrets to anyone who would listen. Shh, shh, shh, they said, over and over. It made me realize just how big the ocean was. And how insignificant I was in comparison.

Cool sand sifted between my toes as Jason said, "Okay."

My mom removed her hands from my eyes. It took a second to make out what was in front of me in the dim moonlight. There was a large blanket spread out on the sand. A telescope was sitting in the middle of it, surrounded by what looked like constellation books and star charts and a paper plate filled with round chocolate-looking discs.

I peeked at Jason, who was watching me from the other side of the blanket. He rubbed the back of his neck.

"What's all this?" I asked.

"I overheard you telling Dante in that assembly that you wanted to visit a planetarium. So I asked my mom if we could make one instead." He gestured to the spread on the blanket.

I glanced at our moms, both standing by the edge of the blanket.

"Don't look at me," Jason's mom insisted. "It was Jason's idea. I just helped bring it all together. Except for the homemade MoonPies." She pointed to the plate. "You know I can't resist themed snacks."

I bit back a smile.

Jason rolled his eyes. "She means she borrowed the telescope from a friend, drove me to the library to get the books and helped me search online for the star charts."

"Jase, there's a life lesson here," his mom said as she placed a hand on my shoulder. "When someone lets you take all the credit for doing something nice for a pretty girl, you take it."

Jason and I both blushed.

"I just thought this would be way better than a planetarium." He *looked up at the sky. "You wouldn't be able to hear the waves or feel the sand at a planetarium."*

I gazed at the stars winking at me in the darkness like they were in on the secret too.

"Do you like it?" he asked.

I tore my eyes away from the stars and grinned at him. "I love it."

"I knew you would. You totally geeked out during the whole planets unit in science."

My mouth dropped open. "Shut up!"

Jason smirked. "I don't think Mr. McCreedy has ever had anyone in the history of all the sixth graders he's ever taught so interested in class before."

A warm sensation filled my chest. There may have been an infinite number of stars in the sky or millions of miles of ocean, but there was only one person in the whole world who smirked at me like that. A slow smile formed on my lips. I didn't feel so insignificant anymore. "Come on, Mr. Science Guy. Show me some stars."

"Now I'm not going to have a date for prom," Livie whined, pulling me out of the memory.

She leaned over the sink and I rubbed her back just like I remembered my mom doing when I was upset. "Prom's still a month away," I pointed out.

"Yes," Kiera agreed. "There are tons of guys who don't have dates yet." She smacked a hand on the sink. "What you need to do is ask someone else, arrive all gorgeous and show Jason what he's missing."

Livie stood a little taller. "Yeah? Like who?"

"Someone better than Jason."

I pursed my lips.

"How about Justin Parker?" Kiera offered.

Livie wrinkled her nose.

"Austin Zimmerman?"

Livie rubbed her bottom lip. "I heard he was taking Katrina Carr."

"Oh yeah." Kiera tapped a finger against her chin. "What about Sawyer?"

"Been there, done that," Livie mumbled, then glanced at me with wide eyes. "Don't tell Jason, okay? It was just a one-time thing. A…moment of weakness last fall."

Holy cow. "Um, yeah. Sure."

Kiera pushed herself off the sink and held up two fingers. "I have two words for you—Oliver Clarke."

Livie's gaze darted to me.

I held up my hands. "We're just friends."

"You're only *friends*? After that totally romantic serenade in which he called you *his* brown-eyed girl? Why?"

I sighed. "It's just a song, Livie. It's not like that."

A gleam of something I couldn't quite place flashed in Livie's brown eyes. "So you don't mind if I ask him to prom?"

"No. Go ahead."

"Although you do risk Chloe's wrath," Kiera reminded Livie.

"If it makes a difference," I said, "she broke up with Oliver, not the other way around."

Livie's mouth dropped open. "Why didn't you tell me this?"

"I didn't think it was important."

Livie smiled at her own reflection in the mirror. "I'm *so*

asking Oliver Clarke to prom." She spun on her heels and marched out of the bathroom.

I watched her go. *How can she replace Jason with someone else so quickly?*

"I hate this screen door!" Mark yelled a few hours later.

I chuckled and followed his grunts of frustration into the kitchen. He was standing by the back door with about six overflowing grocery bags in each hand. The ones in his left hand were safely inside the house while the ones in his right hand were either trapped outside or being smushed by the screen.

Mark gave another big tug to no avail and his shoulders slumped. "It's trying to eat the groceries."

I laughed as I squeezed behind him. I untangled the bags and pushed open the screen door. Mark collapsed into the kitchen.

"Maybe it's been smelling all your delicious cooking and it wants you to share," I said.

"Maybe if it stopped trying to bite my ass every time I went through it, I might."

I shook my head and started emptying groceries out of the bags now slung across the kitchen floor. "How was work?"

He glanced at his watch. "Fine. Had a broken pipe that took longer to fix than I expected. How was school?"

"High school drama is *intense*." I put a gallon of milk in the refrigerator. "Jason broke things off with Livie and I found her crying in the bathroom right before lunch. But five minutes later she was all excited about asking another guy, a *better* guy, to prom. Then neither Jason nor Livie showed up at lunch, and Oliver got stuck finishing some lab experiment, so I was left with Sawyer and his grand plans for this weekend. We're going out to dinner on Saturday, by the way." I placed a bag of apples on the island. "Was high school that dramatic when you were there?"

Mark shrugged. "I wouldn't know. I was homeschooled."

"What? Why didn't I know this?"

He placed a package of chicken on the island and studied it. "I had trouble with the other kids. I never really fit in. It was easier to stay home."

I watched him, still studying the food. "Did you not like it? Is that why you never suggested homeschooling me?"

He looked up. "I never suggested homeschooling you because you're not me. You've always fit in. And I didn't want you to feel any more isolated than you already were."

"Oh. Well, things got better when you went to college, right?"

"Yeah. Once I left, things got a lot better. But from what you're telling me, it sounds like I didn't miss out on much. High school sounds exhausting."

"It is," I agreed. "And I don't even participate that much."

"It seems like you're settling in though. Making weekend plans? You haven't done that in a while. That's…good." He piled a package of sausage and a bag of uncooked shrimp on top of the chicken.

I eyed them with delight. "Are you making paella?"

Mark placed his hands on either side of the meat pyramid and nodded slowly. "I thought bribing you with the promise of making one of your favorites soon would soften the blow of what I have to tell you."

I smacked the island with both hands. "We're not moving! You just told me it was good I'm settling in here!"

"No, no," he assured me. "We're not moving. I just have to leave. For the night. I have a meeting about my next assignment, the one after you graduate."

"Oh." I fiddled with the bag of apples. "You have a meeting after six on a Friday night?"

"No. I have a meeting early tomorrow morning at the regional office. But it's a lot easier if I leave tonight."

I shoved a box of cereal in the pantry.

"Are you going to be okay?" He bit his lip. "I know we've never spent a night apart, but you've got that senior trip coming up and... If I didn't absolutely have to go, I wouldn't." He turned and started stacking yogurts in the refrigerator. "Hopefully this is the only time I'll have to leave."

Until you have to leave for real. But not forever, I reminded myself. *I'll still see you.* "I'll be fine. It's just one night. And I have paella to look forward to when you come back."

Mark smiled at me over his shoulder. "That was the idea." He gathered up the empty grocery bags and stuffed them in our to-be-reused drawer, then peeked at his watch again. "I'm actually running late. I need to get going if I want to get there before the middle of the night. You can fend for yourself for dinner, right? I bought enough food to feed an army."

I made an offended sound. "You're not the only one who can cook in this house, you know."

He held up his hands as he backed out of the kitchen. "Sorry for doubting your culinary excellence."

If he'd still been in the room, I would've rolled my eyes

for dramatic effect. But really, I was debating whether Cocoa Puffs or Lucky Charms would make a better dinner.

Mark reappeared two minutes later carrying a small duffel bag. "For my own peace of mind, remind me of the emergency plan."

"You mean the plan we created after I thought I saw my old neighbor in Arizona but probably didn't and have never had to use once?"

He shot me a look.

"Fine. I text 911 to you, destroy the phone, take the long route through many public places to our meeting place and wait for you if you're not there already."

"And where's our meeting place here?"

I sighed. "That takeout Mexican place on the corner of our block, in the back by the Dumpsters."

Mark nodded once, satisfied I knew the plan, then handed me a slip of paper. "Since graduation is less than eight weeks away, I set up a new email account for each of us—totally untraceable. I thought we could use them to keep in touch after you graduate. Or, you know, in case we get separated during an emergency so we don't have to spend days wandering around looking for each other."

My eyes skimmed over the paper. There was an email address for Mark, one for me, and next to mine, an eight-digit code of random numbers and letters. "Wait—" I couldn't stop the grin that took over my face "—are you setting up an emergency plan for the emergency plan?"

His cheeks reddened. "No. It's mostly for after. Or if we haven't been able to get in touch for a day or two."

"Oh, now I get it. It's an *emergency* emergency plan."

Mark shook his head. "You need to use that code the first time you sign in to activate the account, then you can pick any password you want. Just memorize it and dispose of that properly, please."

I drew an X over my heart with one finger. "I promise to memorize this address and nonsensical code, burn this offensive paper and scatter the ashes across the ocean so they may travel to the four corners of the world as proof that your double emergency plan never existed."

Mark stared at me with a slightly unreadable, vaguely amused expression, then scooped me into a hug, his arms strong and safe. "If anything ever happens, I'll find you," he whispered in my ear. And then he was gone.

THIRTEEN

Nothing was right.

The house had been too quiet without Mark, so I decided to escape to the backyard, blanket in tow. But the lights from the neighbors' houses made it difficult to see the stars and it wasn't the same without the sound of the waves and Jason beside me. I could've gone down to the beach, but that didn't feel right either. And the mouth-watering smell of Mexican food hanging in the air was both making my stomach growl and annoying me. I didn't like the way it reminded me of the last time I'd been in a Mexican restaurant.

"Do you need anything else, Miss Phoebe?"

I spun around and grinned at the way Manny's frown of concentration creased his jet-black goatee. He was as worried as I was about everything being perfect. "It looks great, Manny." I gestured to the rectangular table set for two with a dozen candles glowing softly at one end. "The candles are a nice touch."

"It's not every day one of my favorite customers asks to rent my

private room to surprise one of my other favorite customers on his birthday."

"And it's not every day she's told off in Spanish about how you'd never take her money. Thanks again."

Manny stepped farther into the room, squinting at the items I'd set up along the table. When he realized what they were, he laughed so hard it made his round belly shake like Santa Claus. "Oh, Duke is going to love that."

I smiled. Duke loved Mexican food, Manny's in particular, but he always complained it wasn't hot enough. No matter how much hot sauce he used, he always wanted it hotter. So, in honor of his seventeenth birthday, I'd rounded up seventeen of the hottest hot sauces I could find on the internet.

Manny placed a gentle hand on my shoulder. "I'll let you finish setting up. He should be here soon, right? The food's prepared. Just call when you're ready, okay?"

I nodded as he walked through the bead curtain that separated the small room from the rest of the restaurant. There wasn't much else to get ready. I'd managed to save enough babysitting money for the hot sauces, the colorfully wrapped present sitting on an extra chair in the corner and a large tip for Manny. And my outfit.

I ran my hands along the pale pink sundress. It was totally inappropriate for the February weather, even in Texas, but I didn't care. It was the first time Duke would see me in a dress. And it was a miracle I'd found it and the cowboy boots I was wearing at the first thrift store I tried. I would've worn this outfit even if it snowed.

The clattering of beads made me look up. My heart sank. "Mark?"

He stood in the entrance to the room and took everything in: the candles, the present, me, in what was probably the first dress he'd seen me in too. "Shit," he mumbled. "I'm sorry, Kid. But we have to go."

I gripped the back of a chair. "Right now? But…"

He moved swiftly to my side. "There was someone at your school today asking about you," he said in a low voice.

My heart skipped a beat. "How do you know?"

"That secretary called me. You know, the one with the big hair?"

"The one you took out on that date?"

Mark waved a hand dismissively, but the hint of a blush appeared on his cheeks. "I don't know who was asking about you or why, but we can't stick around to find out."

I looked at the row of hot sauces and felt sick to my stomach. "No." *This couldn't be happening. "We've been here for fourteen months, longer than anywhere else," I said, fighting to keep my voice low. "We're safe here. That's why…"*

"I don't think the school gave out any information, but we can't be sure. I already have all of your stuff packed." He started pulling me toward the back door.

"Wait."

Mark spun on me. "I'm sorry. I'm so sorry. But we need to go before Duke gets here. It's going to be harder to leave after you see him. And you don't want to put him in any danger."

Fear shot through me. I couldn't put Duke in danger. I took one last look at the candle-filled table, then followed Mark out the back door without a sound.

"Screw it," I muttered as my stomach growled again. "It's been long enough. If you want to eat Mexican food again, do it. Stop being such a baby." I gathered up the blanket, took ten dollars out of the rainy-day money stash in the kitchen and locked up the house.

It almost felt like an adventure as I snuck through the thicket of trees that ran between the backyards of the houses on either side of my block. I popped out at one end and walked down the sidewalk to the opposite corner.

It smelled even better inside the restaurant. I stood off to the side, out of the way of the long line of customers, and pretended to study the menu while really checking for exits and scanning the crowd.

"The burritos are my favorite."

I jumped at the voice right next to me.

"Sorry." Jason failed at actually looking sorry. "I didn't mean to scare you."

"Hey," I breathed as my heart started again. I glanced behind him. "What are you doing here?"

"My mom's away this weekend visiting family so I'm cooking dinner," he said with a grin, like he'd come to the same conclusion I had about actually cooking. "I was in line when you walked in."

A mixture of relief and annoyance flowed through me. Relief because his mom wasn't in the restaurant too. Annoyance because I'd forgotten to check the people in line first.

"How about you?" He looked around. "Are you here with anyone?"

I hesitated. "Um, no. I was out for a walk and I followed the smell."

He bit his lip. "You're alone tonight too?"

"Yup."

"Do you…" Jason looked down and toed the ground with one shoe. "Do you want to come to my house?" He peeked at me through his eyelashes. "We could take the food with us and maybe watch a movie?"

There's no way this person who gets shy asking a friend to watch a movie is the player Livie described. There had to be more to the story and I wanted to know what it was. "Two burritos to go?"

"You know," Jason said as he put the food on the bar in his basement rec room, "I was kind of surprised to see you at the restaurant. I didn't know you came out in the wild on weekends."

I stopped searching his collection of action adventure and superhero movies and glared at him. "Did you forget that we're going out to dinner with Sawyer tomorrow? At a diner. *In the wild.*"

He stared at me, a foil-wrapped burrito in each hand. "We are?"

I furrowed my eyebrows. "Sawyer didn't tell you?"

"No." Jason grabbed two sodas out of the mini fridge.

I sighed and turned back to the movies. "It's supposed to be a group thing. He said he'd tell you guys about it." A movie caught my eye and I chuckled. *"The Notebook?"*

"Hey, I have a romantic, sensitive side."

"Is that what you're hiding in your bedroom? Evidence of your romantic side?"

Jason's cheeks turned pink. "Sawyer and Livie give me so much crap about that. I just want one place that doesn't belong to anyone else. Where I can be myself and not worry about what everybody else thinks. Is that so weird?"

My fingers stilled on the DVD cases. I wanted that too. One place where I could stay and just be myself. "No. I get that." Our eyes locked for a second and I looked away. "And

don't try to pretend you're all sensitive. *The Notebook* is totally your mom's, isn't it?"

He laughed. "Yeah."

Images of our moms laughing and crying at movies we
were too little to watch, while Jason and I tried to sneak into
the room and steal their popcorn, danced at the edges of my
memory. Something tugged at my chest. Being in Jason's
house, seeing a movie I know his mom probably watched
with mine, only two days before my mom's birthday made
my chest ache. I quickly pushed the feeling away and pulled
out a movie I didn't recognize. *"The Usual Suspects,"* I read
aloud. "What's that about?"

"It's this good old-school crime thriller where you don't
know who anyone really is."

That sounds familiar. "Can we watch it?"

"Sure."

I started the movie and sat on the couch as Jason carried the
food over to the coffee table. When he handed me my burrito, his fingers brushed against mine, lingering for a second
longer than they had to. A thrill shot through me.

I swallowed hard and concentrated on unwrapping all the
foil from my burrito, picking it out of the tiny tortilla crev-
ices. When I started peeling the burrito apart to peek inside,
the room went silent. I glanced up to find Jason watching me
with an amused expression.

"What's going on there?" He nodded at a sliver of tortilla
I'd pulled back.

"I like to eat the guac first because it's the best part."

He eyed the tightly wrapped, near-bursting burrito, that

half smile teasing me. "You realize it's going to fall apart if you do that, right?"

"You just worry about your own food," I said with a small smile of my own. Duke used to give me a hard time about the same thing.

I crumpled the foil into a ball. I could feel Jason's eyes on me as my gaze landed on the trash can by the bar, a good twelve feet away. *Elbow straight, exhale, shoot.* I tried not to laugh as the foil soared right into the middle of the trash can.

Jason raised an eyebrow at me.

Let that convince him I'm not the same girl who once managed to hit two students and our gym teacher with a single misthrown basketball. "So I heard you were busy last night."

Jason stopped unwrapping his burrito. "What?"

"You broke up with Livie?"

"Oh. Yeah." He was quiet for a moment. "We'd been dating for a while but it just wasn't working anymore."

"She said you'd say it was never serious."

Jason pursed his lips. "No, it was. At first." He put down his burrito and studied me. "What else did she say?"

I held his gaze for a moment, trying to decide how to phrase it. "That you were a bit of a heartbreaker."

Jason snorted. "I'm quite certain she did not use that word."

"Okay, she said you'd slept with half the girls in school."

He winced. "I didn't sleep with all of them. Or *any* of them. I've never…"

My eyebrows shot up.

"Don't look so surprised! Do you really think I'm like that?"

"No."

He made a doubtful sound.

"*No.* I didn't believe Livie, all right? But I am a little surprised. Not because I think you're the type to sleep around with lots of girls, just because—" I waved a hand at him, sitting on the floor four feet away from me "—look at you."

He peered down at himself. "What about me?"

Just kill me now. "You're *you*. It's hard to believe you're still a virgin at the end of your senior year."

He wrinkled his forehead. "I'm *me*?"

I stared at my burrito and tried to stop the images of Jason that began flashing in my head as soon as I said the word virgin. *Talking. Talking would help.* "You're ridiculously handsome and sweet and up for anything. You have this way of making the people you're with feel like they're the only people in the world that matter. You're super competitive yet still a good sport when you lose, and that's such an amazing combination. You smell like cookies and the beach and…" *And you need to stop talking now.*

Jason was silent. Dead silent.

When I couldn't take it any longer, I glanced up. He flashed a sexy grin. "Did you say *handsome*?"

"Shut up," I muttered, desperate to change the topic. "If the stories aren't true, you really should set things straight."

"What stories are those?"

I went back to studying my burrito. "There was one about homecoming and an afterparty."

"Did Livie tell you that ten minutes after we got to Josh's afterparty, I found my date making out with him in his bedroom? That's why I left."

I knew it.

"What else?" Jason prompted.

"New Year's Eve dinner?"

He picked at his burrito. "I barely knew Lauren. We didn't have any classes together but she seemed nice, so I said yes when she asked me to come to her New Year's Eve party. Except when I got there, she and her friends were already drunk. Her older brother had gotten them hard lemonade or something. It wasn't any fun being the only sober person, and she kept trying to take me to her room so we could be 'alone.' She said she wanted to ring in the new year by doing something special and she wanted me to be her first."

My eyes widened.

"I know some guys wouldn't have hesitated, but I didn't *know* her. And she was drunk. That's not cool and not what I wanted my first time to be like."

"So why would Livie lie about it?"

Jason paused, a deep line creasing his forehead, like he was weighing his words carefully. "Liv can sometimes be a little cruel when she's mad or feels like someone's been mean to her. And I'm probably not her favorite person right now."

Okay, so no getting on Livie's bad side. "If the rumors aren't true, then why didn't you correct them?"

He glanced at the TV, but he wasn't watching the movie. "I didn't want to trash those girls' reputations. Plus, I'll be the first to admit that I've gone on a lot of first dates and not very many second ones. Having a reputation as a heartbreaker, as you put it, made it easier for me to bail after the first date."

"Why don't you like second dates?"

Jason's cheeks flushed a bit as he ducked his head. "This is going to sound weird, but I have this perfect girl in my head that I measure all other girls against." The tiniest smile played at the corner of his mouth. "No one's measured up yet."

I was mesmerized by what that half smile did to his lips. "What about Livie? You two went out on more than two dates."

He turned his whole body to me. "Livie and I were friends first. I thought that's what had been missing with all the other girls. Things seemed easier with her because I already knew her." His eyes locked on mine. "But it turned out that just being friends first wasn't enough. She still wasn't the right person for me."

His gaze felt heavy, like it was pinning me in place. I chuckled nervously. "I didn't realize you had such impossible-to-meet high standards."

Jason's sly half smile reappeared. "Not impossible," he said softly. "Not for the right person."

A warm sensation filled my chest, just like that night we watched the stars. I looked away.

"What about you?" he asked. "What kind of guy is your type?"

A few boys flashed through my head, all guys I'd hung out with casually. But that was only because they were nice enough and I felt like I needed to in order to fit in, not because I'd actually liked any of them. And they had nothing in common, physically or personality-wise. Then there was Duke: average height, dirty-blond hair, light brown eyes with hints of green, built from years of helping on the ranch. He was quiet and loved the same things I did, like reading and the outdoors and trying new things. I'd been drawn to him because I'd been able to show him tiny bits of myself. But in the end I'd realized that's all it had been: tiny bits of a real relationship. Because he never knew the real me. He only knew Phoebe.

I faced Jason, who was somehow both smirking and shaking his head. "That many boyfriends to remember, huh?"

"No. I've never had a boyfriend, not really."

His eyebrows shot up.

"Don't look so surprised! I've gone out on dates and stuff. But I want someone who likes me for who I am, who knows the real me. And I haven't found that yet."

"I thought maybe Oliver was your type."

"A girl can only be serenaded so many times before it gets old," I joked.

A hint of a smile brushed Jason's lips. "What about Sawyer?"

"Sawyer?"

"Yeah. You laugh at his pickup lines."

"Because they're hilariously awful."

He took a bite of his burrito and chewed for a moment. "You're going out to dinner with him tomorrow."

"It was supposed to be a group thing! You didn't show up at lunch today so I couldn't tell you about it." Jason looked at me and this time I held his gaze. "Will you come tomorrow? Please?"

He nodded.

"Sawyer likes me, doesn't he?"

"Yeah. He wanted me to find out if you like him," Jason said. "I think he wants to ask you to prom."

I fiddled with my food. "He's not really..."

"He doesn't know you?" Jason offered.

"He doesn't know me."

"Don't worry—I'll talk to him. Hey, I can be *your* wingman. Maybe I can mummify him in rolls of duct tape so he stops touching you."

I laughed, remembering our conversation about Livie at the Kissing Tree. "You'd do that for me?"

Jason grinned. "Of course. What are friends for?"

Friends. Just like at the Kissing Tree, hearing that word in connection with Jason made my pulse race. But this time, it was for a completely different reason.

FOURTEEN

When I walked into the diner the next evening, the first thing I noticed were the locations of possible exits: the kitchen to the left and the unmarked door by the bathrooms in the back. The second thing I noticed was the diner itself.

It looked like something straight out of the past. Waitresses in 1950s-style uniforms were scurrying around the black-and-white-checkered floor with steaming hot plates of food. Booths lined the perimeter of the restaurant, each with its own tabletop jukebox. And for the tables in the middle without jukeboxes, oldies were playing softly from overhead speakers. I grinned. I recognized Bobby Darin's "Dream Lover." Jason's mom had always played oldies when we were younger and I was surprised to still remember the words.

I bobbed my head to the beat and searched the crowd. I spotted Jason and Sawyer in one of the front booths by the windows, but no one else. At lunch yesterday, besides saying he'd tell Jason, Sawyer promised to tell Oliver and Livie about our dinner plans because we didn't want either of them to feel left out. But Sawyer hadn't told Jason. And that was before I found out Livie had been so angry at Jason she'd lied about him. Now I wasn't sure whether she'd even want to come. Or whether Jason would want her to.

"I see my friends," I told the hostess, who looked like she'd stepped right out of an *I Love Lucy* episode. She grabbed a ringing telephone and waved me past.

Jason and Sawyer were sitting on opposite sides of the booth, leaning over the table examining something. When I got closer I saw they were crowded around Sawyer's phone, studying a picture of a girl about our age. She had long blond hair, blue eyes and a smile that lit up her whole face. She was wearing a pretty blue-and-white-striped shirt and holding a red plastic cup out to the camera with her right hand. A wide silver ring glinted on her ring finger. It was an intricate fili-gree pattern that looked like a piece of silver lace. "Who's that?" I asked.

Jason and Sawyer both looked up, startled. Jason scooted over and I slid into the booth next to him. To my surprise, Sawyer didn't frown or protest or grab me and pull me into his lap. *Maybe Jason talked to him already.*

"Her name's Miranda Mills," Sawyer said. "She's a friend of my cousin's and she's missing."

I gasped. "What happened?"

"She was at this big party last night a few towns over where my cousin lives. She went outside to get some air and just disappeared."

"That's horrible." I glanced at the girl's picture again. "No one saw anything?"

Sawyer shook his head. "Her best friend took this picture

around two this morning, right before Miranda went outside. My cousin sent it to me. They're trying to get it to as many people as possible. They're hoping someone's seen her."

A petite girl in a pale-blue-and-black poodle skirt stopped at the edge of our table. Her light brown hair was pulled up in a perky ponytail and her brown eyes were surrounded by tortoiseshell cat-eye glasses. "Is that Miranda Mills?" she asked. "My cousin was at that party."

"Mine too," Sawyer said. "Who's your cousin?"

"Bryce Anderson."

"No way!" Sawyer grinned at her. "I've hung out with Bryce before. My cousin's Dylan James. They're good friends."

Her mouth dropped open. "I know Dylan. He's sweet."

"It runs in the family," Sawyer assured her.

The waitress smiled. "It's weird we've never met before. I'm Kylie." She held out her hand.

For a second, I worried Sawyer was going to do something goofy like kiss the back of her hand, but he just shook it. "I'm Sawyer."

Kylie's eyes lit up. "Like from the TV show *Lost*? My brother and I binge watched the whole thing last year. Sawyer was my favorite character."

I widened my eyes at Jason.

Sawyer's face practically glowed. "Yeah. Exactly like *Lost*." He held Kylie's gaze for a moment, then glanced at his phone. "It's really bad about Miranda, huh? Have you heard anything new?"

Kylie shook her head. "It's all rumors at this point. Some people are saying she had this huge fight with her boyfriend yesterday afternoon and maybe she bailed on him. Others are saying she's been hooking up with his best friend and they're holed up in a motel room somewhere. Who knows what's true?" She shrugged. "I hope they find her soon though. I heard her parents are freaked."

"Yeah," Sawyer agreed.

"So." Kylie tapped a pen on the pad in her hand. "What can I get you guys to drink?"

"Is anyone else coming?" I bit my lip, not sure who to look at. "Oliver? Or maybe Livie?"

Jason held up his phone without a word. On the screen was a picture Livie had texted him ten minutes earlier of her and Oliver smiling and eating ice cream. *Yikes.*

I turned to Kylie. "I think we need some milkshakes."

After she took our drink orders and left, I wiggled my eyebrows at Sawyer. "She's cute."

His cheeks turned bright red. "I'm going to the bathroom," he muttered. He watched Kylie out of the corner of his eye as he crossed the diner.

I turned to Jason with a huge smile. "Was he flirting with her?"

Jason laughed. "I don't know. I talked to him this afternoon about how you weren't interested and how he needed to stop touching you all the time, but I didn't think it was sinking in. Maybe I was wrong." He shifted and his leg brushed against mine under the table. He didn't move it away.

My heart tripped. "Um, thanks for being such a good wingman."

"You should see how much duct tape I have in my car right now. I figured I'd need a lot to mummify him because he's *so damn tall.*"

I laughed and a tingling sensation flowed from my heart to the spot where Jason's leg rested against mine.

Jason watched as Kylie walked by with a large tray balanced on one hand. "We should tell Sawyer to—"

Ding!

My leg reflexively jerked away from Jason's.

He glanced at me, eyes curious. "What was that?"

I shrugged. "I don't know." But I did know. I knew the sound of an incoming text on my phone. In fact, I'd been expecting one from Mark.

I'd taken my phone off vibrate when I returned from Jason's house late the night before to make sure I wouldn't miss a call or text from Mark while I slept in. And he had woken me up when he called after his meeting was over to tell me he'd be home around dinnertime. I'd left a note on the island telling him the name of the diner and asking him to text when he got back so I knew he was okay. And then I forgot to set my phone back to vibrate.

Jason checked his phone. "It wasn't me."

Of course he knows it was a text. I tried to think of a way to silence my phone, but all I could come up with was escaping to the bathroom to do it there, which seemed too obvious.

I turned to the booth next to ours, hoping to blame the texting on someone there. Except the only people in the next booth were an elderly couple sharing a piece of pie and reading a newspaper. *Yeah. No texting there.*

Ding! Ding!

I had to stop myself from flinching. *Jesus, Mark! Stop texting!* I wanted to slide my hand into my pocket and turn the phone off, but I was afraid Jason would notice.

Jason's eyes narrowed. "Is that—"

"Here you go!" Kylie announced as she placed a chocolate milkshake in front of me.

Ding! Ding!

Luckily, the sound of Mark's latest texts were drowned out by Sawyer's return to the booth. "Hi, Kylie," he said without any trace of the embarrassment he'd had when he left the table.

Kylie set a strawberry shake on his side of the table. "What's your shirt mean?"

Sawyer peeked at his gray T-shirt, which had the words *I'm the Real Dread Pirate Roberts* in plain black letters, then back at her. "You've never seen *The Princess Bride?*"

She shook her head.

"You're missing out on a classic. I make everyone I know watch it."

"It must be good if they make shirts about it."

Sawyer fingered the hem of his shirt. "Do you know what this shirt's made of?"

A cute bewildered expression crossed her face. "No."

Sawyer grinned. "Boyfriend material."

A slow smile spread across Kylie's face.

Jason bumped his leg into mine in a way that said, *She actually liked that.*

It took Kylie a minute to tear her eyes away from Sawyer and remember to pull out her order pad. She cleared her throat and turned to Jason and me. "Do you know what you want?"

Sawyer ignored her prompt for orders. "Do you go to school with Bryce and Dylan?"

Her eyes locked on Sawyer again. "Yeah."

"What grade are you in?"

"I'm a junior. How about you?"

"We're all seniors," Sawyer responded. "You should come along the next time I hang out with Dylan."

Kylie glanced over her shoulder at the front door, where the hostess was studying her through narrow eyes. She fidgeted with her order pad. "Um, I have a boyfriend."

"And I have a math test on Monday," Sawyer said without missing a beat.

The confused expression returned to Kylie's face.

Sawyer winked at her. "I thought we were talking about things we could cheat on."

Classy, I thought. But Kylie giggled. Actually *giggled*. And she continued to giggle the whole time she took our orders.

After she disappeared into the kitchen, I pounced on Sawyer, all worries about Mark and his texts completely forgotten in my excitement that Sawyer might be interested in someone who wasn't me. "You have to get her number."

Sawyer ducked his head. "Nah."

Jason stared at Sawyer. "Why not?"

"She said she had a boyfriend."

I made a skeptical sound. "That was a lie and you know it. You saw the way she peeked at the hostess. She's probably not supposed to flirt with customers or something."

Sawyer rubbed at an invisible spot on the back of his hand. "She's not really my type."

"What?" I shook my head. "She's *exactly* your type. She was interested in your shirt, she liked all of your pickup lines, your cousins are friends, she was giggling nonstop and Sawyer is her favorite character from *Lost*. She couldn't be any *more* your type."

Sawyer took a long sip of his shake, not looking at me.

He just needs a little push. I leaned back against the booth and crossed my arms over my chest. "Huh."

Sawyer's brown eyes met mine. "What?"

"Nothing." I waved a hand in his direction. "I just didn't realize."

He frowned. "Realize what?"

I leaned over the table. "That you're all talk and no action," I said slowly, the challenge clear in my voice.

Jason gave a low whistle.

Sawyer's mouth dropped open. "I am not."

I planted my hands on the table and leaned even closer to Sawyer. "Bet you can't get Kylie's number."

He inched toward me. "I could totally get Kylie's number if I wanted to."

I half stood. "Then prove it. Show me some action."

Sawyer mirrored my position. Our noses were only inches away. "You want action?"

"Yeah."

Faster than I could blink, Sawyer kissed me.

I jerked back in surprise, hand covering my mouth.

"What the hell, man?" Jason exclaimed.

I stopped my free hand from forming into a fist. Because hitting Sawyer right after Jason yelled definitely would've qualified as making a scene. And I couldn't make a scene.

I turned to tell Jason to calm down and saw Mark through the large window next to our booth. He was standing across the street, jaw clenched tight. *Crap.* I had more damage control to do than I thought.

Without saying anything, I jumped out of the booth and walked to the back of the diner, where I knew Mark would go. I didn't even stop to wonder whether an alarm would sound when I shoved open the unmarked door by the bathrooms.

As soon as I stepped out into the quiet, cool evening, a hand wrapped around my arm. Mark led me a few feet away to a hidden spot between two Dumpsters. "What was that?" he hissed.

"I don't know," I shot back. It's not like I had a lot of kissing experience to draw from, but that felt more like creepy Ben from the waterfall, more like a kiss to prove something than like Duke's kisses. "I was teasing him to get our waitress's phone number. I didn't think—"

"Did you want him to kiss you? Because it didn't look like you wanted him to kiss you." Mark looked like he wanted to strangle someone. "Who was that?"

"Sawyer," I mumbled.

"I thought you said there were no stalkers here."

"He's not a stalker." I sighed. "He's just annoyingly persistent."

Mark raised his eyebrows, clearly about to point out how stalkerish my explanation made Sawyer sound, when the back door I'd escaped through banged open. Mark pulled me farther into the Dumpster shadows.

"Sloane!" Jason called. It was quiet for a moment, then Jason muttered, "Damn it, Sawyer." The door slammed shut and based on the silence, I knew he'd gone back into the diner.

"Who was that?" Mark asked.

"Jason. He's just a friend—he's fine."

Mark peeked his head out between the Dumpsters. When he was satisfied the coast was clear, he nodded toward the sidewalk just beyond the edge of the diner's lot. "Come on."

I followed him as we walked the few blocks home, daylight quickly fading around us. About halfway there, Mark whirled on me. "Do you want me to call in reinforcements on this Sawyer kid?"

I snorted at the image of Sawyer being surrounded by a team of Marshals in the middle of the cafeteria and hauled away. "That's one way to blend in."

Mark frowned.

"Look, it's no big deal. I thought it would be enough to have Jason tell him I wasn't interested, but maybe he needs to hear it from me. I have an idea. Let me handle it, okay?"

He shifted, his expression unreadable. "You're not interested in him?"

My mouth twitched at the memory of my conversation with Jason the night before. "He's not my type."

"Hmph." Mark started walking again.

As I hurried to catch up, I pulled my phone out of my pocket and read Mark's texts for the first time. The first one was basic:

I'm home.

Followed two minutes later by two more in rapid succession:

That diner is close.

Are you up for some company?

His last two texts came less than a minute later.

Screw it. I'm coming.

Last chance to stop me.

"Hey." I wrapped my hand around Mark's wrist to stop him. "You wanted to have dinner together?" I held up my phone as evidence.

He closed his eyes and when he opened them, I was surprised to see hazel instead of his natural brown. I'd forgotten for a moment. "I didn't remember you were going out with your friends tonight. I thought maybe you'd gotten tired of feeding yourself." He looked down the block. "I'm sorry. I didn't mean to interrupt. I was about to turn around when…"

"Hey," I repeated. "You don't have to apologize for wanting to eat out with me. We should try that place sometime. It's neat inside and the food…" I paused. "I can't say what the food's like because I left before it arrived. Crap!" I searched his face in alarm. "I think I just walked out on my check."

"Don't worry," Mark growled. "Lover boy can pick up the tab. They won't let all of you leave without someone paying."

I remembered the observant hostess and figured he was probably right. I released Mark's wrist and we walked side by side in silence, Sawyer's kiss replaying in my head. "I wanted to stab him with my fork. Or maybe punch him in the throat," I admitted as we turned onto our block.

"Maybe it's good you didn't." There was a smile in Mark's voice. "We know how well that worked out for you last time."

I bit my lip to keep from snorting.

I let the water run into the sink, pretending to wash my hands to waste a few more minutes. What was Mark thinking? *I knew there were times we needed to play along, to say yes to invitations in order to fit in and not raise suspicions, but this? This was cruel and unusual punishment.*

A shrill shriek followed by a chorus of giggles made me jump. I ran a hand down my black hair, watching my reflection in the mirror. Autumn was turning thirteen—too old to need a babysitter, too young to be someone an almost sixteen-year-old would actually hang out with. The only reason I was even at her party was because her dad was Mark's boss and an invitation from the boss couldn't be ignored. The fact she'd only invited me in some misguided attempt to look cooler to her friends—apparently claiming that the sophomore you think of as a "big sister" can't wait to come to your party gives you some middle school cred—didn't matter.

I turned the water off, slid my phone out of my pocket, and texted Mark: You owe me. Big time. Like fettuccine alfredo and chocolate mousse from scratch big.

Making sure the phone was set on silent, I hid it away and mentally prepared myself for more gossip about middle school boys and questions about popular clothes in high school and how far I'd gone with a guy. I shook my head. If that was what Autumn wanted to know, she'd definitely picked the wrong fake "big sister." I didn't know how to do the friend gossip thing. If they'd been paying even the slightest bit of attention, they would've known from my nondescript wardrobe that I wasn't exactly following fashion trends. And my only experience with a guy had ended with me kneeing him in the balls.

A small smile tugged at the corners of my mouth at the image of telling them that story. I bet Mark's boss would love that. *Instead, I opened the bathroom door, plastered on my this-is-so-much-fun grin, and stepped into the hall.*

It was darker than it had been a few minutes before. And quieter too. Other than the one burst of laughter I'd heard in the bathroom, the ten girls at the party had suddenly become oddly silent.

I eased down the basement hall into the playroom. Bowls of chips were still overflowing on the pool table, balloons were still dancing along the ceiling, a super sappy romantic comedy was still playing on mute on the TV, but no girls. The fact they'd all disappeared together wasn't too unusual; they seemed to travel in packs. But the lights were out. The life-size cutout of that teen heartthrob Autumn wouldn't let go of was missing. And it was quiet.

The hairs on the back of my neck stood up.

I edged around the pool table to get a better look out the sliding glass door. Maybe they went outside. *But the light was fading too fast for me to see very far into the yard. Squinting, I took a step closer.*

A shadow in the yard moved.

I scrambled backward and bumped into a large body right behind me.

Without thinking, I crouched down and swung my leg around in an arc just like Mark taught, sweeping a man's legs out from under him. He crashed onto his back with a loud oof and before he could blink, my hand was hovering over his throat, ready to crush his windpipe.

There was a collective gasp.

I looked up to find ten girls huddled in the entrance to the playroom, all staring at me with varying degrees of shock. They must've come from somewhere down the hall, beyond the bathroom I'd just left. I glanced at the man on the ground beneath me and saw Au-

tumn's dad—Mark's boss—*sprawled on the ground surrounded by a very large pile of scattered birthday presents. There was no way he would've been able to see me over all of those presents, let alone avoid coming too close to me in the dark.*

The sliding glass door slid open and the lights flicked on. "What are y'all doing in the dark?" Autumn's mom asked. Her eyes widened as she took in the scene in front of her. Her grip on the sprigs of holly—the ones she must've just cut from the backyard bushes—slackened.

"What was that, Olivia?" Autumn exclaimed.

"Um." I stood and smoothed my shirt. Think, think, think. *"Well, you were asking me about guys earlier, and that—" I stared down at her dad, who was staring back at me with the reddest face I'd ever seen "—is what you do when a guy won't leave you alone. I thought it'd be easier to understand with a real-life example."*

A tiny "oh" escaped Autumn's mom.

I held out a hand to her dad. "Sorry about not warning you, but that move really only works when the person isn't expecting it." I put on my best fake smile.

He sat up, his eyes narrowing before he took my hand. How is it possible for his face to be getting even redder? *"Gotta teach these girls how to protect themselves, am I right?" I said as I helped him stand.*

"That was awesome," Autumn muttered.

Another girl pulled out her phone. I angled myself behind Autumn's dad right before she snapped the picture. "I'm posting this right now. Wait until we tell everyone at school what she can do."

"Ooh," the girl next to her said as she tapped on her phone. "I'm calling my sister. She's a senior and said some guy keeps bugging her. If she can come over, can you teach that to her?" She looked at Au-

tumn. "Maybe my sister could invite some of her friends too. Everyone should know this."

Several of the girls nodded their agreement.

Crap.

"Is it presents time?" I asked, picking up two packages from the floor and placing them on the pool table next to the chips. "I left mine in my jacket pocket, but I'll go get it right now."

I brushed past Autumn's dad as I headed for the stairs and took one quick glance back at the room. Autumn's mom and the girls were talking excitedly, words like spy and ninja jumping out of their conversation, but he was watching me with hard eyes.

Crap, crap, crap.

I took the steps two at a time, snatched my jacket off the chair by the Christmas tree, and slipped out the front door.

Running as fast as I could, I covered five blocks before I even broke a sweat. I kept the same pace, my breath making puffy clouds in front of me, until I'd made enough twists and turns that no one from Autumn's house could've kept up. I slowed down and called Mark.

"I'm already making the pasta," he said as a greeting.

I didn't bother with a greeting either. "Start packing."

Something clattered in the background. "What happened? Are you okay?"

"I'm fine. No one's here. I just…"

"If you don't start explaining, I'm coming to their house in full Hulk mode."

"No!" I peeked over my shoulder at a car driving by. "You'll only make it worse."

"What happened? I wasn't supposed to pick you up for another hour."

"Okay. Um, I may or may not have gotten a little spooked and thought something was off and…knocked your boss flat on his back and been about to punch him in the throat right in front of everyone." That last part came out all in a rush.

I winced, waiting for Mark to start yelling.

Instead, he laughed. "Oh my God, you knocked Doug down? He's almost a foot taller than you and has gotta weigh at least two hundred pounds."

"Sorry."

"No. Never be sorry for trying to protect yourself, okay?"

"But we're going to have to move now! The girls wanted to post stuff about it online and get me to teach everyone at school and Doug definitely thought something was up. I tried to spin it but I don't think it worked. I just screwed everything up."

Mark's voice was calm. "Are you close?"

"Three more blocks."

"Good. When you get here I want you to tell me the exact look on his face when he realized he was on the floor."

I cracked a smile. "You're not mad?"

"He's an ass. Worst boss I've had so far. And I hated sending you to that stupid party. It's fine, Kid."

The tightness in my chest loosened a bit. "What's the reddest you've ever seen a person's face?"

"Oh, now you're just teasing me."

I bumped Mark's shoulder with mine. "What about you? Your reaction back there definitely wasn't dramatic enough. There was this giant window just ripe for destruction. You could've stormed inside and thrown Sawyer through it. Gone into Marshal-turned-overly-protective-fake-dad mode. That's a thing, right?"

Mark didn't respond, but I could see his grin in the dim

light. He pulled out his phone and the glow from the screen lit up his face. A second later, my phone chimed.

I snorted. The only person who had my number was walking right next to me. But I still read the three words Mark sent:

I missed you.

FIFTEEN

My fingers drummed against the steering wheel in Mark's car the next morning. I patted my pocket to make sure the paper was still there, the buzz from just successfully completing phase one of my repel-Sawyer plan making me feel like not going home yet. Without consciously deciding to, I turned out of the diner's parking lot packed with Sunday brunch-goers and headed for the ocean.

It wasn't hard to find a parking space by the nearest beach access, a wide swath of sand surrounded by grassy dunes on either side. I turned off the engine and listened to the waves through the open windows. *Shh, shh, shh*, they said, whispering their secrets. Suddenly, I couldn't get to the water fast enough.

I kicked off my flip-flops and crossed to the beach, smiling at the way the cool sand squished between my toes. I climbed the slight incline of the beach access until I passed the dunes and saw the ocean spread out before me. I gasped.

It was massive and blue and peaceful and endless, gentle

waves crashing while wispy clouds watched overhead. The beach was deserted, which wasn't surprising given it was mid-morning on a Sunday in early April. April 10, to be exact. My mother's birthday.

I grinned and ran toward the ocean, sucking in a shocked breath when my feet finally reached the cold water. I closed my eyes and let the spray of salt water cover my skin and the briny breeze ruffle my hair. When my feet turned numb, I backed up and sat on the sand. I picked up a handful and let it sift between my fingers. It had been almost six years since I'd been at a beach, *any* beach, but it felt exactly like I remembered. It felt like home.

Because my mom's birthday was only six days after mine, we always celebrated together at the beach. We would set up camp on the deserted sand—early April was too cold in New Jersey for anyone except the most diehard beach-goers like us—and spend the day playing in the waves and building sandcastles and reading curled up on fuzzy beach towels, just the two of us. It was right to come to the beach today, to come home, on my mom's birthday.

I leaned back on my hands and stretched out my jean-covered legs. I was contemplating the possibility that some of the water in front of me could've been the same water I once played in with my mom hundreds of miles up the coast when a hesitant voice interrupted my thoughts.

"Hey."

I turned and saw Sawyer standing a few feet behind me. Warning bells went off in my head. *This Repel Sawyer plan better work.* "What are you doing here?"

"I followed you." My alarm must've been written on my

face because he quickly added, "Not like that. I was driving by when I saw you get out of your car. I parked but it took me a few minutes to work up the courage to come over." He pointed to the sand. "Can I sit?"

I glanced at the empty stretch of beach behind him, then nodded.

He sat a safe distance away and watched the ocean for a minute. "I want to apologize about last night." He faced me. "I'm sorry about the kiss."

Just hearing him mention the kiss made me want to smack him all over again. But that's why I had a plan. Because I wasn't running away this time. I had to learn how to deal with the stupid things people did instead of leaving. But I wasn't letting him off that easy.

"That was seriously *not cool*, Sawyer."

"I know. You weren't giving off kiss-me vibes so I should've stopped. And J told me you weren't interested but I… I don't know, I thought maybe you were playing hard to get. And then Kylie was there and I wanted to make you jealous by flirting with her. I thought you'd change your mind if there was someone else into me." He hung his head. "I swear this all sounded better in my head yesterday."

"I wasn't playing hard to get. And you really need to make sure someone wants you to kiss them before you do, okay?"

"Yeah, definitely. No yes, no kiss. Got it." He buried one hand in the sand. "J threatened to duct tape my mouth shut after you left. Any idea why he actually had a roll of duct tape in his car?"

I remembered Jason's promise to be my wingman and bit back a smile. "Nope."

We were both silent, listening to the waves, but I felt Sawyer's eyes on me.

"Can I ask you something?" he said.

I smiled at him. I didn't need things to be any more awkward between us. "Sure."

"Are you not interested in me because you're holding out for someone better?"

I picked up a handful of sand and threw it at him.

He ducked, but his shoulders shook with laughter.

"What is it with you people and *better*? No, Sawyer, I don't think someone's better than you. You're cute and goofy and happy. I mean, I've never seen anyone grin as much as you do. And, okay, maybe you're a little too touchy-feely for my taste..."

His gave me a sheepish grin.

"But that's just who you are," I continued. "You're exuberant. It's like you can't keep it all inside yourself. You're a great guy, Sawyer. I just don't want to date anyone right now."

After another few moments of silence, he said, "What about prom? That's just one dance. We don't even have to call it a date."

I threatened him with two fistfuls of sand.

Sawyer held up his hands and grinned. "I'm kidding."

I reached into my pocket and pulled out the slip of paper. "Here." I handed it to Sawyer.

"What's this?"

"This is me showing you that I think you're a good guy." I waited for him to unfold the paper. "That's Kylie's phone number. I stopped by the diner before I came here."

He raised his eyebrows at me.

"I apologized to her for leaving so suddenly last night and told her how much you've been talking about her ever since. She said she was bummed you didn't ask for her number yesterday. And her next door neighbor owns the diner and tells her overprotective parents everything she does there. That's why she was acting all nervous and making up boyfriends. I wouldn't be trying to set you up with someone if I thought you weren't worth getting to know."

Sawyer stared at the paper, a slight blush on his cheeks. "Thanks, Sloane." He pulled out his phone and programmed Kylie's number in. Before he could put it back in his pocket, his text notification, which sounded like a train whistle, went off. "Good news!" he exclaimed after reading for a second. "My cousin said they found Miranda yesterday."

"The missing girl? That's great. Where was she?"

"She woke up in some woods about a mile from the house where the party was."

I frowned. "Was she okay?"

Sawyer scrolled down and read for what seemed like forever. "Yeah, sort of. Her parents took her to the hospital because she couldn't remember anything, not even leaving the party. She had some drugs in her system. They think someone must've slipped something into her drink."

I remembered the red cup she was holding in the picture.

"Whatever it was seriously knocked her out. Other than that, she was fine. No injuries or evidence of sexual assault or anything, thank God." Sawyer shook his head. "It's weird. She woke up by some berry bush and had red juice dried in her hair and on her clothes. She was pretty freaked out it was blood at first."

I shuddered. "I'm never going to drink anything at a party again."

"Yeah."

"You know who you should tell the good news to?" I nodded at the piece of paper still crumpled in Sawyer's hand.

"Kylie was pretty cute, wasn't she?"

"She's totally cute. And totally into you. You should call her."

He studied his phone for a moment, then nodded. "She's at the diner now? I was on my way to help look for Miranda but since that's no longer necessary, maybe I'll go talk to Kylie in person." He stood.

"Sawyer?"

"Yeah?"

"Maybe take her out a few times before you ask her to prom or try to kiss her. You know, build up to the touchy-feeliness."

Sawyer chuckled. "Got it. Thanks, Sloane. You're really great, you know that?"

"Save the sweet talk for Kylie."

He saluted and walked back toward his car.

I turned back to the ocean. I hadn't expected to see Sawyer until school on Monday, but it felt good to have this over with. "Phase two accomplished," I told the waves. "Nothing like a little ego boost. Should be smooth sailing from here on out."

SIXTEEN

I was officially exhausted. I'd gotten up early for the senior trip bus ride to Charleston, toured a bunch of historic homes, visited Fort Sumter, shopped the stalls in City Market and had dinner in an awesome restaurant. My legs ached, my eyes were itchy and I really wished I could take out my contacts. "I don't want to do anything except watch some mindless movie, eat this chocolate we bought today and pray my legs hold up for the city walking tour tomorrow," I said.

Livie appeared around the corner of the small hallway that led to both the bathroom and the door of our hotel room. Her brown hair had more waves than usual and her brown eyes looked striking surrounded by glittery gold eyeshadow. She was wearing the deep red lace tank top she'd bought earlier that day and jeans so tight I wasn't sure she'd be able to sit down.

I examined my own outfit: blue plaid flannel pants and a navy camisole. "Wow, Liv. Your pj's are fancy."

Livie rolled her eyes. "I'm going to Oliver's room. He's kicking his roommate out."

That explains the tight pants. I knew Livie and Oliver had gone out once or twice the past few weeks, but I hadn't realized things had moved so quickly. He'd been pretty quiet whenever I brought Livie up.

"How do I look?" she asked.

"Great," I said. "I like your new shirt."

Livie smiled. "Thanks. I like the one you got too. It's about time you owned something other than cotton and denim."

I glanced at the top by my duffel bag. It was pale lavender satin with sequins and spaghetti straps. It was the only fancy thing I'd owned since the sundress I'd worn for Duke. The sundress I'd burned the day after I left him. "Yeah, all I need is someplace to wear it."

"I can ask Oliver if he has any lonely friends…"

"I don't want some random trip hookup, Livie." I quickly changed the subject. "How are you going to get around the bed check?"

Livie batted her eyelashes at me. "That's where you come in."

I didn't think that suggestion to visit Oliver's friends was real.

"Mr. Pruitt should be coming soon. I was hoping you could turn on the shower and tell him I'm in there? I'll owe you one."

I sighed. Everything had been going well the last three weeks since Sawyer apologized at the beach: he genuinely seemed to be into Kylie; I'd hung out with Jason and Oliver a few times, although I'd also said no to a couple of invitations so I could have some extra Mark time; and I was *so* close to making my final college choice, which was good since the deposits were due in a few days. I didn't want to do anything to jinx it, lying to a teacher included. But I found myself saying, "Yeah, sure. Just don't forget your key. I really don't want to have to get off this bed to let you back in."

Livie clapped. "Thanks!" She turned to go.

"Hey," I said, stopping her. "Are you sure about this? Going to Oliver's room, I mean?"

"It's *Oliver.* Of course I'm sure." And with that, she was gone.

I'm so glad she's not with Jason anymore. And if things don't work out between her and Oliver, I'm slightly worried for Oliver, I thought as I forced myself to get off the bed and turn on the shower.

When Mr. Pruitt knocked on the door five minutes later, wisps of steam were curling out from under the bathroom door. "Hello, Sloane." He gazed at the clipboard in his hands. "You're rooming with Liv Dawson, correct?"

"Yes, sir."

"Where is she?"

I pointed to the closed bathroom door. "Shower." *The fewer untruthful words, the better.*

Mr. Pruitt eyed the steam and light leaking out from under the bathroom door. "Okay. You girls have a nice night. And don't forget—we're meeting in the lobby at eight for breakfast."

"We'll be there!" I called as I shut the door. I waited until Mr. Pruitt knocked on the door to the next room, then shut off the shower. After turning off all the lights except the tiny lamp on my bedside table—I figured Livie would need something to see by when she came back—I climbed into bed. But the more I flipped through the TV channels in search of a movie to watch, the more my eyes bothered me.

I examined the dimly lit room. Livie was gone and would probably be so tired whenever she came back that I would have to drag her out of bed to make it to breakfast on time.

All I had to do was get up early and put my contacts back in before Livie woke up. I decided a decent night's sleep was worth the risk and dug my contact lens case out of its hiding place in my bag. When I returned to bed contact-free, I felt so much better. I popped a piece of chocolate into my mouth and settled on an action movie with lots of gun fights. A few minutes later, I was fast asleep.

Dad ruffled my hair as he crossed to the front of the car. "I'm glad we get to spend the day together, kiddo."

I hurried to catch up to him on the sidewalk, sucking in a ragged breath. It had rained earlier, but the air was still muggy and stale. "Yeah, but when does the fun stuff start?"

"What? Watching me get my hair cut wasn't fun?"

"Um, no. Fun is the burgers and shakes and mini golf you promised me. I bet Jase I could get a hole in one!"

Dad chuckled. "I hope he didn't take that bet. You're the hole-in-one queen."

I grinned up at him.

"You can cream me in mini golf after we drop this off." He shook the padded envelope in his hand.

I rolled my eyes. When he came into my room that morning and said, "Mom's working. Want to have a fun day with me?" I hadn't expected it to start with so many errands.

As we rounded the corner of the warehouse, I trailed my fingers along the rough brick wall, darker in spots from the rain. Then Dad's arm flew out to the side, stopping me in my tracks. He silently shifted in front of me and I peered around him to see what was going on.

Two men stood with their backs to us. The taller of the two, whose short brown hair was peeking out of a blue baseball cap, stared down at the ground and said something I couldn't hear. That's when I no-

ticed the older man slumped against the warehouse at their feet. His blond curly hair was matted with blood and his face was swollen and bruised. I'd never seen anyone so beat up before.

The older man's mouth moved with difficulty as he said something.

"Shut up!" the shorter standing man yelled. He tugged up his bright orange polo shirt, pulled a gun from the waistband of his shorts, and pointed it at the man on the ground.

I gasped, my heart pounding so hard in my chest I thought it would explode. Dad shoved me behind a tall stack of wooden crates leaning against the edge of the warehouse, and we both crouched low to the ground.

"Shh."

The whispered hush sounded loud in the cramped space. My knees scraped against rough broken pieces of crating as I covered my nose and mouth with my hands. I was breathing too loud and too fast. I had to be quiet.

Dad's wide back, covered in his favorite black Bruce Springsteen concert shirt, blocked my front and something sharp and jagged from one of the crates was poking my back. I knew Dad was trying to protect me, to hide me from whatever was happening with those men, but I couldn't stop myself. I needed to see what was going on. Even though it was nearly impossible, I tried to move. Dad reached back. His hand clamped down on my arm and it hurt. There was no way I was going to be able to move now. So I turned my head and peered through the slats in a crate.

Polo Shirt, the shorter of the two guys, still had his gun pointed at the man on the ground, but now his hand was shaking.

"Please!" the man on the ground cried in a surprisingly high-pitched voice. He tried to sit up a little and winced, a crazed almost smile-like expression crossing his face. "Please don't do this!"

Polo Shirt dropped his gun to his side and his shoulders slumped forward. There was a sudden blur of movement.

Pop! Pop, pop!

The explosions were so loud, so close, that my hands flew to my ears. Dad spun around in the tiny space. His nose was practically touching mine and his eyes were wild with fear. He whispered a single word: "Run."

I took off after him, one foot slipping on a broken piece of wood on the ground. It skittered into the stack of crates with a thunk.

A prickly sensation crept up my neck at the feeling of eyes on my back as I ran.

"Hey!"

Dad's grip on my arm tightened as he pulled me forward, but I instinctively peeked over my shoulder at the surprised shout. The taller guy with the baseball cap was pointing a gun at the head of the now unmoving man on the ground. But Polo Shirt, whose gun still hung limply at his side, was looking straight at me. Our eyes locked and several emotions flickered in quick succession over his face: fear, then anger, then recognition.

I bolted upright in bed with a gasp. A trickle of sweat ran down my back.

Boom, boom, boom.

My gaze fell on a TV I didn't recognize. I switched it off with the remote by my hand, eager to stop the booming sound so I could think for a minute.

Boom, boom. "Sloane! Livie!"

I glanced around, trying to figure out where I was and why I could hear Jason's voice, and spotted my duffel bag. It clicked into place: the senior trip, my hotel room and the interior door that connected my room to Jason and Sawyer's room.

"Are you guys okay?" Jason yelled. A second later, still too loudly, he said, "It's fine, Sawyer. I've got it."

The illuminated clock on the bedside table read 1:02 a.m. I groaned. If Jason didn't stop yelling he'd wake up the whole hotel. I forced myself out of bed, fumbled with the lock, and finally managed to get the door open. As soon as I turned the knob, Jason pushed his way in.

He grabbed my shoulders with both hands. "Are you okay?" The interior door clicked closed behind him.

"Yeah," I croaked. "Why?"

He saw Livie's empty bed and flew around the corner to the bathroom, flicking the light on even though obviously no one was in there, then off again. "Where's Liv?"

I pushed the heels of my hands into my eyes. Things had been tense between Jason and Livie lately and I couldn't deal with their crap right now. "She went to hang out in…another room."

Jason made a disgusted face that said, *That didn't take long*, then the concern returned. He ran a hand through his black hair, making it stick up even more than it already was. "So it was you screaming?"

"Screaming?"

"Someone was in here yelling, 'Run!' or 'Gun!' or something like that over and over."

Oh no. I swallowed hard. "I had a nightmare."

And it *was* a nightmare. Now I understood why Mark never wanted me to remember. Because I knew the guy in the orange polo shirt, the one who'd recognized me. His name was Lorenzo Rosetti.

"Hey, Dante, wait up!" I rushed down the hall and caught up

with him just outside the cafeteria doors. "Why didn't you wait for me? We always walk together when parent pickups are called."

Dante shuffled his feet and eyed the stream of kids going into the cafeteria to be driven home by their parents. "Lorenzo's picking me up," he mumbled.

I took a step back. "Oh." Seeing Dante's brother always made my stomach drop.

Billy Burke, from one of the other fifth grade classes, passed us. "Hi, Dante!"

"Don't talk to him," hissed the boy next to Billy. "Don't you know who that is? He's Dante Rosetti. My older brother told me his dad, Angelo, is like the boss of a mob family. He said his dad kills people."

Billy peeked at us over his shoulder as he entered the cafeteria.

"My brother goes to school with his brother, Lorenzo," the boy continued, not yet out of earshot. "Lorenzo's the oldest Rosetti kid and my brother said he's just as bad as his dad."

Dante frowned and stared at the floor.

"Here," I said over the boy's voice. I pulled the princess coloring book out of my bag and handed it to him. "I heard Ms. Stohl say all the girls in her kindergarten class are really into that princess right now. I don't use it anymore, but I thought Sofia might like it."

Dante perked up. "Sofia can have it?"

I smiled. "Yeah."

"I should've known." The mocking sound of Lorenzo's voice made me stiffen. "Here I am," Lorenzo said, "wondering what happened to my baby brother when all you're doing is flirting with your girlfriend. Come on. Show me your moves, little man."

"Cut it out, Lo." Dante's eyes darted to mine, full of apologies. "She's not my girlfriend."

I felt a bit shaky inside as my gaze bounced between the two of them.

Lorenzo leaned against the cafeteria doorjamb. He was barely six-teen, with the same brown hair as Dante, but his thick facial hair made him look much older. "That's good. You know she's not good enough for you."

Dante faced his brother. "Leave her alone!"

"Ooh, standing up for her. Definitely not something a boyfriend would do." He sneered and stared at Dante's hands. "Hold on! Are you holding a coloring book? *What are you, five?"*

"I gave it to him. It's for Sofia," I snapped.

Lorenzo narrowed his eyes and focused on me. "Is it now? And what makes you think you can give anything to my sister?"

My pulse raced but before Lorenzo could say anything else, Sofia came walking up in a single-file line behind her kindergarten teacher. Dante grabbed her hand and showed her the coloring book. "This is for you. Want to color when we get home?"

Sofia's face lit up as she followed Dante into the cafeteria. Dante didn't look back. But Lorenzo did. He gave me a long scornful glance before disappearing into the crowd.

"Sloane?"

I blinked and Jason came back into focus. "Sorry. It was just a nightmare. I'm fine."

He moved toward me. "You're not fine. You're shaking."

I examined my shaking hands. *Of course I'm shaking! I saw an innocent old man get murdered and Lorenzo Rosetti was involved! I understand now why we've been running for six years! Because even at twelve years old, I knew to be afraid of Lorenzo Rosetti.*

Jason peeked at the tangle of sheets on my bed and away again quickly. "Um, do you want to sit and talk about it?"

The idea was laughable. There was no way I could talk about it with Jason, even if he knew who I really was. I wouldn't put him in that kind of danger. I couldn't even talk about it with Mark. Not after the overly confident way he'd said it wouldn't change anything if I remembered what happened. He hadn't been sure if that was true, and I wasn't going to tell him anything that might jeopardize my release from WITSEC. But sitting sounded very good right then.

I moved to the bed and buried my face in my hands. "I don't remember what it was about."

I felt Jason tugging on the sheets and looked up. He pulled until the bed was covered, then sat against the bed's headboard, his legs stretched out in front of him. He patted the empty spot beside him. "You're still shaking. Let's just talk for a few minutes until you calm down."

I numbly crawled next to him. "What do you want to talk about?" There were so many things I *couldn't* tell him, it felt like I didn't know what we would ever talk about again.

"Me."

Despite everything, I cracked a smile.

Jason took a deep breath. "Remember how your first day at school Livie told you my parents were divorced?"

I grew still. I'd been expecting him to keep joking around. "Yeah."

"They're not. Not really. That's just what my mom and I told everyone when we moved here."

I glanced at his profile, silhouetted by the dim light of the bedside lamp. "Where's your dad then?"

"In prison." The words hung in the air. Jason continued without looking at me. "He got mixed up in some bad stuff a few years ago and made some really poor decisions. My mom and I moved here, where my aunt lives, to get away from it all. We stayed with her for a while until we got back on our feet."

I closed my eyes. I'd completely forgotten about his aunt Jill, the one who lived at the beach in North Carolina.

"I wish they'd gotten divorced," Jason muttered.

"Why?" I was shocked by everything coming out of Jason's mouth. There must've been some explanation for whatever Jason's dad did. He'd always been a great guy, like a second father to me. And Jason had always been super close to him.

"Because I can't forgive him." Everything about Jason's expression was dark. "For getting locked up and taken away from us. How could he not think about how his actions affected us? What about my mom? How could he leave her like that?"

"What does she think about it?"

"She's supported him through everything. Refused to divorce him. Even drives to visit him once a month on visitation weekend. That's where she was a few weeks ago when you came over, visiting *him*." He scrubbed a hand over his face.

"You don't go with her?"

"I can't do it," he admitted quietly. "I haven't seen him in years."

The very thought of Jason not seeing his dad for so long broke my heart. I'd give anything to see my dad again. "Why are you telling me this?"

He studied my hands resting in my lap. "Because we all have secrets, and now you know one of mine. I trust you. And you can trust me if there's anything you ever want to talk about."

My heart raced. "Like what?"

"Like your secret cell phone that was blowing up with texts at the diner."

I opened my mouth to deny it, but nothing came out.

"It's okay—that's all I'm trying to say. Secrets are okay."

I wanted to tell him. Oh my God, I'd never wanted to tell anyone anything more in my life. But I couldn't. I'd heard the stories, just like everyone else in my hometown. I could never put him in the Rosetti kind of danger I was in, the we-annihilate-your-whole-family-if-you-cross-us kind of danger. Still, one secret popped into my head. "I have a tattoo," I blurted.

Jason stared at me for a long second, then laughed his chipmunk laugh. "Are you serious?"

I grinned and nodded. "No one else knows."

His eyes scanned my body. "Where is it?"

"On my hip." *In a place that could always be covered, even by a bathing suit, because Mark would kill me if he knew I'd created an "identifying mark."*

Even in the dim light, Jason's deep blue eyes glinted with amusement. "What is it? When did you get it?"

"A few months ago." In February, a few days after the Sloane Sullivan fake ID I hadn't used yet said I turned eighteen. "And it's three tiny stars."

Jason's gaze softened. "Do they have any significance or do you just like stars?"

I stared down at my flannel pants so he couldn't see me blush. "Both, I guess. They represent people important to me." *My mom, my dad and you.*

I felt Jason's eyes on me. "Why stars for people?"

I thought about the day I'd gotten the tattoo, the day the memory of Jason showing me the stars had first come back. "To remind myself that even though I couldn't see the people, they are always there, just like the stars." *Inside me, like my memories.*

Jason's voice was rough. "Which hip is it on?"

"My left," I whispered.

He touched the outside edge of my left hip with a single finger. "Here?"

I grabbed his finger and slowly slid it down, closer to the top of my pelvic bone. "Here."

Jason laced his fingers in mine and rested his hand against my hip, right above my tattoo. His hand felt warm and solid and safe. "Your secret's safe with me."

Those were the sexiest five words I'd ever heard from a boy.

Click. Something bright made me scrunch up my eyes before opening them. The bedside lamp cast an eerie glow on Livie standing at the foot of the bed, sneering.

I lifted my head and winced at the crick in my neck. *Why am I sleeping sitting up, leaning against…* I peeked sideways. *Oh shit*. Jason was asleep, resting against the headboard of my hotel bed. My head had been on his shoulder and our hands were still clasped on my hip.

"Hey, kids," Livie said in an unpleasant voice. "Fun night?"

That's when I noticed the phone in Livie's hand. *The sound. The bright light.* "Did you just take a picture of us?"

Jason stirred. "What's going on?" he mumbled.

"You bet I just took a picture," Livie replied. She sounded way too bitter for someone returning from a "better" guy's hotel room at—I glanced at the clock—3:47 a.m. Livie shook her phone at me. "You're going to want this memento of your time together after Jason dumps you like all the other girls."

Jason sat up, fully awake. "Hey. I'm sitting right here."

"It's not like that," I said. "I had a nightmare and I was yelling and Jason came to make sure we *both* were okay."

"Yes," Livie agreed, "Jason's very thoughtful at first."

"Knock it off," Jason grumbled.

"Why? Don't like hearing the truth?"

Just put the phone down, I silently pleaded. *Put it down so I can erase the picture. I don't want to have to leave again.*

Jason stood and moved toward Livie. "What would you know about the truth? You told Sloane I slept with half the girls in school when you know that isn't true."

Livie just shook her head.

"Where were you tonight, Liv?" Jason continued. "Who's the one sleeping around, huh?"

Livie shot me a death glare. "Nice, Sloane."

"I didn't tell him anything," I insisted as Livie stormed out. With her phone.

Jason began pacing. "I can't believe she—"

"Think she'll do anything with that picture?" I interrupted, remembering what Jason said that night at his house about Livie sometimes being mean when she's mad.

He froze. "Yes. *Shit.* It won't be hard for her to use it to start of bunch of rumors. And with my reputation…" He rubbed the back of his neck. "I don't want to drag you into all of that."

I made my way to the door as fast as possible without looking like I was running. "It's okay," I lied. "I'll go after her."

Jason followed me. "No, let me. I'm the one she's mad at. I'll get her to delete it." He stepped into the hall.

I hesitated in the doorway as bright light from the hall spilled into my dark room. "I can handle it."

Jason spun around, his mouth set. "Would you just let…"

His voice trailed off and he stared at me for a moment before the hint of a smile appeared on his lips. "Let me help you for once. It's what friends do." He started down the hall.

I frowned. "Hey, Jase?"

He grinned at me over his shoulder. "Yeah?"

"Remind Livie she owes me one."

"Got it."

I closed my door and leaned against it, letting my head fall back against the metal. *Stupid, stupid, stupid. It was stupid to fall asleep next to Jason. You knew Livie was coming back. You knew she was still upset about Jason breaking up with her, even if she acted like she wasn't around Oliver. She's barely said two words to Jason the past three weeks. And it was stupid to tell Jason a secret, even if it wasn't a big one, because now he's being all weird and smiley and feels like he has to help you. And it was really stupid for your stupid brain to randomly remember what happened. You don't want to know secrets about the Rosettis! Not now. Not ever.*

"Ugh!" I kicked the door, then groaned again at the pain that shot up my leg.

I flipped on the bathroom light and hobbled my way inside, eager to splash some water on my face and clear my head and stop groaning before the whole hotel heard me. I glanced in the mirror, eyes widening at the complete mess my hair was in, and froze. Because the eyes staring back at me weren't brown. They were green. Non-contact-wearing, natural green. *Stupid, stupid, stupid.*

SEVENTEEN

"**G**ood morning."

My whole body tensed at the sound of Jason's voice. I placed the serving spoon back into the large bowl of scrambled eggs and glanced around the hotel's buffet table. Most everyone else had finished eating breakfast long ago and there was no one getting food except us. I took a deep breath.

It seemed like forever since I'd realized my mistake and put my contacts back in, but it hadn't even been five hours. Five hours that I'd spent creating excuses to explain why Jason was wrong when he brought up my green eyes. Because I was sure he was going to bring it up. I'd expected him to say something as soon as he got back to my room with Livie. But when they walked in, Jason gave me a tiny nod to tell me the evil picture had been taken care of and retreated to his room without another word.

Maybe he'd been tired or just didn't want to be around Livie any longer than he had to after the way she'd acted. I didn't mind. It gave me extra time to craft elaborate explanations involving things like shadows and cheap hotel lighting playing tricks on your eyes and the way sleep deprivation can make you think you're seeing things. Then Jason was late to breakfast. I'd been sitting at a table with Sawyer and Oliver for the past half hour, breathing in the scent of their bacon and coffee, leg bouncing furiously, while I waited for Jason to show up, waited for the inevitable confrontation. And now here he was.

"Good morning," I replied. I looked at him, trying to widen my eyes to prove their brownness, but he was checking out the food.

"Okay everyone," Mr. Pruitt called from the other side of the room. "The buses are here. Let's go."

Jason grabbed two waffles off the platter next to me. His shoulder brushed mine as he spun around and headed for Sawyer by the door. I watched him walk away. *He didn't say anything. Why didn't he say anything?*

Oliver grabbed my hand, pulling me away from the buffet. "I call dibs on Sloane today!" he yelled toward Jason's back. The day only got stranger after that.

Jason walked with Sawyer and people I didn't really know during the city tour and sat with Sawyer on the bus ride home. Not only did he not talk to me, he never even looked at me.

Then there was Livie. She acted like my best friend the whole day, like she hadn't gotten all mad just hours before. It was totally weird. And it made me wonder what Jason said to appease her. Did it have something to do with my eyes? She was talking to Jason again but since Jason wasn't talking to me, I had no idea what went down between the two of them.

So I spent the day with Oliver, joking around and pretending I wasn't eavesdropping on Jason's conversations. We'd actually had fun on the bus ride home, debating which past era had the best music. I'd lobbied for oldies from the '50s and '60s while he'd argued for '90s alternative. But even a fun bus ride couldn't completely get rid of my jitters.

As I rounded the back of the bus, bag in hand, I spotted Jason leaning against his car. His eyes locked on mine for the first time that day and my pulse raced. Then someone threw their arms around me from behind.

"I had so much fun this weekend!" Livie squealed in my ear.

This girl is like Jekyll and Hyde. I spun around and nodded. "Yeah. It was great." I noticed Oliver a few steps behind her. "Are you headed home?"

"I'm going to hang at Oliver's for a while." Her eyes shifted over my shoulder to Jason. "Want to come?"

I glanced at Oliver, who shook his head. He must've wanted some alone time with Livie, probably to figure out what was going on with her. It was obvious something had happened between Jason and Livie from the way Livie kept sneaking peeks at Jason throughout the day, but it seemed like Oliver couldn't figure out *when* it could've happened since Livie had been in his room most of the night. I couldn't blame him for wanting to get any potentially awkward conversations over with. I winked at him. "I think three straight hours on a bus is all I can take of this guy and his misguided musical taste."

Oliver grinned. "Maybe tomorrow I'll wear my Pearl Jam shirt in your honor."

I half laughed, half groaned as Oliver and Livie walked

away. But when I turned around, my smile disappeared. Jason was gone.

I climbed into Mark's car, which he'd been more than happy to drive to the school and leave for me so he could do a long run back home, and drove out of the parking lot. But I didn't go home. I made random turns and wandered all over the little beach town as I thought about what to do. Because I couldn't go on like this.

It was *my* cover story, *my* future hanging in the balance, and I needed to take control. I was tired of waiting on pins and needles to see what Jason was going to do. I needed to spin this my way and I was ready. And maybe if I got Jason alone, like Oliver was trying to do with Livie, he'd finally mention my eyes. Maybe he'd been waiting for me at his car, waiting for a moment when there weren't so many people around. And if I got him talking, maybe he'd also tell me how he got Livie to erase the photo. I just had to come up with a way to get him alone that didn't involve my house, where Mark was, or his house, where his mom was.

I turned onto a street I'd never seen before. It was lined with souvenir shops and clothing boutiques and a tiny bookstore with a coffee bar. On the corner was a small yellow building with a large glass window filled with cake stands in various colors. I pulled into a parking space facing the building and searched the window.

In the center was a large decal of a yellow bird sitting atop a blue three-tiered cake with the bakery's name written like it was coming out of the bird's beak: *Sweet, Sweet!* Below the decal were the cake stands. They were filled with cupcakes and brownies and the exact item I was looking for: M&M's

cookies bigger than my hand, piled high on a bright blue cake stand. I grinned. Jason had loved M&M's cookies, always begging his mom to make them when we were little. And now I had a plan: go into the bakery, borrow their phone and call Jason to tell him I was in desperate need of sugar and someone to share it with. *Friends can meet up for dessert on a Sunday evening, right?*

Little bells rang as I entered the bakery. I was enveloped by the scent of sugar and vanilla and it made me feel at home. I examined the small store, trying to figure out why it was so inviting. There were cheerful yellow walls, display cases full of delectable deserts, a handful of black metal tables and chairs with brightly colored cushions, and shelves filled with every kind of sprinkle and candle you could imagine, all of which was charming but not necessarily like home to me. Then I noticed the music. "Little Bitty Pretty One" by Thurston Harris was playing from speakers set up on the counter. An image of me and Jason's mom dancing around his kitchen to that very song flashed in my head. I smiled and tapped my foot and for a split second, imagined pulling out my own phone and calling Jason to ask whether he remembered that day. Instead, I listened as another of my favorite oldies started: "Twistin' the Night Away" by Sam Cooke. That song had always made me want to dance. I swayed my hips as I waited for someone to come to the counter so I could ask to borrow the phone.

My gaze drifted over a display case and landed on a tray of black-and-white cookies, perfectly aligned in two straight rows. I stopped dancing. Those were my mom's favorite cookies.

I remembered the first time I'd ever eaten one, the time she brought a box of them home from a trip to New York

City when I was nine. We sat at the kitchen table with glasses of milk as she taught me about icing versus fondant and how they're really more like a cake than a cookie and that the best ones always taste slightly lemony. Even during all those years in all the different places we'd lived, if I saw a black-and-white cookie, I ate it. They were never as good as that first time. But I had to admit, these looked amazing.

I took a step toward the display case. A slight squeaking sound came from the direction of a swinging door I'd assumed led to the kitchen (and most likely an exit). Before I could even turn toward the sound, a large *clang* drowned out the Sam Cooke song still playing. I saw two metal baking sheets lying haphazardly on the floor surrounded by scattered white cookies, and the very startled face of Jason's mom.

EIGHTEEN

Jason's mom covered her mouth with a shaking hand. "Oh my God."

Lesson number six: take control of the situation. I took a few steps toward her so she'd be able to see my eyes—my brown eyes—better. "Sorry, I didn't mean to scare you. I was—"

The swinging door squeaked again and Jason appeared. "Mom? Are you—" He noticed me, frozen in the middle of the store. Something flashed in his eyes. "Hey."

His mom's eyes darted between the two of us. She pointed in my direction. "Do you—"

"Sloane, can you excuse us for a second?" Jason interrupted, pulling his mom back through the swinging door.

I waited until they disappeared into the kitchen and rushed to the swinging door, sidestepping the white cookies on the floor so I could get as close as possible to eavesdrop.

"Is that…?" Even astonished, Jason's mom's voice was as sweet sounding as I remembered.

Jason was quick to reply. "No."

"But she looks just like—"

"Don't," Jason snapped.

"Don't what? She's a dead ringer for—"

"Don't," Jason repeated with more force. "You promised you'd never say her name again."

"Jase, come on."

"It's not her, okay." Jason sighed, a long, frustrated sound. "I know they look alike. I thought it was her at first too. But that girl out there's got brown eyes and a different name and no mole on her neck and her mom's still alive."

I flinched. *That girl?*

"I didn't realize you were still so upset about this," his mom said softly. "It's been almost six years. You have to let it go, Jason."

"I can't."

I involuntarily took a step back from the intensity of Jason's voice.

"Six years," he repeated. "Without a single word. She could've found me by now if she wanted to. It would only take *one* internet search. But she hasn't. She never looked back. And I'll *never* forgive her for leaving me like that."

I backed away from the swinging door. I should've been happy. Jason hadn't seen my eyes after all. His smile in the hall had been about something else completely, probably the complete disaster my hair was in, fully visible for the first time in the hall's bright lights. But I didn't care about that anymore. I didn't care about blending in or following the rules or taking control of the situation. I simply ran out of the bakery as fast as I could.

He'll never forgive me. I drove home in a daze, repeating

those words over and over. All this time I'd been worried Jason might recognize me. It never even occurred to me to worry that he wouldn't want to see me again.

I should've left that first day after running into him. At least then I still would've believed he missed me as much as I missed him. That would've been better than knowing he hated me, knowing I was never going to measure up to the girl in his head either. My dad's words rang in my head, reminding me of the single lesson I'd learned from him: *"Bad things happen when you don't follow the rules."*

I took a deep breath and typed the name into the internet browser: Julia Abbott. Thousands of results popped up, for doctors and teachers, videos and blogs, but they weren't what I wanted. It took until the fourth page of hits to find what I was looking for: a newspaper article from my hometown.

I clicked on the link and my breath caught in my throat as a picture of my mom materialized on the computer screen. It was the one from our last Fourth of July party, when she had sun-kissed highlights in her blond hair and even more freckles than usual. I glanced around to make sure no one was watching, then scanned the article as fast as I could.

Words jumped out at me: car accident, fire, funeral, closed casket. I shivered. The one time I'd asked, Mark told me the Marshals created a cover story so no one would know she'd been murdered. An accidental death made an easier explanation for our sudden disappearance from town than us leaving in the middle of a murder investigation. I'd just never known what "accident" they'd picked.

"What are you doing?" my dad whispered. In an instant, Mom's smiling face vanished.

He deleted the browser history and shut the computer down. Then he grabbed the sleeve of my hoodie and pulled me into the stacks in the back of the library. "Jesus, Elise!"

I flinched. I hated when he used my fake name. He had to sometimes, of course, but I wished he'd come up with something universal like Mark's "Kid."

"What were you thinking?" Dad asked. I didn't know a whisper could sound so angry. "You know the rules. No contact with our past lives, ever. Bad things happen when you don't follow the rules."

"It's okay," I insisted. "We're in a public library in the middle of Wyoming. No one's going to find us."

He shook his head. "There are ways of tracking what people search for on the internet. You know that. The...people we're dealing with are very thorough."

My neck grew hot. "That's why I used a fake name when I got the temporary computer pass. So even if someone did track it, it wouldn't come back to me."

"And what if it's not only the name that matters? This is a public library, remember? Lesson number three: know where the cameras are likely to be."

I tugged on the hood of my sweatshirt, still up around my red hair. "That's what this is for."

"But what about me? You didn't let me in on your plan and I'm not wearing a hood. Plus, you look conspicuous all bundled up inside." He leaned against the metal shelves and scrubbed his face with his hands. "I can't keep doing this. It's been ten months and we're in our fifth town. Do you want to keep moving around like this?"

"No," I mumbled.

"If Mark found out..."

I hung my head. "Are you going to tell him?"

"I'll figure something out." It was an effort for him to even push *the words out. "Come on. We need to leave. Probably shouldn't come back either."*

He stalked off, glancing around like he expected someone to jump out of the stacks and haul us away.

"Sorry," I whispered to his back. "I just needed to see her one last time."

I slammed the car door shut, just like I wanted to slam a door on that memory. Dad had figured something out all right. Three days later, he killed himself.

Deep down I knew it wasn't entirely my fault. He'd been depressed, although I hadn't realized just how sick he was at the time. It was a serious mental illness and he should've been getting help. But I also knew I'd helped push him over the edge by breaking the rules and making him decide whether to tell Mark and have to move again or not. *Bad things happen when you don't follow the rules.* Just like now. I didn't leave when I first saw Jason and because of that, I now knew he hated the real me. It was my own fault my heart felt like it was breaking.

I tossed my bag onto the kitchen floor and stormed toward the bathroom. I wanted to take a shower, the hotter the better. Anything to wash away the whole trip. I threw open the bathroom door and found a glistening half-naked Mark standing in front of the sink, a towel wrapped low around his hips. "Oh God! Sorry!" I spun around as fast as I could.

"You're back! Just…give me a sec."

I inched away from the bathroom threshold as fabric rustled behind me.

A minute later, Mark appeared in front of me in a faded

red T-shirt and ripped jeans, drops of water still scattered in his hair and eyelashes. "How was the trip?"

"Fine. Great."

"What'd you do?"

I showed someone my real eyes. I pissed off my roommate and got my picture taken sleeping next to a boy. I told that same boy a secret because I thought... Hell, I don't know what I thought, but then I found out he can't even stand to hear my real name. I remembered what happened, and I want you to tell me everything's going to be all right and that Lorenzo Rosetti is in jail and the guy with the baseball cap is in jail and I'm still getting out of WITSEC.

Concern settled in Mark's eyes. "Are you okay, Sloane?"

I blinked. "I think that's the first time you've called me Sloane."

"It's about time, don't you think?" Mark grinned. "You're doing it. We've been here over a month. Graduation's only a month away. Time's flying by and we haven't had any problems. So I'm calling it. You are officially Sloane Sullivan now."

That's right. I didn't come here to make friends. I didn't come to get Jason back in my life. Did I actually just think I should've left that first day because he doesn't like the girl he grew up with anymore? Forget her. She died right along with her parents. I came here to turn eighteen, graduate and get the hell out of WITSEC. And that's exactly what I'm going to do. I nodded. "I'm officially Sloane Sullivan. Now and forever."

NINETEEN

As I pulled my physics book out of my locker the next morning, I felt someone hovering behind me.

"Hey." The voice was soft and low, meant only for me in the bustling hallway.

I closed my eyes and took a deep breath. *Sloane Sullivan, Kid.* "Hey, Jason," I said as I spun around.

He searched my face. "Where'd you go yesterday? At my mom's bakery, I mean. You just…disappeared."

I raised my mouth in what I hoped was a playful smile. "I got a call on my secret bat phone. I would've let you know I had to leave but you disappeared too."

Jason nodded slowly. It made him look surprisingly like Mark. "Important superhero stuff, huh?"

"Yup. Saving the world one high school at a time."

"Sloane and J," Sawyer said as he strolled up and tossed an arm over my shoulder. "My two favorite people."

Sawyer's ratio of physical to nonphysical interactions had much improved in the three weeks since he'd started dating Kylie, but at that moment I was happy for the way he pulled me closer to him and away from Jason, ending any further phone talk.

Sawyer peered down at me. "Are you coming to prom this weekend? Kylie was hoping you'd be there."

Prom. I hadn't even thought about the prom since getting Sawyer and Kylie together. Part of me wanted to go—I mean, it *was* my senior prom—but with everything that had gone wrong on the trip and at the bakery, I didn't want to push my luck at a big public event. And considering Sloane wasn't one to come out in the wild that often, I could probably get away with skipping it. "Tell Kylie I'm sorry. I'm not going."

Sawyer's arm dropped away from my shoulder. "Why not?"

I said the first thing that popped into my head. "I don't have a dress." Which was true.

He frowned. "Maybe you can borrow one from Livie or something. Girls borrow each other's clothes, right?"

"It's okay," I said. "Dances really aren't my thing."

"Well, what about the party at J's house after?" Sawyer pressed. "Kylie's really nervous about not knowing anyone. She said you two got along well at the diner."

I looked at Jason. "I didn't know you were having an after-party."

"I decided ten minutes ago. And it's not really a *party* party, more like a few people coming over. I was just about to ask you to come. Actually, I was—"

"What's up, Buttercup!" Oliver's grinning face was visible above the crowd as he worked his way toward us. He stopped in front of me and tugged on the hem of his black Pearl Jam T-shirt.

I held up a hand. "I've already successfully defended the

merits of 'Build Me Up Buttercup.' It's better than anything Pearl Jam did."

Oliver arched an eyebrow. "Did you know Pearl Jam did a cover of 'Last Kiss,' which was originally recorded by Wayne Cochran in 1961? That 'oldie' was one of Pearl Jam's highest-charting songs in the US."

I tried to stop it, but a smile spread across my face. "I did not know that."

Oliver smoothed his T-shirt. "I think I may force you to listen to it so you can appreciate how much better Pearl Jam's version is than the original. Slower and more soulful. It's good."

I shook my head. "All this proves is that you like oldies."

"All this proves is that I don't have misguided musical taste." He smiled an adorable dimple-filled smile and turned to Jason. "So, party at your place after prom? Livie just told me." Before Jason could answer, Oliver's green eyes brightened and he pointed at me. "I'm bringing the song and making you listen to it then."

"We don't know if she's coming yet," Sawyer said. "She's not going to prom."

Oliver looked at him. "What? Why not?"

"She doesn't have a dress."

"Who cares what she wears?"

"*She's* right here," I said. "And I care."

Oliver leaned toward me and pressed his palms together like he was begging. "If you don't want to come to the dance, at least come to Jason's after. You helped get me out of my funk after Chloe, and I want you there. It wouldn't be the same without you. And I refuse to experience prom day without seeing you eat your anti–Pearl Jam words."

Sawyer copied Oliver's begging position. "Come on,

Sloane. Come hang out with Kylie and get a musical smack down. What more could you want on a Saturday night?"

I pursed my lips and peeked at Jason.

His fingers brushed the small of my back. "Please come. You don't have to dress up. There's something I want to show you."

His eyes were bluer than normal and my back was tingling and I couldn't help it, curiosity got the better of me. "Okay," I agreed. Because I was dying to know what Jason could possibly have to show the girl he was convinced was Sloane.

"I think if you ever have to pick a new name, you should be Duckie Markovitch."

Mark and I were watching the end of *Pretty in Pink*, the fourth movie in our prom-themed prom day movie marathon, and Duckie was my favorite character.

Mark's mouth dropped open in mock horror. "I should be the guy who *doesn't* get the girl?"

I waved a hand at him dismissively. "Oh you could get the girl." I pressed my lips together to stop from smiling at the faint trace of pink that appeared on his cheeks. "Just how cool of a name would that be?"

He snorted. "I'll keep it under consideration."

I watched as movie Duckie told the girl he loved to leave their prom to chase after the boy she loved. "I never knew there were so many movies about prom. How'd you find all of these?"

Mark popped a piece of popcorn into his mouth. "I've seen them all before."

"I know you love movies but I never took you for the girly prom-movie type."

He threw a piece of popcorn at my head. "I wanted to see what I was missing out on."

"Because you were homeschooled?"

"Because I was stuck at home all the time with a family that didn't understand me any better than the kids at school did. I was pretty isolated, so I read a lot of books and watched a lot of movies."

I hugged my knees to my chest and studied his profile. "You didn't have anyone you liked in your family? What about your sister?"

Mark's gaze dropped to the bowl of popcorn. "You remember I mentioned a sister?"

"It was the only other time you talked about your family."

He took a deep breath. "She was great, but she was younger and didn't really understand. I had a cousin that was pretty cool though. We talked all the time when I was growing up. But he lived far away so I didn't get to see him very often."

I stretched out across the couch and nudged his leg with my foot. He glanced at me. "I'm your family," I said quietly. "Don't forget about me."

He placed a hand on my bare foot and squeezed gently, a silent gesture that said *I know* and *Thank you* and *I could never forget about you*. A smile played at the corner of Mark's mouth. "So I was thinking…"

"Oh Lord, what now?"

"After graduation we should take a trip. Anywhere you want to go, except someplace we've lived before."

I grinned. "Like a real vacation? No new names, no new schools? Just hotels and sightseeing and touristy crap?"

Mark's smile grew. "The crappier, the better."

"What about your next assignment?"

"I haven't had a vacation in six years, Sloane. I think they owe me a week or two off."

I sat up. "There are still like twentysomething states I've never been to. Can we do a *real* road trip? Windows down, music blaring, too much junk food, the whole nine yards? Stopping to see the world's biggest ball of yarn just because we have the time and aren't running for our lives?" I'd just started looking for a summer job. And when we sent in the deposit to Vanderbilt a few days ago, Mark told me as a graduation present he'd rented the house through August so I could stay until I left for Tennessee. But even as excited as I was about being on my own and doing normal, everyday teen summer stuff, a road trip with Mark before he started his next assignment sounded amazing.

His eyes lit up. "You really want to go?"

"I'd *love* to go." A tingly feeling swept through me. It was really happening. We were planning things for after graduation, *after* I'd be released from WITSEC, and it was only a few weeks away. So many of the end-of-year senior milestones had already happened: the scavenger hunt, the trip to Charleston and now prom.

My gaze drifted back to the TV, to the fancy dresses and the people dancing and the girl kissing the boy. I slid my foot out from under Mark's hand and tucked both knees under my chin, not taking my eyes off the movie. "Do you think I should've gone? To prom?"

He was silent for a moment. "Are you having second thoughts?"

I shrugged. "It's supposed to be one of those quintessential high school events, right?" I looked at him over the tops of my knees, eyebrows scrunched together.

Mark's eyes never left mine, but his hand slipped into his pocket and pulled out something small and shiny. "It's not too late."

I stared at the silver rectangle and the words printed across the top in bold black letters: *A Night to Remember.* I sat up straighter. "Where'd you get that?"

The corner of his mouth twitched. "The school sent an email about buying prom tickets. I know you said you weren't going, and it's totally your choice, but I got one, just in case…"

I checked the time on my phone. It was close to ten, but the dance didn't end for almost two more hours. I bit my lip as the credits on the movie started rolling.

Mark grabbed the remote and clicked back to the menu to search for another movie—another prom-related movie.

My mouth dropped open. "Were you using all these movies today to convince me I was missing out?"

He grinned his giving-me-a-hard-time grin.

I shook my head.

He shook the ticket in his hand. "Prom is supposed to be *a night to remember.* It wouldn't hurt to give yourself one of those big-deal types of high school memories, would it?"

I leaned over and snatched the ticket out of his hand. "You could've just told me you thought I should go."

"Nope. You needed to decide this one all on your own."

I stood, mentally calculating how fast I could make it to the ballroom where prom was being held.

Mark put down the remote and began collecting empty

soda cans and candy wrappers from the coffee table. "What are you going to wear?"

Oh shoot. I looked at my outfit, the one I'd picked for Jason's afterparty: jeans and the top I'd gotten in Charleston, the pale lavender satin one with sequins and spaghetti straps. It wasn't a prom dress, but at least it was a little fancy. And it's not like I had any other options. "This, I guess."

His eyes shifted to me and away again. "You look…really nice," he said as he picked stray popcorn pieces off the couch.

I grinned. "Thanks."

"Here." He handed me his car key. "Go make some epic prom memories so you can tell me about them on our trip."

I started toward the back door but paused in the doorway. "Mark?"

He stopped cleaning and looked up. "Yeah?"

I tapped the edge of the ticket against my bottom lip. "Thank you for a great prom day."

Mark held my gaze. "It was my pleasure."

The street was dark and deserted when I pulled out of the driveway a minute later. I couldn't stop thinking about places we could go on our trip, places I'd never been to: Disney World, the French Quarter, Mount Rushmore, the Statue of Liberty. I was so deep in thought I didn't notice the car behind me until its headlights were blinding me through the rearview mirror.

The back of my neck prickled. I hadn't seen any cars on the road when I left the house. There was no way a car could've turned onto the street and caught up to me that quickly. I paused at the stop sign at the end of the block, unsure whether I should turn around or continue to prom. *It's late on a Satur-*

day, I rationalized. *Probably someone speeding home to make curfew or rushing to the drugstore before it closes.*

At the end of the next block, I turned right. So did the car. When I made a left turn a mile later and the car followed, I pulled my phone out of my jeans pocket. My thumb hovered over Mark's number as I neared the ballroom. The lights shining from the building and the students gathered by the doors screamed *people* and *safe*, but I didn't pull into the parking lot. I drove past, deciding to circle the block to make sure the car was following me. If it copied two more of my turns, I was calling Mark.

I turned right at the end of the block and so did the car. When I made the next right, however, the car kept going straight. I released my death grip on the steering wheel as I watched my rearview mirror to make sure it didn't turn around. *You're getting paranoid in your old age, Kid.* But I didn't put my phone away until I locked the car right in front of the ballroom.

I squeezed past a group of girls I didn't know by the front doors. They were a giggling mass of chiffon and curls and dramatic makeup. A few of them glanced in my direction, their gazes lingering slightly too long on my jeans and flip-flops. My cheeks grew hot as I stepped into the lobby. *Maybe I should've thought about the whole what to wear thing a little more because this is definitely* not *blending in.*

My chest tightened when I spotted Principal Thompson next to a pair of double doors that must've led to the actual ballroom. Her shimmery cocktail dress and signature stiletto heels looked way too elegant for the rickety folding table she was sitting behind. My footsteps echoed in tune to my pounding heart as I crossed the lobby's inlaid wood floor and handed her my ticket without a word. She eyed my outfit as she punched a hole in the ticket, then handed it back to me. "Purple's a good color for you," she said with a genuine smile.

A slow grin made its way onto my mouth. *At least she's not going to bust me for some prom dress code violation.* "Thanks."

She gestured to the double doors. "Everything's in there," she said as her eyes narrowed at something over my shoulder.

I took a deep breath and opened one of the doors.

"Stop right there, you two..." But the rest of Principal Thompson's command was drowned out by the music and heat and excitement that instantly engulfed me. The door swung shut and I let out a little laugh. Because the room looked exactly like something from a movie.

There was a fountain and trees draped with paper flowers and twinkle lights hanging from the ceiling. A dozen tall lamp posts with three lights apiece marked a pathway to a square wooden floor, where a DJ had a crowd of kids dancing to a song I could feel thumping in my chest. Round tables and chairs dotted the back half of the ballroom, and a photographer in the far corner was snapping pictures in front of a backdrop that looked like a city park at dusk. And it was *packed*. More people than I expected were dancing and talking over the music and completely ignoring me.

It was perfect.

I walked under a balloon arch—a *balloon arch*—and scanned the dimly lit faces. Before I took more than ten steps, a voice called out over the music: "Avoider of Senior Proms!"

I grinned and turned to find Oliver standing at the edge of the dance floor in a black tuxedo and matching bow tie. Livie was next to him, looking like glamorous old Hollywood in a long, fitted gold dress and her hair in pin curls.

"I think you mean *Attender* of Senior Proms," I said after I made my way to them.

Oliver leaned closer. "I knew you wouldn't be able to resist seeing me in a tux."

I gave him a little shove just as a new song started.

Oliver rolled his eyes. "We need to teach this DJ about good music!"

"Who cares if it's good? Dance with us!" Livie yelled as she pulled me onto the dance floor.

So I did. For five straight songs, I jumped and thrashed and lost myself in the music and the crowd and the knowledge that, at that moment, I was nothing but a typical high school senior dancing with her friends at prom.

Then a slow song started. Oliver glanced at me and raised his eyebrows in question just as Livie wrapped an arm around his waist. "You two go ahead," I said, fanning myself with my hand. "I'm going to find something to drink."

I wound my way off the dance floor and headed for a long table full of bottled waters and sodas. I smiled at the sign behind the table counting down the days until the remaining senior events: "career day: 2; finals: who cares; graduation: 25."

Grabbing a water, I turned and watched couples dancing as I drank. Some of them looked like they belonged in a movie too, gazing into each other's eyes, seemingly unaware they were in a room surrounded by hundreds of other people. A girl in a short strapless silver dress came spinning into my field of vision. I followed her as she spun back to her dance partner, and I froze, water bottle halfway to my mouth. She was dancing with Jason.

He was wearing tuxedo pants and a white dress shirt with

the sleeves rolled up to his elbows. His black hair was perfectly disheveled and his smile reached all the way to his deep blue eyes. A lump formed in my throat. If he was that gorgeous in half a tuxedo, I couldn't imagine seeing him in the whole thing. And he was dancing with a beautiful brunette.

He leaned in and said something close to her ear. She tipped her head back and laughed. Even though I couldn't hear her over the music, I felt each chuckle like a tiny stab in my chest. His head started to turn in my direction and I fled, suddenly eager to be back on the other side of the dance floor.

"Sloane!"

I kept walking, pretending I hadn't heard Jason yell my name.

"Sloane!" A hand brushed the back of my arm.

I spun around.

His eyes widened as he took in my fitted top.

"Hey, Jason."

He bit his lip. "You came."

I glanced over his shoulder at the girl in the silver dress. She was smiling at me. Not like I was someone who'd just interrupted her dance. Like she knew me.

I blinked. It took me a second to realize it was Kylie. I hadn't recognized her without the tortoiseshell glasses from her diner uniform.

She scooped me into a hug. "The boys told me you weren't coming but I'm so glad you made it!" She released me and patted Jason's arm. "This one needs a new dance partner. I've been hogging him too much tonight."

Jason opened his mouth but I spoke first. "Where's Sawyer?"

Jason pursed his lips. "In the bathroom."

"I should probably check on him," Kylie said. "Wanna come?"

218

Being part of a group check-in on Sawyer in the bathroom wasn't exactly something I'd imagined doing at prom, but I nodded at the serious expression that fell over Jason's face.

I followed them out a side door I'd noticed when I first arrived to the hallway where the bathrooms were. Just as the door clicked shut behind me, it opened again, music blaring into the hall, as Livie and Oliver joined us.

"We saw you heading this way. Is it check-in time again?" Livie leaned against the wall and slid down to a sitting position. "My feet are killing me."

"Geez, Sawyer."

I turned toward Jason's irritated voice and gasped.

Sawyer was slumped against the wall opposite Livie, half sitting, half lying down, his skin pale and clammy.

Jason glanced down the hall toward the front of the building, where a single turn separated us from the lobby where Principal Thompson was stationed, then back at Sawyer. "You promised you'd stay *in* the bathroom."

I squatted in front of Sawyer, careful to face away from the camera I'd spied at the end of the hall. "Are you okay?"

His eyes were slow to focus on me. "Do you...have a name?" The words came out sluggish and slurred. "Or can I call you—" he lifted a clumsy hand and tried to point at himself "—*mine*?"

I stood and took a step back. He wasn't sick—he was drunk.

I stared at Kylie, who was shaking her head at Sawyer. "Did he drive here like this?"

"He was totally sober when he picked me up."

"Ha. Ha. Ha." Sawyer's laugh came out more like individual words as he tried to point at himself again.

A muscle in Jason's jaw tensed. "We didn't know he brought a flask with him."

"Crash and burn," Livie said without looking up from her phone.

Oliver leaned over and offered a bottle of water to Sawyer, who winced. "By the time they announced prom king and queen," he said as he straightened, "Sawyer was smashed."

What was Sawyer thinking? It was one thing to have a drink when you were at a hotel and not going anywhere for the night, like I saw Sawyer do on the senior trip, but getting so drunk during a school dance that you couldn't even stand or figure out a way to get home was just plain stupid.

Sawyer tried to sit up and groaned. "I'm…" His eyes fluttered closed before he could say anything else.

Oliver frowned. "Maybe we should get him out of here before he gets in trouble."

Jason nodded. "I was just thinking the same thing." He looked at Kylie. "Would you mind if we left now?"

"No, of course not."

He faced me. "How'd you get here? Do you need a ride?"

I shook my head. "I drove."

His eyes darted to Livie and back again. "But you're still coming to my house later, right? For the party?"

"Um, yeah."

"You're welcome too, Kylie, but I'm bringing Sawyer home with me so…"

Kylie snorted. "I think I'm ready to call it a Sawyer-free night." She wiggled her bare toes. "Just let me go find my shoes in that massive discarded shoe mountain in there, which should only take, oh, a half hour or so."

Jason chuckled. "I'll send a search party if you don't return."

The *thump, thump, thump* of another song filled the hall as Kylie walked through the door to the ballroom.

"Ooh, this is a good song." Livie stood and took Oliver's hand. "Let's go dance."

Oliver nodded at Jason. "You need help with Sawyer?"

"No, I'm just going to sneak him out the side door." Jason pointed to an exit halfway down the hall. "See you at my place later?"

"Sure." Oliver grinned and pointed at me. "And you need to save me a dance. I can't leave prom without dancing with the prettiest flip-flop-and-purple-sequin-wearing girl here."

A cloying smile formed on Livie's lips as she latched on to Oliver's arm. "I told you that top was made for you. If it had fit me—" she glanced at her own chest, then at my noticeably smaller chest "—I would've snatched it up for myself." She pulled Oliver into the ballroom and waved over her shoulder.

I stared after them. Even with the muffled sounds from the dance, the hall seemed oddly quiet now that the people and explanations and backhanded compliments were gone.

I ran my hands down my jeans and peeked at Sawyer, who looked like he was sleeping. I could feel Jason's closeness, feel his heat filling the space between us, the weight of his eyes on me. I swallowed. "You were dancing with Kylie because Sawyer couldn't."

Jason's voice was soft. "Yeah. Oliver did too, but...yeah."

I glanced at him. He stood a foot away, studying me.

The echoes of prom music shifted to something softer and slower. Jason held out a hand in my direction. "Do you want to dance?"

The nervous, vulnerable expression on his face exactly matched the one he wore that night so long ago under the stars. *You're Sloane*, I reminded myself. *You don't know that.* But I couldn't *not* remember. That look tugged at my heart, and I placed my hand in his. *Just once, for old times' sake.*

He pulled me close, wrapping both hands around my back. It was more of a hug than a slow dance, but I couldn't make myself pull away. Instead I wound my arms around his neck.

"I've been debating the best way to say this." Jason's voice was just a whisper in my ear. "There's something I was going to show you later at my house and let it speak for itself. But this?" His arms tightened the tiniest bit around me. "This might be better."

I could feel his heart pounding in his chest.

"Because I'm not sure how you're going to react and if I'm holding you, it might be harder for you to run away."

I grew very still.

He pulled back and searched my face. I'd never been this close to him before, so close I could see every swirl of blue and green in those eyes I loved. He rested his forehead against mine and took a deep breath. "I—"

"I forgot my phone."

Jason jumped away from me at the sound of Livie's voice.

Livie was standing by the still-closing ballroom door with a blank expression. I hadn't even registered the increase in sound until she spoke, but now everything was too loud, too harsh compared to Jason's whispers.

Livie wordlessly crossed to where she'd been sitting and grabbed her phone off the floor. She hesitated for a moment, her back to us, then whirled on Jason. "I can't believe you."

"Livie," he warned.

"Don't *Livie* me. You *promised* me there was nothing going on between you two. Twice. When you broke up with me *and* when you chased me down at the hotel and told me you missed me." Her voice rose. "I deleted that picture because you said there was no chance you'd *ever* date her." Livie stepped closer to Jason, her eyes narrowing. "You said you felt *sorry* for her because she didn't have any other friends. You thought she had *serious issues* because of how she freaked out when Oliver sang to her and never wanted to go out on weekends and made up all that shit with the cop at the carousel."

My mouth dropped open.

Livie poked a finger into Jason's chest. "You are so going to regret lying to me. And you." She faced me. "Some friend you are."

"I didn't…"

Livie spun on her heels and stormed down the hall into the lobby.

Jason rushed after her. "Livie, wait!"

I stared at the carpet, my cheeks hot. Tears pricked my eyes. *He thinks I have* issues. *He hates the girl I used to be and thinks the girl I am now is a freak. And he* misses *Livie. What was I thinking, dancing with him like that?* I took a step toward the ballroom door and found Oliver standing in the hall. He must've come out at some point during Livie's rant.

"Is that what's been going on?" He glanced toward the lobby. "Livie and Jason are still hung up on each other and she's trying to make him jealous? Is that why she asked me to prom?" His voice was timid and unsure. Something shifted in his eyes and he frowned. "Did you know that's what she was doing?"

I shook my head and moved toward him. He took a step back.

"What picture was she talking about?"

I ran my hands over my face. "She found Jason and me asleep in my hotel room on the senior trip."

Oliver's eyes widened.

"Not like that. Fully clothed, sitting up, on top of the covers. I had a nightmare and I was screaming and he came to check on me. She got mad and took a picture, but I didn't think... She thought you were *better* than Jason. And she was coming back from *your* room, after you two... I didn't know..." But I did know. I saw the gleam that flashed in Livie's eyes when she decided to ask Oliver to prom to show Jason what he was missing. I knew something happened between Livie and Jason after Livie took the picture. And I knew Oliver could read it on my face.

He opened his mouth and shut it without saying anything. Then he tried again. "Nothing happened with Livie on the senior trip. She asked if she could come to my room so we could *talk*. My roommate was there the whole time. We've never even kissed."

I closed my eyes.

"I only started spending time with her because she seemed sad about the breakup and I knew what that felt like. That's why I said yes to her prom invitation too, not because I was into her. I would've been fine coming by myself or hanging out with you."

I knew he didn't want anything serious after being hurt by

Chloe and her games. And I never warned him about how Livie liked to play games too.

"I really like being your friend, Sloane," Oliver continued. "And, as my friend, you should've told me what was going on. Remember 'points for being honest'? And for the record, I want you to know I *never* would've said things like what Jason said about you. That's not how friends treat each other."

I didn't move as the ballroom door opened and Oliver's footsteps faded away.

"Found them!"

My eyes snapped open. Kylie was standing in the exact spot Oliver had just left, dangling a pair of black heels from one finger. She scanned the hall. "Where's Jason?"

"Oh...um." I had no idea what just happened, or if Jason was even coming back, but I was ready to get the hell out of there and I wasn't going to leave Kylie stranded. "Change of plans. Jason had to help Livie with something so I'm going to take you home, okay?"

She smiled. "Sure."

She'd just taken a step toward me when something shifted in my peripheral vision. *Sawyer.* With all the dancing and revelations and people storming off, I'd completely forgotten he was there.

I looked down. Just as he lifted his head and vomited on me.

TWENTY

Flip-flops and really drunk boys don't mix.

"Oh my God." Kylie's hands covered her mouth like she couldn't believe what happened, but her eyes were shining, like she was trying not to laugh.

I swallowed hard. Luckily my jeans saved me from the worst of it, but still. "You know," I said, locking eyes with Kylie, "they weren't kidding when they said this was going to be 'A Night to Remember.'"

A muffled giggle escaped her.

I shook my head and started laughing. "It's so disgusting I have to laugh or I'm going to be sick too."

Sawyer groaned, his eyes still closed.

"He doesn't even know what he just did!" Kylie wiped a tear away from one eye. "This whole night is so awful, it's funny."

I stepped out of my flip-flops. "I am never wearing those again." We both broke into another round of giggles as I picked them up and tossed them in the trash can by the bathrooms. I pointed at the girls' room. "Just give me a second."

I sat on the bathroom counter and with a ridiculous amount of soap, cleaned myself better than a doctor prepping for surgery. But when I came out of the bathroom a minute later, my wet jeans rolled up to my calves, it was like I'd also washed away my ability to laugh at it all. Even Kylie seemed more serious as I stood next to her, both of us staring down at Sawyer.

"We could leave him here," she said without malice. "He ignored me most of the night and drunk-flirted with every girl he saw and threw up on you. I've heard of girls abandoning dates for lesser things than that. If we tipped off one of the chaperones, he'd be safe here until they found him."

I considered it, but prom was a school event, which meant school rules applied. And being caught this drunk had to come with some serious consequences. Maybe even serious enough to involve the police. I shifted, keeping my back to the camera at the end of the hall. "You get one arm, I'll get the other?"

"Sounds like a plan."

"You're lucky I wasn't in the mood to meet your parents tonight, Sawyer."

A snore from the backseat of the car was his only response.

After driving Kylie home, with Sawyer passed out in the back the entire way, I'd thought about trying to track down his address so I could dump his drunken butt on his doorstep and ring the doorbell. But I didn't want to chance someone seeing me and then having to explain to his parents not only who I was, but why I was lugging their comatose son to their front door barefoot. And honestly, the detective work involved in finding his address seemed like too much trouble when all I wanted was to get home and take off my gross wet jeans.

So I headed for Jason's. He was supposed to be having people over after prom. Who knew if anyone was actually still coming, but his mom didn't know that. If she heard a noise outside, she probably wouldn't come investigating. At least, not before I could sneak away.

I glanced at the dashboard clock as I turned onto Jason's street. There were still fifteen minutes until prom ended. That was plenty of time to leave Sawyer on the porch and get out before anyone—especially Jason—showed up. I was dreaming of warm showers and comfy socks as I pulled into Jason's empty driveway.

I opened the back door and shook Sawyer's leg. When he didn't stir, I tried again. "Sawyer." I leaned in and smacked his cheek, maybe a little harder than necessary.

His eyes flew open. "Wha—"

"Come on."

His wide eyes focused on me.

"We're at Jason's and I can't carry you by myself. You have to help me."

Sawyer managed to fold himself out of the car and get an arm wrapped around my shoulder. I sagged a bit under his weight, but his steps were steadier than when Kylie and I practically dragged him to Mark's car.

Halfway up the path to Jason's front door, Sawyer lurched to the side, leaning over like he was going to be sick again. I scraped my foot on the rough concrete as I held him steady, but he straightened almost immediately. "False alarm."

I peeked at my foot, a raw line running along one side. "Super."

I hesitated when we reached Jason's porch, trying to decide where to put Sawyer so he could fall asleep again and not roll over and hurt himself. *Why didn't I get a lesson on how to handle drunk boys?* Before I could set him down, the front door swung open.

Jason's mom stood on the threshold in yoga pants and a faded blue Atlantic City T-shirt I recognized as one Jason's dad used to wear around the house. Her brown hair was knotted messily at the nape of her neck and she had a dusting of flour on her cheek. She smiled. "I was walking by and thought I heard footsteps out here." Then she noticed the way Sawyer was leaning against me. "Oh." Her gaze swept over Sawyer's still-too-pale skin, my rolled-up jeans, the scratch on my foot where tiny drops of blood were beading, and I saw the moment it clicked in her eyes. *"Oh."* She rushed to Sawyer's other side. "Let me help."

We squeezed through the door. "Um, sorry about lurking on your porch. I didn't…" *What? Think you'd be awake? Want you to catch us? Want to see you after what happened at the bakery?* There was no good way to finish that sentence.

"Don't worry about it," she said as she glanced around the living room, then pointed. "Basement." After shuffling Sawyer down the stairs, she peeked at me around his torso. "Couch or bathroom?"

"Bathroom. Definitely."

Despite overhearing Jason convince his mom I wasn't really me, fear edged its way into my chest as we passed the pictures in the hall leading to the bathroom. I avoided the one of my mom, focusing instead on keeping my foot balanced so I wouldn't spill any blood on the carpet. Jason's mom eased Sawyer onto the bathroom floor.

"I think I'm feeling better." It was mumbled, but it sounded more like Sawyer's usual voice.

"That's wonderful, Sawyer," Jason's mom said as she tucked a towel under his head. "That means you and I can have a nice long chat very soon about your choices tonight."

Sawyer squeezed his eyes shut and groaned. "Still. Woozy."

"Nice try." Jason's mom shook her head and motioned for me to follow her back to the rec room. "Where's Jason? Was he…" She gestured to the bathroom.

"Oh. *No.* Jason wasn't drinking at all. He's…with Livie. But I'm sure he'll be here soon. People are coming over, right? But not me. I mean, I can't stay." *Why are you babbling?* "I'm just going to go." I took a step toward the stairs.

"It's Sloane, right?"

My heart stopped. "Yes."

"Well, Sloane, Sawyer smells like the back alley of a bar and I'm assuming the rolled-up pants and lack of shoes aren't a fashion statement." She smiled. "I think you've at least earned a bandage before you go."

"It's really not a bad scratch."

"Then it will only take a second to clean up. I'll be right back." She disappeared down the hall past the bathroom.

I eyed the stairs, wondering whether I should make a run for it, but decided the girl she thought I was, a girl who wasn't concerned about hiding her past, would wait for the bandage and then leave.

"Here you go," Jason's mom said a minute later. She was holding a box of bandages, a tube of antiseptic ointment, and a pair of fuzzy blue socks.

The fuzzy socks did me in.

Jason's mom gave a little laugh at what must've been longing in my eyes. "I thought so. I'm going to see if I can find some pants you can change into also." She was up the steps before I could stop her.

I cleaned my scratch and covered it with a bandage. I wasn't sticking around for a whole new outfit, but the warmth of the socks as I slid them onto my feet made my still-damp jeans so much more tolerable.

Jason's mom reappeared with a pair of gray sweatpants and what looked like two chocolate chip cookies on a plate. "I have a totally selfish reason for bringing you baked goods," she said as she placed the plate on the coffee table in front of me. "I've been testing out a new recipe to keep myself awake and I need someone to be my taste tester. Are you up for the job?"

I was already thinking up polite excuses when she continued.

"Plus, I thought it might give us a moment to talk."

I tensed.

She gave me a sheepish grin and sat on the couch next to me. "I was actually waiting for you to show up tonight. Jase told me you were coming."

My heart jumped into my throat. "You were?"

She nodded. "I feel like I should explain what happened the other day."

"Oh no, Ms. Thomas. There's no need—"

She held up a hand. "Please call me Stacy. That's what Jase's friends have always called me."

Actually, when we were little we called you Mrs. Stacy, but who's counting? "Okay, Stacy. There's nothing to explain."

She was silent as she grabbed a cookie, broke off a tiny piece, and chewed it thoughtfully. "Jason had a really good friend when he was younger," she said once she'd swallowed. "Someone I was certain was going to be a part of his life, one way or another, for a *really* long time."

I stared at the coffee table, wanting a happy ending to her story, but I already knew what happened next.

"Then one day there was a family tragedy and she moved away suddenly. We haven't seen her since."

I closed my eyes. "I'm sorry to hear that."

Stacy sighed. "It was a rough time, but for Jase in particular."

I fiddled with the remaining cookie on the plate. "Really?"

"He became so withdrawn, which wasn't like him at all. Stopped making bets, stopped letting anyone in his room." I glanced up to see Stacy shaking her head. "Things got better after we moved here. I think it was easier for him not to be reminded of her everywhere he looked, you know?"

I nodded. I was very familiar with the effectiveness of a change of scenery as a coping mechanism.

"You look like her," Stacy admitted. "That's why I reacted the way I did at the bakery. I'm sorry if I startled you."

More than anything in the house, the sound of Stacy's voice made me miss my mom the most. Their voices were tangled together in so much of my childhood that it almost felt like I could be sitting with my mom instead. My voice was rougher than I wanted when I said, "You don't have to apologize."

I wasn't sure what else to say, how else to push those feelings away, so I took a bite of my cookie. "Mmm."

She smiled widely. "Do you like it?"

"Yeah. It's got..." I tried to identify the slightly unusual flavor I tasted. Then I remembered one of Mark's recent baking adventures. "Avocado."

She raised an eyebrow. "I'm impressed."

"My dad's been on a health kick lately. Hey, if you put these in the bakery, you could sell them as healthy."

Stacy grinned. "I like your thinking. I may have to keep you around." Her eyes danced. "I know Jase would like to."

"I'm sorry?"

"He'd kill me for telling you this, but he talks about you all the time."

Yeah, because he thinks I have issues.

"He thinks I don't know about all the dates he goes on." She tsked. "I never worried though, because the fact he never talked about those girls told me all I needed to know. And don't even get me started on Livie. But you?" She placed her hand on top of mine. "*You* he talks about."

I studied Stacy's hand. That same hand taught me how to bake brownies and plant flowers, hunt for shells and write cursive, make friendship bracelets and play tennis. All the times Jason's mom had touched me lingered on my skin and I had to blink back tears because it felt too real. Except I was Sloane.

Stacy squeezed my hand and I looked up. "Just do me a favor, okay?"

I nodded.

"Be gentle with his heart. I can't watch him go through another loss like that again, S—"

Footsteps thundered down the stairs and I jumped up. Jason burst into the basement, his shoulders sagging the moment he spotted me. His gaze darted to the tiny amount of space between his mom and me, then back to me.

"I've been looking everywhere for you. I couldn't find you

at prom so I called Kylie, but she wasn't sure where you were going after you left her house."

Stacy took a few steps in his direction. "Jase."

"I need to explain," Jason continued as if his mom hadn't spoken. "What Livie said, I didn't…"

My cheeks grew hot as all the things he'd said to Livie about me came rushing back. *I should've gotten out of here when I had the chance.*

"Jason."

His back stiffened. Even my stomach twisted at the familiar too-calm voice Stacy used when she was particularly upset. He looked at her for the first time since rushing into the room.

She inclined her head toward the steps. "Can I have a word upstairs, please, about why Sloane was hauling your drunk best friend here by herself?"

Jason closed his eyes for half a second then turned to me. "Just… I'll be right back."

I waited until Jason and his mom were all the way up the stairs before I started moving. Stacy had gone somewhere down the hall past Jason's room and the bathroom, and I was going to find out where. There had to be another way out of this basement.

I spun around and startled.

Sawyer was slumped against the entrance to the bathroom hall, eyes bloodshot. "I heard what Livie said back at prom, when I was on the floor. All those things J was just trying to apologize for." The corners of his mouth turned up. "He's not so great now, is he?"

Something about the sight of him enjoying my embarrassment in a wrinkled, halfway unbuttoned tuxedo shirt made me snap. "What is wrong with you?"

Sawyer retreated a few steps.

I came straight at him down the hallway. "You asked me to come to prom because you were trying to make it more fun for Kylie, and then you get drunk off your ass? That's not how to show a girl a special night, Sawyer. You're not so great either."

He backed into the bathroom and stumbled into the sink. His eyes grew dark. "You want to know what's wrong with me?" he asked, stepping closer to where I was hovering in the bathroom's doorway. "*Jason*, that's what. He did what he always does, Mr. Knight-in-Shining-Armor. Dancing with Kylie at prom, offering to drive her home. I know what he's up to."

I threw my hands up. "Jason danced with her and offered to drive her because you were too drunk to!"

"Are you seriously defending him right now? After what Livie said he said about you?"

I pursed my lips.

"Why do girls think he's so great?" Sawyer half fell, half sat on the closed toilet. A clump of red hair flopped onto his forehead. "It's like Livie all over again." He looked up at me with watery, pitiful eyes. "Did you know I liked Livie when she first moved here? I thought she was into me too. We slept together." He threw his hands out to the side as if to say, *Means she likes me, right?*

An image of Livie in the bathroom the day after Jason broke up with her, calling Sawyer a "moment of weakness," flashed in my head. I already knew where Sawyer was going with this.

"Then, as she was getting dressed, Livie told me we couldn't tell anyone. That it was a *mistake* and Jason could never know because then she wouldn't stand a chance with him." Sawyer sniffed and shook his head. "It hadn't even been five minutes and I was a mistake."

I stood in front of him and sighed. "That was a shitty thing for Livie to say, Sawyer. And if you want my opinion, she's not a nice person. You could do a lot *better*," I added, using the word everyone here seemed to use. "I think Kylie's a lot better."

"*Kylie*. She probably thinks I was a mistake too. She's probably at home dreaming of *Jason*."

"Not if you do something about it. Call her and apologize. *After* you sober up."

"Yeah." Sawyer was silent for a moment before he repeated, "Yeah. I need to do something about it." He stood and stalked out of the bathroom, ricocheting off the door frame as he passed.

I followed Sawyer down the hall, trying to figure out what he was planning to do—I definitely wasn't letting him drive anywhere in his condition—only to find Jason rushing down the stairs by himself. His eyes locked on mine and I shifted, eyeing the easiest route around him and out of the room. *Sawyer can be his problem now.*

"Please just let me explain." Jason blocked my path to the stairs. "What Livie said wasn't what it sounded like." He never took his eyes off me, which was why he didn't see Sawyer barreling toward him until it was too late.

Sawyer planted his hands on Jason's chest and shoved with

all his drunken might. Jason stumbled backward, but caught himself before he fell over.

I froze, hesitating between escaping or breaking up whatever was about to happen with the boys.

Jason stared at Sawyer. "What's your problem?"

"You," Sawyer replied, his voice icy. "*You* are my problem." He lunged at Jason. It was slow and uncoordinated, and Jason easily dodged out of the way.

"What the hell, Sawyer?"

Sawyer spun around and faced Jason. "I am so sick and tired of watching you steal every girl I like. Every. Single. Girl."

Jason's stance looked casual, but the muscles in his arms were strained. "What are you talking about?"

"Anna Kaplan in eighth grade, Courtney McManus sophomore year." Sawyer ticked the names off on his fingers. "Sammy Hayes."

Jason's mouth dropped open. "*She* asked me to homecoming. I never knew you liked her."

"That's because you don't think about anyone else. You swoop in with your *hair* and your *charm* and you make it impossible for the rest of us. Just like you did tonight with Kylie."

"I wasn't trying to steal Kylie away from you. I felt bad for her because she was stuck at a dance with nobody she knew while you were puking." Jason shook his head. "I didn't make Kylie impossible for you, Sawyer. You did that all on your own."

Sawyer growled and plowed into Jason, knocking him off his feet.

"Guys, stop!" I stepped toward them, searching for a way to pull them apart without getting hit by the tangle of arms and legs flying around, but Jason was back on his feet before I could do anything.

"Don't blame me for your own stupidity, Sawyer," he panted.

Sawyer stood slowly. He touched a finger to the corner of his mouth and pulled it away, staring at the blood on his fingertip. "What about Livie?"

Jason threw his arms up. "What about Livie?"

Sawyer cut his eyes from the blood to Jason. The corners of his mouth rose in a cruel sneer. "I slept with her."

The words had their desired effect. Surprise flashed in Jason's eyes before they hardened. He leaned forward, ready to spring.

I rushed between them with my arms spread wide, trying to keep them apart. "It was a while ago, before you and Livie got together," I told Jason. "Last fall."

A strange expression, like something clicking into place, flickered on Jason's face. He looked at me. "You knew?"

"I found out after you and Livie broke up. I didn't want—"

"I liked her first," Sawyer whispered. "And you made her want you instead."

I turned my head to Sawyer, arms still outstretched. "Go lie down somewhere and sleep this off, Sawyer. You're not thinking straight."

Jason sighed. "Jesus, Sawyer. If this is about Livie, you can—"

"It's *not* about Livie," Sawyer snapped. "It's about you always getting what you want. You want Kylie now? Fine. Then I'm taking Sloane."

My whole body tensed.

Jason took a step forward, his chest brushing against my fingertips. "She's a person, not something you can just *take*."

Sawyer barked out a single harsh laugh. "Oh really?"

I dropped my arms, watching Sawyer through narrow eyes, waiting to see what he meant.

"*I* bought her lunch that first day. *I* offered to give her a ride when we were decorating T-shirts. And what did you do? The very next day you picked her as your scavenger hunt partner. You made this *grand gesture* of surprising her at the carousel. You broke up with Livie." He wiped the corner of his mouth with his sleeve, leaving a trail of blood on his white tuxedo shirt. "You *took* Sloane away from me, like all the other girls."

I balled my hands into fists. "He didn't take me away from you, Sawyer. I'm not interested in you. I *told* you that. I set you up with Kylie so you would understand that."

"And he went and stole her too!"

"I wasn't trying to steal Kylie. I don't care about Kylie." Jason's voice was so tight I turned to face him, worried he might be about to hit Sawyer.

Sawyer shifted behind me. "There was one thing different with Sloane though. One quick, but *oh so sweet*, thing that didn't happen with any of the other girls."

Jason's face went scary still.

Sawyer wasn't touching me, but I knew he was close. It was the sour smell of the alcohol on his breath, the charge in the air between us, the way the hair on the back of my neck stood up. Every inch of me wanted to move away, to turn and confront him. But my self-defense lessons taught me it was better to wait and make my move at the right moment.

Sawyer leaned close and trailed his fingertips down my bare left arm. His breath was hot on my neck. "Tell me, J. How does it feel to know I kissed Sloane first?"

I grabbed Sawyer's wrist with my right hand, pulled his arm across my chest, and flipped him over my shoulder in one impossibly fast movement. He hit the ground with a loud *smack*.

For a few seconds, Sawyer stared at the ceiling, dazed. But he didn't stay down for long. He rolled over onto his knees, shaking his head slightly, and got to his feet. When his eyes met mine, they were cold and calculating. Then he lunged at me.

Faster than I could react, Jason jumped in front of Sawyer and punched him so hard his teeth clicked together as his head snapped back. Blood gushed out of Sawyer's nose and he dropped to the floor. His chest was moving up and down, but he was out cold.

I covered my mouth with my hands as Jason bent over Sawyer, making sure he could breathe. *How did this night go so wrong so quickly?* I'd promised to be gentle with Jason's heart. Instead, I was screwing everything up for him. I'd set Livie off and apparently I'd been causing problems between her and Jason for a while. Jason and Sawyer were literally *attacking* each other because Sawyer thought he had some sort of prior claim on me and tried to use me to get back at Jason. And to top it all off, I'd just done a fairly advanced jujitsu throw on his best friend that your average eighteen-year-old girl probably wouldn't know.

No wonder Jason thought I was a freak.

I spun on my heels and raced for the stairs. I needed to get out. *Out of this house, out of this town, out of this way-too-complicated life.*

"Wait!" Jason's fingers gently circled my wrist as my foot hit the first step. "Don't go."

I couldn't look at him. "It's too much, Jase. I can't…" I

closed my mouth before I said something I shouldn't. "I need to go." I turned and tried to smile. "I'll see you later, okay?"

Jason's eyes grew wide. "No." He glanced at Sawyer, who had already stopped bleeding, then back at me. "I—I have to show you something. Two minutes. That's all I'm asking for." He released my wrist and held his hands up, making it clear it was my choice. "Two minutes," he repeated. "If you want to leave after that, I won't try to stop you."

I'd never seen his eyes so wild before. Or so beautiful. "What could possibly be that important right now?"

"It's in my room. Come on."

I hesitated. Jason didn't let anyone in his room. Except, apparently, me. I closed my eyes. "Two. Minutes." I'd meant it as a reminder, a warning that I wasn't staying. I just wasn't sure if I was trying to remind Jason or myself.

I breathed in the unmistakable *Jason* smell as the door to his room clicked closed behind me. My eyes skimmed over a bed with navy sheets, a window easy to climb out of, a soccer ball resting in a corner, a plate dusted with crumbs, a trophy sitting on a low dresser, a photo of his parents. My breath caught in my throat as my gaze returned to the trophy. I wasn't close enough to read the piece of paper covering the plaque, but I knew what it said: #1 Best Superstar at Everything.

Jason's voice was rough behind me. "Please don't leave me again, Sasha."

TWENTY-ONE

Fear crept down my spine at hearing my real name for the first time in almost six years. Someone knew who I really was.

I stared at the trophy, searching for a way out. Behind it, tacked to the wall, were three pictures. Two of me and Jason growing up: him making a silly face behind my back at my dance recital; and the two of us covered in bubbles the day we'd gotten in trouble for washing his dad's car with the windows down. And in between those two, one of me talking to Oliver in the lunch line. Jason must've taken it when I wasn't looking. Surrounded by the other photos, it was so obvious I was the same person. Silent tears ran down my face. I hadn't fooled him for a second.

"I've known the whole time," Jason said softly behind me.

I turned and opened my mouth, but nothing came out.

When Jason saw my tears, he wrapped his arms around me, cocooning me in his cookie-and-cologne smell. "Did you really think I wouldn't recognize you?" He pulled back so he could see my face. "Just because you grew up gorgeous and came here with a different name and different eyes?" He shook his head. "You could dye your hair pink and get contacts to match and I'd still know it was you." He placed a finger above my heart, the heat from it radiating through my chest. "I know what's in here. I'd always recognize that."

A lump formed in my throat. It wasn't just *someone* who knew who I was. It was *Jason*. "But you didn't say anything."

"I knew it was you but I didn't know what was going on. You weren't using your real name, you were acting like you didn't know me. So I played along and tried to figure things out. And then you were late for the scavenger hunt on your second day." He rested his forehead against mine. "I thought I'd lost you again. I thought you'd left." He chuckled and stepped back. "I practically chewed off my entire nail waiting to see if you'd show up. I was so relieved when you called my name, I promised myself right then and there that I'd do whatever I had to to get you to stay."

I shook my head. "But what about what you told your mom at the bakery?"

Realization flickered in his eyes. "Is that why you left?"

I studied the pictures of us as kids. "You said you'd never forgive me."

"I didn't mean it. I knew you didn't want to be recognized. I only said that to convince my mom you weren't…you."

"You're not mad?" I hadn't realized I was holding my breath until the words were out.

Jason brushed a lock of hair behind my ear. "Oh, I'm mad. I'm mad I lost so much time with you. I'm mad I don't know what happened to the mole on your neck. I'm mad I missed you somehow becoming actually good at basketball."

I cracked a smile.

"But I'm not mad at you. I've never been mad at you. I've always just wanted you back."

I exhaled slowly. All this time I thought I'd been fooling Jason when really, I'd been fooling myself. The relief that flowed through me told me the truth: I'd needed him to know who I really was.

Jason rubbed the back of his neck. "I tried giving you clues so you'd know I knew it was you."

I frowned. "What clues?"

"I took you to the Kissing Tree with our same initials carved into it, like I did that one spring."

I gave Jason an *Are you serious?* look. "That was on your scavenger hunt list. It was a coincidence, not a clue."

"I drew our made-up superhero symbol on the scavenger hunt shirts."

"That was a clue? It was *your* made-up symbol. You used it every time you played superheroes with anyone."

Jason's mouth twitched. "Okay, fine. What about the ear pulling?"

I laughed. "Jase, come on! You and your dad did that to everyone. That's not a clue. That's just annoying."

Jason grinned and took a step closer to me. "I took you to a *carousel*. With *rings*. On your *birthday*."

My smile vanished. "Sawyer told me it was his idea to go there. He said he wanted to do something special for me."

Jason glanced over his shoulder at his closed door, as if he could see Sawyer through it. "I can't believe he…" He turned back to me with a fierce expression. "You should go to the cops. He kissed you when you didn't want him to. He was about to *attack* you. That has to be assault or something."

I ran my thumb gingerly over the knuckles on Jason's right hand. They were red and raw. "I can't do that," I said without looking up.

"Why not?"

"Because the police can't get involved."

Jason placed a finger under my chin and pushed up until I was looking directly at him. The longing and concern and desire in his eyes almost undid me. "Where have you been, Sasha?"

I held his gaze. "I can't tell you."

"You can trust me. I thought we established that on the senior trip."

A vision of Lorenzo Rosetti in an orange polo shirt, holding a gun and glaring at me, flashed in my head. "It's not that I don't trust you, Jase. The less you know, the safer you are."

Jason took a deep breath and searched my eyes. "Okay," he said after a long moment. "If that's how it has to be for you to stay, I can deal with not knowing." He crossed to his bed, sat back against the headboard like he had in my hotel room during the senior trip, and patted the spot next to him.

I mirrored his position, staring at the trophy we'd loved as kids.

He slipped his hand into mine. "I'm sorry about your mom. I went to her funeral. Tons of people showed up."

I took a shaky breath. I'd always wondered what her funeral was like.

"My mom had that couple from church your mom liked so

much sing during the service," Jason continued. There was a long pause before he spoke again. "I wouldn't leave the casket. When it was all over, I mean. I'd convinced myself that you were going to show up, just sneak in so you could say goodbye and sneak back out. I thought if I didn't take my eyes off the casket, I wouldn't miss you. Your aunt told me you and your dad weren't coming. She said you were taking things really hard and couldn't handle the funeral. Everyone said you were moving away."

I nodded. That fit with the cover story the Marshals created.

"But I didn't believe them. I didn't believe you'd miss the funeral, no matter how hard it was. But then the casket was in the ground and you still hadn't shown up. My mom sat with me for hours at the cemetery before she could convince me to leave."

I rested my head against Jason's shoulder. "I wanted to be there. I never wanted to leave."

He rested his head against the top of mine. "I never stopped looking for you. I Googled your name all the time. I've spent more hours than you could imagine searching random pictures on the internet for you."

"You wouldn't have been able to find anything."

"Yeah." His laugh was more of a sigh. "No pictures."

"No pictures," I agreed.

Jason brushed his thumb along the back of my hand. "What happened to your dad?"

My heart jumped. This was venturing awfully close to can't-talk-about-it territory. "How do you know he's not here with me?"

"Remember that night we got the Mexican food and you came over and watched the movie and told me I'd been busy the night before?"

"Yeah."

"Well, I hadn't only broken up with Livie the night before. My aunt Jill is a real estate agent and I used her database password to look up which houses had been rented or bought in the past six months that were walking distance from mine."

I stared at him.

"You didn't drive to my house that first day after school," he explained with a shrug. "Anyway, there was only one rental I thought would've worked. So I did a stakeout. And saw you and a guy in the window who looked nothing like your dad."

I couldn't believe he'd taken a picture of me and watched my house without me knowing. "I never realized you had an inner Sherlock Holmes."

"Yup," Jason said. "He's good at tracking down rental properties in small beach towns and packing food for short-term stakeouts. He's also good at knowing when you're trying to dodge the question."

I hesitated. Not because I was trying to think of a way out of the question. Jason had already seen Mark, so I was going to have to tell him something. It was just that I'd never said the words out loud before. I took a deep breath. "My dad committed suicide."

"I didn't… Shit. That sucks."

I rested my head on his shoulder again.

Jason's voice was gentle when he asked, "What happened?"

That I definitely couldn't explain. I shook my head, knowing he would feel it against his shoulder.

"So who was that guy I saw at your house then?"

I gave him the truest, most simple answer I could: "He's my family."

Jason shifted a little and I could tell there were more questions building up inside of him. I decided to change the subject before they made their way out. "Can I ask you something?"

"Of course."

I lifted my head and looked into those deep blue eyes. "What's going on with you and Livie?"

Jason flipped my hand over and traced the veins under my wrist. I'd never had a single touch make me want to kiss someone so badly before.

"The thing with Livie," Jason said, "is that she shows you what she wants you to see. With me, that was the sweet friend who started having feelings for me."

Livie's words in the school bathroom popped into my head: *"Friends for a couple of months, then slowly show him I was interested, like I couldn't help developing feelings for my best friend."*

"And at first, things were good. Then, not so much. And I thought it was because of me." His fingers stilled on my wrist. "I knew I never took any of those first dates seriously, never gave anyone a real chance. And I thought that's what I was doing with Livie too." His voice dropped to a rough whisper. "I'd started to lose hope I was ever going to see you again and I *needed* to be able to forget you. So I promised myself I'd stick it out and try to make it work with Livie. And then you showed up."

Jason lifted his eyes to mine with that half smile that wrecked me.

"And there you were, making bets and racing me to the Kissing Tree and looking at me the way you are right now and…" He swallowed hard. "Jesus. When you look at me like that?" He closed his eyes for a second. "It was like everything came rushing back at once and I remembered how much I *didn't* want to forget you."

My heart felt like it was about to explode out of my chest.

"And when I ended things with Livie, she thought it was because of you. She said she'd seen the way I looked at you. So I told her what she needed to hear so she wouldn't blame you. With my mom, the only way to get her to stop asking whether you were Sasha was to make her believe I was upset about it. With Livie, the only way to stop her from taking her mean streak out on you was to make her believe I didn't have any feelings for you."

My stomach flipped.

"That's why I've been so distant since the senior trip. I had to lay it on thick after she took that picture of us at the hotel. I made her think I regretted ending things, that I was jealous after seeing her with Oliver. But I figured acting like I only liked you as a friend was a small price to pay for Livie deleting that picture."

I swallowed. "Acting?"

Jason ran his thumb over my cheekbone. "I thought I could keep my distance, at least until school was over and we didn't have to see Livie again. But it *killed* me walking away from you at the hotel without explaining why. I wanted to be the one sitting next to you on the bus ride home from the trip. I wanted to take you to prom. I wanted to be the one complimenting you tonight."

I shook my head slightly.

"Yes," Jason insisted. "Don't you get it? *You* are the girl I've been comparing everyone else to, Sasha. My best friend, the person who gets me better than anyone. That's what I want."

I closed my eyes. "Say my name again."

"Sasha."

Jason's breath tickled my lips, his mouth only inches from mine. I grabbed a fistful of his shirt, pulling him the rest of the way to me.

When we kissed, I knew there was no going back. I could pretend to be a thousand different girls, but none of them would ever be real. This was what was real. I was the girl who made bets and climbed through bedroom windows and ate themed snacks with the boy who'd given me the stars. It didn't matter what my name was, I was Sasha, and Jason had my heart.

So when I finally pulled away from him, breathless and dizzy from the amazing softness of his lips and the feeling of his hands against my skin, dread filled me. Because now, without any doubt, I'd broken the only rule I'd ever made for myself: don't have anything you can't leave behind.

TWENTY-TWO

I knew the moment Sawyer entered the hallway Monday morning by the way Jason tensed before pushing off the locker next to mine.

Sawyer paused when he spotted us, but squared his shoulders and kept walking in our direction. He was wearing cargo shorts and a frayed navy T-shirt that was slightly too small. His normally clean-cut hair was disheveled, making him look younger. The bruise spreading from the bridge of his nose to under his left eye made him seem fragile, almost breakable. And his eyes weren't cold anymore. They were filled with regret and shame and apologies. "I'm sorry," he said as soon as he was close enough.

Jason crossed his arms. "I can't— I don't want to do this right now, Sawyer."

Sawyer's shoulders slumped. "Look, I'm sorry, okay? I don't know what else to say. I was drunk and stupid and I wasn't thinking straight. I didn't mean it."

"You were about to hit her," Jason growled. He took a deep breath and turned to me. "Let's go."

Sawyer reached out as if to grab my arm but stopped himself, his hand hovering inches away from me. "I'm sorry, Sloane. I don't know why I came at you like that. I'd never actually hurt you."

I thought about his unwelcome kiss in the diner *right after* Jason told him I wasn't interested, the way he'd talked about me like a consolation prize for the taking, the creepy feeling of his fingertips trailing down my arm and his breath hot on my neck. "I'm not sure I believe that, Sawyer. No means no. It's a simple concept, but you don't seem to get it."

He hung his head as we walked away.

When we reached Jason's locker, he let out a long breath. "I don't even know what to think. I mean, he's always been a mean drunk. But we've been friends since the first day of eighth grade. Does he really think I purposefully stole every girl he's liked?"

"I don't know."

Jason stared at his feet. "There has to be some truth to it. He never could've just made that up when he was that drunk." He toed the edge of his locker. "Maybe it is true. I know it killed me every time he touched you. And did you see his face? God, I did that."

"Hey." I squeezed his hand until he looked at me. "You did that to protect me."

He pursed his lips.

"Did he say anything to you after I left your house Saturday night?"

"No. I told my mom he passed out and left him on the floor to sleep it off. He was gone by the time I woke up on Sunday."

I squeezed his hand again. "You don't have to figure it all out right now. There's time."

Jason moved to pull me into a hug but I stepped back and slid my hand out of his. "Livie might see," I whispered. "We don't need to antagonize her."

"Livie won't do anything."

I frowned. "I thought the whole plan was to make her think you didn't like me."

Jason stuffed a book into his locker and slammed it shut. "That was the plan when I broke up with her and when I got her to delete that picture. But that was before she saw me with my arms wrapped around you and wanting to kiss you so bad it hurt. There wasn't any way I was going to convince her I didn't like you after that." He leaned against his locker with a slight smirk. "So when I chased after her at prom, I used my ace in the hole."

"Your what?"

Jason glanced around and lowered his voice. "Livie's the one who made Chloe break up with Oliver."

I scratched my head. "I'm not following you at all."

"When Livie started here last fall, Chloe began picking on her. She was an easy target, the new girl with no friends yet. By the time Livie started hanging out with Sawyer and me, Chloe had moved from making fun of Livie's clothes to spreading rumors about her sleeping around with guys she barely knew. I assumed it was a lie, like all of Chloe's stories, but…" He shrugged one shoulder.

253

"But maybe she knew Livie and Sawyer slept together last fall?"

Jason nodded. "Chloe has a knack for learning secrets and talks crap about everyone, including me with my reputation. I learned a long time ago that she's only in it for the power trip. If she doesn't think she's getting to you, it's not fun to her anymore, you know? So I told Livie to ignore Chloe and act like it didn't bother her."

"Did it work?"

"I thought so. Chloe wasn't getting the reaction she wanted so she stopped. Things seemed calm between them for months. Then the night I broke up with Livie, we were hanging out in her room. She went to tell her parents something and her laptop dinged. We were waiting for an email from Sawyer so I assumed that's what it was." Jason pushed off his locker and took a step closer. "But when I went to read it, there was this email account open in some name I'd never seen Livie use. And the email that had just come in was from Chloe."

I raised an eyebrow.

"Exactly. It was this long email chain in which it was very obvious that Chloe had no idea who she was really talking to. And it all started with a photo Livie anonymously sent of Oliver kissing a blonde girl that definitely wasn't Chloe."

"But Oliver told me he didn't cheat on Chloe."

"He didn't," Jason said. "Not a lot of people know that Liv's a whiz when it comes to photo editing."

"I like to get creative with reality." I remembered Livie's words from my first day, when I'd seen her doctored sunset picture at Jason's house. "Wow."

Jason nodded. "I opened the editing software on her lap-

top to make sure. She had a picture of Oliver and Chloe kissing and a picture of some random blonde and somehow she
made a new picture that switched out Chloe for the blonde."

I peeked down the hall to make sure none of the people
we were talking about were within earshot. A middle-aged
woman in a navy suit walked past us, deep in conversation
with Principal Thompson, who was equally decked out in a
tailored charcoal gray suit and her usual stilettos. "So Livie
waited until no one would suspect her of seeking revenge on
Chloe, sent Chloe fake evidence that Oliver was being un-
faithful, and pretended not to know why they broke up?"

"Pretty much, yeah."

The shift in Livie's eyes when she decided to ask Oliver
to prom took on a whole new meaning. "And *then* she asked
Oliver out to get back at Chloe even more! That's so messed
up."

"I know," Jason agreed. "But when I saw that email, I was
thrilled. It felt like I was finally seeing the *real* Livie, not just
the one she wanted me to see. And I was going to call her on
it, use it as an example of why I was ending things. But then
I thought of you." He gave me a sexy grin he definitely didn't
have when we were twelve. "Which happens a lot, actually."

My cheeks grew warm.

"I knew Livie would be suspicious that you were the reason I was breaking up with her. And I figured it would be
good to have a little insurance in case she decided to get revenge on you the way she had on Chloe. So I didn't tell her
I saw the email."

Now I understood. "When you chased after Livie on prom

night, you told her that if she did anything mean to me you'd tell Chloe everything."

Jason stood a little taller. "Yup," he said with a grin.

"Did you tell Oliver?"

Jason's smiled faltered. "Not exactly. And before you say anything, I know he deserves to know how horrible Livie really is. But I told you I'd do whatever I had to to get you to stay. And if that includes blackmailing Livie and leaving Oliver in the dark for now, so be it."

Oliver's voice echoed in my head: *"Remember 'points for being honest'?"* I wasn't sure if he was mad at me after the semiargument we'd had at prom, but I needed to tell Oliver somehow. I frowned as a man in army fatigues strolled past us.

"We'll figure out a way to let him know," Jason promised. "After we're sure Livie's calmed down. But not now. Now all I want to do is this." He grabbed my hand. "And this." He tucked a lock of hair behind my ear. "And especially this." He leaned in and kissed my cheek, right by the corner of my mouth.

I blushed all the way to my toes.

"Do you know how often I've wanted to make you blush like that?" Jason whispered in my ear.

Movement in my peripheral vision made me pull away from Jason. Even though he felt confident about the Livie situation, I wouldn't be surprised if she had more tricks up her sleeve. We still needed to be careful around her. But it wasn't Livie I'd seen. A man with short salt-and-pepper hair stopped at the end of the hall next to the woman I'd seen earlier walking with Mrs. Thompson. They said a few quiet words to each other, then disappeared around the corner. "Okay. What's going on with all the weird adults here today?"

Jason pulled me down the hall toward the auditorium. "It's senior career day, remember?"

I groaned, then squeezed his hand. "Wait. Does that mean I don't have physics with Sawyer and Livie?"

He chuckled. "Yes. Instead you get to sit with me all morning while people describe *in great detail* what they studied after high school to get the delightful jobs they have today."

"That sounds perfect."

Jason gave me a disbelieving glance. "Really?"

"Not the detail part. The *with you* part."

"Are there a lot of seniors who want to be embalmers at mortuaries?" I asked as the balding man with glasses left the stage.

Jason shuddered. "There must be at least one. That's how they find the speakers for career day. Seniors fill out a questionnaire listing the types of careers they're interested in, and the counselors try to find representatives from as many of those careers as possible."

"I think I'll pass on that one."

Jason nodded his agreement as the man I'd seen in the hall with the short salt-and-pepper hair strode onto the stage. He adjusted his suit jacket and took a microphone from Mrs. Thompson. He cleared his throat once, then said in a commanding voice, "My name is Agent Kessler, and I'm with the US Marshals Service."

I froze.

"The Marshals Service is the enforcement arm of the federal courts. It is the nation's oldest federal law enforcement agency and the most versatile."

I ran a hand over the phone hidden in my pocket. I was positive I'd set it on vibrate, and I hadn't gotten any texts or calls from Mark. *Why didn't Mark tell me Marshals were coming?*

"It serves our country in a wide variety of ways," Agent Kessler continued, "but the most well-known, and the one of interest here today, is the witness protection program, which is officially called the Witness Security Program or WIT-SEC for short."

My heart pounded in my chest. Something was wrong. Even if every senior had stated they wanted to be a Marshal working with WITSEC, there was no way they'd send Marshals into a school where they were actually hiding a witness. Not as publicly as this. Not without letting me know first. It could lead to questions that shouldn't be asked. It wasn't blending in. And Mark never would've allowed it. Which meant Mark didn't know about it.

I peeked at Jason. He was studying me with narrow eyes.

"Since the WITSEC program began in 1971, Marshals have successfully protected more than 8,600 witnesses and 9,900 of their family members," Agent Kessler said as he paced the stage. "As you are probably aware from portrayals in movies and television shows, participants in WITSEC are given new identities and can never have contact with anyone from their past lives again."

Jason's eyes grew wide. I held his gaze, pulled it into me, until I saw the realization settle on his face. Until I knew I could finally tell him the truth. "I wanted to tell you, so many times. I just…" I slowly turned my head in both directions to check all of the auditorium's exits, two in the back and two on the sides. My stomach dropped. Each exit was being guarded by a person in a suit. "I wasn't allowed."

"Why are they here?" Jason's voice was as unsteady as my heartbeat.

I eyed the youngest-looking agent blocking the side exit closest to me. He looked to be in his early twenties, but I knew from Mark that looks could be deceiving. His brown hair was short and neat and his brown eyes were scanning the crowd of students. As his gaze swept in my direction, I inched down in my seat to hide behind Jason. "I don't know. This isn't right."

Agent Kessler's voice boomed from the stage. "We are very proud of the fact that no WITSEC participant following program guidelines has ever been hurt or killed while under the active protection of the Marshals Service."

I closed my eyes. *Following program guidelines.* And here I was, sitting next to someone from my past life. I was breaking the rules, they knew and they'd come to stop me.

"To become a Marshal…" Agent Kessler's voice echoed through the room but I tuned him out.

I could count on one hand the number of Marshals I'd had contact with besides Mark. I wasn't about to deal with agents I'd never seen before without talking to Mark first, especially not agents whose ill-conceived public presentation just caused Jason to figure out I was in WITSEC. Together maybe Mark and I could convince them that Jason would keep my secret, that I didn't have to be yanked out of here or kept in WIT-SEC forever. And if Mark was in trouble for me having contact with Jason, if that's why Mark wasn't here, then I had to find a way to explain what I'd done, to apologize to him before they never let me see him again.

Something inside me grew very still. *What if they never let me see Mark again? What if they never let me see Jason again?*

I had to find Mark.

My breath caught as I wrapped my fingers around Jason's wrist. "I need you to help me get out of here as fast as possible."

His pulse tripped but he slid his fingers through mine. "Anything."

"Ask to go to the bathroom. Say it's an emergency or something. And once you're out, pull the fire alarm, okay?"

He nodded and started to stand.

"Wait!"

He leaned close and brushed his lips against mine, quick and sweet. "I'll find you." Then he was gone.

Fear crept up my throat. I wasn't going to let this be another Duke. It couldn't be.

I wasn't going to lose Mark *and* Jason.

The youngest agent's eyes swept over the students sitting by the stage as Jason made his way to the side door. I realized, too late, that if they knew I'd been in contact with someone from my past, they'd know exactly who that person was. And if they knew who Jason was, seeing him leave the audience, seeing where he'd been sitting, might lead them to me before I had a chance to get out of here and find Mark.

Every step Jason took closer to the agent sent a new round of icy tingles shooting through me. But after a few quick words to the teacher leaning against the wall by the exit, Jason slipped out of the auditorium without a second glance from the agent. I let out a silent breath, thanking whatever luck made the agent more interested in the audience than the guy who had to use the bathroom.

Thirty-six seconds later, the fire alarm sounded.

Agent Kessler paused midsentence and made a quick gesture to the other agents. The two by the side doors exited swiftly while the two in the back held their positions. "Stay calm, everyone," Agent Kessler said in a soothing voice. "It appears we need to evacuate. If you could please exit through the rear doors, we'll get through this in an orderly fashion."

Thankfully, no one listened to him. Seniors started pouring out of the side doors and the teachers didn't stop them. The pulse of the alarms and the crowd and my heart made my chest vibrate as I folded myself into a group of taller people—lesson number five: how to disappear in a crowd—and headed for the unguarded side exit.

I followed the flow of students out of the auditorium, ready to make a quick escape. Instead, I cursed under my breath.

Forty feet in front of me, at the intersection of hallways where I needed to turn left to get to the girls' bathroom with the window big enough to climb out of, teachers were herding everyone straight. Straight toward the front doors, where I could see agents, including the youngest that left his post at the auditorium's side door, scrutinizing the students as they exited. There was no way I was going to be able to slip past those teachers and down the now deserted hall into the girls' bathroom without being spotted.

I blocked out the blaring sirens and searched my memory of the night I'd toured the school with Mark. There was a boys' bathroom coming up with a window. It was a little higher and smaller than the window in the girls' bathroom, but it could work if I had someone to give me a boost. Someone like Jason.

He wasn't anywhere in front of me that I could see. I peeked over my shoulder, hoping maybe he'd been hiding somewhere, waiting for me to pass, and was now behind me trying to catch up. And that's when I saw him, sandwiched between a goth guy dressed completely in black and a tall, skinny girl in a UNC shirt. Not Jason, but someone else from my past I recognized just as easily.

Someone who shouldn't have been there.

My knees almost buckled and a gasp escaped my lips. Maybe I shouldn't have been so surprised, but a high school in North Carolina teeming with US Marshals was the last place I expected to see Lorenzo Rosetti.

TWENTY-THREE

How did he find me?

I pushed the question out of my head. I didn't have time to figure it out right then. I needed to get out of the hall, and I needed to do it right away.

Even if I trusted these Marshals—and honestly, the fact Lorenzo was roaming around my school didn't exactly instill a lot of confidence—the closest agents I could see were by the front doors, a good eighty feet away. And Lorenzo was only fifteen feet behind me. I didn't like those odds. I quickly shifted all the way to the right side of the hall. At the doorway to the boys' bathroom, I pushed the swinging door open as narrowly as I could and slipped into the room.

A second after the door swung shut, it began to open again. I didn't have time to hide anywhere but behind the door. I held my breath and got ready to put my self-defense skills to use.

"Sloane?" a familiar voice called over the muffled sound of the fire alarm blaring in the hall.

I peeked around the closing door and saw Oliver standing

a few feet away with his back to me. I inched forward and touched his arm.

He jumped. "I thought I saw you come in here. What are you doing in the boys' bathroom?"

Before I had a chance to answer, the bathroom door squeaked its opening again. *I'm not here*, I mouthed as I dashed into one of the stalls and stood on top of the toilet, crouching low so I wouldn't be seen above the stall walls. The door swung shut and I could feel the tension in the room building. There was a long moment of silence before someone finally spoke.

"Is anyone else in here?"

My heart spasmed at the sound of Lorenzo's voice, the same voice I now realized I'd heard in my head after the scavenger hunt say, "You can't hide." I cupped my hands over my mouth. Just like the last time I was in Lorenzo's presence, I was breathing too loud and too fast. I had to be quiet.

"No," Oliver said. "Just me. I stopped to pee since who knows how long it's going to be before they let us back in, you know?"

There was a shuffling of feet, but no response.

"Are you looking for someone in particular? Maybe I can help you find them outside," Oliver said.

I leaned the tiniest bit to the right, trying to peek out of the sliver of space between the stall door and wall. I wanted to see where Lorenzo was, see whether it was working.

"You don't go to school here, do—"

Boom!

I jumped and my foot almost slid off the toilet as the thin stall walls around me shook. I didn't need to see to know what caused that sound: Lorenzo had pushed open a stall door.

"I told you no one's in here." Anyone else probably would've thought Oliver sounded bored, almost annoyed. But I heard the hint of panic in his voice.

Boom!

The noise was louder this time, closer. There were only four stalls in the bathroom, and I was in the third one.

My heart was in my throat and my fingers tingled from all the adrenaline, but I shifted my weight onto my toes and forced my body to go loose, ready to attack. If it was going to come down to a fight, surprise was all I had going for me.

A dark shadow passed over the crack by the door and I realized it was Lorenzo's black shirt. He was standing a foot away from me.

Images of self-defense moves were flashing through my head as the door swung open. But it wasn't the door to my stall that opened.

"Hey, Oliver," Sawyer said over the squeak of the bathroom door. "And...some guy I don't know."

Lorenzo turned and I could see his profile, one eye narrowing to size up Sawyer.

"I hate to break this party up, but you guys need to leave." Sawyer's voice was even. He had no idea what he'd just walked into. "Principal Thompson told me to clear out the bathroom and she's seriously out for blood. She'll probably be in here herself any minute. Apparently someone's hiding in the girls' bathroom."

Lorenzo straightened. "Where's the girls' bathroom?"

"Around the corner to the left," Sawyer replied.

In a blink, Lorenzo was no longer in front of my stall door. I held my breath, praying he'd taken the bait. But instead of the squeak of the bathroom door, I heard his voice, low and suspicious. "What happened to your face?"

"I tripped." Sawyer's voice was defiant, challenging Lorenzo to question him.

My heart stopped beating.

Then Lorenzo snorted and the bathroom door squeaked. After a bit of shuffling, Oliver said, "You can come out."

I eased out of the stall. Oliver was standing by a trash can he must've shoved in front of the swinging door to block it, and Sawyer was hovering by a sink. I shook out my hands and faced Sawyer. "Is the principal really coming in here?"

He shook his head. "I was searching for you and Jason to try to apologize again." He glanced at Oliver, his cheeks turning red, then back at me. "I saw you come in here, and then Oliver, and then that dude, but no one came out. So I thought I'd see what was going on. And Oliver looked kind of freaked out and I didn't see you at all, so I figured something wasn't right with that guy. I was just trying to get him out of here."

I closed my eyes and massaged my temples. Some escape expert I was. Oliver, Sawyer *and* Lorenzo had all found me in the span of a few minutes.

I'll find you. My heart twisted at the memory of Jason's promise. Lorenzo Rosetti was here. He was coming after me. Which meant Jason couldn't be anywhere near me.

"I need you to find Jason," I told Sawyer. "Tell him *not* to look for me, okay?"

A wrinkle appeared in the middle of Sawyer's forehead. "What's going on?"

"Please, Sawyer." I eyed the trash can blocking the door. It didn't look like it would stop Lorenzo if he really wanted to get back in. "If you want to apologize, this is how you can do it. Find Jason before he finds me."

Sawyer nodded. "Yeah, okay." He moved toward the door.

"Sawyer?"

He looked over his shoulder at me.

"Thanks."

He nodded once more, then slipped out the door.

Oliver replaced the trash can blockade and was at my side in an instant. "Why was that guy looking for you?"

"It's a long story. But if you ever see him again, run the other way." I pulled my phone out of my pocket with shaky hands.

"I thought you didn't have a phone."

I didn't look up. I texted 911 to Mark, placed the phone on the bathroom floor, and jumped on it as hard as I could.

"What the hell!" Oliver exclaimed. "What's going on, Sloane?"

I stomped several more times, breaking the phone into tiny pieces. Then I remembered how Mark fried his last phone. I pushed my way into a stall and dropped the pieces into the toilet. I flushed and watched them disappear down the drain.

Oliver was waiting for me when I came back out. He grabbed my shoulders and forced me to look at him. "Why are you in the boys' bathroom in the middle of a fire drill? Who was that guy? And why did you just flush a phone down the toilet?"

"I wish I could tell you, but I can't. I'm sorry." I studied the lone window in the bathroom, then turned back to Oliver. "Can you give me a boost to that window?"

He shook his head. "Not until you tell me what's going on."

I sighed as all the things that made me feel unsettled in the auditorium, before I'd even seen Lorenzo, came back: Agent Kessler on stage; the number of Marshals guarding the exits; the noticeable absence of Mark. "Something felt off about the assembly. Some people who were there may not be who they say they are. I don't know. Jason pulled the alarm to buy me some time. All I know is that guy is looking for me and he *can't* find me. That's not a possibility. So I need to get out that window before he comes back. That's all I can tell you, okay?"

Oliver's expression grew serious. "Okay. Whatever you need."

I turned and caught sight of myself in the bathroom mirror. I'd forgotten I was wearing my bright red V-neck T-shirt. "Shit. I'm like a walking target in this."

"Here." Oliver reached into his backpack and pulled out a white T-shirt with the name of the school's a cappella group written on the front. "It's clean."

I whipped off my red shirt and slipped on the white one, not worrying about modesty, but I couldn't help smiling at the way Oliver immediately averted his eyes. "Got anything else in that bag of yours?"

He pulled out a black baseball cap with a grin.

"I should call you Saver of Lives." I put the cap on and tucked my hair under it so it was completely hidden. After stuffing my red shirt into my own backpack, I faced Oliver.

"Ready for a boost?" he asked.

"One more thing." I wrapped my arms around him and squeezed tight.

Oliver stiffened for a second, then hugged me back.

"Livie was the one who made Chloe break up with you,"

I said into his chest. "She emailed Chloe a doctored picture that made it look like you were kissing a blonde girl. And she also texted that picture of you two eating ice cream together to Jason right after they broke up. I saw it and I thought it meant you were into her. I thought *you* asked Livie to your room on the senior trip. So I didn't say anything about her, but I should've. I'm sorry." I pulled back and searched his face. "You deserve so much better than both of them. You deserve someone who loves sweet potatoes and grand romantic gestures and melts at the sound of your gorgeous voice. Someone who will trust you and believe you when you say you didn't cheat, and who won't use you for revenge or to make someone else jealous. Someone who will always be honest."

A tiny crease appeared in between his eyebrows. "Why does it sound like you're saying goodbye?"

Lorenzo's voice rang in my ears as I stared into Oliver's green eyes one last time. *Because I am.* "I'm not saying goodbye, I'm just being honest in a limited amount of time. Now come on."

Oliver hoisted me onto the windowsill and I paused there, balancing just like I had the last time I had to say goodbye to someone I cared about because of Lorenzo Rosetti. "I really like being your friend too."

He flashed me a sad, confused smile and I dropped to the ground.

I couldn't have asked for a better escape spot. The east wing of the school blocked me from the view of all the students and agents and psychotic mobsters gathered at the front of the school. But I still sprinted as fast as I could for the cover of the woods on the edge of the school property.

My backpack thumped against my back with every stride, but I continued to run until I was closer to home. Then I slowed to a brisk walk, weaving my way through the more populated streets until I came to the takeout Mexican place on the corner of my block. It wasn't open at ten-thirty in the morning, but that didn't matter. I was supposed to meet Mark in the back by the Dumpsters.

When I rounded the corner of the building, my heart sank. Mark wasn't there. I sat on the ground in between two Dumpsters, hopefully hiding myself from anyone except the one person who knew I would be there, and waited.

After what felt like an hour but had probably only been ten minutes, I was officially freaked. I didn't have my phone anymore so I didn't know how long it had been since I'd texted Mark. I figured it had to have been at least forty-five minutes, if not closer to an hour, which was way too long. Mark should've been there by now. It was his day off, and he should've been at home. All he had to do was circle the block or, even quicker, cut through the trees and make a bee-line for the place.

I stood. The Marshal's words from earlier ran through my head: *No WITSEC participant following program guidelines has ever been hurt or killed while under the active protection of the Marshals Service.* I was about to totally disregard program guidelines and deviate from the emergency plan, and with Lorenzo roaming around, I knew it wasn't my smartest idea. But without Mark, I had no protection at all.

I crept out from between the Dumpsters and listened. There was only the sound of the ocean breeze fluttering the tree leaves and the occasional car passing by on the road. I ran to the trees, headed straight for my house, and hid behind an oak tree at the edge of my backyard. Everything was still. There was no movement inside the house, no sound at all. I dashed across the backyard and unlocked the back door.

I held the screen door open so it wouldn't slam shut. The inside of the house was as silent as the outside. I wished I could tell whether Mark's car was parked out front, but I couldn't see the driveway from the back door. After a full minute of silence, I eased into the kitchen and inched the screen door shut with an almost inaudible *click*.

I silently placed my backpack on the floor and studied the backyard, making sure no one had followed me. When I was convinced I was alone, I stepped back into the kitchen and closed the door. I spun around, eager to see if Mark was home, to see if anything was out of place. My foot slipped in something wet and I crashed to my hands and knees. A salty, metallic scent filled my nose as I lifted one hand and watched a warm, thick liquid drip from my fingertips. It took me a few seconds to realize I'd landed in a very large pool of blood.

TWENTY-FOUR

There was a body a foot in front of me.

It was a man lying on his side, his back to me, with short brown hair the same shade as Mark's. A scream died in my throat as I scurried backward, sliding in the blood until I found my footing. I made it as far as the island before nausea forced me to my hands and knees again, retching, but nothing came out. When the convulsions stopped, I sat with my back pressed against the island cabinets and wiped cold sweat off my forehead. My hand left a warm, sticky trail of blood on my skin.

"Oh God." My breaths came fast and shallow as I frantically wiped my hands on Oliver's white shirt, streaking it red over and over. When my hands were raw from rubbing them so hard, I took several deep breaths and crawled around the top of the island, avoiding the pool of blood by the man's feet.

"Mark?" My voice cracked, barely louder than a whisper. I stood and skirted around the body until I could see the face. I dropped to my knees as tears began streaming down my cheeks.

Lorenzo Rosetti's brown eyes were staring blankly at me.

They were dull and empty and I couldn't look at them. I glanced to the side and gasped at the bullet holes gaping in his chest. I covered my mouth with my hand and immediately pulled it away at the rusty smell of blood. There was a dead mobster in my kitchen and I was covered in his blood. I had to get out of there.

I scrambled to my feet and tore out of the house, running so fast across the backyard that Oliver's baseball cap blew off my head. Mark would find me. I knew he would. I came crashing through the thicket of trees, only to find the Dumpsters behind the Mexican restaurant still deserted.

I placed one hand against a Dumpster and leaned over, focusing on tiny, irrelevant details—an ant marching across the pavement, the trail of something white that had run down the side of the Dumpster, the way the breeze made the ends of my hair sway apart and back together again—until my heart slowed and my tears stopped and my stomach quit churning. I straightened and a hand clamped down on my shoulder.

"It's me," Jason whispered.

I whirled around, shock making my mouth dry. "Jason?"

Jason's gaze trailed from my forehead to the bottom of my shirt. His eyes grew impossibly wide. "Is that blood?"

I looked down at my shirt. The front was almost as red as the V-neck I'd had on earlier.

"Are you all right?"

I glanced from Jason to the trees. *How did Jason find me before Mark?*

Jason stepped in front of me and placed his hands gently on either side of my face. "Sasha. Are you hurt?"

I shook my head.

"What happened?"

"He's in there."

"Who's in there? What's going on?"

The question I'd thought of when I first saw Lorenzo returned. "How'd he find me?"

Possibilities began running through my head. Jason didn't tell anyone, I was sure of that. *Jason's mom?* I didn't think that was likely. I hadn't had contact with anyone else from my past, no social media networks, no picture— "Damn!" I focused on Jason. "Do you have your phone?"

"Yeah."

"Check Livie's stuff online."

A minute later, Jason cursed and held his phone out to me. Livie had posted the picture of the two of us asleep in the hotel room with a comment that included Jason's first name, my first name, and a few choice words about us being the scum of the school—the *full name* of the school. I looked at the time of the posting: 1:10 a.m. Sunday morning.

I wasn't sure how that picture had led Lorenzo to my doorstep, but it was too much of a coincidence not to have played a role.

"I deleted that picture myself," Jason muttered.

"She probably emailed or texted it to herself before you deleted it. Whiz with the photos, right? She wanted a little insurance of her own." I shook my head. It didn't matter. What mattered was finding Mark. "How'd you find me? I told Sawyer—"

"I know. But I promised I'd find you. And when Oliver told me you demolished a phone and left through the bathroom window, I wasn't about to stay there and do nothing. So I snuck to my car and started driving around. Then I saw you running through your backyard."

"Did you drive by the front of my house?"

Jason nodded.

"Was there a car in the driveway?"

"No."

"But your car's close?"

Jason bit his lip. "Yeah."

"I need to borrow it."

His hand slipped into his pocket and curled into a fist around what had to be his keys. His expression matched the one he'd had when we first saw Sawyer in the hall that morning, like he knew something was about to change and he was preparing himself for it. "I'm coming with you."

"Jase, no." He thought I was running from some Marshals. He had no idea about Lorenzo or whoever else from the Rosetti family was in town. "I can't—"

"Don't try to talk me out of it." His voice was hard. "I know what I'm saying. I'm in this, all the way. I don't care how dangerous you're going to tell me it is. Where you go, I go."

I pursed my lips.

A smug expression flitted across his face. "I've got a car, an ATM card with about two thousand dollars in the bank and a cell phone. What have you got?"

I narrowed my eyes. We wouldn't be able to use those things for long, but at least they'd get us someplace safer where

I could come up with a plan for finding Mark. "An annoying partner in crime, apparently."

Jason half smiled at my acquiescence. "And as your partner, I deserve to be told what's going on." His face grew serious. "Starting with whose blood that is."

Before I could answer, a tinted older model sedan pulled into the alley behind the Mexican restaurant, blocking the narrow road. The driver's side door swung open. I bounced on the balls of my feet, ready for whatever was about to happen.

The agent with the buzzed salt-and-pepper hair who'd spoken on stage during career day climbed out of the driver's side. A second later, the youngest agent with the brown hair and brown eyes stepped out of the passenger's side.

I shifted slightly in front of Jason but remained silent.

"Sloane Sullivan?" the older agent asked. The expression on his face told me he already knew who I was. When I didn't respond, he continued in an authoritative voice. "I'm Agent Kessler and this is my partner, Agent Dixon." He waved at the younger agent with one hand and pulled a badge out of his suit pocket with the other. "We're with the US Marshals Service. We've been looking for you."

I pretended to study the badge. I didn't know what was going on anymore, but I wasn't about to trust just anyone who claimed to be an agent. Not when at least one mobster who should've been in jail had been close enough I could've touched him. Badges were easy to fake. Who knew who else was in town? And even if they were real Marshals, they weren't *my* Marshal.

I laced my fingers in Jason's. I wasn't leaving his side. Not after the so-called agents had seen us together. They may have had a vehicle they'd left running, but Jason and I could maneuver faster through the cramped beach town on foot than they could in that monstrosity of a car. And there was no way the agents knew the town better than Jason. We were going to run and hide somewhere until it was dark. I was just waiting for the right moment to give Jason the signal.

Agent Dixon eyed my shirt. "Is that blood?"

I needed to draw the agents away from the car a little to buy us a few extra seconds when we escaped. I cleared my throat and asked, in a voice much steadier than I was feeling, "What's your name again?"

Dixon left his open door and took three steps toward me. "Agent Dixon."

I nodded so slowly Mark would've been proud. "Agent Dixon, where is Agent Markham?"

Dixon's eyebrows flattened. "Who?"

Kessler strode to the front of the car and placed his hand on Dixon's arm. His suit jacket spread open slightly, revealing a gun in a holster. "Agent Markham is fine. He's at a safe house nearby. He asked us to bring you to him."

I had to work hard to keep a straight face. They didn't know who Mark was. Because if they did, they would've known there was no way Mark would've sent someone unfamiliar to collect me. Even if he was dead, his ghost would've floated on over to the Dumpsters just to make sure I was okay. I squeezed Jason's hand and, out of the corner of my mouth so my lips barely moved, whispered, "Bet I can run faster."

We took off in the opposite direction of the sedan, heading for the thin layer of trees that separated the restaurant from the house on the opposite corner. I planned on hiding anywhere we were protected from view: backyards with fences, pool houses, inside a house if we were lucky enough to find an open door or window. I was going to be like Ferris Bueller in his mad dash through people's backyards, only I wasn't racing my parents.

As I approached the line of trees with Jason easily keeping pace at my side, I knew I wasn't slowing down for anything. Even if the agents started shooting or a whole fleet of sedans crashed through the trees after us, I wasn't stopping.

"Sasha, wait!"

The clear, melodic voice carried over the ocean breeze. It was a voice I instantly recognized even though I hadn't heard it in almost six years. A voice that, despite what I'd just been thinking, made me jerk to a stop. Because it was my mother's voice.

TWENTY-FIVE

Jason skidded to a stop next to me. A wrinkle appeared in between his eyebrows as we both spun around.

From a distance, the woman standing in front of the sedan could've been my mother. She had the same shade of dirty-blond hair, although it was longer than I remembered my mom's being. But I was too far away to see anything definitive, like my mom's freckles or green eyes or the thin scar that bisected her left eyebrow.

The woman took several steps in my direction.

"Julia," Agent Kessler warned.

She waved him off, never taking her eyes off me. "It's okay, Sasha. It's me."

The voice brought back a flood of memories, of all the little things I missed the most when I lost her: the elaborate stories she made up at bedtime the year I was afraid of the dark and didn't want to go to sleep, the way she sang along to the radio as loud as she could while driving with the windows open, her refusal to eat any kind of ice cream that didn't have chocolate in it, which was the reason I still didn't like vanilla. I opened my mouth, but no words came out.

Heart pounding, I closed the distance between myself and my mom until I was close enough to make out the scar in her eyebrow. "I don't—"

The rest of my sentence was swallowed up by my mom's bone-crushing hug. "It's really you," she whispered into my hair.

It felt like I was drowning, like I was sinking back in time and couldn't breathe and didn't know which way was up.

"But...you're dead," Jason said from my side, his voice unsteady. "I went to your funeral."

Over my mom's shoulder, I saw the agents really *look* at Jason for the first time.

Mom pulled back enough to study Jason but kept both hands on my shoulders. Her head tilted to one side. "Jase? Is that you?"

"You know him?" Dixon asked.

She nodded. "He's our old next door neighbor, Jason Thomas."

I didn't miss the glance the agents exchanged. It made me want to stand in front of Jason again, protect him somehow.

I took a shaky breath. It didn't matter what I was feeling, I needed to take control of the situation. I'd dragged Jason into this, and I needed to keep it together until I understood exactly what was happening.

Jason shook his head. "Everyone was at your funeral. My mom, your sister, your *parents*."

"Everyone except Sasha and her father," Kessler corrected. The annoyed edge to his voice rubbed me the wrong way.

I wiped a tear from my cheek and narrowed my eyes at him. "You need to tell me what's going on, and you need to do it right now."

Kessler opened his mouth, but my mom removed her hands from my shoulders and waved him off again. She stared at me. "If I didn't know better, I'd think those brown eyes were real." She shook her head, as if she was trying to dislodge the sadness in her eyes that said *I missed too much*, then sighed. "My accident wasn't real. The Marshals staged it to protect me from the people who took you."

I turned to Jason. My own confusion was mirrored in his expression. "Let me get this straight," I said, my gaze bouncing from my mother to each of the agents. "The Marshals faked your death to protect you from *the Marshals*?"

There was a full ten seconds of silence before Dixon said, "What?"

I was losing my patience. I didn't understand how my dead mother was standing in front of me, I still didn't know where Mark was and the urge to run was making me antsy. "I've been in WITSEC this whole time!" I snapped.

"Oh, baby, is that what they told you?" Mom brushed her fingers down my arms, leaving goose bumps in their wake. "It's not true."

TWENTY-SIX

One hour. It had been one hour since my mom said those three little words that made me and Jason agree to take a ride in the sedan to the Marshals' safe house two towns over for some explanations. Thirty-nine minutes since she let go of me long enough to give me some extra clothes and a pair of flip-flops and let me take a scalding hot shower, during which I tried to ignore the reason why the white bar of soap kept turning pink as I scrubbed myself clean. And eighteen minutes since I sat at the large square table in the safe house's dining room and Kessler and Dixon began to lay out their theory, a small digital voice recorder documenting everything they said. And I still had no idea what was going on.

"Are you okay?" Jason asked from his seat next to mine at the table.

I reached over and squeezed his hand. From the way he pursed his lips, I knew he was taking my silence as a no. The answer to his question was *no*, but that wasn't why I hadn't spoken. I'd been trying to say as little as possible because of the voice recorder. I didn't like the idea of my words being used against me. Or Mark.

I took a deep breath. "So what you're telling me is that I haven't been in WITSEC since I was twelve. Instead, I was kidnapped by Angelo Rosetti's son. Did I get that right?"

Dixon nodded. "Yes."

"That's impossible."

Directly across the table from me, Kessler sighed.

I glared at him. "We've already established that Lorenzo Rosetti is dead in my kitchen. I know what he looks like. I haven't been with Lorenzo. And I knew Dante Rosetti. He was in my class at school the year I left. I wasn't kidnapped by a sixth grader."

"It wasn't Dante or Lorenzo," Dixon said. "We believe it was Angelo's oldest son who took you."

I frowned. "Lorenzo *is* Angelo's oldest son."

Dixon's gaze dropped to the manila folder on the table in front of him. He stared at it for a second, like he was debating something, then pulled out a picture. Without a word, he slid it across the table to me, facedown. But he didn't take his eyes off the manila folder.

The way he wouldn't look at me unnerved me more than anything. My pulse raced as I picked up the photo.

For one infinite moment, my eyes didn't blink and my lungs didn't breathe and my heart didn't beat.

I was looking at four guys in suits at what seemed to be a wedding: Dante, who was a little younger than I remembered; Lorenzo, whose eyes were bright and full of mischief; Angelo, who looked just like he had the few times I'd seen him pick up Dante at school; and...Mark. He was off to the side, separate from the rest of the group. His thick brown hair was longer than I'd seen it in a while and his facial hair not quite as thick as he'd been able to grow it since I'd known him, but it was definitely him.

"His name is Marco Rosetti."

My chest constricted at Dixon's words.

Kessler cleared his throat. "That's the only picture we have of him. He was a recluse, never out in public with the family, homeschooled most of his life. We know very little about him."

I couldn't stop staring at the photo. *Mark. Marco. It's not possible.*

My mom placed a hand on my arm. "Sasha?"

I blinked. From the way everyone was staring at me, I knew it wasn't the first time someone had said my name.

"Is that who had you?" Dixon asked with a nod to the picture.

I studied the familiar brown of the younger Mark's eyes. "He didn't *have* me. He was protecting me."

"She's brainwashed or something," Kessler muttered.

"I'm not brainwashed!" I insisted. "Every time there was a threat he kept me safe and hidden."

"From his own family?" Kessler asked, doubt dripping from his voice.

Dixon shot his partner a cutting look I wished could've been recorded and turned back to me. "My guess is that those threats were actually times we got close to finding you."

Jason reached over, took the photo out of my hand, and frowned at it. He'd been too quiet since we arrived at the safe house.

I rested one elbow on the table and leaned my cheek against my fist, watching Jason. "It doesn't make sense."

Kessler barked out a laugh. "You know what doesn't make sense? That you could've believed you were in WITSEC to begin with."

Jason's whole body tensed. "What's that supposed to mean?"

"It means that before you can enter WITSEC there are vetting and interviews that have to be done. You don't just magically pop into the program."

I scowled. "There was an interview! Look, my dad and I saw—" my gaze flickered to the digital recorder "—something. We ran. Only, right after it happened, it was too much for my brain to process and I shut down. Dad said I went catatonic, stopped speaking and just kept rocking in the backseat of the car. So he drove around to make sure no one was following us and tried to get me to respond. And after a while I did. But when I started talking again, I didn't remember what we'd seen."

My mom stared at me with tear-filled eyes.

"I didn't remember until very recently, actually."

"The senior trip." Jason's eyes told me he'd just realized that's when I'd remembered. He massaged his temples. "I should've—"

"You did everything right that night," I whispered, then focused on Agent Kessler. "When my dad and I finally got home, there were men in suits waiting for us. They said they were Marshals. They said they'd been surveilling the warehouse we were at and heard the gunshots and found…the body. And they asked my dad all kinds of questions. I don't know what all of them were because they didn't let me stay in the room. Dad didn't want me to remember. But I know they asked him whether he was willing to testify. That much I overheard."

Kessler frowned.

I glanced at my mother. "He said he'd testify if the agents protected all of us. The agents—"

"They weren't agents," Kessler interrupted.

"The *agents*," I continued, "said they were sending some-one to get you from work. We were going to meet up with you at a motel in Ohio."

"Was Marco there?" Dixon asked.

"No, not yet. We picked new names and packed as quickly as we could. They only left me alone for a few minutes. And then we left for Ohio. That's where I first met Mark. In the motel." I turned back to my mom. "He told me you'd been killed, that the bad guys had gotten to you before the agents could."

The look on her face, on all of their faces, said they thought Mark knew he was lying to me. But I'd seen his eyes when he told me what happened. He couldn't fake that. "He said they created a cover story to explain your death. I found out later it was a car accident."

"The car caught on fire," Jason added. "That's why there was a closed casket at the funeral."

"That's because *we* set it up to look like that," Kessler said.

There were so many more questions I wanted to ask him, but he didn't give me the chance.

"So you got to Ohio and met Marco, and he's been with you ever since?"

I glared at him. "Are you accusing him of kidnapping someone else and splitting his time?" And just like that, just by answering a question with an even snarkier question, I was no longer in the safe house.

"*Tell me* exactly *what happened.*"

I grabbed the cookbook from the counter and dropped it into the box by my feet. "They were fighting again—" *I gestured in the direction of the neighbor's house* "—and it kept getting louder and louder. Then there was a big crash. I was afraid someone was hurt, so I peeked out the blinds. And that's when the police pulled up, lights flashing and everything. I don't know who called them, but as one got out of the car he saw me looking out the window."

Mark paused, one of his kitchen knives half wrapped in paper towels. "I knew we should've moved the first time we heard them arguing. How long was it before the officer knocked on the door?"

I put Mark's favorite pan in the box on top of the book. "Ten minutes, maybe. He'd already seen me, so I couldn't just act like no one was home."

Mark nodded.

"I went and got your giant headphones first, looped them around my neck, and shoved the cord in my pocket like I had a phone in there. Then I answered the door. The cop said they'd received a call about a 'domestic disturbance' and asked whether I'd seen or heard anything."

Mark placed his wrapped knives into the box. "What'd you say?"

"I pointed to the headphones and said, 'Do you think I can hear anything with these on?'"

Mark's eyes darted to the front window, then back to me.

"Don't worry. I told him I saw the flashing lights and that's when I looked out the window."

"Did he buy it?"

"Probably not because then he asked if my parents were home."

Mark opened his mouth.

287

I held up a hand. "So I started gawking at all the officers hanging around next door and said, 'What's going on? Can I, like, take pictures and text my friends to come watch and stuff?'"

Mark's eyebrows shot up. "What did he do?"

I grinned. "He rolled his eyes and muttered something about calling the department if we had any additional information and left without even asking for my name."

Mark surveyed the bags by the front door. "Then you called me and started packing while I rushed home from work."

"Yup. And I opened a window, just to make sure I would hear if any of them said anything about us. The neighbor's pressing charges and getting a restraining order, by the way."

He watched me for a moment before breaking into his own grin. "That was pretty smart for a thirteen-year-old, answering all of his questions with questions. Where'd you learn that?"

I shoved him.

"Come on. Let's finish packing so we can get out of here before they come back."

I exhaled slowly. *I don't understand. All those lessons, all the moving. Who were we running from?*

Kessler clenched his jaw, oblivious to my trip down memory lane. "No," he growled, answering my rhetorical question as curtly as possible. "I was simply trying to point out that Marshals only provide twenty-four-hour protection while a witness is in a high-threat environment!"

"What does that mean?" Jason asked.

"It means when the witness is making a court-related appearance, like at a trial or a pretrial conference," Dixon explained, his voice even. "Once witnesses are settled in their new lives, they're on their own. Agents only check in with them about once a year."

Kessler snorted. "It means Marshals don't *live* with witnesses."

"He didn't live with me, not at first!" I ignored Kessler's eye roll and focused on Dixon. "In the beginning, he was just close. In the same apartment building or a block or two over. He didn't start living with me until..." I closed my eyes. I couldn't say it, not with my mom sitting two feet away.

"It's okay, sweetie." She squeezed my hand. "I know Dad's gone."

My eyes popped open. "How?"

She glanced at Kessler.

"We had a phone tap on an associate of Angelo's around that time for...other reasons," he said. "We overheard a conversation that led us to believe your father was murdered."

I shook my head. "He wasn't murdered. He killed himself."

"What?" Kessler, Dixon and my mom all said in unison.

"He committed suicide."

Mom stood and began pacing the room. "That's not possible. He never would've done that." She stopped and faced me, wearing the same expression she'd worn the time I'd broken her grandmother's heirloom china teacup and lied about it. "He never would've left you alone like that, not on purpose. How could you say that?"

I ducked my head and picked at the side of my thumb. After a full minute where the only movement in the room was my mother's pacing, I said, barely louder than her footsteps, "You don't know what it was like. Constantly moving around, constantly looking over your shoulder, especially so much in the beginning. He tried his best, he really did. But he couldn't take it anymore. And he knew I wasn't going to be alone. He left me with Mark."

I didn't look up, but I could feel every pair of eyes in the room on me. To my surprise, it was Jason who spoke first.

"When you showed up and said your name was Sloane, I assumed that's who you'd been since the day you left New Jersey."

My eyes met his.

"It never even occurred to me to think you'd been anyone else. It wasn't until that day at the carousel that I realized how wrong I'd been." He shook his head slightly. "That story you told the cop had just the right amount of quirkiness and plausibility that it had to be true because no one could come up with that on the spot like you did. That's when I knew you'd been making up stories for yourself for a long time."

I held Jason's gaze.

"How many people have you been?" he whispered.

"Counting Sloane?"

He nodded.

I took a deep breath. There was only one other person on the planet who knew the answer to that question. But if I was going to let Jason in, he deserved to know the truth. All of it. "Nineteen."

It felt like all the air had been sucked out of the room.

"Jesus," Jason muttered. His eyes filled with the same regret and sadness they'd had at the carousel. "I should've stopped you. I knew something was wrong when you gave me the trophy that last day. I just didn't… I should've held on to you when you hugged me. It felt like you were saying goodbye, but I didn't understand. I never should've let you go."

Tears filled my eyes. "Jase…" I had to do something to erase that look from his face. To erase all the pitying looks on all the faces in the room. Well, except for Kessler, who mostly looked annoyed at the interruption of his interrogation. "It wasn't your fault. It wasn't anyone's fault. We were in the wrong place at the wrong time. And it was okay, really. I learned to adapt and blend in and become really good at making up stories."

"It was someone's fault." I jumped at the intensity of Kessler's voice. "It was Marco's fault. *Marco* was the one who took you away from your mother and your friend. He was probably the one who killed your father too. And you need to accept that."

I narrowed my eyes. "He *didn't* kill my father."

"How do you know?" Kessler challenged. "Did you see your father's body? Were you there when it happened?"

"Are you kidding me right now?" Jason huffed. "How could you ask—"

"I wasn't there when it happened." I held Kessler's gaze, making sure not to blink. "And neither was Mark."

I glanced around the dining room, letting my words sink in. The Marshal's safe house was nothing more than a beach house filled with the ubiquitous ocean-related decor found in all beach rentals. There was nothing "safe" about it. It certainly didn't feel like the place to spill secrets, but I'd do it if it got me more information on Mark. So I told them about the day Mark took me to the carnival.

"Do you know who the agent was, the one in your kitchen when you got home?" Dixon asked.

"It wasn't an agent," Kessler mumbled.

I ignored him. "No. But I remember exactly what he looks like."

"The phone call we intercepted made it clear your father's death was planned," Kessler said. "*Murder*, not suicide. So even if Marco didn't do it himself, he knew about it."

My heart pounded. But my brain recalled the way Mark tensed when we walked into my apartment and saw the agent, the surprise in his voice, the way he sang to me afterward. "He didn't know about it."

"Why are you defending him?" Kessler snapped.

"Why are you getting mad at me?" I snapped back. "I've lived practically every day of the past six years with Mark. I know when he's surprised or lying, okay? And if everything you're telling me is true, you guys let me be kidnapped by a mob family. Don't think I haven't realized that you somehow had enough warning to save her—" I pointed to my mom "—but not my dad and me. You let me get kidnapped, and you couldn't find me for six years. So I should be the one who's mad!"

Kessler opened his mouth to argue, but my mom reached across the table and turned off the digital recorder. "I think we could all use a little break, don't you?" She stared at him, daring him to challenge her.

Kessler closed his mouth, a hint of contrition in his eyes.

"Good. Let's go make some food."

We all followed my mom into the kitchen even though no one seemed eager to eat. After a moment of standing awkwardly watching her pull things from the refrigerator, Dixon went to help, grabbing plates from one of the cabinets. Kessler sulked by the window and I took a seat at the tiny round table in the corner, not wanting to get in anyone's way. Jason leaned against the counter next to me, lost in his own thoughts.

I don't know how long I sat there, staring at nothing, replaying memory after memory in my head, before a plate appeared on the table in front of me. On it was a ham and cheese sandwich cut into triangles, just the way I'd liked as a kid. I glanced up.

My mom shrugged and for a second, it looked like she was about to smile. Then there were tears in her eyes. "Did he hurt you?"

Everyone in the room looked at her.

"Marco." There was a fierceness to the way she held my gaze. "Did he ever…"

"No." My cheeks got hot as I realized what she was asking. "*No.* Never." I turned to Kessler. "And you can record that if you want."

Jason reached over and slid his hand under my hair, gently rubbing his thumb along the bottom of my neck. A wave of calm flowed through me.

Dixon placed the plate he was holding on the counter. "Agent Kessler has been working on this case—on anything involving the Rosettis—for a long time. I was brought on more recently, but it didn't take me long to get up to speed. And knowing what we both do about the Rosettis, we were operating under the assumption that your life with Marco wasn't as…voluntary as it seems to have been. That's an idea we're going to need a little time to get used to." He looked pointedly at Kessler. "But we know things you don't." His gaze flicked to Jason then back to me. "And you know things we don't."

"Like what?" I asked.

"You know what you and your father saw and you know about Marco."

It was what I'd been afraid of. They wanted intel on Mark.

"But I'm going to guess that, more than anything, everyone in this room wants to know the truth. About what really happened that day at the warehouse, what really happened to your dad, how you ended up with Marco, everything. Am I right?" Dixon raised an eyebrow at me.

For a brief second, his brown eyes looked so similar to Mark's a chill ran down my back. They were full of an eagerness to prove himself, to be good at something, or maybe just to be *good*, but also a lingering hint of amusement that said he knew this whole situation was absurd. I nodded.

"The only way we're going to get to the truth is to tell each other everything we know, without judgment. We have to piece together the whole puzzle."

"Okay." I took a deep breath. "I'll tell you what I saw."

A few minutes later, Kessler lifted his pen from the paper he was using to take notes at the kitchen table even though he'd started recording again. "So you don't know who the taller man was, the one you think actually shot the man on the ground at the warehouse?"

"No. I never saw his face or, if I did, I don't remember it." I frowned. "I guess it's still possible I haven't remembered everything. I mean, I know I got back in the car with Dad, and before that I threw up, but I only know because he told me, not because I remember."

My mom absentmindedly rubbed her thumb over the scar in her eyebrow. "Did you tell Marco you remembered seeing Lorenzo after your school trip?"

My heart skipped. I'd seen her rub her scar a million times when she was trying to figure out something difficult, but until that second, I'd forgotten all about it. I glanced away. "No."

Kessler's eyebrows shot toward the ceiling, although, to his credit, he seemed to consider his words before he barked at me. "You expect us to believe that you didn't tell the man you thought was a Marshal protecting you from murderers that you remembered who the murderers were?"

My face flushed. "Yes. Mark said they got a confession. So even if I did remember, my testimony wasn't necessary anymore. That's why I was getting out of WITSEC. I didn't want to jeopardize that."

"You don't get released from WITSEC," Kessler grumbled. "Once you're in, you're in for life."

I turned to Dixon. "He said I was a special case. I didn't know anything, I was turning eighteen, and someone confessed and was in jail, so no one would be coming after me anymore." I rubbed my temples. "But obviously Lorenzo wasn't in jail, was he?"

"No."

"And since you were asking me about the taller shooter, I'm going to guess whoever that was isn't in jail either."

"Right again," Dixon said.

Jason took the last seat at the table. "Was anyone in jail? Was there even a confession?"

Dixon glanced across the room at Kessler, some sort of

silent conversation occurring between them. "There was a confession to the murder Sasha witnessed, yes," Dixon finally replied.

"Then who confessed?" I asked.

The ticking of a grandfather clock in the hall counted off the seconds that no one answered as the tension in the air grew thick. I peeked at Jason. He shook his head, not understanding what the problem was either.

I cleared my throat pointedly. "In light of the fact we're supposed to be telling each other everything, let's try this one. Who did I see get murdered?"

Dixon's gaze shifted from me to Jason, from calm provider-of-information to wary don't-kill-the-messenger. "He was the head of a rival mob family named Reuben Marx."

The name didn't mean anything to me, so I looked at Jason. All the color had drained from his face and he was gripping the edge of the kitchen table so tightly his fingertips were white. "Jase?"

He blinked at me. When he spoke, his voice was very small. "That's the man my dad is in jail for killing."

TWENTY-SEVEN

"He didn't do it," I told Jason. "Your dad didn't kill Reuben Marx." I turned to Kessler and Dixon, my words spilling out more quickly. "The man I saw had brown hair. I'm positive. Jason's dad has black hair like his." I pointed at Jason. "His dad didn't do it." I knew there had to be an explanation for Jason's dad being in prison. It was a mistake.

Dixon rubbed the back of his neck. "We know he didn't do it, Sasha."

My face fell. "Then why is he in jail?"

My mom poured a glass of water from a pitcher on the counter. Her flower-coconut scent trailed behind her as she passed me to place the glass in front of Jason. She gave his shoulder a quick squeeze. "Scott is in jail because he chose to be."

Jason wrapped his hands around the glass. "I don't understand."

"When Reuben Marx was murdered," Dixon said, "Scott was working with the Marshals to collect evidence against the Rosettis. He'd been wearing wires to work and copying files and telling us everything he could for months."

"Wait. Jason's dad was working for the Rosettis?" I glanced at Jason. "I thought he was an accountant for a shipping company."

Jason frowned. "So did I."

Kessler tapped his pen on his notes. "The shipping company was a front. Angelo used it to smuggle drugs, weapons and cash to international terrorist groups, drug cartels—you name it—which Scott was trying to help us prove. He *was* an accountant for the Rosettis, only one that also used other means when necessary to make sure people paid their debts, like—"

"I don't want to know," Jason said with a grimace.

"But he was trying to turn his life around," Dixon assured him. "That's why he was working with us. We were going to admit him into WITSEC after he testified."

I stared at Jason with wide eyes. *Jason would've been in WITSEC.* He *would've left* me.

"So how did my dad end up in jail?" Jason asked.

"Scott was inside the warehouse when Reuben was killed. He heard the shots and found the body, presumably right after you and your dad left, Sasha, and Lorenzo and the other guy cleared out."

My mom sighed from across the room. "Stacy came over that morning and said Scott had forgotten something he needed for work. She had to take Jason to the dentist, so I told her you and Dad could take it to Scott."

The image of my dad shaking something in his hand flashed through my mind. "It was a padded envelope."

Mom nodded and traced the speckles in the granite counter with a finger. "I sent you there."

"Julia, it wasn't your fault," Kessler said in the nicest voice he'd used all day.

Jason ducked his head. "It was *my dad* who sent her there. If he hadn't been involved with the Rosettis, none of this would've happened."

"True," Dixon said, "but if Scott hadn't been at the warehouse, Sasha would probably be dead right now."

Jason's head snapped up at the same time I whispered, "What?"

"After Reuben was shot, all hell broke loose. Mob killings aren't as common as they used to be, especially not someone that important to a family. And we still have no idea why he was murdered. But during the scramble to hide his body and make sure no one from his family could retaliate, all Scott could find out from the inside was that Lorenzo and Marco had been sent to retrieve something for Angelo. We don't know what."

Kessler tapped the edge of his notepad on the table. "At first we thought we'd finally be able to catch Marco. If he was getting publicly involved in the family business, we wanted him. Then Scott got a call about a 'mess' he had to 'take care of.' A man and a girl, at an address he recognized."

Jason looked at me in horror.

I shrugged. "Lorenzo saw me when we were running away. He knew me from Dante. It wouldn't have taken long to find my address."

Kessler held my gaze. "Thirty-seven minutes from the time Scott heard the shots to the time he got the call."

"Scott called us," Dixon said, "and told us the Rosettis were considering putting out a hit on Julia too, just in case Sasha or her dad told Julia about what they saw. So we got to her at work before they could. And Scott took control of clean up. He stalled for as long as he could to buy us time. Lorenzo wanted to make it look like a random crime, a home invasion or carjacking. Something violent where you two could be executed as soon as possible and it wouldn't be linked to the Rosettis. But Scott talked some sense into Angelo, claiming the murder of a young girl in a violent crime would cause a media frenzy in town, which wasn't something they wanted."

Jason buried his head in his hands. "This is so sick. All of it. That my dad was involved, just all of it."

"Keep in mind," Dixon added, "this was all happening in the first hour after the shooting. And we were scrambling too. Trying to come up with a way to find you before they did and offer you protection."

"And then Scott got a call that the problem had been 'taken care of.'" Kessler made air quotes. "We thought that meant you two were dead. We went to your house to make sure and no one was there. It didn't look like you'd packed and left. I remember your room in particular, Sasha. It was still full of clothes scattered around and a book lying open on the flower bedspread. So we assumed the worst." A look that almost seemed apologetic crossed his face. It almost made him look human.

I studied my mom, who was still tracing patterns in the granite. "How long did you think I was dead?"

She lifted her head, her expression truly apologetic.

"It's okay," I said. "I thought you were dead for almost six years."

The hint of a smile played on her lips. "It was eight months before an agent overheard a phone conversation about Marco and a girl. We didn't recognize the girl's name, but we hoped it was you."

"Couldn't my dad have found out where they were and told you?" Jason asked.

"Things changed for Scott the day Sasha was taken," Kessler said. "We couldn't tell him we'd gotten to Julia in time. We can't divulge information about whether someone is in WITSEC, even to someone who's helping us. So in his mind, in the span of a single day, Sasha and her dad had been murdered by the Rosettis and her mom died in a car accident. It scared him. He was worried about what Angelo would do to you and your mom if anyone found out he was an informant, so he stopped helping us."

Jason shook his head. "He just *stopped*?"

Dixon pushed off the counter he was leaning against and crossed the kitchen. "Come on," he said over his shoulder. "There's something you need to see."

Jason and I looked at each other, then abandoned our uneaten food and followed him back into the dining room, my mom, Kessler and the recorder trailing us.

Dixon reached into his manila folder and pulled out another picture. "About a month after the shooting, the cops anonymously received a video of Scott finding Reuben Marx's body. Who do you think that was courtesy of?"

"The Rosettis," Jason replied. "It was their warehouse, right?"

"Correct. When Scott found Reuben, he immediately began damage control, which included picking up the gun on the ground next to the body to get rid of it. From the angle of the camera and the point where the video started, it looked like Scott was holding the gun over Reuben's dead body." Dixon handed the picture to Jason. "That's a still frame from the beginning of the video."

I took a step forward, my arm brushing Jason's. If I hadn't known better, I would've believed Jason's dad had just killed Reuben Marx from that picture.

"Two days after the cops got the video, what was left of Reuben Marx washed up onshore," Dixon said. "The next day, while the media was buzzing about the body being found, a copy of the video was leaked to the press. And the day after that, the cops got a search warrant and found the gun from the video buried in Scott's backyard."

Jason thrust the picture back at Dixon. "I remember that part."

I wrapped my hand around Jason's, gently rubbing my thumb across the inside of his wrist.

"We tried to explain to the police that Scott had been helping us and was being set up for doing so," Kessler said, "but it was too late. They had a body, a gun, video evidence and media pressure to bring charges. It was too incriminating for them to do nothing."

"That's what the Rosettis did to him when they had no idea he was helping us," Dixon said softly. "Imagine how much worse it could've been if they found out."

Jason leaned into me. "My dad said he was innocent at first, right?"

Dixon nodded. "He got a good defense lawyer, fought it every step of the way." He tucked the photo of Scott back into the folder. "Then one day, out of the blue, he confessed."

"We didn't have any money left," Jason said. "My mom wouldn't tell me a lot about what was going on, but I knew the lawyer was expensive and we had to sell the house."

"That's why your mom *thought* he confessed, to stop the money problems." Kessler looked Jason in the eye. "But that's not the truth. He told us Angelo threatened you and your mom. The Rosettis knew the cops were close to pinning Reuben's murder on them, so they planted the evidence. They needed someone within the organization to take the fall, and your dad was going to be it."

Jason squeezed my hand, then sat at the dining room table. "Did my mom know? About *any* of this?"

"No," my mom replied. "We talked about everything, Jase. If she had known, I would've known. I'm sure of it."

"Scott told me she didn't know anything, even after," Dixon assured Jason. "And don't worry, we've already sent an agent to bring her here just in case any other Rosettis are around."

Jason exhaled. "That's why my dad was so eager for us to move away."

"Wait." I sat next to Jason as I put the timing together in my head. "You moved before eighth grade, right? And your dad confessed before that?"

"Yeah."

"Mark told me the confession happened a year ago. That's when we started planning Mark and Sloane Sullivan. Why would he lie about that?"

Jason pressed the palms of his hands into his eyes. "Because they're all liars. Everything we thought we knew is a lie."

I reached over and placed both hands on Jason's, pressing down on his wrists with my thumbs until he was forced to drop his hands and look at me. "Your dad was protecting you. He was protecting *me*. I don't know how he got involved with the Rosettis, and obviously there's a lot more to him than we knew growing up, but he was trying to be better. He shouldn't be in jail for killing Reuben Marx, and I can prove it."

I closed my eyes for the briefest of moments and let my hands drop into my lap. After wanting to get out of WITSEC for so long, I couldn't believe what I was about to say. But I had to. I opened my eyes and looked directly at Kessler, standing by the door. "I can testify that Jason's dad didn't do it. I can tell the cops what I saw and they can reopen the murder investigation and we can get a hearing or something to prove it wasn't Jason's dad."

Kessler studied me. "There were unidentified fingerprints found on the gun, the one used to kill Reuben Marx. But you can't always just 'get a hearing.' Scott confessed, Sasha. Unless you can also testify as to who really pulled the trigger, give us some concrete evidence we could use to catch the real killer, your saying Scott didn't do it isn't going to help."

Crap. He's probably right. No one said anything as I stared out the dining room window. All I could see was the side of the house next door. I wanted fresh air and the sound of the ocean and time to think. But I still hadn't found out the one thing I needed to know.

Kessler broke the silence. "I'm just going to ask the question everyone here wants to ask." His eyes locked on mine. "Could the man you saw shoot Reuben Marx have been Marco?"

"No," I replied without hesitation.

Kessler folded his hands in front of him, his face a mask of calm. Then he spoke. "Ever heard of Stockholm syndrome?" he snapped.

"Oh my God!" I smacked a hand on the table. "I'm not some hostage that psychologically bonded with my captor."

"You are!" Kessler insisted. "You can't accept even the possibility it could've been Marco. Scott said Lorenzo and Marco went out together. We don't know where to, but you saw Lorenzo at the warehouse. Who else could've been with him?"

"Any guy from fourteen to forty with brown hair and a baseball cap, which probably describes about 50 percent of white males in that age group!" I pointed to the voice recorder, back in its place in the middle of the table. "You want to know about Mark, right? That's what all this is about? The recorder and the interrogation? Fine. I'll tell you about Mark." I leaned closer to the recorder to make sure it captured my words. "He makes the best fettuccine alfredo I've ever had. He plays basketball dirty, all elbows and hip checks. He likes giving me a hard time and when he does, the right side of his mouth quirks up crookedly. He tears up at romantic comedies, even though he totally denies it, and he sings along to Kings of Leon more loudly than anyone should. And he hates guns. As in, he's morally opposed to them. Other than to protect me, there is not a single circumstance I can imagine in which Mark would pick up a gun, let alone shoot someone. *That* is how I know it wasn't him."

The expressions that met me when I finished ranged from surprise to disbelief to concern. The concern was all Jason's.

"He didn't do it," I said softly. *But he might know something about who did.*

"Have you found Marco yet?" Jason asked without taking his eyes off me.

That was the question I'd been waiting for.

"No," Dixon replied. "We have agents scouring the area for him, road blocks set up, ears on the inside ready to tell us if he contacts Angelo, but nothing. It's like he vanished. We don't even know whether he's dead or alive."

I could feel Kessler's eyes on me, feel the way he wanted to dissect my reaction, so I changed the subject. "How did you find me? Now, after all this time?"

Once again, Dixon reached into the manila folder.

"I'm really beginning to hate that folder," I muttered.

Dixon slid over a piece of paper. "It started with that."

I picked up a missing-child poster just like I'd seen in ads in the mail, except this one had my picture on it. Actually, two pictures: a close-up my dad had taken the last day of sixth grade, with me smiling and the tips of Jason's fingers visible around my shoulder, and an artist's rendering of me at eighteen that was surprisingly accurate. I raised an eyebrow as I scanned the information on the poster. "Jennifer Smith?"

"After we realized you might still be alive," my mom said, "we decided to try anything to find you, including putting your picture on a missing-child poster, sending it to all the police stations in the country every few months and hoping something would turn up. We used a fake name so the Rosettis wouldn't catch on."

"We never got a single hit until five weeks ago." Dixon moved to the window, looking out and stretching his back. "I emailed the poster one morning like clockwork, and that afternoon I got a call from Officer Nilson in North Carolina claiming to have seen you at a carousel."

I shook my head. I knew the officer's curious gaze and unusual questions had made me uneasy for a reason.

"The first time we got a hit and it was on your birthday? It seemed like too much of a coincidence so I came to North Carolina." Dixon shot me a look. "Of course, I was busy searching for a girl named Andy who was homeschooled and lived with both her parents that no one in town ever remembered seeing."

A slight smile tugged at my lips.

"And while Agent Dixon was in North Carolina," Kessler added, "I was following Lorenzo. Who, about two weeks ago, took a road trip by himself to a small white house with red shutters in Lexington, Kentucky."

My smile vanished. "With a basketball hoop at the end of the driveway and a large maple tree by the street."

Kessler blinked. "How'd you know that?"

"That's where we lived before we moved here. But we left at the end of March. Why would Lorenzo have gone there at the end of April?"

Kessler narrowed his eyes. "Because I don't think he knew you'd moved." He sat and glanced at Dixon before continuing. "He drove straight to that house and waltzed up like he owned the place. I was watching from down the block. When an elderly man opened the door, Lorenzo was surprised. He kept gesturing and asking the man questions, and all the man did was shake his head. Lorenzo finally gave up and went back to his car. But when he got in, he punched the steering wheel. Then he made a phone call, punched the steering wheel again, and drove back to New Jersey without stopping. None of it made sense until right now."

Jason leaned forward, eyes on Kessler. "So if Marco was keeping in touch with his family, he didn't tell them about leaving Kentucky."

Kessler nodded. "I think you're right."

"Meanwhile," Dixon said, "I was broadening my search for the elusive Andy, working my way town by town, when Agent Kessler called to say Lorenzo was on the move again. Another solo road trip that ended three days ago in a North Carolina beach town. It was too close to where Andy had been to be a coincidence."

"Three days?" I asked. "Lorenzo was here all weekend?" The memory of headlights following me to prom made me shiver.

"He arrived on Friday, drove around for a while, then ended up watching your school all afternoon," Dixon replied. "So we got access to the school records, searched for any recent changes, anything that might have attracted Lorenzo's interest, and we found Sloane Sullivan." He tapped the table with one finger. "With no student ID, no picture on file, no presence online, nothing. But an offhand comment to the office secretary about how strange it was for a senior to transfer so late in the year got me a very helpful story about how she'd set you up with a First Day Buddy named Liv."

Damn, Mrs. Zalinsky, I thought.

"There was only one Liv at the school, and she had *lots* of pictures online."

"Including one of me and Jason she just posted," I said.

Dixon nodded. "I showed it to Julia."

"And I flew in right away because I knew it was you," Mom said, smiling at me. "I would've known your lemonade hair anywhere. But even though the post said *Jason*, I didn't put two and two together. I didn't think it was possible for you two to be in the same place."

I squeezed Jason's hand under the table. "It was a surprise to me too."

"We tried to find you at prom, but I saw Liv arrive and overheard her tell some girl you weren't coming so we left," Kessler said, always eager to get back to business. "Then Liv posted your picture, and we had your address, but we still didn't see either you or Marco at your house on Sunday."

"We were home. We just stayed in all day."

"And we didn't see anyone leave this morning," Kessler added.

The idea of Agent Kessler spying on me made my skin crawl. "I went out the back and Mark was off work today."

Dixon leaned over the back of a dining room chair. "He has a job?"

"He's always had a job, wherever we've been. We were trying to blend in, not pretend to be independently wealthy. Plus, he enjoys it." I held a hand out to Kessler. "And before you say anything, I'm sure agents don't get jobs. You've already noted my failure to recognize nonagent behavior."

Kessler crossed his arms. "We asked the school this morning if we could join career day for two reasons: one, because we hoped a large presence of Marshals would scare Lorenzo away from you; and two, because we hoped you'd seek us out if you were being held against your will. We did it for you."

I rubbed my temples. "I'm sorry. I appreciate that you were trying to help me. But I already told you I wasn't being held against my will."

"Yeah, well, the plan didn't work anyway." Kessler leaned back in his chair. "Just as one of our agents spotted Lorenzo in the auditorium, another agent saw *someone* set off the fire alarm." He eyed Jason.

"Sorry," Jason muttered.

"We lost you and Lorenzo in the crowd," Dixon told me, "but an agent was able to keep tabs on Jason, and we followed him to you."

Jason peeked at me. "Sorry," he muttered again.

Kessler cleared his throat. "Since we've spent many years trying to help you, maybe you could try to help us."

My chest tightened as I turned to Kessler.

"How do you think Lorenzo ended up dead in your kitchen?" he asked.

"I don't know."

"That's an important question, don't you think?"

"Of course." *But it's not the most important question. The most important question is why did Lorenzo show up for the first time in almost six years now?*

"A question I think Marco could help us answer," Kessler continued.

I didn't reply.

"How do we find Marco, Sasha?"

"I don't know."

Kessler stood, his lips pressed into a thin line. "You don't have a phone number, a meeting place, some way of contacting the person who was supposed to be protecting you?"

"I have a phone number, but it won't work anymore. The plan was for him to destroy his phone if he ever got a 911 text from me, which I sent after I saw Lorenzo at school. Then I destroyed my phone too."

"What was the plan after destroying the phones?" Dixon asked.

I frowned. "I was supposed to meet Mark at the restaurant where you found me. He never showed."

"That's it?" Kessler's annoyance was back in full force. "No backup plan?"

Backup plan. An emergency plan for the emergency plan.

My stomach dropped. I'd destroyed Mark's piece of paper about the untraceable email addresses he'd created like I'd promised and then forgotten all about it. I'd never even activated the account. And my mind was now a total blank on what the code I'd memorized was. There should've been a backup plan, a plan for when we hadn't been in touch for a day or two, and I'd screwed it up. Then Mark's voice sounded in my head, like he was talking right into my ear: *"If anything ever happens, I'll find you."*

My eyes locked on Kessler's. "The backup plan is that Mark finds me."

TWENTY-EIGHT

A sliver of moonlight danced on the light blue wall of the safe house's bedroom just like the thoughts dancing in my head. After the interrogation ended, I'd done what I did best: blend in. I'd sat with my mom as she rubbed circles on my back and we told each other what we'd been doing the past six years, talked with Jason about the impossibility of it all, smiled at the best-friend reunion after Jason's mom showed up at the safe house, watched a movie with Dixon and made fun of the horrible acting, listened to Kessler's updates on the search for Mark. Everything a girl happy to finally be in the protection of the US Marshals and reunited with her friends and family should do. Then, when it was sufficiently late, I'd claimed I was tired and needed some time to process everything that had happened that day. They'd given me a bedroom to myself and ever since, I'd been lying in the dark, watching the moonlight inch its way along the wall, listening to everyone settle in for the night. And thinking about all the things no one else in the house knew.

They didn't know Mark the way I did. They didn't know about lesson number four: how to be stealthy like a ninja. They didn't know I'd lied.

At 1:57 a.m., I snuck out of my room. Mark preferred the heel-first-then-roll-your-weight-onto-your-toes method of silent walking, but I'd perfected the slightly-crouched-body-loose-balance-on-the-balls-of-your-feet tiptoe, which I used to slip past the bedroom my mom was sharing with Jason's mom on my way to the kitchen. It was the room in a beach rental most likely to have what I needed—like scissors, a screwdriver or a long thin knife, and some kind of tape—to hotwire a car.

I turned at the end of the hall and froze. Kessler was sitting with his back to me on the couch in the living room, a small lamp glowing on the end table next to him. He muttered something, too soft for me to hear. I inched back into the shadows and watched. After a few moments of silence, he shifted, revealing a slim cell phone pressed against his ear. A muscle in his jaw tensed, then his mouth started moving quickly. His voice rose just enough for me to hear him whisper-snarl, *"—find them."*

I backtracked, trailing my fingers along the wall as I counted doors, my mind scrambling for a new way out. I felt the vibration in my fingertips a split second before I heard it: the sound of rushing water. I paused. The door a few feet in front of me, the one surrounded by inky blackness, belonged to my mom's room. The door I'd just passed led to Dixon's bedroom. And a tiny sliver of light was peeking out from under it.

I grinned. If Dixon wanted to take a shower in the middle

of the night, I certainly wasn't going to complain. Not when there could be something useful in his room.

I pivoted, my fingers closing around the cool metal of the doorknob. Ever so slowly, I twisted. I had to stop myself from snorting when I didn't meet any resistance. *He didn't even lock the door.*

I slid in and swept the door shut in the span of a single breath. Ignoring the faint off-key humming I heard over the sound of the water and what looked like clothes he might sleep in tossed casually over the chair in the corner—*please let me be out of here before he needs those*—I scanned the room.

The contents of Dixon's manila folder were scattered across the cream-colored carpet by his bed, pictures and notes and scribbled-on napkins. *Amateur,* I thought with a smile. Not because Dixon left his evidence out in an unlocked room, but because he'd left the key to his car sitting in the middle of it all.

A new plan formed in my head. I'd been about to hotwire the oldest car I could find on the block. But this? This was too easy. This was not only a way to get out, but also a way to ensure that, at least at first, Dixon and Kessler wouldn't have a car to chase after me once they realized I was gone.

I lifted the key, careful not to disturb anything else on the carpet. As I dropped it into my pocket, I noticed two items on the nightstand: Dixon's gun still in its holster and in the shadow of the holster, the digital voice recorder.

I studied them. The gun was…a gun. But the recorder was as tall as my phone had been and only about half as wide. It would easily fit in my back pocket. Without a second thought, I grabbed the recorder, the slight scraping of metal against wood easily drowned out by Dixon's shower, and slipped back into the hall.

Adrenaline made my muscles buzz as I tiptoed through the dim light. It felt like a practice escape run through one of my new schools only this time, no one was chasing me.

When my eyes had fully adjusted to the darkness in my room, I slid the recorder into my back pocket, stuffed the bent wire hanger I'd taken from my closet and the paper clip I'd found in my dresser into the pocket with the car key, and jammed my borrowed flip-flops into my other front pocket. I slid open my window—thank God for first floor bedrooms—climbed into the windowsill and gracefully dropped to the ground.

The dew on the grass was cool between my toes and the moon was full and bright. My gaze darted to the unlit window directly above mine, the window to Jason's room, but I forced myself to look away. I closed my eyes and took a slow, deep breath of salty air. Then I checked my pockets to make sure nothing fell out when I landed and walked around the house and down the street to where the tinted sedan was parked. I unlocked the door and was just reaching for the handle when I heard a sound behind me. Not sharp enough to be a twig snapping, not heavy enough to be a door closing, but *something.*

The back of my neck tingled. Just like it did when someone was watching me.

I slowly spun around.

Headlights swept across the front of the safe house. I flattened myself against the sedan and crouched low, heart in my throat, as a car began driving down the street.

Kessler's angry words echoed in my head: *find them*. I gulped.

The car crept toward me, moving so slowly I probably could've outrun it. I bounced on the balls of my feet, wondering whether I'd have to. Every inch of my skin prickled, but I slowed my breaths, slowed my thoughts and waited.

The car inched past the safe house. I tensed as it moved out of my field of vision, the sounds of a ticking engine and wheels crunching pebbles the only way I had of knowing it was passing directly on the other side of the Marshals' car—and slowing. I wrapped my hand around the key to the sedan hard enough that it dug into my palm as I got ready to jump in and start the engine and ram into whatever I needed to. Then the car reappeared on the other side of the sedan, pulling into a driveway three doors down. Two girls who looked to be in their early twenties got out, one loudly teasing the other about "driving like my grandma," and disappeared into the house without a glance in my direction.

I let out a shaky breath. This many weeks without any serious lesson practice was making me jumpy. Kessler could've been talking about anything when he said *them*: things he was looking for in our house-turned-crime scene, other Marshals who weren't where they were supposed to be, his missing senses of humor and compassion. He didn't have to mean people who would come looking for me in the middle of the night. In fact, no one had said anything all day about there being any other Rosettis in town. *Besides*, I thought as I glanced up and down the street, *this place is dead*. The only light in any house I could see was the single lit window on the first floor of the house I'd just left, the one that belonged to

Dixon's room. *Dixon's room.* I raised an eyebrow. *Then again, it couldn't hurt to have a little backup.*

The trip back to my window took seconds. I hoisted myself onto the windowsill in one swift move, grateful for my childhood of window climbing, and dropped silently onto my bed. I held my breath and listened, but I couldn't tell whether Dixon was still in the shower.

Easing the door open, I edged back into the hall. The sound of running water greeted me. And so did darkness, even more so than before. As I neared Dixon's room, the only light I could see was the sliver coming from under his door. The lamp in the living room was off, which meant Kessler must've gone to bed.

Perfect.

I was in Dixon's room in a flash. In two swift steps, I crossed the room and slipped the gun out of the holster, checking to make sure the safety was on. It felt solid and familiar in my hand as I examined the holster still in its place on the nightstand. If Dixon didn't look too closely at it, he might not notice the gun was missing. The corners of my mouth pulled up. All of my pockets were full, but I'd been around Duke long enough to know a few places to hide a gun.

The water shut off.

My eyes darted to the clothes on the chair, then to the gun in my hand. I tucked the gun into the waistband of my jeans at the middle of my back, and dashed out the door.

I'd just passed the threshold of my mom's bedroom door when I heard it: "Sasha."

Heart pounding, I spun around, excuses ready to roll off my tongue. But the hall was empty.

"Sasha, no."

It was softer the second time, followed by a long sigh I could tell came from the other side of my mom's door.

I pressed my ear to the door and heard the low murmurings of my mom talking in her sleep. Resting my forehead against the door, I took a deep breath. Before she said anything else to wake herself or Jason's mom up, I was back out my window. I adjusted my shirt to make sure it covered the gun, then made my way back to the sedan.

I got in as quickly and quietly as possible. After wrestling my flip-flops out of my pocket and tossing them on the floor by the passenger seat, I placed the gun on the center console and checked the safety one more time. Then I started the car.

As I pulled onto the road and drove past the safe house, I peeked at the clock on the dashboard. Even with going back to get the gun, it took less than ten minutes to make my grand escape, and no one in the house knew I was gone. Just like no one in the house knew I had a pretty good idea where Mark was.

TWENTY-NINE

Forty-five minutes and a few missed turns later, I cut the lights as I coasted past a two-story house with pale blue siding and white trim. I parked at the end of the block and studied the way it sat farther back from the road than either of the neighboring houses, at the end of a long driveway. Even in the middle of the night, when the windows and porches and charm were harder to see, it looked just like the pictures I'd seen in Mark's safe.

At the time, I'd assumed Mark hadn't picked the blue house because it was in a neighborhood called Avalon. But once Dixon said Mark had vanished—and none of the Marshals mentioned finding a safe in our house—I realized maybe that was exactly why he *had* picked the blue house. Because a neighborhood we never would've gone to under normal circumstances was a perfect hideout. I stared at the deserted-looking house. It was possible I was wrong and Mark wasn't in there. But something deep inside me knew he was.

I stashed the gun behind my back and peeked from my flip-flops still resting on the passenger's side floorboard to the long paved driveway. Deciding they would be too loud, I slipped out of the car and left the flip-flops behind. The breeze picked up, ruffling leaves as I started toward the house. When I was halfway down the driveway, a dull *thud* made me pause.

Goose bumps trailed up my arms. I scanned the neighboring houses and the street, but saw nothing. When the moon slid behind a cloud a second later, darkening everything a few degrees, I made a run for it and snuck around the side of the house, hugging the siding and ducking below the windows. Using the makeshift tools I'd taken from the safe house, I easily picked the lock of the first door I came to. It made a low drawn-out *creak* as I pushed it open. I winced and ducked inside.

I was in the middle of a tiny mudroom. Despite the sharp lemony scent of the cleaning supplies stacked above the washer and dryer, the house smelled stale and musty. It wasn't something I associated with Mark, who more often than not smelled like cologne or whatever yummy food he'd been cooking. It made me wonder how long ago he'd rented this place, how long he'd been planning for the possibility that everything would fall apart.

I shook my head and pushed those thoughts out of my mind. Not wanting to risk the door creaking again, I left it open and used my patented tiptoe technique to sneak farther into the eerily silent darkness. I was all the way across the kitchen before a dim shaft of light became visible from the back of the house. I smiled.

The light was coming from a room at the far end of the hall. I snuck toward it and wedged myself in between the end of a console table and the door frame so I could peek into the room. There was a giant flat-screen TV against the wall to my right, an old-school pinball machine in one corner, an air hockey table centered on the back wall and, sitting in the center of a futon pressed against the left wall, was Mark. His eyes were closed and his head was hanging, elbows resting on his knees, fingers pressed to his temples. He shook his head and muttered something. I narrowed my eyes. I thought he'd been massaging his temples, but maybe he was holding a phone to his ear instead. I inched forward to see his hands more clearly, and stepped on a cluster of large decorative glass seashells I hadn't seen on the floor.

The *hiss* of air I sucked between my teeth was due to both the pain of glass slicing into my bare foot and the knowledge that I'd just broken the number one rule of ninja-stalking a person: watch where you walk.

Mark jumped to his feet and whirled in my direction faster than I could blink. His face was as hard and cold as the gun he was pointing at my head.

I sucked in another breath, as the scene I was seeing shifted.

"Please!" the man on the ground cried in a surprisingly high-pitched voice. He tried to sit up a little and winced, a crazed almost smile-like expression crossing his face. "Please don't do this!"

Lorenzo dropped his gun to his side and his shoulders slumped forward. There was a sudden blur of movement.

Pop! Pop, pop!

The explosions were so loud, so close, that my hands flew to my ears. Dad spun around in the tiny space. His nose was practically touching mine and his eyes were wild with fear. He whispered a single word: "Run."

I took off after him, one foot slipping on a broken piece of wood on the ground. It skittered into the stack of crates with a thunk.

A prickly sensation crept up my neck at the feeling of eyes on my back as I ran.

"Hey!"

Dad's grip on my arm tightened as he pulled me forward, but I instinctively peeked over my shoulder at the surprised shout. The taller guy with the baseball cap was pointing a gun at the head of the now unmoving man on the ground. But Lorenzo, whose gun still hung limply at his side, was looking straight at me. Our eyes locked and several emotions flickered in quick succession over his face: fear, then anger, then recognition.

"We have a problem!" he yelled.

The taller guy spun, his hat a flash of blue against the faded red of the bricks, and pointed his gun at me. His jaw was set, mouth pressed into a thin line. But it was his eyes that made me start to tremble. They were vacant and cold and deadly.

And then he blinked. His eyes came back to life and it was like he saw me for the first time. His gun began to shake.

"What are you doing?" hissed Lorenzo, who raised his gun just as Dad yanked me around the corner of the warehouse.

A bullet shattered a stack of crates behind us as Dad clicked the car remote to unlock the doors. I leaned over and threw up, partially drowning out the sound of a second shot being fired. Dad shoved me in the backseat. "Go, go!"

The door slammed behind me with a loud thud, *but not before Lorenzo yelled, "You can't hide!"*

"I'm so sorry."

Mark's voice snapped me back to the present. He was standing right in front of me, his face full of concern, no gun in sight. "Are you okay? I didn't know it was you. How…?" He tucked a strand of hair behind my ear. "I'm so sorry."

I stared into Mark's brown eyes. The same eyes I'd seen beneath the rim of a baseball cap all those years ago. The same eyes that made me shudder in fear. The same eyes of the man who killed Reuben Marx.

"Oh my God." I stepped back out of Mark's reach and placed my shaking hands into my back pockets. Realization settled in my chest, a hundred icy pinpricks freezing my heart and making it hard to breathe. I'd seen the picture of Mark with his father and brothers. I knew he was Marco Rosetti. I just hadn't realized he was *Marco Rosetti*. "It was you," I whispered. "I remember. You're really him."

Mark stiffened.

"You're Marco Rosetti."

"How do you know that name?"

I cradled my head in my hands. "The Marshals told me. Maybe they're Marshals. I don't know what's real anymore."

Mark's face blanched. "There were Marshals?"

Words came tumbling out of my mouth. "They came to school. So did Lorenzo, but I got away and you didn't show up and they found me and I was covered in blood—"

"What blood? Are you okay?" His eyes swept over my body.

"Blood from the dead body in our kitchen!"

"What… Do the Marshals know about that?"

"Yes!" I threw my arms out to the side. "I was covered in blood!"

Mark grew very still. "What did you tell them? Are they here?"

"No. I told them nothing because I don't know anything to tell. I don't know what's going on!" I was hot and cold all at the same time, like my body didn't know how to react. *Fight or flight? Cry or beat the crap out of him?* I blinked back tears.

Mark took a step forward. "Hey. Don't cry. Just let me explain." He reached for my hand.

"Don't touch me!" I pressed the heels of my palms into my eyes. I wanted to keep everything out, keep everything I thought I knew from changing again. "How could you shoot that man? How could you be Marco Rosetti?"

"I'm *not* Marco Rosetti."

A tingly sensation flowed through me at the intensity of his voice. I dropped my hands from my face, unsure if the feeling was confusion or hope.

Mark sighed at my expression. "That's my name, but I was never one of them." He scrubbed his hands over his face. "All my life I was expected to go into the family business. There was never any question about it. As the oldest son, I would eventually take over everything my father had built, end of story."

It was just like what Kessler and Dixon had expected.

"I got lessons growing up too," Mark said. "Only mine weren't about protecting myself. Mine were about how to make a drop without getting caught, which of our *business partners* were the ones you really didn't want to piss off." He lowered his voice. "How to hurt people to make them talk." He laughed once without humor. "For my tenth birthday, my uncle Gino taught me the best places to cut a person so it would hurt like hell but they wouldn't bleed out before they confessed."

I shuddered.

"It was sick." He searched my face, trying to make me understand. "I asked to be homeschooled because I got so tired of everyone staring at me and being afraid to talk to me. Even teachers wouldn't tell me when I did something wrong because of who my dad was. All I did was look forward to the day I could leave for college and never come back."

This sounded like the Mark I knew. "So what happened?"

Mark's hands dropped to his sides. "Reuben Marx kidnapped my baby sister."

I gasped. "Sofia?"

Surprise flashed in his eyes. "You knew her?"

An image of Sofia's eyes lighting up at my coloring book popped in my head. "A little. Dante talked about her all the time."

Mark rubbed the back of his neck. "I was so frantic that day. I just wanted to find her. I loved that kid. I mean, I half raised her myself because I was home all the time and my parents were too busy with *the family* to take care of their family. So I went looking for her with Lorenzo."

Lorenzo and Marco had been sent to retrieve something for Angelo, Dixon's voice reminded me in my head.

"We were too late," Mark whispered.

My stomach dropped. "What do you mean?"

His face grew hard again. "I mean, Reuben Marx killed my sister, then told us where we could find her body. He even mocked the way she'd begged for her life."

My hand flew over my mouth. I'd heard Reuben beg in a high-pitched voice, seen the way he'd smiled almost teasingly despite the gun pointed at him. I felt like I was going to be sick.

"He murdered an innocent six-year-old girl," Mark spat, "and I have no idea why. There wasn't some ongoing feud between our families. The last time someone from one of our families killed someone from the other had been *years* before. And Sofia didn't have anything to do with all that mob shit. She was sweet and funny and loved Frosted Flakes and unicorns." His voice broke and his gaze dropped to the floor.

I walked farther into the room, closer to him.

"Lorenzo and I were both in shock. We thought they took her to send a message to our father, maybe to back off a deal or something. But we never expected... I think Lorenzo even lowered his gun." He furrowed his eyebrows. "And then Reuben Marx pulled a gun on Lorenzo. He must've had it hidden somewhere. Lorenzo had searched him but..." There was a long pause. When Mark spoke again, his voice came from someplace far away. "I fired. I didn't think—it just happened. I never meant to kill him. I was only trying to protect Lorenzo." He glanced up. I'd never seen him look so lost.

It's too easy to make a mistake with a gun, I thought.

Mark stepped closer. "Then Lorenzo saw you and your father running away. He recognized you and called our dad. They wanted to kill you." He shook his head. "I couldn't just stand by and let that happen."

My eyes grew wide. "*You* came up with the witness protection scam?"

He nodded. "I'd turned eighteen a few weeks before the shooting." He opened his mouth to continue, but paused at the surprise on my face.

I'd always known his birthday was June 1. But I never knew how old he was until now. *He's only twenty-three. He won't even be twenty-four for three more weeks.*

"I told you I wasn't as old as you thought," he said softly.

I just stared at him. He'd been the same age I was now when he had to search for his missing sister, face her killer, protect his brother. It put college acceptances and prom in a whole new light.

Mark looked down at his hands. "Because I would've been tried as an adult if the cops found out what happened, my dad wanted me to lie low. Go into hiding. And I convinced him to let me take you too."

"Why?" My voice came out rough.

He held my gaze, eyes open and honest and gleaming with tears. "Because I couldn't protect Sofia."

A tear ran down my cheek. "Mark..."

"The least I could do was protect you. No other kids had to die." He wiped his eyes with the back of his hand. "I knew there were surveillance cameras on the warehouse. I watched the feed. Your dad only saw the back of me. But you—" his eyes locked on mine again "—you saw me."

I nodded.

"I wasn't sure how to spin that, but I knew I had to. I was going to dye my hair or cut it all off or something." He shrugged. "I...knew some things about the witness protection program, so I sent three of my dad's guards to talk to you, the ones I trusted the most. To find out what you two knew, if you'd be willing to 'testify'—" he made air quotes "—about what you saw. I thought that might be the only way to get you to come voluntarily. And then they called and told me you couldn't remember anything. I took it as a sign. I told my dad this way we'd always know where you were, what you did, who you talked to. We'd control everything about you, and you'd trust us with your lives."

I shivered.

"I had to put it in terms he'd like to get him to call off the hit. But it worked." Mark inched closer. "I'm sorry. I'm so sorry. I never meant to hurt you, I only wanted to keep you safe." He reached out and took my hand.

This time, I didn't stop him.

I stared at his fingers, wrapped securely around mine. There were so many questions bouncing around my head, but there was only one I needed the answer to before anything else could happen. "Did my dad really kill himself?" I whispered.

"No."

I flinched at the directness of his reply.

"I'm done lying to you." His voice was quiet but steady. "I'm putting it all out there. You deserve the truth. And you deserve to know everything about me. I want you to know the real me."

My head snapped up as my own words echoed in my head: *"I want someone who likes me for who I am, who knows the real me."*

Mark searched my face. "Your dad was murdered, but I had no idea it was going to happen. I thought I'd convinced them to leave all of us alone. But they had some plan to blame Reuben's murder on someone else and they wanted anyone who could ruin the plan eliminated."

"Who was that guy we found in the apartment?"

"Franco, one of my cousins. I was furious. I couldn't believe he... I threatened him. I told him if anyone from the family ever came near you, they'd have to deal with me. But I didn't know anything about your dad before it happened. You have to believe me."

I opened my mouth, then closed it. I'd been about to ask Mark if he'd known my mom was still alive when he told me she was dead that day at the motel. Instead, I studied his eyes. They were the eyes of a killer. But they were also the eyes of the person who'd protected me. A warm sort of certainty settled in my chest. I believed him. About all of it. About my dad and my mom and in that moment, he didn't need me to tell him about another lie he'd been told, about the fact my mom was alive. He needed me to tell him the truth. "I believe you."

He let out a long breath. "How'd you find me?"

I shrugged, slipping my hand out of his. "I was going to hotwire a car, but it seemed easier to borrow the key to the Marshals' car since it was just sitting there waiting for me to take it. Then I snuck out of their safe house and picked the lock on the mudroom door here. Oh, and I snooped through the safe you had hidden in your bedroom a few weeks ago and found the printouts about this place." I glanced around. "Avalon, huh?"

Mark half chuckled, half stared at me in awe. "You're amazing. I've been here all night panicked that my family somehow had you, trying to come up with a way to find you, and you found me, just like that."

"They think you've disappeared, but I knew you hadn't gone far." I shifted and for the first time, felt the pain of the cut on my foot. I winced.

Mark looked down. "What's wrong with your foot?"

"I cut it on glass in the hall. It's nothing."

"Let me see."

"Mark—"

"Let. Me. See." I lifted my foot and he bent down to examine the cut. "It's not that deep. I don't think there's any glass left in it. Come on." He motioned to the futon. "I had to find some bandages before."

I followed him to the futon, wondering why he'd needed bandages. He rested my foot in his lap and began cleaning the cut. After a minute of silence, he said, "We could do it."

"Do what?"

He stuck a bandage in place and lifted his eyes to mine. His hands felt warm stretched over the top of my foot. "Disappear. Like everyone already thinks we've done."

I lifted one eyebrow. "Everyone?"

"This last identity switch wasn't just about getting you out. It was about getting me out too. Out of my family for good."

Lorenzo's trip to Kentucky suddenly made sense. "They never knew we became Mark and Sloane Sullivan."

Mark shook his head. "I wanted you to have options. You could live a normal life, graduate and go to college and stop moving all the time and be *safe*, without them ever being able to find you. Or," he said, dropping his gaze back to my foot, "you could be safe and disappear with me."

I studied the pattern on the futon. I felt the moment Mark glanced at me, but I didn't look up.

"I've been saving the money they've sent all these years. It's enough for a while, at least. We can pick new names. I'll be Duckie Markovitch." He let out a single shaky laugh. "We can go where we want, do what we want. It'll be like that vacation we talked about. We can be on vacation permanently." He squeezed my ankle, trying to get my attention. "I know things weren't like that between us when you were younger. But lately... I..."

I scrunched my eyebrows together at the hope in his voice and lifted my head.

"Just you and me," Mark whispered. "Who needs anyone else, right? That's all that matters. We'll be together." His thumb ran slowly down the side of my ankle and back up, sending tingles up my leg. "We can leave right now. There's nothing for us here, nothing holding us back."

My pulse tripped, rapid and uncertain.

"Don't listen to him, Sasha."

I jumped and turned my head. Jason was standing in the doorway.

THIRTY

Mark shot up, knocking my foot out of his lap. By the time I regained my balance a second later, Mark's gun was pointed at Jason. "Who the hell are you?"

"Whoa!" I jumped up and placed myself in between Mark and Jason.

"I'm the son of the man who's in jail for the murder you committed," Jason snarled over my shoulder.

Jesus, Jason. Way to escalate the situation. I held my hands out to Mark, heart pounding in my chest. "Put the gun down."

He motioned with the gun, eyes on Jason. "Get out of the way!"

"I'm not moving." I waited until Mark's gaze locked on me. "So unless you want to keep pointing that thing at me, you need to lower the gun."

Mark grimaced, then slowly lowered his arms until the gun pointed at the floor.

I turned to Jason. "What are you doing here?" I snapped.

Hurt flashed in his eyes before they hardened. "I followed you. Then I hid in the back of the car."

The noise I'd heard when I first left the safe house, when it felt like someone was watching me. The *thud* that gave me goose bumps as I crept down the driveway here. It had all been Jason.

"You didn't honestly think I believed you needed time to 'process' everything in your room, did you?" he continued. "I know you better than that. A master storyteller like you should've come up with a better excuse."

I flinched.

"I knew you weren't telling them everything about where *he* could be." Jason glared at Mark. "So I snuck out before you did and waited on the porch. When you left, which I knew you would, I was going to follow you somehow." He shook his head. "And then you made it easy. You left the car unlocked when you went back in the house."

Oh my God. I unlocked the car before I backtracked to get the gun and I never even looked inside when I returned. I just drove away as fast as I could and I brought Jason with me.

Mark's eyebrows shot up. "He knows you 'better than that'?"

Jason's jaw clenched. "I've known her my whole life, since long before you kidnapped her."

Mark narrowed his eyes, studying Jason. "I remember you. You were at that diner." His gaze cut to me. "You've been hanging out with someone from your past this whole time and didn't tell me?"

I shot him a withering look. "Do you really want to play the who-didn't-tell-what game right now?"

"I think that's a great idea," Jason said. "Why don't you start by asking him who killed Lorenzo."

It was only there for a split second before Mark regained control over his expression, but the look that flashed across his face made my stomach drop. I'd seen photographic proof of his real identity, I'd remembered him shooting Reuben Marx, but it still hadn't crossed my mind that he'd been the one to kill Lorenzo.

Horror rose up inside me. "You killed your own *brother*? The one you protected that day?"

Mark's eyes were pleading. "He'd found you at school. He knew you were still alive. He said he was going to kill you."

I took a step back. "So you killed him instead?"

Mark kept his eyes on me, as if we were the only two people in the room. "I'll do anything to protect you."

"I don't want you to do *anything*! I don't want you to do *that*!" My head was dizzy, like it couldn't keep up with the awfulness of everything and each new revelation sent it spinning all over again.

"What do you mean Lorenzo knew she was *still* alive?" Jason asked.

I blinked.

Mark didn't reply, but he balled the hand that wasn't holding the gun into a fist.

"Could it have anything to do with this?" Jason pulled a plastic bag stamped with the word "Evidence" in red across the top from his pocket. "The infamous manila folder was just sitting on the dining room table while everyone else was distracted after dinner, so I took a little peek. They found this picture in Lorenzo's back pocket." He held the bag out to me. "Take a look."

I took the bag from Jason. The photo inside was well-worn and looked like it had been folded and unfolded many times, but I could clearly see a girl with long blond hair lying face-down in what appeared to be a pool of blood. I frowned.

"There's more," Jason said. He handed me a second evidence bag.

Inside was another picture, this one of a string of texts on someone's phone. I looked at the top of the screen. The texts had been sent from a very familiar number. And at the bottom, next to the same photo of the blonde girl I'd just seen, was a text that read: Told you I'd do it my way.

The memory of hovering in the kitchen, listening to Mark pace came at me in a rush. *She doesn't know anything...You promised I could do this my way...Yes, it'll be soon. Have a little faith.* My throat grew tight and I had to force my next words out. "What is this?"

Mark's expression softened and, in a quiet voice meant only for me, he said, "Where's the faith, Kid?"

"Don't *faith* me right now!" I shook the evidence bags at him. "What is this?"

"They were pressuring me to stop playing games and come home. Apparently their 'generosity' toward you was over. They wanted me to...hurt you." Mark's gaze fell to the gun in his hand. "I had to make them believe you were dead so we could get out. So, no matter what, they'd never come looking for you."

"Look at the girl more closely," Jason said from right behind me.

I studied the photo. There were splatters of red on the back of the girl's blue-and-white-striped shirt. Her long blond hair was disheveled, spread out so it both covered the side of her face that was visible and fanned out behind her head to tangle in the fingers of her right hand, which was lying palm down on the cold, dark ground. But her hair didn't cover the wide silver ring on her ring finger. It was an intricate filigree pattern that looked like a piece of silver lace. A lump formed in my throat. *They found Miranda*, Sawyer's voice reminded me. *She woke up by some berry bush and had red juice dried in her hair and on her clothes. She was pretty freaked out it was blood at first.*

I swallowed hard. "You made an amateur mistake, Mark. You forgot to take off Miranda's ring. It's too much of an identifying mark."

Mark glanced from me to the picture and back again.

"It didn't occur to you that I'd hear about a missing high school student from a few towns away? You underestimated the power of texting." A chill ran through me. "I saw a picture of her from right before you…took her. *That's* what you did the night you left? You told me you were getting ready for what was next."

"I was," Mark said quietly.

"By kidnapping an innocent girl?"

"I didn't hurt her," Mark snapped. "I…borrowed her. I drove around until I found a party in full swing, found the girl who looked the most like you, and brought her safely to the trees behind our house to take a picture. And then I returned her unharmed."

"She's not a library book, Mark! She's a person. One you *drugged*, who can't remember what happened, who's probably been scared ever since!" I stared at the photo of Miranda through the plastic bag. I couldn't imagine waking up covered in what looked like blood, not knowing where you'd been or what had been done to you. "Did you text this picture to Lorenzo?"

Mark nodded.

My mind began to race. "When?"

"A few days after I took it."

Everything clicked into place. I'd overheard the phone call where he'd promised to do things his way the day before he supposedly dropped his phone in the toilet. Then he'd gotten a new phone with a new number. And a week later, he'd taken Miranda and texted her picture to Lorenzo, using his old number. "Your old phone wasn't dead. You got a new one because you didn't want your family to know your number if you were trying to disappear. But you kept the old phone just so you could send this picture to them. You planned this all along."

Mark frowned. "I had to use the number they knew, just one last time. But then I destroyed it. Then I disappeared."

I threw my hands up in the air. "You didn't disappear! You made Lorenzo suspicious! He went looking for you, Mark. He went to Kentucky two weeks ago."

Mark's mouth dropped open.

"The Marshals followed him there. And what do you think he did when you weren't where you were supposed to be? He found a way to find you, just like I did. He used this picture."

"What do you mean? You can't tell anything from that picture."

"You can when you text it! Why would you have left Kentucky if I was actually dead? Why wouldn't you have gone home if you'd done what they wanted? Too many questions made Lorenzo look for answers. And unless you disable the location services on your phone, every picture you take has the longitude and latitude of where you take it embedded in the photo's properties. All Lorenzo had to do was open the properties to know where to find us."

Mark ran a hand through his hair.

I stared into the eyes I thought I knew so well. "You kidnapped a girl and for what? To lead your brother here? To *shoot* him? I never asked you to do that for me."

Mark edged closer to me. "Everything I've done has been for you! For *us*, so we can—"

"There is no *us*." Jason's voice was low and calm, but I felt the strain of each muscle in his arm as he stepped next to me and rested his hand against the back of mine.

Mark made an annoyed sound and raised his gun to Jason's chest.

I dropped the evidence bags. "Mark, stop! Put the gun down."

He didn't listen. "You," he said to Jason, pointing to the other side of the room with his gun. "Move away from her."

"No," Jason replied. He took a slight step in front of me. "I'm not letting you take her away from me again."

The muscles in Mark's arms flexed as he tightened his grip on the gun.

"Mark," I warned. My heart felt like it was trying to escape from my chest.

"I'm not taking her away," Mark told Jason. "It's her choice."

"And you think she's going to pick you?" Jason scoffed.

Mark's eyes narrowed as he stared down the sight of the gun.

I jumped in front of Jason and pointed Dixon's gun at Mark. My hands shook slightly, but I still remembered what Duke taught me. *Grip. Sight. Trigger.* "Please, Mark. Don't do this," I whispered.

Mark tensed and the skin around his eyes wrinkled the way it did when he was surprised. "What are you doing with a gun?"

"I borrowed it from a Marshal."

Mark shifted. "It's not safe. You don't know what you're doing."

I took a deep breath, trying to keep my voice steady. "Maybe I do know what I'm doing. Maybe you're not the only one of us who kept secrets."

Mark studied me. "You're bluffing."

I clicked the safety off.

Jason stepped next to me. "I think she just made her choice."

"Shut up!" Mark growled.

"Why? You think she'd actually pick you?" Jason laughed. "What can you offer her? More living on the run? Because that's what your life is going to be now that you killed Lorenzo. The Marshals *and* your family are going to be after you."

Mark kept his gaze and his gun trained on Jason, but I saw doubt creep into his eyes.

"Everything Sasha needs is here." Jason turned to me. "Stay." The word felt more like a promise than a request. "Your mom's here."

Mark's eyes locked on mine. He shook his head. "I *saw* her car on fire. My family… Lorenzo said they did it. As a warning to you *and* me if I couldn't keep you in line."

"I'm here," Jason continued as if Mark hadn't spoken. He reached up and smoothed a piece of my hair.

"That's it. I don't know what game you're playing, but back off!" Mark's voice was steely.

"No!" Jason faced Mark. "I'm not afraid of a sorry excuse for a person who kidnaps and drugs and murders people, then runs away and lets others take the fall. My dad's been in prison for *five years* because of you!"

I couldn't react, couldn't take my eyes off the gun, off Mark's face. *Easy*, I thought. *Don't push him too hard.*

But Jason didn't get my telepathic message. "I'm not the one playing games. I came to protect Sasha from *you*. Because you're no better than the rest of your pathetic criminal family."

I saw the change in Mark's eyes, from angry and annoyed and *there* to vacant and cold and deadly, a split second too late. "Mark, no!"

A gunshot rang out. My whole body tensed and I felt the recoil of a gun. And the boy I loved dropped to the floor.

THIRTY-ONE

My ears were ringing. I wasn't sure whether it was from the explosive sound of two gunshots in the small room or from the sickening *thud* of Jason hitting the floor.

"Jase!" I dropped next to him, my knee landing in blood already pooling under his left shoulder. "Can you hear me?"

His eyes were closed, his light blue T-shirt was plastered to his shoulder with blood, and he was paler than I'd ever seen anyone before.

"Jason?"

He groaned so quietly I almost didn't hear it. I cradled his head in my hands and moved my ear closer. There was only silence as his body went limp.

"Jase?"

Nothing.

Dread filled every pore of my body. "You're okay." I gently placed his head back on the floor. "You're okay." I didn't know whether he'd passed out or...

I grabbed his wrist to check for a pulse, but my hands were

shaking too hard for me to feel anything. I released his arm and leaned forward, ready to listen for a heartbeat, when I saw the bloody fingerprints I'd left behind on his wrist. *How did my fingers get bloody?* All I'd touched was his head. *Jesus.*

A strangled noise escaped me as I patted Jason down, searching for a phone to call 911. All of his pockets were empty. *Mark.* Maybe Mark had a phone. I turned to him for the first time since Jason collapsed.

He was sprawled on the floor in front of the futon, one arm above his head, one arm flung out to the side, his gun a few inches away from his empty hand.

"Mark?"

I stood on wobbly legs and approached him slowly. My foot brushed against something. I looked down at Dixon's gun spinning slightly on the floor from the gentle kick I'd just given it, then back at Mark. He wasn't moving.

"Mark?" My voice broke.

He didn't moan, didn't flutter his eyelids. I watched his chest, waiting for it to move up and down, even the tiniest bit, but there was nothing. His shirt was black so I couldn't see any blood, but I knew where I'd been pointing Dixon's gun.

I covered my mouth and shook my head. The room began to spin. I hadn't thought, hadn't meant to pull the trigger. I didn't even remember dropping Dixon's gun. But I couldn't have done this. I couldn't have killed Mark. No matter who he really was, he'd always protected me. Always kept me safe. And I shot him for it.

"Mark?" I tried again. Black spots bloomed at the edges of my vision. "You can't…" I forced a gulp of air into my lungs. I couldn't lose it now. I had to help him, *both* of them.

"I can't do this without you," I whispered hoarsely. "I don't know what to do." I took another deep breath. *Find his phone. Call 911.*

I knelt next to Mark and reached for his jeans pockets.

Bang!

The sound of a door flying open, followed by hurried footsteps, came from somewhere down the hall. I jumped back from Mark and tripped over Dixon's gun. I picked it up and scrambled until I was facing the door to the room, my back pressed against the wall.

The footsteps grew louder. I didn't know who they belonged to—more Rosettis?—but I wasn't going down without a fight. It was up to me to protect everyone in the room. I blinked away more black spots and tried to steady my shaking hands. *You've already pulled the trigger once, you can do it again if you have to.*

I tightened my grip on the gun, aligned my sight on a point in the middle of the open doorway, and squeezed out the slack in the trigger. My heart pounded in rhythm to the quick footsteps just outside the door. My trigger finger twitched as a man with a gun flew into the room.

"Whoa!" Dixon yelled. He threw his hands up and ducked at the sight of his own gun pointed at his chest.

I jerked my finger off the trigger and raised the gun to the ceiling. "I almost shot you!" I cursed and tried to slow my pounding heart.

Dixon stepped farther into the room. "What is go—" His eyes widened as he took in Jason's still body on the floor. His gaze cut back to me.

I pointed toward the futon.

Dixon's eyes grew even larger when he saw Mark. He

pulled a phone out of his hoodie. "I found them. Send an ambulance ASAP!" He rushed to Jason's side. "What happened, Sasha?"

I held my breath as he placed two fingers on Jason's neck.

Dixon looked up at me. "He has a pulse, but it's weak."

I slid down the wall and crumpled to the floor, all of the breath and warmth and determination rushing out of me.

Dixon crossed to Mark. "Stay with me, Sasha. What happened?"

"Mark had a gun," I whispered. I was so cold.

Dixon leaned over Mark for an infinite moment. I didn't know whether he was checking Mark's pulse or listening for a heartbeat, but I couldn't look away.

"I tried to stop him." The spots in my vision weren't going away. "I—I shot him." The words echoed in my head.

Dixon rocked back on his heels and peered over his shoulder at me. "*You* shot him?"

A cool sweat broke out all over my body. "Is he…?"

Dixon only nodded once, but that tiniest of movements made my chest compress so painfully I couldn't breathe. "He's dead, Sasha."

Those were the last words I heard before everything went black.

THIRTY-TWO

When I opened my eyes, everything was white. The fluorescent lights above my bed were bright white. The ceiling and walls of the small room I was in were a slightly duller white. The linoleum floor was a scuffed dingy white. The sheets covering my legs were a warm soft white. The blinds in the single window on the wall to my right were a shiny plasticky white. Even the sun filtering in through the blinds, making shadows across the floor, was so brilliant I almost had to squint.

I liked it. It felt like I was in the middle of a blizzard. Or a cloud. It was quiet too. So quiet that if it had been snowing, I probably could've heard the snowflakes falling. I snuggled into the soft sheets and traced my bed's shadow with my eyes. It was long, stretching out across the floor and bending up the closed white door. I shifted and looked around. All of the shadows in the room were long, which meant the sun was low in the sky. Either it had just risen or was about to set. I frowned. Something about that didn't feel right.

I leaned forward to get a better view out the window and felt a tug in my left arm. I glanced down and saw an IV needle in the inside of my forearm, held in place with tape. A tube ran from the needle to a bag of clear fluid hanging from an IV pole next to my bed. I moved around a little. I didn't *feel* sick. Nothing hurt. I wasn't even tired. *Why do I have an IV?* I twisted my arm to examine the needle. There was a tiny drop of dried blood trapped under the tape. I stared at it. *Blood!*

I jumped out of the bed, dragging the IV pole with me. There were no other machines in the room, nothing else attached to my body, so I ripped off the tape and yanked out the needle in one swift movement. I crossed to the door, stepping over the long shadows on the floor, and threw it open.

Dixon's head snapped up. He was sitting in an uncomfortable-looking blue chair directly across from my door in a narrow, white hallway. He closed the manila folder in his lap. "You okay?"

"Where's Jason?"

Dixon held up a reassuring hand and pointed to the door next to his chair, diagonally across the hall from me. "He's fine. He's in there."

The top of a medical chart peeked out of a plastic bin attached to the wall next to Jason's room. I scanned it and pursed my lips. I took a step toward the door.

Dixon wrapped his fingers around my wrist to stop me. "You can see him very soon. He's been asking for you nonstop. But we need to talk first." He nodded to the blue chair next to his.

I flopped into the chair with a resigned sigh. It was as uncomfortable as it looked.

"A lot's been going on while you were out," Dixon began.

"How long was I out? And why was I out? I wasn't hurt."

He glanced at his watch. "About sixteen hours."

My eyebrows shot up.

"You were in shock and the doctors thought it was best to knock you out for a while and give you some fluids." His gaze drifted to the spot on my arm where the IV had been. A small trail of blood had taken its place. "You don't do anything by the rules, do you?"

I wiped the blood away with the edge of my hospital gown. "In case you've forgotten, I was never told what the real rules were."

Dixon smiled but it didn't reach his eyes.

I stared at the blood on my gown. "How much trouble am I in?"

"You're not in any trouble."

My head snapped up. "How could I not be in any trouble?" I lowered my voice. "I—I *killed* him." Guilt burned in my chest, working its way up my throat. I tried to swallow it down.

Dixon watched me for a long moment before responding. "You know, not many people would blame you if you meant to do it. Marco kidnapped you and kept you from your family for almost six years."

"He didn't kidnap me," I insisted. "And I didn't mean to do it. Not *that*. I never meant to fire the gun at all. I just wanted him to think I could." I closed my eyes. "I don't know what happened. I don't know if my finger slipped or some instinct to protect Jason just took over, but I didn't mean to hurt him."

"Well, either way, it's been officially ruled self-defense."

I searched Dixon's eyes the same way I'd searched Mark's eyes right after remembering Mark was the one who shot

347

Reuben Marx. Which was right before I'd stepped out of Mark's reach, placed my hand into my back pocket and started the digital voice recorder. "It worked?"

Dixon nodded. "It recorded everything up until you collapsed on the floor, right before you passed out. Kessler thinks it stopped somehow when you landed on it."

I rested my elbows on my knees and stared at the floor, exhaling long and slow.

"I don't know whether sneaking out like that to record Marco was one of the stupidest things I've ever seen or one of the bravest."

"I had to try," I said softly. "Kessler was right. With what I remembered when we were at the safe house, I couldn't have testified about Reuben Marx's killer. I couldn't have helped Jason's dad at all. And I only had a picture in my head of the man who possibly killed my father. No name, no proof that's what really happened."

"So you stole a Marshal's car, gun and voice recorder, found Marco, whom you supposedly had no idea how to find, and secretly recorded his confession to murder and various other crimes?"

I leaned back against the hard chair. "*Stole* is such a strong word. I was thinking *borrowed*."

Dixon huffed. "Yeah, well, you're lucky your *borrowing* worked out. It could've ended a lot differently."

I don't feel lucky. "I didn't know I was going to be recording his confession to murder. I just thought maybe he knew something about who really did it. I went there to get a name or a description, something we could use to help Jason's dad. And then I remembered and started the recorder and…" I gazed across the hall into my all-white hospital room, bare and deserted-looking. "Did you listen to the whole thing?"

"Yeah."

"It wasn't as black-and-white as you guys thought. He wasn't—"

"I know," Dixon admitted. He gave my hand a little squeeze. "I know."

"What happened to him?"

Dixon shifted in his seat. "Both his and Lorenzo's bodies are being processed, then they'll be returned to the Rosetti family."

I pressed the heels of my palms into my eyes. I could already feel it, this empty hole inside me getting bigger by the minute.

"Listen," Dixon began.

I shook my head. I couldn't talk about it. Not yet. I uncovered my eyes and changed the subject. "How'd you find us?"

He frowned but let it drop. "The car you borrowed had a tracking device. I was outside by the car when I heard the gunshots."

"I didn't think of a tracking device," I said with a slow nod. "That was an amateur mistake."

Dixon chuckled quietly. It was a knowing laugh, like he was familiar with the feeling. "Believe me, it's not as bad as forgetting to lock your bedroom door, having half your equipment and evidence stolen—I mean, *borrowed*—by your prime witness and having your gun used to shoot your main suspect."

I winced. "Sorry, Dixon. If it'll help, I can tell them the part about me not following the rules well."

"You can call me Tony, you know."

I studied him. He didn't look anything like a Tony. "I think I'll stick with Dixon."

Dixon bit back a smile, then sighed. "It's actually a bit of a sore spot that we lost you and your dad all those years ago. With the way everything played out this morning, I think it'd be best if you basically never talked to anyone about what happened again." He searched my eyes. "You'd be doing me a big favor."

I couldn't deny him that. Not after all the trouble I'd caused. Not after the way his eyes looked like Mark's again, pleading yet aware that what he was requesting was impossible. "Of course."

A door creaked open to our left. Kessler marched into the hall, followed closely by my mom, then Jason's mom and finally, the female agent I'd seen at career day, still wearing the same navy suit. None of them looked in my direction. I opened my mouth to call out to my mom, but stopped myself. I recognized her frazzled expression, the nervous clenching of one hand while the other clung to Jason's mom, the hurried way she walked away from me, both freaked out and with purpose. I watched them turn the corner.

A weariness settled over me. Their little parade confirmed what I'd known was a possibility when I'd left the safe house in the middle of the night. When I'd started recording my conversation with Mark. When I'd read the name *John Doe* at the top of Jason's medical chart. Now I understood what Dixon meant when he said a lot had been going on while I was out. I stared at the spot where my mom disappeared around the corner. "I'm going into witness protection, aren't I?"

Dixon's voice held the apology he didn't say. "You and Jason both are."

THIRTY-THREE

The door to Jason's hospital room felt heavy, much more substantial than the thin wood looked, as I rested my palm against it. I adjusted the clothes Dixon had given me to change into, stalling. *Just do it. Get in and get out. See him one last time so your final memory won't be of him bleeding and passed out on the floor—do what you need to do and keep your distance. The longer you stay, the harder it will be to leave. And do not, under any circumstances, tell him how you feel about him. Because then he might tell you how he feels, and knowing that will only torment you once you're gone. You can do this.*

I took a deep breath and pushed the door open.

"Oh thank God!" Jason exclaimed.

The expression on his face did me in on the spot. I was going to remember that look forever. He didn't need words to tell me how he felt, and there was no way to unknow it now.

Give it up, Kid. You can't do this.

I rushed to his bed and threw my arms around him. Jason hugged me back as fiercely as he could with one hand. Pulling back, I looked away from his face for the first time. His left arm was still and there was a large white bandage peeking out of his hospital gown. I lifted a hand to touch it, but didn't want to hurt him. "Are you okay?" I whispered.

"I'm fine. The doctor said the bullet went straight through and didn't hit anything important. Just lost a lot of blood."

"But your head was bleeding too."

"It busted open when I hit the ground. They think I passed out because I hit my head, not because of the gunshot."

I closed my eyes. *Of course Mark didn't hit anything important. He probably had an aunt who gave him a places-to-shoot-people-that-do-the-least-amount-of-damage-but-still-shut-them-up lesson when he was twelve.*

"I was so worried about you," Jason continued. "They told me you were okay, but I heard two gunshots. And they wouldn't let me see you."

Mark purposely shot Jason somewhere the bullet could go straight through and I'd been aiming right at his heart. "He shot you," I said with my eyes still closed, "and then I...shot him. I killed him." The words burned in the back of my throat.

"Sasha." Jason cupped his right hand against my cheek. "Look at me."

I slowly opened my eyes.

His blue eyes were more intense than I ever remembered seeing them. "I'm *so* sorry. I shouldn't have acted so possessive and goaded him like that. I never should've put you in that position."

"Jase, I'm the one—"

His words rushed out on top of mine. "I just wanted you to see the type of person he really was."

I blinked. "What?"

Jason ducked his head. "I was out in the hall for a while. I heard a lot of what you guys said. You believed him about your dad. And he wanted you two to disappear on a permanent vacation together. I was afraid that's why you went there, because you wanted that too." His voice grew quiet. "I thought if you could *see* what he was really like, you'd change your mind. I wanted you to pick me."

"I *did* pick you, Jase. That's why I went there."

His head snapped up. "What?"

"I took some things from Dixon before I left the safe house too. I had the voice recorder in my back pocket the whole time. I didn't find Mark because I wanted to disappear with him. I went so I could record everything he knew about Reuben's murder to help your dad."

"Really?"

Jason's voice was so hopeful I couldn't help but lean forward and kiss him. "Really," I said when I pulled away. "Mark confessed. And Dixon said he thinks the recording will work. With it and my testimony, he thinks we can get your dad out soon."

"Wait." Jason sat up straighter. "You have to testify?"

I swallowed hard. "I remembered what happened, so I can. It will help."

"But if Lorenzo and Marco are both dead, who are you going to be testifying against?"

The hem of my T-shirt suddenly became fascinating. "Well, I don't have to testify *against* anyone to get your dad out. But it's not just him. I can..."

"Who, Sasha?"

"Angelo, for starters. He covered up Reuben Marx's murder, ordered my dad's murder, framed—"

"No."

"Jason."

"No." He wrapped a hand around his left arm, hugging it to his body. "If you testify against Angelo Rosetti, you'll..."

"Have to go into witness protection," I confirmed.

"No," he repeated. "You wanted out when you only *thought* you were in it. What's it going to be like to actually *be* in it? You can't get stuck in WITSEC for the rest of your life because of me."

"I have to!"

"No you don't!" he shot back. "Let the recording get my dad out of jail. Let someone else testify against Angelo. It doesn't have to be you."

The beeping of Jason's heart monitor picked up speed. I eyed him meaningfully. He sighed, then rested back against his bed and took a few deep breaths.

"It's not just your dad, Jase. I have to stop running."

"What does that mean?"

"All I've ever done, every time something bad happened or even if we weren't sure—" a picture of Duke flashed in my mind "—was run. And I kept doing it even after I came here. When Oliver sang to me in the hall, I ran. When I overheard what you told your mom at the bakery, I ran. When Sawyer kissed me at the diner and got all creepy at your house after prom, I ran. I can't keep running. I can testify about who killed my dad. I can bring justice to both our fathers. I have to do this or I won't be able to live with myself, whoever I end up being."

He pursed his lips.

"Plus," I said, "I just killed Angelo Rosetti's oldest son. I'm the reason that son killed his younger brother. I'm pretty sure that puts me at the top of Angelo's hit list."

Jason opened his mouth to protest, but I spoke first.

"You heard Mark. They wanted me dead before. Nothing that's happened in the last day is going to change that." I shrugged. "My testimony is really just a justification for the Marshals' protection."

"I can't believe this," Jason muttered.

I took his right hand and traced random patterns on the back of it. "There's more."

His eyes grew wide.

"Some Marshals already paid your dad a visit. Apparently he hid some of the stuff he took from the Rosettis before they threatened you and he confessed. Now that he knows about Mark's recording and that there's proof he's innocent, he's promised to give it over and testify against Angelo as long as you and your mom are protected first."

Jason furrowed his eyebrows. It took a second for what I'd said to sink in, but I saw the moment it clicked in his eyes. "My family's going to be in WITSEC too?"

"Yes."

He broke into a huge smile. "Why didn't you start with that? That's good! I mean, it sucks, but we'll be together. We can handle anything if we're together." He laced his fingers with mine. "We can pick new names and go to the same college somewhere."

My breath caught in my throat. "No, we can't."

His smile faltered. "Why not?"

"Because we're not related. They don't put unrelated witnesses in the same town. Or school."

"So what?" Jason huffed. "We'll ask Kessler or Dixon to make an exception."

"Our moms already tried that. Kessler and Dixon aren't the ones who make the exceptions. And the higher-ups are concerned that Lorenzo might have seen us together and figured out who you are. If he reported back to his father before he died, they might already be looking for us." His grip on my hand tightened. "With our moms and your dad, who they know well, we've been deemed 'too large and conspicuous a party' to be placed together."

"No," Jason insisted again. "This is not happening. We'll... we'll get married." His eyes brightened. "We're both eighteen. They can't stop us. Then we'll be related."

"Jason, be serious."

"I am serious!" He sat up. "We can do it before anyone finds out. Hospitals have priests or ministers or someone usually, right? This can work." He started climbing out of bed.

I put my hand on his arm to still him. "Jason. We've never even been on a date and you want to get married?"

"Oh crap! That wasn't exactly the most romantic way to propose, was it? Hold on." He glanced at his IV tube. "Let me see if this thing will reach far enough for me to get down on one knee."

The desperation in his voice broke my heart. "Jase."

He leaned forward and rested his forehead against mine. "When?"

"My mom and I leave tonight. She's waiting for me in the hall."

He closed his eyes.

"And you and your mom are leaving tomorrow as soon as the doctors release you."

Jason's voice was a whisper. "So by this time tomorrow we'll have different names and be in different places and won't know how to find each other?"

I couldn't answer.

"It's too soon," he said. "I just got you back, Sasha. I'm not losing you again."

I pulled back and pushed the waist of my yoga pants down to reveal the tattoo on my left hip. I placed his fingers on the three tiny stars. "You're always with me, Jason. Like the stars, far away but always there. And I'll always be with you too."

He brushed his fingers over my stars.

"We found our way back to one another before when I didn't think it was possible," I reminded him. "We can do it again."

Jason's deep blue eyes locked on mine. "I love you, Sasha. I've always loved you."

And I kissed him and told him, again and again, "I love you too."

Eight months later

That was the day Sloane Sullivan disappeared. And the day I got my twentieth identity. Well, twenty-first, if you count Sasha Abbott. I'm doing my best to remember who she is these days.

It's been eight months since I last saw Jason. Eight months that I've had to settle into this new state, one I'd never been in before. Eight months since the Marshals worked their magic and got me into this fine institution of higher learning, which has bestowed upon me these spacious living accommodations. Eight months to get to know my mom again. And eight months to play *what-if*.

I testified, just like I promised I would. Thanks to my testimony—and the recording of Mark—his cousin Franco, my father's murderer, is in prison. And Angelo Rosetti is headed to the same place. I only had to testify a single day at his trial. The trial is dragging out, and his lawyers are putting on an impressive defense, but from all the live-from-outside-the-courthouse updates I've been watching on TV, it's not looking good for him. There was a small part of me—okay, a huge part—that hoped I'd see Jason when I testified. But those Marshals are sticklers for their rules. I never even saw Jason's father and he testified the same day I did.

All these bad guys getting locked up is a good thing. I know that. But it doesn't make it any easier every time I bet my roommate to do something silly and she just looks at me like I'm weird. It's those little reminders of the things from Sloane's life I miss, like making bets, that make me wonder what would've happened if I'd walked out of school that first day and told Mark about Jason. If I hadn't decided to make my own decisions and play God with all three of our lives. Mark and I would've moved for sure. I wouldn't have gotten to know Jason again, but at least I would've known he was there, as Jason Thomas. I would've had an easy way to find him again whenever I wanted. And most likely, Mark would still be alive. That's the *what-if* that gets me every time.

Maybe Lorenzo would've tracked us down somewhere else.

Maybe I never would've learned the truth, never seen my mom again, never been able to help put the bad guys away. But I also wouldn't have killed Mark. That's the part I'm sure of, the part that keeps me up at night. The one time I didn't run away, and I end up killing someone.

The *what-ifs* are the worst.

An unexpected *click* makes me turn my head. My dorm room door flies open and blond ringlet curls bounce on my roommate's shoulders as she jerks her head back in surprise. "Hey," Celeste says as the door falls shut behind her. "I thought you'd be in chem lab."

I shrug. "I wasn't feeling it today." She has no idea I officially withdrew from school this morning. "What about you? Shouldn't you be on your way to sociology?"

She snags a paper off her desk and shakes it at me. "I forgot this. And now I'm super late." She throws the door open but peeks her head back around. "We're still on for tennis tonight, right, Faith?"

"Yup. See you then."

Her fingers wave goodbye around the door frame, then disappear right before the door shuts. I hate lying to her. She's been pretty great, all things considered. Especially with the nightmares I have practically every night. She's gotten really good at waking me up, joking around to calm me down and pretending she believes my excuse that I've suffered from night terrors since I was a kid. In reality, they're all different versions of the same thing: me killing Mark.

I've shot him in my dreams, of course, but I've also strangled him, drowned him, stabbed him, killed him in more ways than I could possibly imagine awake. I finally realize what Mark meant about guns. The mistake part was easy to get—I proved that one myself. But I didn't fully understand what he meant about the consequences being too permanent. At the time, I thought he meant death. But now I know that's not the only permanent part.

Out of everything that happened, that's the thing I can't change, the thing I have no control over: I can't unkill Mark, and I can't stop reliving it. God, *what-ifs* suck.

Sighing, I stand and reach between the pages of my thick chemistry book for the letter I wrote Celeste a few days ago. I lift the edge of her monogrammed comforter—turquoise blue with a hot pink coral pattern—and place the letter on her pale pink pillowcase, covering it back up. I'm so busy trying to imagine what her reaction will be when she reads it that my phone's on the second chorus of my ringtone by the time I realize it's ringing.

I snatch it off my tiny desk and smile, both at the time and the person calling. "You're so punctual. Kessler would be proud."

Dixon chuckles, and it makes me smile even wider. "What, no hello? *You* sound like Kessler now. I knew I should've been the one to guard you at the trials."

Just like Kessler explained, the only time I've had around-the-clock Marshal protection in the past eight months was when I testified, first against Mark's cousin and then against Angelo. And both times it was Kessler and an agent I didn't know who escorted me, not Dixon. But we've been emailing, and thankfully my request for Dixon to be my contact for this, my first official check-in call after I fulfilled my testimonial duties, was approved. After this, he'll check in with me once a year. Still smiling, I say, "It's good to hear your voice, Dixon."

"You too. So how's college life? How's the dorm room?"

I make an exaggerated stretching sound. "Wait…almost… *there*. I'm touching both walls of my room right now."

"Sounds like my dorm room in college." I hear the grin in his voice. "And how's the roommate? Still perky?"

"Annoyingly so."

"She can't be that bad," Dixon replies. "I don't hear anyone playing the bouzouki in the background, which is what my freshman-year roommate did at *all hours of the day*."

"Oh. Well, that's only because Celeste's in bouzouki class right now."

Dixon laughs again, but it doesn't last long. "Seriously, how are you?"

I shrug even though he can't see me. "I'm hanging in there."

"Have you seen the therapist I emailed you about?"

Definitely not. I don't need someone psychoanalyzing why I picked the name Faith Peterson. Or why I still refer to myself as Kid sometimes. "I don't need to talk to a therapist. It was only me for many years. I'm good at dealing with things myself."

"No," Dixon corrects. "It was only you and Marco for many years. *That's* what I'm worried about."

"Can't we talk about something else? Isn't there, like, a checklist of stuff you should be asking me or something?"

There's a loud ruffling of paper on his end. "As a matter of fact, there is. But just know I'm allowing you to change the subject for now. The topic will be broached again in future irritating emails."

I grin. "Duly noted."

"Any problems I should know about?"

"Nope."

"Any contact with anyone from your past?" This question is followed by a pointed cough.

"Nope."

There's a pause in his questioning and I know he's waiting for me to ask, so I do. "How is he?" No need to use a name, he knows who I mean.

"He's doing as well as can be expected for someone going through this for the first time."

I close my eyes and picture Jason. Dixon technically isn't supposed to tell me anything about Jason, but he's one of the good guys who doesn't mind bending the rules a little every once in a while.

"I just talked to him a few days ago," Dixon continues. "He asked about you."

I bite my lip and say the most honest thing I'm probably going to say to him in the whole conversation. "I wish things had turned out differently."

"Me too," he admits. "But you did the right thing."

"I know."

"And this is the safest place for you," he reminds me. "But don't get complacent."

My smile in reply is sad. I remember lesson number eight.

"Watch your back, okay? Things may be calm right now when the family's focused on the trial, but there are still many people loyal to Angelo who would love to get their hands on you. I know Dante may be little in your memory, but he's a full-fledged member of the family now."

Like I could forget the sole remaining Rosetti son. He's half the reason I'm doing what I'm about to do. "Got it."

"You never know when someone might pop up and surprise you."

My heart thumps in my chest and for a second, I'm positive he knows. But I'm just being paranoid. There's no way he could know what I have planned. "Okay."

"You have my cell number, right? I'll answer it anytime, day or night."

"Yes. And thank you." And that's the truth. I do have his number. It's the only one programmed into the new, secret phone packed away in one of the duffel bags under my bed. I may be about to do something that totally breaks all the rules, but I'm not foolish enough to do it without a backup plan.

"If you ever want to talk or just…have any questions, please call. I'll even promise not to mention the therapist during the first call."

I chuckle. "With that generous offer, how can I resist?"

I hear more paper shuffling, then Dixon says, "That's all I've got. But let's keep talking. Tell me about the most disgusting thing you've seen at a frat party."

I glance at Celeste's alarm clock's glowing pink numbers. "It would take me *forever* to describe all the disgusting things I've seen at parties here, and I have a class soon."

"Fess up, that roommate of yours signed you up for bouzouki class, didn't she?"

I snort. "Is that even a real thing?"

"Why am I the only person that's happened to?"

Out of nowhere, there are tears in my eyes. It's not like I actually get to see Dixon, or even communicate with him, that often, but I'm going to miss him. "Thank you for everything," I say softly. "I mean it."

The teasing disappears from his voice. "You're welcome, Sasha."

That little slip in the rules, the tiny reminder of who I am, is exactly what I need. "Going all out with the first names, huh, Tony?" Before he can answer, I groan. "Sorry. I just can't do it, Dixon."

His tone is light again when he says, "I'll talk to you later, *Peterson*."

No you won't, I think. But all I say is, "Bye," and the line goes dead.

Before I do something stupid and give in to the urge to hear Dixon's voice one last time, I place the phone on my desk, pick up my massive chem book, and smash the phone to pieces. Then I scoop up all the bits, run down the hall to the bathroom, and flush them down the toilet. Hey, it worked the last time I had to destroy a phone.

As soon as I'm back in my room, I check Celeste's clock again. Everything's going according to plan, but I still feel jittery. I lean under my bed and pull out two nondescript black duffel bags. Two small bags that contain all I'll need in my new life. Everything else on my side of the room is disposable—souvenirs from a life I never intended to live.

Don't get me wrong. I really like college. And I intend to go back. Just on *my* terms, at a school *I* picked, not one someone deemed to be the safest or the farthest away from anyone else in WITSEC. Not one where my admittance was required by the flash of a badge.

I couldn't have packed more of my stuff anyway. Once Celeste reads her letter, she has to believe that, after finding out my mother just died, the only thing I would've done was throw a few clothes into a bag and bolt. The dead mother story should buy me a few days, maybe even a few weeks, of time in which she won't be suspicious about my lack of response to her attempts to contact me. And by the time she does a little digging, the school will tell her I officially withdrew.

I unzip one of the bags and pull out the fake ID I got during a road trip to a school across the state line a few weeks ago. It's not great, but it will do until I get to one of the places Mark and I used before. We always had the best fake IDs. A soft, hesitant knock on my door makes me grin. *Right on time.* I put the fake ID back in the bag, take out an envelope, and open the door.

I nod at the guy standing on my doorstep. He looks even better than when I found him early this morning roaming aimlessly around the student parking lot on the other side of campus: pale skin, long brown dreadlocks, massive beard, baggy cargo pants, T-shirt for some band I've never heard of and about twenty hemp bracelets piled up one arm. My Lilly Pulitzer–wearing roommate would *never* talk to this guy.

"You're here," Dreadlocks says. "It's Jessica, right? I didn't think you'd actually be here."

"I'm here," I confirm.

He looks over my shoulder at Celeste's side of the room and his eyes widen in obvious pastel overload. He shifts uncomfortably, like being that close to so much pink is making him itch.

I bite the inside of my cheek to stop from smiling at my sheer luck in finding him. "Here it is," I say, holding out the envelope.

He glances back at me and blinks a few times, like he's been looking at a bright light for too long. "So all I have to do," he says as he takes the envelope, "is drop this off at this address?" He points to the address typed on the outside of the envelope. "And you're going to give me $400?"

I pull four $100 bills from my pocket. "Yup."

Dreadlocks takes the money with the same reluctant expression he gave Celeste's lime-green inspiration board. "That's it? There's nothing, like, illegal in here, is there?" His forehead creases. Trying to imagine the types of illegal activities preppy girls could be caught up in must be hard work.

"Of course not," I assure him. "It's just something my aunt and uncle need by tonight. I forgot to mail it and I don't have a car. Plus, I can't spend four hours driving there and back today. I've got a test this afternoon and a bouzouki lesson I can't miss."

His head tips to the side. "Bouzouki. Right on," he says with an approving nod.

Thank you, Dixon. "I told them you'd put it in the mailbox."

"Sure thing, Bouzouki Jess."

This is going better than I imagined. If he ever comes back here looking for Bouzouki Jess, Celeste isn't going to have a clue who he's talking about. "Thanks. You're doing me a big favor." And he is. I couldn't risk this letter getting lost in the mail or arriving faster than I expected. And I couldn't deliver it myself.

"No, thank you. It's like I'm getting paid to skip class." He gives me a mini salute with one hand and saunters down the hall.

After he disappears, I close the door and sigh. Celeste isn't the only person I wrote a letter to. I just hope that when my mom reads hers after he delivers it, she'll understand why I'm doing this.

I know the Rosettis will come after me. Putting Angelo in prison won't stop them, and anyone who knows where I am is someone they could potentially use to get to me. Not only the Marshals, but also my mom or her new boyfriend, Celeste, maybe even Jason and his family. They could all be kidnapped or hurt or killed for information about me. Payback is a matter of when, not if. I mean, no one even knows why Reuben Marx killed Sofia. Maybe just to prove he could. Even though Mark said that was unusual, I won't take the chance of that happening to the people I love.

Leaving my mom behind will be the hardest part of this, but she won't be alone. Her boyfriend's a good guy. When I was over at their place last weekend, he asked me if he could propose and I gave him my blessing. He'll help her get through it. Although the first thing she's going to do is call Dixon. He's the wildcard.

In one of his many lessons about the *real* WITSEC, Kessler confirmed what I'd already figured out: WITSEC is voluntary. I'm eighteen, I can leave the program if I want to, and there's nothing they can do about it legally. But I know Dixon would break the rules and search for me even if his bosses told him not to. And he's the only one with the resources to possibly find me. All I can do is hope he realizes that this way, I'm the only one who knows who I am and where I'll be.

There's more knocking on my door, louder and more emphatic than the last time, and butterflies dance in my chest. Make that *two* people who'll know who I am and where I'll be.

I throw the door open, faster than I've moved in eight months, and the first thing I see are his eyes: pools of almost green around his pupils that melt into a deep ocean blue set against even darker blue rings around the edges. The unmistakable deep blue eyes of Jason Thomas, and they're smiling at me.

I grab him and yank him into my room. He's wearing a baseball cap that covers most of his black hair, but a little is peeking out the back. I reach up and rub it in between my fingers. It's soft and smooth and proof that he's really, finally here. And then Jason is kissing me.

His kisses are urgent at first, insistent, like he's trying to erase the last eight months. Then they slowly turn soft and sweet and gentle, a promise that from here on out, we'll never have to make up for lost time again. It leaves me breathless.

He pulls away first and runs a thumb across my cheekbone. He half laughs, half shakes his head.

"What?" I ask.

"Your eyes are green again." He brushes a lock of my pale blond hair behind my ear. "You're more beautiful than I remembered."

I lean forward and kiss him again and this time, it's my promise that he's more beautiful than I remembered too.

It didn't take me long between all the kisses and *I love yous* in Jason's hospital room eight months ago to realize that, even though I hadn't actually been in WITSEC all those years, I had a pretty good idea how the whole witness protection thing was going to work. And that, as Sloane Sullivan, I'd starting doing things *my* way, the *Sasha* way. And, as Dixon had pointed out outside of Jason's hospital room, Sasha was the girl who didn't do anything by the rules.

So I came up with a way for the two of us to communicate after we'd been placed. It was simple, really: we picked a popular social media site, created profiles in fake names we picked that day, and posted random, seemingly innocuous messages that contained clues as to who we were, where we were, and when we were ready to put the plan into motion. Something as simple as Can't wait for the FSU-Florida game tomorrow. Go Gators! can tell a lot to someone who needs to know where you go to school. We only accessed our profiles from computers in public places like libraries, never posted anything on each other's profiles, and it worked. Jason's here.

"I'm glad I understood all your clues and found the right room," he says with a sheepish grin. "I was a little worried I'd be wandering around campus for days searching for you."

Something tugs at the back of my mind but I'm too excited to pay attention. I'm looking at Jason and I still can't believe it. This time I'm the one half laughing, half shaking my head. "I can't believe you're really here."

He leans his forehead against mine. "I'm not going anywhere." Then he pulls back and winces. "Except maybe to the bathroom. I've been driving for hours." His face lights up. "Bet you have to make more bathroom stops than I do on our road trip."

I tsk in mock disapproval but really my insides are all glowy and warm. "You are so on."

I open my door and point Jason to the bathrooms at the end of the hall. He stands on my threshold and cocks one eyebrow. "Both doors have a picture of a girl on them."

"A welcome gift at the beginning of the year from the guys on this floor. They were hoping some girls would get confused and end up showering in the boys' bathroom."

Jason snickers.

"You want the one on the right." I watch him for a moment as he heads down the hall. Even though I haven't seen him in months, he still walks the same. And kisses me the same. And makes ridiculous bets the same. I hadn't realized until this second how worried I've been that something would've changed between us. But it hasn't.

I let the door fall shut and take one last look around my room. Goodbye preppy, hello possibility. Anyone, anywhere, anything. It's all possible.

A contented sigh leaves my mouth as I cross the room and close my open duffel bag, the one that had my mom's letter in it. There should be something satisfying to the steady *zip*, like a soundtrack to me closing this chapter of my life once and for all, but it sets me on edge. I move both bags closer to the door, closer to freedom, but something's still off.

I glance around the room, trying to figure out why it feels like I've forgotten something. I triple-checked my bags so I know I haven't, but this nagging sensation isn't going away. My gaze lands on the aqua spot in the middle of Celeste's hot pink rug where Jason and I stood a minute ago. His kisses and his sheepish grin and his words all mix together in my head: *"I was a little worried I'd be wandering around campus for days searching for you."* Then the voice I hear isn't Jason's, it's Mark's: *"In case we get separated during an emergency so we don't have to spend days wandering around looking for each other."*

The paper Mark gave me with the code and the untraceable email addresses flashes in my mind. I haven't thought about those emails since that day in the safe house, when I was too stressed-out to remember how to even sign in, and now I can remember them perfectly. My chest tightens. I gave Mark such a hard time about making an emergency plan for the emergency plan when really, he wasn't wrong about needing more backup.

I study the bags by my door, filled with clothes and cash and, yes, notes about some places I've scoped out online as possible emergency meeting spots in towns we may stop in, but that's it. *Maybe it wouldn't hurt to have more of an emergency plan than just Dixon's phone number.*

My eyes dart to my laptop. Usually I wouldn't do this kind of thing on my own computer, but I didn't spend last night in the library researching the easiest ways to destroy a hard drive for nothing.

I'm at my desk in a flash. The email Mark created for me is as good a place as any to start. If it still works after not being activated for so long, then all I'll have to do is create the same type of account for Jason. My fingers tingle as I type in the eight-digit code to sign in. And my heart stops beating.

There are four emails in my account, all from Mark's email address.

I zero in on the last one in the list, the one that came in first. It's from the day the Marshals showed up at school. Since I destroyed my phone that day, the exact timing of things before we got to the safe house has always been a little fuzzy. But it was sent probably right around the time Kessler and Dixon found me. With a shaking hand, I click it open.

Don't come home. It's not safe.
    Don't go to our meeting spot—it's too close to home.
    Lie low and reply to this so I know you're okay.

That's it. No greeting or names or explanations. I can picture Mark, panicked after Lorenzo showed up at our house, scrambling to figure out what to do next. My pulse races as I click on the next message.

I know you gave me crap about the double emergency plan or whatever, but seriously? Why haven't you responded yet?
    Are you okay?

I look at when it was sent: 5:33 p.m.

I open the third message, checking the time first. It came in at 2:16 a.m., not long after I snuck out of the safe house. My mouth goes dry as I read Mark's words:

I can't wait anymore, I'm coming to find you.
    Please be okay.

I close my eyes. He thought his family was in town and he didn't try to leave or save himself. Instead, he stayed and tried to figure out a way to find me, to protect me when he thought they had me. Because he wanted me to be okay. And less than an hour after that email, I was in the Avalon house shooting him.

A feeling of dread settles deep inside me as I hover the cursor over the arrow that will open the last message. I almost don't want to read it, to know what his last thoughts were before I showed up and everything went to hell, but I force myself to keep going.

Right away something's different.

Sloane,

I don't know if you'll ever see this email but just in case you do, I need to say thank you. For saving my life and for helping me find a way out.

Wait, what? My eyes fly to the date on the email and a cold sweat breaks out across the back of my neck. It was sent eight days ago, the day *after* I testified at Angelo Rosetti's trial.

Without your 911 warning text that day, I never would've put on the bulletproof vest I bought before we left Kentucky. And without that, I wouldn't have survived the shots Lorenzo fired at me before I stopped him. Or the one you fired at me, for that matter.

I understand why you did it, even though I wish things had turned out differently. I wish you would've picked me. And I definitely wish your aim wasn't so spot on. Even with the vest on, that *hurt*. But I get it. You made the choice that helped make the bad guys pay. And in the choice I offered you, the bad guys wouldn't have been held accountable. I'm glad that recording you made of me helped with that part.

There's more you need to know, but I'm leaving it up to you. If you want answers, you know what to do.

Duckie Markovitch

Under the signature is an address. In a town only half an hour away.

I stand up and take a step back, the chair squeaking against the hard floor. *It's a trap.* Someone in the Rosetti family is messing with me, trying to lure me out of hiding. The Marshals said Lorenzo was in town on prom day, the day I made up the Duckie Markovitch name. Maybe they had our house bugged and overheard it. *But how would they know about the email accounts when Mark gave me that piece of paper weeks before prom? How did they know to pick an address in Florida? And why would they wait to send this until* after *I testified?*

The memory of standing over an eerily-still Mark, waiting for his chest to move up and down, searching for blood but not finding any, makes me shiver.

But it *can't* be true. I mean, sure, Mark could've owned a bulletproof vest I didn't know about. But I wasn't the only one to see him dead. There were Marshals all over the Avalon house, way more than just Kessler and Dixon. Mark was described as *deceased* by everyone at the trials. And I saw Angelo's face when they mentioned Mark's name—he wasn't faking his grief.

It doesn't make sense.

Before I consciously realize what I'm doing, I'm back at

my computer, typing in the address from the email. I half expect some horror-movie shack of torture in the middle of a swamp to pop up. Instead, I frown at what appears on my screen. *Okay, that's…weird.* I click through picture after picture, trying to get a feel for the layout of the place, until a quick knock pulls me back to the present.

"Your bathrooms are way nicer than mine were," Jason says when I open the door.

I pull him inside, leaving him standing in the midst of Celeste's Technicolor side of the room. "Really? Maybe I *should've* tried the boys' room." I was going for light and teasing rather than *I just read an email supposedly from a dead person,* but my voice sounds off.

He notices right away. "What's wrong?"

I should push him right back out the door and leave. Just go and forget I ever saw the email. Which might be possible, if I could get one word to stop bouncing around my head: *answers.*

I hold Jason's gaze. "There's a stop we need to make on our way out."

"I don't like it."

Jason cranes his neck to get a better view of the small brick building that's halfway down the block on the other side of the busy four-lane road we're facing. "Explain to me again why I can't go with you?"

"It's a bank, Jase. It's crawling with cameras. And you came here today wearing a baseball cap for a reason." I tap the brim of his hat. "Even if it's not my school, we don't need to be caught on camera together the day we both go missing."

He bites the side of his lip. "But why that old one? Why

not *that* one?" He gestures to a large white two-story building almost directly across the road from us, all marble and columns and impressiveness. As far as banks go, it does look a little more *safe* than the run-down one I'm heading to.

"I don't know, but that's what I'm going to find out." I lean over and kiss the side of his mouth, right where he was biting his lip. Then I snatch the hat off his head. "I'll—"

"Don't say it." There's a half smile on his face, but a tightness to his voice that takes me a minute to understand. He's thinking of the words I said when I wasn't coming back: *I'll see you later, okay?*

I lean my forehead against his and breathe in that Jason smell. "I'm not going anywhere," I whisper, echoing his words from earlier. "Except maybe to do a little recon on a bank."

He snorts.

I pull back just enough to stare into those deep blue eyes and start a new goodbye tradition, a new promise. "I'll be right back."

My pace is slow and steady as I cross the street and walk down the block, but really my heart's beating a mile a minute. Jason's hat is doing a good job of hiding my face from the cameras, but my hand still shakes the tiniest bit as I open one of the bank's double doors. I flex my fingers, trying to get rid of the twitch, but stop short when I see a second set of doors a few feet in front of me.

Double locking doors. Don't let the shabby exterior fool you.

The door behind me *clicks* as it locks shut. I have just enough time to think *here goes*, then the door in front of me buzzes open and I'm in.

It looks just like the pictures I saw online: a long, chest-high counter where tellers sit to my right, two large wooden desks with several chairs arranged in front of each of them to my left, and two doors straight ahead at the far end of the room, one unmarked, the other with a small sign that reads: Safe Deposit Boxes.

My feet follow a well-worn path in the navy carpet to the first available teller. She has short hair that's dyed a shade so red it's almost burgundy and lips that match. "Can I help you?"

The teller at the next station hands a deposit slip to an elderly man with a cane and says, "See you next week, Walter."

I take a deep breath and pray I'm about to say the right thing. "I need to get into a safe deposit box."

"Okay. Do you have your key?"

Key? Shit. The email didn't say anything about a key.

When I saw the photos earlier, the safe deposit boxes were the only thing that made sense. Short of some Rosettis popping out from behind the counter or a silent alarm being tripped that will make mobsters magically appear in the next few minutes like cops responding to a robbery, what else could I be here for? I don't know how a bank account could give me answers, but something in a safe deposit box could.

"Um, no."

The redhead frowns. "You can't get in without your key. That's the way it works. The bank has one key and you have the other and both are needed to open the box."

For half a second I wonder if I should just pretend I have it and try to pick my way into the box. Then I peek at the other tellers and all at once I understand why I'm in this bank and not the fancy chain one up the block. All of the women are older than fifty. They've probably worked here their whole careers. Because this is the mom-and-pop local bank. The one that's been a part of this community for as long as anyone can remember. The one where the tellers know their customers by their first names. The one where someone could be talked into breaking a rule under the right circumstances.

"Actually, I was told I didn't need a key. That this was a special case."

The teller's already shaking her head. "I don't know who told you that, but—"

"Would you mind checking for me?" I smile sweetly. "It'll only take a second."

She purses her lips, but years of customer service override her annoyance. "What's the box number?"

A string of possibilities flashes through my head: the number of towns Mark and I lived in together, the address of our place in North Carolina, our last cell phone numbers. It's impossible to guess the right one—I don't even know if it's something related to Mark. I don't even know how many digits I'm supposed to be working with. *But the email said I would know what to do.*

Then it clicks. "911." The only number in the email.

My heartbeat takes off as she types three digits on her keyboard.

Her eyes skim over her monitor, then she *really* purses her lips. "Wait here," she says, her words clipped, then disappears through a door in the back.

Before all the ways I can spin getting caught breaking into a safe deposit box that isn't really mine fully play out in my imagination, a different older lady comes back through the same door. Her gray hair is pulled into a bun at the base of her neck and her brown eyes are shining behind wire-rimmed glasses. She marches over to me, clasps her hands together at her chest and says, "I was wondering how long I'd have to wait to meet you."

A grin takes over my face.

"When your brother came in and asked about setting this whole thing up, I'll admit, as the bank manager, I was a little skeptical at first."

Brother? I have to bite the inside of my cheek to keep from hurling questions at her rapid fire. *What did he look like? Was he alone? Did he seem oddly murderous every time my name was mentioned?*

"But then he explained you were on a mission trip in Africa building schools for orphans—*orphans!*—and there was no way for you to receive packages so he couldn't just mail the key to you. And how he was getting ready to leave for his own mission and you wouldn't be back before he left, so this was the only possibility."

Mission trips? Someone put a lot of thought into this. I nod. "He's in a remote village in Costa Rica right now." *That plausible, right?*

But the corners of the woman's mouth turn down. "He made it seem like it might be a while before you made it in though. He paid enough to have the box for *years*. I'm not sure—"

"I had to end my trip much earlier than expected," I blurt, trying to cut off the doubt creeping into her voice. "Because of the accident."

Her face blanches. "Accident?"

379

I put a little wobble in my voice. "Our parents were the ones that organized all the mission trips for our church, so they basically just traveled from one mission site to another. They were on their way to the airport in Haiti and..." I shake my head.

One hand splays across her chest. "Oh, you poor thing."

"My brother had just gotten to Costa Rica and he didn't feel right leaving. They would've wanted him to stay and finish the mission, you know?"

She nods.

"So here I am." I take an exaggerated deep breath. "But now I need what's in the box more than ever. You can keep whatever he paid. It's not important."

"Of course." She types something on the teller's computer and looks at me, a hint of guilt in her eyes. "Your brother and I set up a few security questions you have to answer first. It was the only way I'd allow access without the key."

I swallow hard, but flash her a smile. "That's fine. Thank you for doing this at all."

Relief flashes on her face. "Okay. So I probably should've started with this one when I first came out here, but what's your name?"

That probably wouldn't be a difficult question for most people, but when you've had as many names as I have it makes things a little trickier. Like with the box number, there are too many possibilities. Then I remember who the email was addressed to. "Sloane Sullivan."

"And your brother's name?"

For a second I'm about to say Duckie Markovitch, but that wouldn't make sense if he was my brother. "Mark Sullivan."

"And what is Mark's favorite sports team?"

I grin. I would've known this one even without the hint in the email. "The University of Kentucky basketball team. Go Wildcats!"

She checks the screen and nods approvingly. "What nickname did you give him?"

So this is where it comes in. "Duckie Markovitch."

She shakes her head good naturedly. "There must be a cute story behind that one."

"It involves a malfunctioning rowboat and a runaway hot-dog cart."

We both chuckle together. "Okay, only two more," she says. "Which of his injuries hurt the most?"

I know the email told me the answer, but it doesn't lessen the way guilt makes the words burn as they come out. "Being shot."

Her eyes widen even though the answer must've been on her screen.

I shrug. "Sometimes mission trips can be dangerous."

She nods and takes a deep breath. "Last one. What did you do for Mark that he's the most thankful for?"

I drop my eyes. Out of all the things I've said since I entered the bank, this is the one that most *feels* like a lie. "I saved his life."

She places a cold hand over the one I have resting on the counter. "Hold on to your brother now that your parents are gone."

I nod, because I'm not sure I could say anything with the way my throat is closing up.

"Meet me by the door in the back and I'll be there in a minute."

Exactly as promised, a minute later she opens the door from the inside and leads me into a musty-smelling room lined on three sides with rows of shiny metal doors. The top few rows are tiny boxes, about two inches by five inches, all numbered in the three hundreds. Then two rows of medium-sized boxes, numbered in the six hundreds. And on the bottom is a single row of large boxes, about ten inches square, all with numbers in the nine hundreds.

The woman inches around the small metal table and chair in the center of the room and kneels in front of box 911, inserting the two keys she pulls from her pocket. She turns each key slowly, like it's a sacred act, a ritual to release the secrets of the box. My head feels light with the possibilities of what I'm about to see when she opens the door, but she removes each key and stands, holding one out to me. "You can keep this now that you're back."

I shake my head. No matter what's in the box, I can't come back here again. "I'm not going to need it anymore. But thank you."

She looks like she wants to say more. Instead, she nods once and leaves, closing the door behind her.

My eyes land on box 911 and suddenly the room feels too tight, too *quiet*. My heart is pounding so hard in my chest I can hear it in my ears as I bend down and place my hand flat on the cool metal. I don't know if it's anticipation or dread that's making my whole body buzz. I try to swallow down the feeling, to stay focused, and pull the door open slowly.

All I see is black.

I reach into the space and my fingers brush against a rough, canvasy material. I grab a handful of it and pull. Whatever it is, it's heavier than I was expecting. After a few good yanks, it finally breaks free.

It's a small black duffel bag.

I examine the outside. No tags or labels or markings of any kind. I frown and glance around the room. No cameras either. So I place the bag on the metal table and unzip it. And all the air leaves my lungs at once.

It's not the stacks and stacks of $100 bills that have made my body forget that breathing is something it actually needs to do. It's the piece of paper on top of the money, neatly folded in half, with the words *Read me* scribbled in very familiar cramped, slanted letters.

All the blood feels like it leaves my head as I open the paper.

Hey Sasha,

If you've made it this far, you just talked your way into a safe deposit box without a key. I would say I'm impressed, but I knew you could do it.

So let's get the obvious out of the way. No, you're not hallucinating this letter. And no, I'm not dead.

I force a shaky breath into my lungs. *How is this possible?*

Remember how I told you no one in my family understood me except for one cousin I didn't get to see very often? He's six months younger than me, and growing up he was more of a brother than any of my real brothers were. And like all of us, he was given a traditional Italian name by my uncle Gino: Antonio.

As soon as he turned eighteen, he left home and never looked back, just like I'd always wanted to do. He changed his last name from Rosetti to his mother's maiden name: Dixon.

My legs buckle and I plop down hard in the metal chair. *Holy shit.*

You have no way of knowing this, but I used to call Tony "Dixon" when we were younger, and he called me by my mother's maiden name. It was our way of distancing ourselves from the family. I'm glad you've kept up the tradition. And don't worry—Dixon's not a double agent or anything. He's truly one of the good guys. He'd always talked about us joining the Marshals one day so we could help people trying to stop families like ours. He learned everything he could about them and taught it all to me. That's how I got the idea to pretend to be a Marshal when I was trying to protect you and your dad. Only Dixon actually did it. He became a real Marshal, just one with a little built-in knowledge about the Rosettis.

I never had any contact with Dixon after we went into hiding. The family disowned him when he left, and I didn't know what had happened to him until that night in Avalon. Needless to say, I was shocked when I heard his voice. And even more shocked when he told you I was dead after just asking me whether I was okay.

That moment Dixon had leaned over Mark's body seemed to last forever. But I thought it was because Dixon was checking Mark's pulse or listening for a heartbeat and wasn't finding anything, not because he was *talking* to Mark.

After you passed out and I made sure you were okay, Dixon gave me the quick version of everything that happened. How they'd sent him to North Carolina when they thought they were closing in on us because, if it came down to it, he would've had the best chance of talking me into returning you peacefully. How they found you. How they told you about me. He said you stood up for me with the Marshals, didn't automatically think the worst. Thanks for that. But he knew you needed answers and that you'd try to find me. So he intentionally left things you might've wanted to see unguarded several times throughout the day, didn't bother to put away the car key, and tracked the car once you took it. And then he gave me a choice: join WITSEC and testify against my family or disappear for good.

I wasn't as brave as you. We'd found the voice recorder in your back pocket, so I knew that would be almost as good as my testimony. I saw my chance and I took it. I couldn't stand up to my family, not after I'd killed Lorenzo. And, after shooting Jason, I didn't think you'd want to see me again. I just wanted out. I'm sorry.

Tears prick at my eyes. I want to tell him he is brave. He's the one who protected me from his family, who taught me how to protect myself, who helped me make my own choices and become Sasha again, even though it meant I might choose to leave him behind. And who's risking his secret just so I don't feel guilty anymore.

I was long gone by the time the ambulance and backup arrived in Avalon. Dixon told the other Marshals that I knocked him out and got away. They stayed with you and Jason while Dixon allegedly left to chase me. Really, he helped me stage a fiery car crash. By the time Dixon supposedly found me and reported the accident to the local cops, there wasn't really anything left of my body to return to my family. At least that's what everyone was told after a rather large bribe to a rather corrupt coroner. And a crash was an easy lie for the Marshals to believe when they thought I'd been driving while suffering from a gunshot wound. My family, the Marshals, everyone thought I was dead. Including you.

My mind reels as everything clicks into place. How Dixon said it didn't take him long to "get up to speed" on the Rosettis. How his eyes reminded me of Mark's. How he told me the recording stopped when I collapsed, *before* he said Mark was dead. How quickly he'd dismissed what I'd done as self-defense. How he didn't come with me to the trials, where his family would've been. How he said I'd be doing him a favor if I never talked about what happened that night again. How no one ever asked me during my testimony about how Mark died. All this time I thought Dixon was a slightly careless young agent when really, he's the most devious one of us all.

I'm sorry you had to think I was dead for so long. I wanted you to be able to testify truthfully, without having to lie to cover for me. I didn't want to put you in that position. But now that you're done testifying, I had to contact you one last time to tell you the truth. I promised no more lies. And I wanted to give you your share of the money. I saved it for both of us, for our futures, so it's yours. Well, some of it is rightfully Jason's too.

I blink at that last line.

When we first started planning Mark and Sloane Sullivan—when I knew we were getting out for good—I sent Scott Thomas an anonymous letter. I'm not proud of letting someone else take the fall for my mistake, but, like I've always told you, I wanted to protect you. I let Scott be framed so I could stay with you. Didn't mean I didn't feel guilty though. So in the letter I said I was someone familiar with the Rosettis who wanted to help him, any way I could. I gave him a PO box as a return address (totally untraceable, of course) and waited. I wasn't sure he'd trust an anonymous letter enough to reply, but he did. With a single handwritten sentence, "Take care of my family," and an address. That's why we moved to North Carolina.

A long, slow breath escapes me.

I wanted to see Scott's family and figure out the best way to secretly give them some money. Not that money would make up for what they lost; it was just the best I could do under the circumstances. But the address he gave me was for a real estate agent named Jill who lived with her husband and no kids. When Scott said "family," I pictured more than a possible ex-wife who'd remarried. I didn't know whether I had the wrong house entirely or what. I was so focused on figuring out how Jill fit into the picture—she's Scott's sister-in-law, as you probably already know—that I didn't even think to research where Scott's family lived in New Jersey. Or, more specifically, who they lived next to.

I wonder whether Jason's dad didn't know Jason's address after he and his mom moved out of his aunt's house, or whether his dad didn't trust an anonymous letter as much as it seemed he did.

You're not the only one who broke the rules. I didn't know Scott was your next-door neighbor, I didn't know he had a son your age and I definitely didn't know you knew that son so well. But I knew we were moving to a town where someone from our hometown lived. I guess I figured if anything suspicious happened, you'd let me know. That's why I rented the house in Avalon; just in case you recognized someone and we needed to move quickly. We'd never had a backup house before and because I didn't want to tell you why we had one this time, I kept it a secret. I didn't put everything together until Jason showed up at the Avalon house. And, well, you know how that turned out. I suppose there's some irony to the fact I'm the reason you and Jason found each other again. But thinking like that hurts my head. The what-ifs are the worst, you know?

The corner of my mouth twitches.

Don't worry—I'm not a what-if you have to worry about. I don't know who you are now. Dixon told me I could use a bank in this town, but I have no idea why. I'm not trying to be part of your life again. Not unless you want me to be, on your terms. There's a number on the back of this letter. If you ever need me for any reason, please use it. I'll keep the phone on 24/7, just in case. Maybe our paths will cross again someday. Until then, know you'll always be in my heart. You'll always be my family.

Mark

A half amazed, half disbelieving sound leaves my mouth and I shake my head slowly, holding the letter up to my face as if feeling it with some other body part besides my fingers will help convince me it's real. And as soon as I take my first breath, I'm convinced. Because after being trapped in the airtight safe deposit box, the paper still smells, just a hint, like the spicy cologne Mark always wore.

So many emotions flow through me I don't know what to do. Wherever Mark is, I want to yell at him for keeping me in the dark and hug him because he's alive and smack him for shooting Jason. But mostly I want to thank him for giving me a way out. Because the money will definitely come in handy. Because now I know Dixon won't try to find us. And because, for the first time in eight months, I feel like I can finally breathe. *I'm not a murderer.*

My body's buzzing again, but this time it's a good feeling, an I-need-to-tell-someone-about-this feeling. And suddenly I can't be in this tiny room a moment longer.

I stuff Mark's letter back in the bag, toss the bag over one shoulder and across my body to distribute the weight so it won't look so heavy and slip out the door.

Everyone—the tellers, the bank manager, even the woman by the counter with the fussy baby squirming in her arms— looks first at me, then at the bag. I pull the baseball cap a little lower over my eyes.

"All set?" the manager asks from behind one of the wooden desks.

I nod and flash her a quick smile as I cross the room. "Thanks again."

Before she can come up with any more questions, I'm through the first set of double doors. I force myself to stand perfectly still while I wait for the second set to unlock. *Come on, come on, come on.* Then there's a *buzz* and I'm free.

I'm finally free.

Jason's whole body sighs in relief when he spots me coming his way. He's sitting on the hood of his car, still parked in the restaurant parking lot I left him in, with a milkshake in one hand and another sweating in a plastic cup on the hood next to him. His eyes never leave mine until I'm standing right in front of him, setting the bag on the ground.

He holds out the extra milkshake. "I figured they might get suspicious if I didn't go in and order something."

It's cool and minty and chocolatey going down my throat and I vow to have one of these every single day on our road trip. I smile and lock eyes with the boy I've loved since I was little. The boy who knows to buy milkshakes to keep up appearances. Who knows the real me. Who thinks I killed someone and still wants to be with me. "You won't believe what just happened."

"What?"

I pick up the duffel bag and shove it in the backseat. "I'll tell you all about it in the car." Holding a hand out to him, I ask the question I already know the answer to. "Are you ready to disappear forever?"

Jason's smile is dazzling. "Absolutely."

"Then let's go."

★ ★ ★ ★ ★

ACKNOWLEDGMENTS

It takes a lot of people to make a book, more than I can thank here, but to everyone who helped turn *Sloane* from an idea in my head into an actual book, I'm eternally grateful. And super special thanks to:

My agent, Steven Salpeter, for pulling me from the slush, reading my manuscript at the speed of light and making me an offer that changed everything. Your enthusiasm for this book has never let up, and I wouldn't want anyone else guiding me through the publishing world. Thank you for finding *Sloane* such a wonderful home. And thanks for taking a chance on me!

My editor, Lauren Smulski, whose hard work and amazing insight helped strengthen *Sloane*. Thank you for jumping in headfirst and making this a better book! And big thanks to the rest of the Harlequin TEEN team for working tirelessly on my behalf: Natashya Wilson, Bryn Collier, Evan Brown, Krista Mitchell, Siena Koncsol, Linette Kim, Sean Kapitain and Mary Luna for your editorial, marketing and publicity genius; an amazing cover; and all the things I don't even know about but am still grateful for. Thank you all for helping make my dream come true!

The wonderful team at Curtis Brown, for everything you've done to help me on this amazing journey: Tim Knowlton, Holly Frederick, Maddie Tavis, Jonathan Lyons, Sarah Perillo and Laura Blake Peterson. And special thanks to Holly for the time and thought you've given to *Sloane*. I'm so honored to have you all in my corner!

Michael Strother, for loving *Sloane* first and for the feedback that helped me start revising this book into what I wanted it to be. And to the stranger who sat next to Michael on the subway, read my submission over his shoulder and told him you liked it, thank you too. Speaking of strangers, big thanks to Gaby Salpeter, for taking the time to do a super quick read of a portion of *Sloane* even though you didn't know me or that Steven was my agent yet. I appreciate your time and hope you get a chance to read the whole book now!

All of the people involved in the online writing contests I entered this book in during various stages of drafting and revising. Your tips and feedback helped both me and this story along the way, and for that I will always be grateful.

Jennifer Spina, who read the very first thing I wrote—which was bad—and still sent me the loveliest words of encouragement. I pull out your note and read it sometimes when I'm positive I have no idea how to write. Your words inspire mine, so thank you. And stop living so far away.

My family—you know who you are—for encouraging me in countless ways, being my biggest cheerleaders and knowing that books always make the best presents. Thanks to my brother, Marc, for letting me borrow your name for one of my favorite characters in the book. And to my mom for letting nine-year-old me go into that bookstore and pick out any book I wanted. You probably didn't know what you were starting, but I loved it. And I love you all.

My husband, Erik, for the millions of things you've done to support me and this whole writing thing, like cooking dinners when I'm lost in a fictional world, reading every word I've ever written, making me *Sloane* swag before it was even a completed manuscript and not batting an eye the day I said, out of the blue, "I think I'm going to write a book." There aren't enough words to say how much your support means to me. You're the best husband a girl could ask for and I'm so glad you're mine. I love you.

My daughters, for sharing me with the characters living in my head, talking about them like they're real people and being just as excited as I am whenever I get good book news. I may always be creating new characters for new stories, but you two are the best things I've ever made. I wrote this book for you, knowing that even if it never got published, I could give it to you as proof that you can't be afraid to chase your dreams. I hope you like it. And I love you both to pieces.

Last, but certainly not least, thank you to my readers for picking up *Sloane* and giving it a chance. I'm so excited to be able to share it with you.